HOVER

HOVER

ANNE A. WILSON

A TOM DOHERTY ASSOCIATES BOOK
NEW YORK

HOVER

Copyright © 2015 by Anne A. Wilson

A Forge Book
Published by Tom Doherty Associates, LLC
175 Fifth Avenue
New York, NY 10010

www.tor-forge.com

Forge® is a registered trademark of Tom Doherty Associates, LLC.

The Library of Congress Cataloging-in-Publication Data is available upon request.

ISBN 978-0-7653-7849-1 (hardcover)
ISBN 978-1-4668-6193-0 (e-book)

Forge books may be purchased for educational, business, or promotional use. For information on bulk purchases, please contact the Macmillan Corporate and Premium Sales Department at 1-800-221-7945, extension 5442, or write to specialmarkets@macmillan.com.

First Edition: June 2015

Printed in the United States of America

0 9 8 7 6 5 4 3 2 1

For Bill,
who said, *Go for it.*

ACKNOWLEDGMENTS

I will be forever grateful to my gem of an agent, Barbara Poelle. She is, without question, the captain of this ship, setting the example with her consummate professionalism and contagiously positive attitude. If only I had a tenth of her wit. . . . Thanks for taking the leap, Barbara.

To Kristin Sevick, my ace editor, who saw Sara's path so clearly and pushed me to get inside her head to bring more of her to the page. At the end of one scene, she commented, "I don't love this." She liked it, but she didn't *love* it. She challenged me to step up, stretch my wings, and make her love it. Thank you, Kristin, for your patience, for everything.

I had the good fortune to collaborate with a gifted couple, Jamie Warren and Steve Youll, on the cover design. Thanks to you both. I was humbled by your vision and avidity for the project. In the end, you nailed it.

Thank you to my copy editor, Christina MacDonald, for the spit and polish. If there's one thing I appreciate, it's attention to detail, and you have this in spades.

To everyone who worked so tirelessly behind the scenes at Tor/Forge Books to bring this novel to life, I offer my heartfelt thanks.

This acknowledgments section wouldn't be complete without mention of my first readers. You answered the call, when out of the blue, I plunked four hundred fifty pages in front of you and asked if you could read "this thing I wrote." Thank you to Sandy Annos, Terri Vaughn, Dimitra Sampson, Tracy Poulos, Jen Green, Cassie Woo, and Lisa Carlgren.

Special mention to my cousin, Deanne Poulos, who suffered through the first line-by-line edits of the manuscript. You opened my eyes, Deanne, in so many ways. Thank you for your candor, your insightful suggestions, and the time and effort spent shaping the manuscript in its nascent stages.

To my baby sister, Karla Delord, a brainy attorney who dove into the minutia, completing horribly time-consuming line edits to bring the manuscript to its ready state for submission. Thank you, Karla, for your attention to detail, your chocolate chip cookies, and your exuberant enthusiasm for this entire endeavor.

To my next-to-baby sister, Alexia Haugen, for her input to the manuscript, and—this is a big one—for babysitting my kids so I could have time to write. Thank you forever for your support.

To my mother-in-law, Laura Seidelman, thank you for your outstanding feedback and willingness to read more than one version of the manuscript as it took shape. And to Paul Seidelman, who ardently supported this novel from the beginning. I wish you were here to read the final version.

Thank you to my sister-in-law, Deborah Wilson, my go-to girl in New York. Your comments on the first draft were right on the money.

This book would not ring as authentically if not for the members of my extended Navy family who graciously gave of their time and offered the benefit of their experiences. Thank you to my Naval Academy classmate and former Navy SEAL John Czajkowski. To my Naval Academy classmate and surface warfare officer Captain Clint Carroll, USN. And to my HC-11 squadron mate Pete Martino, USN, retired. Due to story requirements, it was necessary for me to deviate at times from the accurate information these individuals provided, so all errors, intentional or otherwise, are mine.

While the characters in this novel are entirely fictional, two were inspired by the real thing. To Vince Wade and Marty Naylor, the real-life inspirations behind Lego and Messy, I could always count on you in the riskiest moments.

To Jim "Jolly" Rogers, my Naval Academy classmate and squadron mate, Sara's gifted piloting skills were modeled after yours. To Sara Applegarth Joyner, Naval Academy classmate and F/A-18 pilot, your list of accomplishments would fill far more space than I'm allotted here. You are, in a word, extraordinary. My protagonist was named in honor of you.

To my fellow helicopter pilots, it was an honor to fly with you. And an enormous thanks goes to each and every one of my aircrewmen. We all know it's you who make the pilots look good.

To the folks at DJ's Bagel Café, for supplying the carbs and caffeine that kept my writing brain fueled.

To my parents, Ruth and Tony Hotis, thank you for . . . well, cripe, just about everything. Genes, right? Love you immenso!

I owe my biggest thank-you to my sons, who were only seven when I started my writing journey. You've shown obliging patience with Mom's "needing-to-write time," and gone beyond that with your active engagement—brainstorming titles, cover artwork, and even content. "Mom, you should have, like, this huge battle at the end. . . ." I treasure your suggestions and accept them all gladly. Thank you for your understanding with all of this. I love you more than you can possibly know.

And finally, to my husband, Bill. My best friend, my partner, my everything, who has supported me from day one.

HOVER

1

Frigid water fills the cockpit. It seeps into my boots and crawls up my flight suit, slipping through the zippers and finding every seam. I struggle against the straps that bind me to my seat, the water moving steadily upward, flowing around my waist, sliding up my torso, encircling my chest. It is dark. I can't see the water, but I hear it, sloshing over my shoulders, licking at my neck, splashing and gurgling, inching toward my ears. The cockpit rolls right. I crane my helmeted head upward, stealing one last breath before I'm pulled under.

The aircraft tumbles. I grab at the seat rails, muscles rigid, holding myself in place. My instincts scream to disconnect the harness and free myself. Immediately. But I remember the instructions from my training. *Wait until all violent motion stops.*

Shivering, I continue to roll. God help me. Seconds stretch to eternity when you're strapped in and held underwater upside down against your will.

I tighten my face, wincing to keep the water out, but it percolates into my sinuses anyway, stinging like a thousand pinpricks.

With an abrupt shudder, the motion stops. I search wildly for the harness-release mechanism and pull. My arms flail as they maneuver to free themselves from the straps. But once I'm free, it's worse. Now I'm floating up. Or is it down? I'm already disoriented.

Whack! My hand is ripped from its hold by a swift unintentional kick from my copilot, who, like me, searches in the blind for an exit to the aircraft. Only now, I have no reference point, floating free.

I remember the procedures for egress, an exit strategy ingrained over so many years of navy training. *Reach left hand behind you. Grab bulkhead. Right arm across torso to bulkhead on other side. Pull forward.* I do the actions my hands have memorized, grabbing two structures I pray are the walls to the passageway, and pull hard.

My helmet crashes into something unmovable. I've missed the passageway. *Oh shit, oh shit, oh shit! Where is it?* My hands frantically grope, searching for an opening. And already, I feel it—the slow-building pressure that squeezes my chest.

You can do this, Sara. You can do this. Keep it together.

My hand lands on a seat. I'm not sure which one, but the exit must be behind me. I try again. *Left hand on bulkhead, right arm across torso, grab and pull.* There is no resistance. Still clinging with one hand to the bulkhead, I move to the next steps. *Left hand down to crew chief's seat. Hand-over-hand to main cabin door.*

An overwhelming heaviness settles over my body. My chest tightens . . . constricting . . . squeezing . . . searching for oxygen that it won't find. I know what's coming next. My mouth is going to open and it's going to look for the air. I'm going to inhale the moment it opens.

I bolt forward. I don't remember my route. I don't remember anything. My hands are swimming and pulling and grasping at everything and anything. My head is getting light. . . .

I break through the surface with a spastic splash, my lungs heaving with effort to suck in oxygen. I rip the blackout goggles from my face. As I guessed, I'm the last one to surface. I do a sad imitation of a dog paddle to get to the side of the pool, almost kissing the deck when I reach it.

My roommate, Emily Wyatt, waits at the edge, patting me on the back when I arrive.

"Just shoot me, Em," I say in a spluttered gasp.

"Hey, you did it," she says. "You always find a way."

I don't have the energy to tell her that I didn't find anything. Some cosmic deity somewhere pulled me to the surface, because I sure as heck didn't find it myself.

I've barely gotten my breath when the clanging that has permeated so many of my nightmares begins again. The helo dunker is hoisted to the surface and into the ready position.

The helo dunker. God, I hate this device. Every two years, I strap into this heinous contraption designed to simulate a helicopter crash landing in the ocean. You can't fly as a navy helicopter pilot unless you ride this thing, and so, I haul myself out of the pool and return to the holding area to await my fourth and final ride.

The group ahead, aircrewmen and pilots, file into the twenty-foot-long metal drum barrel that mimics a helicopter cabin. Large, square cut-out sections of the barrel serve as windows and, therefore, possible exits. It is through these openings that I watch eight people find their seats and fasten their harnesses.

A metallic clang echoes in the enclosed natatorium as chain-linked metal ropes holding the barrel begin reeling upward, hoisting the dunking apparatus over the water tank. Ten seconds later, the hydraulic pulleys powering the ascension wrench to a halt.

The barrel silently sways, suspended at a height six feet above the surface.

Then, with a quiet click, the chains release, and the drum free falls to the water, a liquid hiss echoing through the chamber on impact.

You never know which way the barrel is going to roll. On this run, it rolls left, rapidly filling with water, continuing to roll until it hangs upside down, completely submerged.

You must wait until all motion stops before you disconnect your harness—probably the longest twenty seconds you will ever experience in your life. Safety divers ensure that no one begins their egress too early, which would lessen the odds of successfully navigating your way out.

In the sudden quiet, those of us on the pool deck hold our collective breath as we wait for helmets to begin popping to the surface.

"Port side—clear!" shouts one safety observer, reporting that all occupants on the left side of the barrel have exited.

"Starboard side—clear!"

We silently count. One head, two heads, three, four, five, six, seven, eight.

"Eight souls accounted for!" the lead diver reports. "Clear to lift!"

"Next up, last ride for Petty Officer Legossi, Petty Officer Messina, Senior Chief Makovich . . ." The names run together, my eyes fixed on the water that spills from the inside of the helo dunker, draining as it ratchets upward. ". . . Lieutenants Wyatt and Denning!"

I have to choke down what's rising in my throat.

"Come on, Sara," Emily whispers in my ear. She knows I struggle with this—the only one who knows why.

On a day-to-day basis, Emily tends to overwhelm—extroverted, extra-loud, extra-everything—but this is one place where she shows a softer side. I think her maternal instincts must take over or something, because she knows how to soothe my fears, just like a mother would. Just like the best friend she is would.

She places her hand lightly on my back. "Let's get this over with."

I swallow hard and move forward with her gentle prod from behind.

For these rides, we are clothed as we would be for flying—standard olive green flight suits, black leather steel-toed boots, gloves, and helmets. Emily and I step into the barrel and take our places in front, in the cockpit. As we did for the last ride, I slide into the right seat, Emily climbs into the left. We fasten our five-point harnesses and tighten them down hard.

You would think that taking this ride once would be enough, but we're required to do it four times in one afternoon. As an added challenge, the pilots aren't allowed to egress out the cockpit escape hatches—the ones right next to us, less than an arm's length away. To simulate a jammed hatch, we must instead find a way through the main cabin door behind us. Like before, we must wear blacked-out goggles to simulate crashing at night.

Once I affix my goggles, I sit in darkness, my hands white-knuckled, gripping the sides of my seat.

The clanging starts. With a lurch, we are pulled upward, metal rumbling, seats vibrating, the discordant jangle of chains echoing loudly now. I open my mouth wide, drawing deep, full breaths. Over and over I do this, as if it will make a difference.

And the reward for all of this? Congratulations, you've earned your way onto a ship for eight months at sea on a Western Pacific deployment.

The dunker jerks to a stop.

Swinging lightly, we hang.

All is quiet.

Until the bottom drops out . . .

2

"*Kansas City* Tower, Sabercat five five, one-mile final, request green deck for landing," I say.

"Sabercat five five, Tower, we have you in sight, winds two seven zero at two six knots, green deck."

"Tower, five five, copy, green deck," I reply.

Nervous perspiration trickles across my neck, saturating the collar of my flight suit. I stare at the teetering flight deck of the USS *Kansas City*, the ship rolling up, over, and sideways through waves that could swallow a semi-truck whole. It's pinky time—that small window after official sunset when it's still light enough to see—and thank heavens, in conditions like these.

I begin a gradual flare to slow the helicopter, the crew chief directing my movements as we approach the flight deck. Because we fly such a large aircraft—a tandem-rotor design capable of carrying twenty-five passengers—there's a whole lot of helicopter behind me that I can't see, so the crew chief hangs his head out the main cabin door to position me for landing.

"All right, ma'am, easy does it," says Petty Officer Kyle Legossi, otherwise known as Lego—one of the best in the aircrew business. "Over threshold. Up two. Steady. Forward five, forward four, forward three, two, one. Steady. I'll call it on the rise. Steady. You're gonna need to get this one down quick. Steady. Back one. Steady. Back one. Steady. Steady. Down now! Three, two, one. On deck!"

The chock and chain runners sprint under the rotor arc.

"Keep on the controls, ma'am. Cyclic forward, easy forward. We're pitchin' up pretty good here. Chocks are in. Steady. One more chain to go. Easy back on the stick. Steady. Okay, we're good."

I let out the breath I was holding.

"Hoo wee! This ship is rockin'!" Lego says in his slow Alabama drawl. "Sweet landing, ma'am."

I allow myself a satisfied smile. I nailed the landing. No bounce on the deck and the nose gear exactly on target.

I look expectantly at the pilot seated to my left, Lieutenant Commander Nick Claggett, the officer in charge of our detachment.

"That approach was . . . fair," he says. "But you're still too tentative on the controls and you landed with your nose too far aft."

Tentative. I bite the inside of my cheek. He shoots words like that at me all the time. If by tentative, he means not over-controlling the aircraft, then yes, I would agree. If by tentative, he means using fine motor control when it comes to hovering or precision approaches or any number of things requiring a touch of finesse, then yes, I would agree. But I know he doesn't mean that.

I let out a long exhale as we shut down, unplugging my helmet and disconnecting my harness.

Swiveling my legs to the left, I climb over the center console and step into the main cabin. Lego has opened the main cabin door, one constructed with built-in stairs and hinged along the bottom so when it's flipped open, the pilots and aircrew have a ready platform for exiting the aircraft. I make the small leap from the bottom step to the unforgiving steel of the flight deck.

A crisp February sea breeze pricks at my face. It's refreshing in one sense, yet the salty air can't mask the overpowering smells of a navy ship—smells that assault my senses. Jet fuel, exhaust, and paint, among other odors, combine to form a potent—uniquely navy—mix.

Emily is here to greet me, wearing her khaki uniform and trademark aviator sunglasses. "Hey, nice landing," she says.

"Thanks a lot, Em." I clear my throat. "Someone might want to let Commander Claggett know."

"Let me guess. Too cautious? Too gentle?"

"Too tentative."

"Ah, yes, my personal favorite," she says. "Fucking asshole."

I don't know how the word "tentative" could possibly find its way into an assessment of Em's performance, whether in the aircraft or on the ground. But she gets it in spades just like I do.

"And I landed with the nose gear too far aft," I say.

"What? You've gotta be shittin' me."

We walk together to check the front landing gear, inspecting the distances closely. "Yeah, I think he's right," Em says.

"What?"

"I'd say you're about two millimeters too far aft. That's pretty shoddy flying if you ask me, Denning. Better step it up next time," she says with a wry smile.

"Thanks a lot."

"Okay, so forget that," she says as we walk the twenty or so feet to the hangar door. We step inside and turn left, ducking into the aircrew locker to deposit my flight gear. "You need to look at this instead!"

She hands me several sheets of official navy message traffic as we begin the walk across the cavernous aircraft hangar that allows side-by-side parking for our two helicopters. Sabercat 54 is already inside, every panel and door flipped open like an advent calendar on Christmas Eve.

"What happened here?" I say, pointing to the aft ramp of the aircraft. Maintenance personnel are clustered around two giant, jagged holes.

"They were in a low hover," Em says. "Lieutenant Taylor hit a stanchion."

"Zack did that?" I say.

"Indeed he did," Em says with a chuckle. "Oops."

"I'd say."

"So never mind the holes," Em says. "Look at the message!"

I start to walk again, head down, perusing the contents. "Okay, so we're officially halfway between Honolulu and Hong Kong—"

"Three thousand miles from Hong Kong, to be exact," Em says.

"Okay, so three thousand miles . . . and Valentine's Day will be celebrated in . . . September?" I look up. "I know the U.S. Navy is capable of many things, but moving Valentine's Day?"

"My dear, today you took off on February thirteenth, and while you were out turning circles in the sky, the battle group cruised across the international date line," she explains. "You have just arrived on February fifteenth."

I follow her as she steps through the forward hatch of the hangar and begins climbing the steep and ridiculously narrow ladder to Officer Country. I grip the rails as the ship seesaws beneath us, the sheets of messages tucked awkwardly under my arm.

"So to preserve the integrity of this most important of holidays," she continues, "we'll celebrate when we pick up an extra day on our return transit in September."

"This is absurd. How does garbage like this make it into official navy message traffic?"

"Valentine's Day is not garbage, at least not for *normal* people," she says with a pointed look over her shoulder. "But that's not the news."

We step off the ladder, entering a rat's maze of passageways en route to our stateroom.

"Okay, let's see," I say, continuing my scan. "Rear Admiral Carlson extends his official welcome to the Sabercats and the newly refurbished H-46 Sea Knight helicopter, combining unmatched maneuverability with enhanced lifting capabilities, blah, blah, blah."

"Yeah, big fuckin' deal," Em says. "But how sweet is this!" She points to the bottom of the news feed. "An all-officer Hail and Farewell for the battle group the first night we pull into Hong Kong!"

She reaches over and flips the page for me. "At the Hyatt Regency in Kowloon!"

I sigh. At functions like these, welcoming new officers and saying goodbye to those moving on, the alcohol flows freely, the food is plentiful, and so are the civilian women.

I hope I don't have to go. These things are usually mandatory, though.

"I said, 'how sweet is this!'"

"It's not, really," I say.

"Oh, no. Still?"

"Well . . ."

"Well what, Sara? So we're in civilian clothes. So the guys are in civilian clothes. So everyone is drinking. So they don't realize you're an officer. So what?"

"So it's weird. They act differently because they think they're talking to a civilian. I hate it."

"You act like you're the first woman who's ever gone through this."

I shove the papers back in her hand.

"So don't go, then," she says. "I bet I have duty that day anyway, so you can switch with me and stew in our room all night."

"Deal."

"God, Sara, you're fucking hopeless! Seriously, you have *got* to lighten up!"

I turn to face her. "How many times do I have to say this? I am who I am. This is just me, so get over it."

"Bullshit! You're a fuckin' Academy grad! You've had plenty of time to get your head around this."

I shrug, too tired to argue, and Em gives me a look I've come to know well.

"You're a mental case, Sara. Seriously. And it's only the first fucking month of cruise."

"And this mental case is in desperate need of a shower."

Rounding the final passageway that leads past the wardroom to our stateroom, I slow, allowing my eyes to adjust to the dimness.

"Emergency lighting?" I say.

"Yeah, while you were gone."

"Again?"

"The wardroom's dark, too. We had to eat dinner holding flashlights."

I let out a tired groan. "Please tell me the lights are working in our room."

"They were when I left," she says, opening the door of our stateroom. "Sweet. And still are."

I waste no time, peeling off my flight suit and throwing it onto the top rack—my rack—of our heavy-duty bunk bed. Barefoot, I pad across the floor to the head. We're lucky to have our own restroom and shower—a perk of being deployed on a large ship.

I say a small thanks for this as I turn on the water and step in. The mundane shower always turns into an adventure when the ship is sustaining fifteen- to twenty-degree rolls. Fortunately, they thought of hand rails for the shower stalls. I hang on for dear life as I wet my hair, timing it right to let go and squeeze shampoo in my hand. I do it quickly and grab the rail again as I rinse.

After drying, I slip into my pajamas—an oversized Minnesota Vikings football jersey—and stuff my dirty laundry into the net bag that hangs at the end of our bunk.

Em changes, too. As always, it takes me a second to adjust to the sight of her in a long pink nightgown complete with lace around the collar. There's just so much . . . pink. Except for the socks. Those are fuzzy and purple.

She unwinds the braid that keeps her long auburn hair neat and tidy while in uniform and shakes it free, then grabs a book from her personal library that she'll fall asleep reading—one of hundreds of Harlequin romances she has brought along with her.

It doesn't compute with me. It has never computed. In fact, I can't reconcile it at all.

"Em, how many of those books did you bring with you this time?"

"Oh, fuck, I don't know. Eighty? Ninety? I didn't want to run out. But I can already see these are only going to last until midway through cruise, if I'm lucky. Why? Tempted to read one?"

"No, definitely not."

"You know, I think this is one of your problems, Sara Denning. You can't even chill long enough to read a romance novel."

"How is that a problem?"

"Allowing yourself to escape to a place that connects with your inner femininity is important to your well-being. You're gonna lose yourself otherwise."

"What? I'm not losing myself. I don't need to read that stuff to remind me I'm feminine."

"I think you do."

"Please."

"They all have happy endings, you know. A guaranteed you're-gonna-feel-good-at-the-end perk."

"I don't need a Harlequin romance to make me feel good."

"You need something."

I glare at her.

"And not just that, you need . . . well, you need to put away your systems manuals and let go of yourself."

"I'm not having this conversation," I say.

"Fine," Em says, fluffing up her pillows before scooching under the covers. "I'm transporting myself to a happy place now. Good-bye."

Climbing into my rack, I flip the switch for the tiny light above my bunk. As it flickers and yawns to life, I cross my arms behind my head, fixing my gaze on the miscellaneous ducting and wiring snaking across the overhead. The ship vibrates, hums, churns, and whines, but not loudly enough to block the sustained ringing from Emily's comments.

Allowing yourself to escape to a place that connects with your inner femininity is important to your well-being.

Not *my* well-being. I can't succeed in this world and maintain that connection. It started the day I entered the Naval Academy, when I began a journey I had never intended, stepping onto a career path carved for someone else. To survive, the walls went up. And to get to where I am now, they stayed up.

I shift my focus to my stack of journals. If I did need an escape, I certainly wouldn't find it here. The pages don't contain a lot of pleasant thoughts. But then, that's silly. Why do I need an escape? I don't need that.

Maybe a letter home? It would be easy enough. My über-practical mother pre-stamped a box worth of envelopes so I would write to her—physically write, as in nothing electronic—insisting a letter means more if it's handwritten.

My mom . . . I miss her. I've lived away from home for eight years, but for some reason, when floating on a hunk of steel in the middle of the Pacific Ocean with nobody who "gets" me, the loneliness becomes acute and nostalgia reigns. I miss my dad, my old bedroom, movie nights, my dog, my cat, green leaves—colors in general—home-cooked meals, and walks in our tree-lined Minneapolis neighborhood. I also miss the simple things—things you take for granted until you're isolated on a ship at sea—like taking a drive, ordering out for pizza, and even shopping at the grocery store.

But most of all, I miss my brother, Ian.

I let out a long sigh, too tired to pick up the pen. Instead, I stare at my bunk light until my eyes blur and close.

3

A prolonged screeching rakes at my ears and my eyes fly open. *What the . . . ?* I turn in time to see our desk chairs accelerating across the floor.

Gripping the side rails tightly, I lower myself, peeking at Em as I do so. Somehow she's sleeping through this. I find my bottom drawer where I have several bungee cords stowed, pull our chairs to the end of our bunk railing, and tie them to the support posts. There.

I climb back in bed. It's 0130.

I toss and turn and so does the ship.

I look at my watch. 0200.

It's going to be one of those nights.

"God, I feel like crap," I say, foraging through my metal closet for some workout gear.

"Well, you had a busy night rearranging the furniture," Em says, reclined in her rack, her nose in another Harlequin.

"I can't believe you didn't wake up. The chairs were sliding all over the place."

"Didn't hear a thing," she says, not looking away from the pages.

"Well, I'm going to squeeze in a short run before the Operation Low Level brief. I've gotta do something."

"Actually, that got pushed back. It's at seventeen hundred instead."

"Excellent. More time on the treadmill."

Em rolls her eyes.

"It really does help with stress," I say.

"So does smoking."

"Oh god, Em, you haven't started smoking again, have you?"

"Well . . ."

I open my mouth, but she interrupts before I can say anything. "Go," she says, obviously not in the mood for another lecture.

I open the door and jump back slightly. Lego stands in the passage-way, his hand poised to knock.

"Whoa, sorry about that, ma'am," Lego says.

"We didn't mean to spook ya," Petty Officer Joe Messina adds, mov-ing into view. Known to all as Messy, he's an Alabama-born crew chief just like Lego.

"No, that's okay," I say, gathering myself. "What's up?"

"They need us to fly, ma'am," Messy says. "Gotta pick up the skipper of the *Lake Champlain.*"

"But I thought *their* guys were bringing him."

"Last-minute change, ma'am," Messy says. "We have thirteen people to deliver to their ship, so I guess they figure since we're comin' anyway . . ."

"Yeah," Lego says. "We're briefin' in five minutes."

"Damn," I say, my shoulders slumping. I really needed that run. "Well, if I have to fly, at least it's with you two."

"Hey, that's just what we said." Lego grins.

"Okay, guys, I'll be right down."

"C'est typique," Emily quips as I change into my flight suit.

"Yeah. Guess I'll see you in a few."

"Lace, your heading is two eight zero," Commander Claggett says. "Cham-plain is at ten miles."

I scan the vast, undulating horizon, seeking a gray hull under a gray sky on a gray ocean—the ship further camouflaged by a sea that seems to breathe, rising and falling with fifteen-foot swells. We're flying low, as we always do, about two hundred feet above the water.

En route, we pass the four other ships in our battle group, technically known as a carrier strike group—one cruiser, one destroyer, one frigate, and the aircraft carrier, USS *Nimitz*—pitching and heaving in the heavy seas. The ocean tosses the smaller ships like play toys between its massive swells, and I think once again how fortunate I am to be stationed on the *Kansas City*, a ship second in size only to the *Nimitz*.

Our ship, a replenishment oiler, is so large because it carries the food, fuel, and ammunition necessary to supply the six ships in our group, in addition to the USS *Birmingham*, the submarine that cruises with us. All total, our contingent counts about seven thousand people. But even for a mobile force as large as ours, we're dwarfed by the Pacific, a fact suddenly more relevant in weather like this.

As I search for the *Lake Champlain*, I silently curse Emily, as I often do. The nickname Lace was her brainchild, derived from her staunch and continuing belief that I need to lighten up. Wearing a lace bra and underwear underneath my flight suit would facilitate this, she said. Naturally, I took offense, so *naturally*, she told the pilots in our detachment . . . who told the aircrewmen . . . who told the maintenance guys. Now, not only does the name tag on my flight suit say LACE, but so does the lettering across the back of my helmet, courtesy of the parachute riggers who maintain our flight equipment.

The fun ran out of it for Emily a long time ago, so I'm Sara again to her. I still hear it occasionally from the other pilots and aircrew, but curiously, Commander Claggett uses it exclusively to address me. If he can find a button of mine to push—and this is a big one—he doesn't hesitate to slam it home.

"Sir, did maintenance have an estimate for repairs on the ramp?" Lego asks.

"They think they can have it done by tomorrow morning," Commander Claggett says.

"Man, the air framers are gonna be up all night," Lego says.

"Ever heard of somethin' like that happenin' before?" Messy asks. "Holes in the ramp? I know I haven't."

"No . . . no, I haven't," Commander Claggett says.

"You know, the aircrew said they barely felt it," Lego says.

"Which is surprising when you see the size of the holes," Messy says. "They were huge suckers—"

"All right, that's enough about the holes!" Commander Claggett barks.

Same old story. His short fuse strikes again, and this will set the tone for the rest of the flight.

An uneasy silence ensues.

And this has me worried. Normally, Commander Claggett fills transit time with aircraft systems questions, so as the minutes tick by, I wonder what has his mind occupied. Probably holes and maintenance reports and—

I see the orange flash from the master caution panel out of the corner of my eye. *Shit!* "Sir, transmission chip light!"

"Shit!" Commander Claggett says. "Lego, got anything back there?"

"Checking," Lego says. "Mess, get the aft tranny. I'll get the forward."

"On it!" Messy says.

"Sir, did you jiggle the light?" Lego asks.

Sometimes, this actually helps. Funny to think how many pilots and aircrewmen, despite how highly trained, or how well versed in scores of exacting emergency procedures, throw in this extra "step."

"Stand by." Commander Claggett reaches over and messes with the light, but it remains illuminated. "Still solid."

"I don't have anything in back," Messy reports.

"Oh, shit, we've got smoke!" Lego says. "Forward tranny!"

"Sir, do you want the controls?" I say. It's not a requirement that the aircraft commander take the controls in an emergency. It depends on the circumstances. But with the bad weather today and the rough seas, experience counts. Of course he'll fly it.

"No, you keep the controls," he says. "I'll go through the emergency checklist."

Hmm. That's odd. There's only one item for the transmission chip light emergency procedure—land immediately.

Okay, Sara, enough dallying. Just get on with it.

As I key the mic, the sleek gray hull of the *Lake Champlain* finally, gratefully, comes into view.

"*Lake Champlain* Tower, Sabercat five five, one mile to the south. Declaring an emergency," I say.

"White smoke, sir!" Lego says, interrupting my radio call. "Fuck! And a lot of it! We need to land! Like right now!"

"Sabercat five five, *Lake Champlain* Tower. State the nature of your emergency."

"Do you hear anything?" Commander Claggett asks.

"Nothing, yet," Lego says.

We're listening for the grinding noises that come next—when the transmission gears begin to shear.

"Sabercat five five, *Lake Champlain* Tower. Repeat. State the nature of your emergency."

"Shit, sir, we can't see much of anything now. This is gettin' bad!" Messy says. "And the pax are gettin' panicky."

We call our passengers "pax" for short, and right now, we have thirteen of them in our aircraft. A wall separates the cockpit from the cabin, the two areas connected by a narrow passageway, so unless I lean far toward the middle, the passengers remain hidden from my view. They sit on bench-like troop seats that run the length of the cabin, a distance close to thirty feet, allowing them an all-too-clear view of the smoking transmission. No wonder they're panicking.

It's up to Lego and Messy to keep them calm and strapped into their seats, and it sounds like they're having a difficult time of it.

"Tower, five five," I say between the chatter. "Transmission chip light with visible white smoke. We need to land immediately, half-mile final, over."

"Roger, five five, your deck is green."

The *Lake Champlain*, a guided-missile cruiser with a flight deck half the size of the *Kansas City*'s, lifts and falls, disappearing and reappearing in an ominously churning sea, the water foaming white along the crests.

I spread my fingers on the control stick, trying to loosen them, to relax, but as white tendrils of smoke begin to weave their way into the cockpit, my grip tightens, my stomach twisting into a hard knot.

"You're a hundred feet above the water," Commander Claggett says. "Ninety knots on the airspeed."

Just keep it steady, Sara. Focus on the horizon. Not the water. The horizon.

The smoke is getting bad now. What was initially wafting into the cockpit is now rushing in. I wish I could open my window, but I can't take my hands off the controls. I shift to short, shallow breaths, bringing my tongue to the roof of my mouth to act as a barrier. Next to me, Commander Claggett shakes as he coughs, hand over his mouth.

"Okay, ma'am, lookin' good," Lego says, keeping a calm voice even though I know he's inundated with smoke. "A hundred yards to the deck."

The smoke is swirling and I move my head side to side to find an opening. Oh my god. The smoke has just obscured everything. Shit! I move my eyes to the gyro, the one instrument that can tell me if I'm flying level. My hands slip inside my gloves, slick with sweat.

"Kyle . . . ? Kyle, I can't see," I say. My voice sounds like someone else's. Monotone. Too calm.

"Just keep it smooth like you always do, ma'am," Lego says. "I'll be your eyes once we're over the deck. We can do this."

I imagine Lego leaning over the rim of the main cabin door—a door that rises to waist level—his body half in and half out of the helicopter, peering into the clear air.

"Sir, is your window open?" Messy asks.

"Yeah—" Commander Claggett says, his answer cut off by another spate of coughing. "And I can't see shit!" he finally finishes.

"Can you jettison your escape hatch?" Messy says.

"Just a sec."

"Okay, ma'am, still lookin' good," Lego says. "We're about fifty yards out. Nice and steady. Lookin' good."

"The hatch's gone," Commander Claggett says roughly, then clears his throat. "You're fifty feet above the water."

"Okay, ma'am, steady on the descent and let's slow it down," Lego says. "Mess, can you see if you can pull her window open?"

Messy pokes his head into the cockpit and reaches over me to grab the window handle. He starts coughing and has to pull back. "Shit! I couldn't get it."

"How you doin', ma'am?" Lego says.

"I still don't have a visual," I say.

I don't think I've ever gripped the controls as tightly as I am now. I'm flying on instruments, we're approaching the back of a ship, one with a very small flight deck, a deck that is anything but stable, and one that I can't see. I breathe through the narrowest slit in my teeth. I know I'll start coughing if I open my mouth any wider.

"Ma'am, we need to descend, nice and easy," Lego says. "We're almost at threshold. Keep it steady. Steady. There. Crossing threshold. Steady. We're fifteen feet above the deck."

I look up. Thank God. The ship's superstructure and the stabilization bar—a horizon reference. It's moving in and out of the smoke. Oh, crap. Now it's gone. I can't see the deck below me at all, which is probably a good thing because frankly, I don't want to know. My eyes go back to the gyro.

"Okay, ma'am, back two. Steady. Left one. Steady. The deck's movin' like a motherfucker. Steady. I'll try to call it on a rise. Steady. Back one. Steady."

I'm swimming in sweat and my hands are starting to cramp. *Come on! Get this down!*

Because Commander Claggett has jettisoned his escape hatch, the sound of the rotors echoing against the metal of the aircraft hangar doors resonates like thunderclaps. Wind gusts through the cockpit, rushing across my face, yet doing nothing to rid the aircraft of smoke.

"Once you're on deck, you'll need to keep flyin'," Lego says. "There's a good chance we might have to pick up again. Back one. Steady. Up one. Steady. Left one. Steady. Steady."

I don't know how much longer I can hold this. My throat is scratchy and I can't start coughing now. Commander Claggett is hacking next to me. Oh please, let us get down fast.

"Sorry, ma'am. Left one. Steady. Left one. Steady. The deck's just . . . goddamn it! Steady. Left one. Okay, steady. Steady. Now! Down, down, down!"

I drive the helicopter to the deck, landing firmly. The chock and chain men run under the rotor arc to secure us.

The ocean lifts the ship, tossing it down the steep backside of a colossal swell, the wheels of the helicopter perilously close to slipping. If they do, we would slide straight across the deck and topple over the edge. So I move the stick like I'm flying, to keep the wheels in place while the men underneath work to tie us down. I'm still operating in the blind, so the manipulating of the controls is happening by feel. Shit. This is *not* good.

"Easy back on the cyclic," Lego says. "Stay with it."

Come on! Come on! Come on!

"Stay easy back," Lego says. "We're still pitchin' down. Stay with it. Stay with it."

God, this is taking forever!

"Damn it already! Come on!" Lego says, imploring the chock and chain men to hurry. "Okay, steady, ma'am. We're starting to pitch up now. Easy forward. Easy forward. You've got this. Steady. One more chain to go.

You've got this. Steady. Steady. Okay, we're chained. Shut the bird down ASAP!"

You don't have to tell me twice.

I slump in my seat. *Holy hell . . .*

4

"Mess, get the pax out the back!" Lego shouts.

Commander Claggett reaches by feel for the switches to kill the engines, while at the same time, Lego, who has jumped down to the deck, yanks on the outside handle of the pilot's escape hatch until it falls free. I breathe deeply, pulling in a lungful of smoke, and immediately begin coughing.

I rip out my radio cord, undo my harness, and fumble to get out. It's about a five-foot drop to the deck from where I'm sitting, so Lego helps me down. Smoke is billowing out of the aircraft, and through the haze, at least a dozen sailors run toward the bird, some in flight suits, some with firefighting gear. I double over, racked with a fit of coughing. Lego keeps one hand on my back and the other on my arm as he leads me away. Several people rush to my side, supportive hands, ushering me along. The ship is pitching so violently, I'm having trouble balancing.

I need some space. I need to sit down.

"Fuck!" Lego shouts, looking behind us. "What the fuck are they doin'? Shit, they're comin' with fire extinguishers!" Lego is in a panic. They don't need fire extinguishers for this, and the chemical would be a nightmare if it got into the control box.

"Sir, can you watch her?" Lego says. "I'll be right back."

"I've got her. Don't worry," an unfamiliar voice says.

A man wearing a flight suit has me by the arm, leading me away from the aircraft. I quickly read the name tag—Lieutenant Marxen. The logo on the tag is instantly recognizable. Shadow Hunters.

He guides me toward a metal box near the railing that houses deck-edge lighting and I lower myself to sit. Dropping my elbows on my knees, I hold my helmeted head in my hands.

I need to get myself together. I've experienced my fair share of emergencies with this aircraft and it's always an out-of-body experience. I drift away from myself and watch the ultra-focused person that's left shut out all peripheral noise and execute.

The only problem with this ultra-focus is that once we've made it through safely, the extraneous noise I had kept at bay rushes into my brain all at once—the noise of what could have happened—a transmission grinding itself into oblivion and the rotors seizing, an aircraft breaking apart and freefalling, aircrew screaming.

But the worst part is knowing what waits below—an insidiously patient, always-hungry ocean. This fact alone is responsible for my physical reaction now—hands shaking, breath accelerating, body shuddering.

"Are you okay?" Lieutenant Marxen asks, putting a hand on my back.

No, I'm not okay. The enormity of what just happened, what could have happened. That god-awful water just laughing as it waits. I'm not handling it well. Damn it. I hate this about myself. *Just handle it, Sara!*

"You're shaking," he says.

"I'll be fine in a second. Just give me a second!" I say a little too sharply. He removes his hand.

Lego returns, squatting down to my level. "How ya doin'?"

"Not so good," I say more honestly.

With Lego, I can be totally open. Same with Messy. When we fly together, one risky mission after another, I entrust them with my life each and every time. Operating in close quarters, I move the controls almost instantaneously with their calls, not questioning, not hesitating, trusting that they're going to get it right. It's hard to hide anything from them, but even so, as a friend, I would never try to.

"Well, you fuckin' rock, ma'am! That's all I gotta say. I've never seen flyin' like that in my life. Hell, I still can't believe what you pulled off. Seriously, you were flippin' amazing!"

"She was flying?" Lieutenant Marxen says. "We couldn't see who it was through the smoke."

"Fuck, yeah. And thank god she was at the controls. Smoothest pilot we got. Fuck, we woulda gone in the drink otherwise."

"Kyle," I say. "Thanks. I couldn't have done that without you."

"Shit, that was all you, ma'am. But we do make a good team, don't we?" He flashes his crooked smile.

Messy runs toward us, breathing hard. "Hey, ma'am. Doin' okay?"

I nod.

"Kyle, I need you back at the bird," he says. "Commander Claggett's recovered, and fuck, is he wound up!"

Lego looks to Lieutenant Marxen, who answers his unspoken request. "I'll stay with her," he says.

With a gentle squeeze on my shoulder, Lego stands and sprints off with Messy.

The flight deck remains in a state of chaos, people running to and from the bird, the ship pitching and rocking to scary degrees I've never experienced before, seawater and salt spray showering us from the edge of the railing. Surely they can't leave the weather decks open much longer.

I turn to Lieutenant Marxen as the coughs begin to subside, embarrassed by the tone of voice I just used with him. *It's not his fault you were shaking.*

"Thanks, for just . . . for sitting here with me," I say. "I'm feeling better now."

"You're welcome." His eyes remain on mine. So steady. I blink and look again. Strong eyes. What a strange thought.

"Eric Marxen." He holds out his hand and I take it.

"Sara Denning."

He releases my hand, but not his gaze. As his eyes move across my face, I have the strangest sense that something's not right.

"What is it?" I ask.

"You're, uh . . . you're not what I expected."

"Expected? What do you mean?"

He studies me in a bubble of drawn-out silence, oblivious to the frenetic activity surrounding us. His olive-green eyes move quickly, purposefully, sharp like a hawk's. Light brown hair worn in typical military fashion, close cropped, but slightly longer on top, frames an angular face. Several inches taller than I, he has broad shoulders and a lean build, and I have to admit, he's strikingly handsome. And this throws me. I make it a point not to notice the looks of the officers I work with and it usually doesn't take much effort. But I have indeed noticed Eric's, so much so that it's hard not to return his stare.

"It's nothing," he says finally. "Never mind."

I don't dwell on the comment, because my attention has been drawn to my hand, the one I hold in front of me, trembling. I make a fist and tuck it into my lap, disgusted by what I'm seeing.

"You know, most of us mere mortals would have been shaking during the emergency itself and probably botched the landing," he says. "But you held it together when it counted. That's the definition of a pressure player."

I wish I felt that way.

"You certainly know how to make an entrance!" The man who approaches wears a flight suit, lieutenant commander insignia, and an easy smile. His dark brown skin is slightly lined, his black hair sprinkled with a touch of gray. He holds out his hand. "Brian Wilcox."

"Sara Denning, sir." I shout to be heard over the wind.

"Brian is our officer in charge," Eric says.

"Nice to meet you, sir."

"Nice to meet you, too. And it's just Brian."

I've known Brian for exactly two seconds and I instantly like him. Far more relaxed and easygoing than Commander Claggett.

Brian waves over the rest of the Shadow Hunter pilots, and as they encircle us, Eric makes quick introductions. "This is Rob LeGrand," he says, motioning to the pilot standing next to Brian.

"Hey, Sara," he says, ducking to avoid a shower of seawater.

"And Ken Watkins, Ben Holcomb, and finally, Stuart Grady," Eric says, pointing to each. "So get this, did you know that Sara was the one flying just now?"

"Yeah, we found out from the crewmen," Brian says. "All I can say is *wow*."

The others nod in agreement.

This is new.

"Let's get out of this weather," Brian says. "Nick has already gone in. I think he's calling the *Kansas City* to let them know what's up."

Funny, I can't bring myself to think of Commander Claggett as "Nick." It would make him too . . . normal.

As I push myself to my feet, Brian adds, "We'll head to the wardroom. We can get you some coffee or something."

"Sounds great. Let me just run by the bird first," I say.

I zigzag toward the aircraft on unsteady legs, removing my helmet. The wind promptly whips my hair into a frenzy, wild strands blowing across my face and sticking to my mouth.

The only way I can wear my helmet with any degree of comfort is to have my hair down. I tuck it in my flight suit for flying and then tie it up before I leave the aircraft because it's too long to wear loose. I'll need to grab my hair tie from my helmet bag first thing.

As I corral my hair with my free hand, I look back to see the group following me. Maybe they're curious about what happened to the transmission just like I am.

A crowd of maintenance guys from the Shadow Hunters cluster inside the aircraft, Lego and Messy in the middle of it all. I poke my head in the main cabin door and make eye contact with Lego.

"Ma'am, the tranny just basically shat itself! We're gonna have to replace the whole fuckin' thing!"

"What?"

"Yeah, we're gonna have to do it right here, too."

"But how are we going—"

"Five four's gonna have to deliver it all—the parts, our maintenance guys. Good god above, it's gonna take fuckin' forever to get this done."

I turn to Brian and the rest of the pilots. "And we're going to be clogging your deck the whole time."

With our helicopter taking all the space on the flight deck, there won't be room to move their helicopters out of the hangar. This sucks for them. Oh, and I bet their captain is pissed. He won't have his air assets available to him the entire time we're here. Not good. That means the whole maintenance effort is going to be performed in a pressure cooker. The only concern of the *Lake Champlain*'s captain is going to be how soon we can get off his deck.

"You know, it's not like it matters," Brian says. "There's no way we're running flight ops in this weather anyway. We were just about to cancel everything when you guys showed up. And the weather's only getting worse."

"So that means our guys won't be able to deliver anything. Or deliver anything right away, anyway."

"I doubt it," Brian says.

Visions of a stranded Commander Claggett race through my head. He's so tightly wound anyway, this is definitely going to set him off.

"Lego, do you need anything?" I say.

"No, ma'am. We're just removing some panels here to get a better look-see."

"Okay. I'm going to head in for a moment."

"No problem. It's not like we're goin' anywhere soon."

I start to turn away, but stop. "How long do you think we'll be here?"

He looks at his hands, wiping them with a grease rag, as he considers it. "Let's see. . . . We'll have to pull the rotor head, the flight controls, all of it, just to get the tranny out. If we work through the night, we can probably get that done. Then if we get the parts in the mornin', the tranny change itself is easily over ten hours of work. And then we'll have to do the check flight, too."

He looks up. "I'd bet a paycheck we're lookin' at two nights on this ship."

5

Two nights—as in, we're going to be spending the night. And this is one time I'm not prepared. Normally, I keep a toothbrush, extra hair ties, and a few toiletries in my helmet bag just for instances like this, but I cleaned my bag the flight before last and never got around to resupplying it.

But what a dumb thing to be worrying about in light of what just happened.

"Come on," Brian says. "We'll show you to the wardroom."

I shove my helmet and gloves in my bag and follow the group into the hangar. We maneuver around two tightly packed H-60 Seahawk helicopters, turning sideways to squeeze between the bulkhead and an auxiliary power unit crammed in the corner. This is a far smaller space than our hangar on the *Kansas City*. I vow right then that when I return to our ship, I will never complain of claustrophobia again.

As we walk, I think about the fact that we're stuck on this ship and are going to need a place to stay. For the guys, it won't be a problem. For me? Different story. In an anomaly that has yet to be explained, the *Lake Champlain* has deployed without any women. Granted, women make up only roughly 15 percent of a carrier strike group, but the *Lake Champlain* has deployed with them in the past, so I'm not sure why it would be any different this time.

I'm no stranger to being in the minority, though. I've been assigned to short deployments as the only woman in the detachment, or perhaps as one of only two. But I haven't minded. I put my head down and do my job with two goals. Be competent and blend in—be the small dot.

Unfortunately, finding berthing for me in this instance is going to be a big dot thing. It's not like they have guest rooms. If Zack was here in my place, they would throw down a cot in one of the pilots' staterooms and he'd be set. Not so with me. They're going to have to jump through hoops to accommodate me. Someone is going to have to move out of his room. Shoot. I hate this. It's such a glaring you-are-not-part-of-the-fraternity moment. Special treatment for the female. The guys are going to groan. Shoot. Shoot. Shoot.

We enter the *Lake Champlain*'s wardroom, a tight, confined space, with one long, rectangular table running down the middle. The mess cranks— what the navy calls its cooks—are preparing for dinner and these guys barely have enough room to squeeze behind the chairs. They're also having difficulty keeping their feet, leaning and stumbling due to the ship's unpredictable movements—an always delicate balancing act.

"Why don't you have a seat here," Brian says. "I'll grab some coffee."

I take a seat at the far end of the table, the other pilots dropping into chairs around me. But curiously, Eric stands apart, moving to the other side of the room. Brian returns, coffeepot in hand, followed by one of the mess cranks, Seaman Ogilvy, who holds several mugs.

"So, welcome aboard the *Lake Champlain*," Brian says with a grin.

Seaman Ogilvy takes over, pouring the coffee—only halfway, so it doesn't slosh out—and serving. I don't think a cup has ever tasted so good.

"We've worked it out so that you'll take my room and I'll move in with these guys," Brian says. "Nick will stay with the XO," he adds, referring to the executive officer, who is second in command of the ship.

"I'm sorry about this," I say. "I don't want to kick you out of your room."

"Hey, it's not a problem. This is a small ship and when we have guests, we have to move to accommodate. It's not just you."

I smile in thanks. It was probably just an offhand comment, rendered without much thought, but Brian has no idea how much what he just said means to me.

The other pilots begin to pepper me with questions about the emergency, and while I'm answering them on the one hand, a separate part of my brain is hyperaware of the man leaning against the opposite bulkhead. Perhaps because he's looking at me. In a watchful way . . . a guarded way.

I sit straighter when his eyes narrow. He shifts to face the wardroom entrance.

Commander Claggett storms into the room like an ice pick in a sea of floating balloons. He dispenses with all pleasantries, not even acknowl-edging the others. "There you are," he says. "I wondered where you'd dis-appeared to." His tone is insolent and rude, like I've purposely been avoiding him. And I've heard this before, unfortunately.

"We need to send out the Hazard Report," he says. "Come on. We're going to Radio."

Keep your cool, Sara. Just keep your cool.

"I'm sorry, Brian," I say. "I have to go. Thanks for the coffee."

"You're welcome," he says. He then looks to Commander Claggett. "We've called a detachment meeting in the hangar in thirty minutes to plan for tomorrow and see what we can do to help. Maybe you can stop by after you finish."

Commander Claggett nods and motions for me to leave. I follow him to the wardroom door where he stops before opening it. "And what's with the hair? You need to put that up."

The blood rushes to my face and I grind my teeth. Hard. What an ass. What a complete ass. Everyone in the room just heard what he said, too. If I pride myself in one thing, it's my professional comportment, in both manner and dress. I can't believe he's zeroing in on this when we're in such a unique situation.

I take another breath—a deep, composing one—gather my hair, and tuck it down the back of my flight suit before starting forward.

Fortunately, the crafting of the message is quick, so we return to the aircraft hangar, where the Shadow Hunters' meeting is still in progress. Maintenance personnel are squeezed into nooks and crannies around their two aircraft, listening to Brian, who stands in the door of the maintenance office on the opposite side of the hangar. He motions for Commander Claggett to join him.

I stay where I'm standing, and thirty pairs of eyes remain on me—I suppose I am a bit of a novelty on this ship—but when Brian gives the floor to Commander Claggett to report on the planned schedule of events, everyone's attention shifts to him. Everyone's attention except one. Eric's eyes haven't moved from my position. I hold his gaze for a moment be-fore returning my focus to the front.

When the meeting wraps, I make my way toward Commander Claggett. I don't want him to complain about not being able to find me. By the time I reach him, he has already ducked into the maintenance office, huddled with Brian and the maintenance crew of the Shadow Hunters.

I slip into the corner to wait and Eric quietly moves to my side. He holds out his hand to give me something. A rubber band.

I stare at it, taken completely off guard. Day to day, the navy throws its share of curve balls, but I'm rarely surprised and almost always prepared. But this small act of kindness stuns me.

I shift my eyes from the rubber band to him, at a loss for what to say. I'm so dreadfully embarrassed about the whole episode, I was hoping everyone would have forgotten. But someone obviously didn't. It takes me several seconds to recover before I mouth the word "Thanks."

I pull my hair back, wrap it tightly in a bun, and fasten the rubber band around it as the rest of the Shadow Hunter pilots file into the office.

"Okay, guys," Brian says, "since flight ops will be on hold the next couple of days, this is going to be a great time for knocking out some training. Grady, do you have your lecture ready on Russian sub profiles?"

"Yep, all set. But be forewarned," he says. "It's Russian subs like you've never heard it before."

The group laughs and Brian joins them. "I don't doubt it," Brian says. "Let's plan on that tomorrow just before lunch, at eleven hundred."

"Brian, would you mind if Lace sat in on that lecture?" Commander Claggett says.

"No, not at all."

"She needs to get her recce up to speed and this will give her something useful to do tomorrow," he says, looking at me directly.

Son of a . . . This is twice now. First the hair and now the inference that my knowledge of submarine recognition is lacking. But the last comment is the worst—like the husband whose wife accompanies him on a business trip and he sends her out shopping to *give her something useful to do.*

Brian gracefully covers the awkward comment. "Sara, we'd love to have you and get your input. It'll be nice to hear your opinion . . . to get a different perspective."

And Brian does it again. I allow myself a small moment to imagine what it would be like to have an officer in charge like him. Open. Progressive. But I quickly banish the thought, knowing I need to remain where I am mentally, so I can deal with reality.

"Well, that should be everything," Brian says before turning to Commander Claggett. "They just started dinner in the wardroom if you'd like to join us."

Commander Claggett agrees, which comes as a bit of a shock. I was sure he was going to find something for us to do that was more pressing.

When we enter the wardroom this time, it's crammed with ship's officers, most of whom are clustered around one end of the table near the ship's commanding officer. Brian walks toward him, motioning for Commander Claggett and me to follow. His name tag reads ROBERT PLANK.

"Sir, this is Nick Claggett—the Sabercats' officer in charge—and Sara Denning," Brian says.

Captain Plank has silver hair worn high and tight—Marine Corps style—his eyes so dark, I can't discern the pupil from the iris. At his side, strapped in a holster, he wears a Beretta M9 semiautomatic pistol. *What is a ship's captain doing with a weapon on his person in the middle of the Pacific Ocean?*

He doesn't bother with pleasantries. "How long until you're off my deck?"

"Sir, we hope to have the transmission changed by tomorrow evening and then fly off the following day," Commander Claggett says.

"Two days . . . Well, ensure that it happens."

"Yes, sir."

The air detachment has congregated at the far opposite side of the wardroom. Brian takes his seat at the head of the table, opposite Captain Plank, and Commander Claggett takes the seat next to him.

Unfortunately, I have to sit next to Commander Claggett. I'm already bracing for the dinnertime conversation and wonder if by some miracle I'll be able to escape more humiliating treatment. Eric sits on Brian's other side, directly across from Commander Claggett.

Seaman Ogilvy rushes over to find out what we would like to drink and gives us the menu selections for the evening. I'm not very hungry, so I opt for a small salad.

The conversation is animated due to the weather. And speaking of weather, boy does this ship move. Everything is tied down because the pitching and rocking would knock anything un-stowed to the ground. I hold my glass so it won't slide, and proceed to eat my salad in a mental cocoon. Conversation hums around me, but tonight, I'd rather just stay out of it.

While I'm eating, I find that I can let go of my glass and it doesn't slide. Hmm. The ship is pitching buckets, but the plates and cutlery are staying put. I finally realize it's the table covering. I run my hand over it, touching my fingers down one at a time. It's sticky. We don't have this on the *Kansas City*.

I look up and see that no one else is holding on to their glasses or silverware either, including Eric, who watches me with a lighthearted look on his face as I explore the sticky tablecloth.

"Culinary non-skid," he says, grinning.

I smile, only to receive a scathing look from Commander Claggett, like I've interrupted him or embarrassed him or something.

But his caustic expression doesn't come close to rivaling Eric's. His eyes have turned cold.

So I'm rather surprised when he starts speaking to Commander Claggett in an upbeat voice. "Sir, I wanted to let you know that we've already started writing up our witness statements to attach to Sara's award recommendation."

I almost choke on the cucumber I'm chewing.

"Excuse me?" Commander Claggett says.

"Sara's NAM for her handling of the emergency today," he says.

NAM? Navy Achievement Medal? What on earth is he talking about?

"Her NAM?" Commander Claggett says.

"Oh, I'm sorry. You probably weren't thinking NAM. You were probably thinking COM, which is certainly understandable given what happened today, and I think our witness statements would support that. Don't you?" He turns to the other pilots.

"Hell, yeah," Stuart says. "That was the most incredible bit of flying I've seen in my life."

"And they had thirteen passengers onboard that were saved due to her flying," Ken adds.

"In addition to the aircrew, so that's actually seventeen souls," Ben says.

"What do you think, Brian?" Eric asks.

"Yeah, I think a COM would go through," Brian says. "Maybe NAMs for the aircrew?"

A Navy Commendation Medal? It's a higher-ranking award than a Navy

Achievement Medal. I can't believe this discussion is happening, and judging by Commander Claggett's expression, neither can he. An award? For me? Initiated by him? It would never happen. No matter the circumstance.

"I would think so," Brian says. "Captain Plank, sir, is this something we could run up our chain of command, since it happened on our ship?"

"That's fine with me," Captain Plank says. I guess he's been listening to the discussion. "I watched it all on closed circuit from the bridge, and awards for that would go through." He turns to Commander Claggett. "Get me those recommendations tomorrow and I'll send it up for approval. Navy COM for Lieutenant Denning and NAMs for the rest."

"Yes, sir. Okay, sir," Commander Claggett says.

I watch, incredulous, as Eric sits back with a satisfied smile.

6

As dinner progresses, I sit next to a hornet's nest, one that's being poked and prodded, swiped and stabbed. Commander Claggett is agitated and angry. His aircraft is down. He's stuck on another ship. The captain wants him off. The weather is lousy, which will cause inevitable delays. He's trapped with the one pilot he likes least, and this same pilot has been recommended for an award that he would never have generated on his own, yet that he now bears the responsibility for writing. I don't see how it could get much worse for him.

But he's not the only one who's bothered. The more I think about what just happened, the more it leaves a sour taste. This isn't how I wanted to get an award—to have Commander Claggett cornered into giving it to me. I want to earn his respect and have it initiated by him.

"Nick, do you want to come with me?" Brian says. "I can get you set up in the XO's stateroom. And Eric, why don't you show Sara around? Make sure she has everything she needs. My stuff is already out of my room, so she can have it."

"No problem," Eric says. He turns to Commander Claggett as the group rises and begins walking to the wardroom door. "Sir, is there anything you'll be needing Sara for tonight? Any messages? Anything? I don't want to inadvertently keep her from something you might need her to do."

Boy, does Eric pick up fast. He has read this perfectly. Because that's how it usually plays out. I'm blamed for not being available or ready or whatever all of the time.

"As a matter of fact, I do," Commander Claggett says. He looks at me directly. "I want those award write-ups in my hand tonight by twenty-one hundred!" His order is accompanied by a noticeable glare of disapproval before he snaps his head and storms out the door.

I put my hands on my hips, sucking in my breath and holding it. I simmer here, staring straight ahead, as the group files out.

When it's finally quiet, only Eric remains.

"I don't want this," I say. "Not like this."

"Not like what?"

"Commander Claggett was forced into this. I want to earn the award straight up, not have him coerced into giving me something."

Eric's hands now go to his hips. "For your information, you legitimately deserve an award for what you did today."

"Regardless, it should have come from him."

He huffs in exasperation. "Okay, I'm sorry. You're right. I shouldn't have interfered. But since I got you into this, since Captain Plank is expecting those recommendations, the least I can do is write them up for you."

"No, you don't—"

"I do," he says firmly. "Come on. We'll type it up in our stateroom. I'll just need some input on the specifics."

As he turns, he mutters under his breath, "And they're gonna be the best damn write-ups Admiral Carlson's ever seen."

He leads me into the cramped passageway and we hold the rails as we walk. Whoa. Pitch. Roll. Rock.

When we reach his stateroom, he opens the door just a crack and looks in. "Guys, I'm bringing Sara in." He turns to me. "Okay, we're good."

He pushes the door open wider so I can step through, and Ben and Stuart look up from their desks. "Hey, Sara."

"Hi, guys."

Yikes, this room is small. Two sets of bunks, stacked three high, fill this micro space. At the far wall, a cot stands on end, crammed between a bunk and a giant metal closet. There's zero room in here already and now they're adding a cot to boot. I feel so bad about this. Maybe I could sleep in the wardroom or something.

"What do you think?" Eric says.

"Are there really six of you in here?"

"Yep. All of the pilots except Brian, and the ship's navigator."

Ben and Stuart are sitting at desks half the size of the one I use in my stateroom.

"There are only two desks," I say.

"Yeah, we have to share," Eric says.

I'm getting embarrassed now. If they could see where I live, well, it's the Taj Mahal compared to this.

"Ben, can we use your desk?" Eric asks. "I told Sara I'd help her with the award nominations."

"Oh, about that," Stuart says. "We didn't write up any witness statements. What were you talking about?"

"Yeah, I just made that up," Eric says casually.

"You what!" I say.

"Lieutenant Marxen . . . showcasing his quick-thinking oratorical prowess once again," Stuart says.

My hands are back on my hips, my mouth open. "You . . ."

Eric smiles conspiratorially.

"So is this a normal thing for him?" I say, turning to Ben and Stuart.

"Yeah," Ben says. "We don't know how he does it, but he can sort of bend anyone to his will."

"It's a bit scary, really," Stuart says. "Must be some special training you ring knockers get at the Academy."

Even though Stuart has said this in good humor, he's referring to one of the nicknames for a Naval Academy graduate, born from the oversized class rings worn by many upon graduation. A small minority of those wearers tend to go a bit overboard, flaunting it as a symbol of their perceived superiority over officers who attended colleges elsewhere. And in some cases, it boils down to an authority thing. You will do this because—*knock, knock* of the ring on the table—I'm an Academy grad and I say so.

Eric doesn't wear a ring and I didn't know he was an Academy grad. But now that I do, I couldn't imagine him wearing one. In just the little interaction I've had with him, he would never have to *remind* anyone of his authority, and he certainly doesn't carry any airs about him.

I don't wear mine either, but not for any stated reason. I think it's just that I have my mom's DNA. Down-to-earth Barbara Denning was never one for wearing jewelry.

"All right, enough," Eric says good-naturedly. "Can we just get this done?"

Ben passes his seat to Eric, who pulls his laptop from the recesses of the desk, opens it, and pulls up the template.

"Okay, we'll do yours first," Eric says. "So, tell me what happened."

"Actually, it was pretty straightforward. We had a chip light with a secondary indication of smoke and we landed."

He gives me a you've-got-to-be-kidding-me look.

"What?" I say. "You asked what happened."

"So I see I'm going to have to write this myself," he says with an exaggerated exhale. "But let's check a few things for clarity and truth of fact, shall we? How many pax were you carrying?"

"Thirteen."

"Thirteen. Good. So you were the pilot at the controls responsible for saving the lives of seventeen souls total. Good."

"But—"

"Next question. Did you or did you not have a cockpit filled with smoke?"

"I did."

"Did you or did you not have a visible horizon?"

"I did not."

"So you flew an instrument approach with a zero-foot ceiling and zero feet of visibility. Good."

"But—"

"Next question. You flew a zero/zero instrument approach to the back of a pitching and rolling ship. Guys?" He turns to Ben and Stuart. "Do you remember the pitch and roll we were sustaining during flight quarters?"

"I think it was pitch four, roll five," Stuart says. "Hold on a sec. I'll call and verify."

"And how about sea state?" Eric says.

"I'll get that here in just a second," Stuart replies.

Eric gives me a look that says he's going to write this whether I help him or not.

"Okay, yeah," Stuart says, hanging up. "Pitch four, roll five, sea state seven."

"Got it," Eric says, typing. "By the way, and this is just out of curiosity, is there any reason Commander Claggett didn't take the controls for that approach?"

"I don't know. I asked him right after we got the caution light if he wanted to fly, and he said no."

Eric shares a puzzled look with the other pilots.

"And besides, he was coughing so badly, he couldn't have taken them if he wanted to."

"Strange," he mutters. "Okay, back to the award. How long would you say you sustained a no-reference hover over a flight deck at pitch four, roll five?"

"I don't know. It seemed like forever."

"She had to have been there close to a minute waiting for the right moment," Stuart says.

"Actually, that was Lego waiting for the right moment," I say. "He's the one who called me in on the approach, kept me steady in the hover, and called me down to land. In fact, Eric, if we have to do these awards, can we put Lego in for the same one I'm getting? Really, he was my eyes. I couldn't have done it without him."

"I totally agree," Eric says. "We'll do his after yours."

By the time Eric completes my citation, it reads more like God was flying the aircraft than Lieutenant Sara Denning, but he's not budging on the edits. I'm pleased most of all with the write-up he creates for Lego. He deserves every word of it. I also think it's great that Lego will be put in for an award higher than Commander Claggett's.

And I have this sneaking suspicion that if Commander Claggett changes the award recommendation for Lego, or any of Eric's wording on any submission, somehow Eric's originals are going to find their way to Captain Plank.

"There," Eric says, handing me the printouts. "And with an hour to spare."

"Thanks . . . sort of."

He rolls his eyes. "So, do you need anything? Do you want to grab a shower?"

A shower would be nice. But then I think it through. I'd be putting on the same stinky T-shirt, shorts, and flight suit that I have on now once I got out of the shower. Yuck. Oh, man. I'm going to be here for two days with no change of clothes, no toiletries, nothing.

"Eric, this is so awkward, but I don't have anything with me. No clean clothes, not a towel, not even a toothbrush."

"Don't worry about anything, Sara," Ben says. "Just sic Eric on it and he'll get you what you need."

"I've got it covered," Eric says. "How about this? Let's go turn in the write-ups to Commander Claggett first to get that over with. That way, you won't have to see him anymore tonight. Then I can get you some overnight stuff."

"Okay," I say. "Ben, thanks for letting us use your desk. I know I've infringed on your time."

"Oh, please," Ben says.

As we leave his stateroom, Eric turns and motions for me to give him the award recommendations. I do, wondering what he's up to, and follow him to the executive officer's stateroom. The nameplate on the door reads COMMANDER HICKS.

"Sir, it's Lieutenant Marxen," he says after knocking.

"Come on in, Eric."

Eric opens the door and looks in. "Sirs, Sara is here with me. May we come in?"

He said "sirs" plural, so I guess Commander Claggett is here, too. I so don't want to see him.

Eric holds the door open wider to let me walk through and actually *that* I do want Commander Claggett to see.

"Sir," Eric says, addressing Commander Hicks. "I helped Sara with these award write-ups. She's a little too modest for her own good." He turns and gives me a look. "Anyhow, I thought you could read them first before I give them to Commander Claggett. I want to be sure that the *Lake Champlain* thinks they're up to snuff before handing them over."

Commander Claggett fumes as Commander Hicks takes the write-ups from Eric and looks them over. He does a thorough job, reading each one carefully.

"Well, you've outdone yourself once again, Eric. This is outstanding work."

"Thank you, sir."

"Nick, you're not going to need long with these," Commander Hicks says, handing the award recommendations to Commander Claggett. "Eric's work is always first-rate. And you know, we could sign these right now and pass them up to Captain Plank. He'd be quite impressed if you had these to him only two hours after his request."

"Sir, I could wait here while you both give your signatures and then hand-deliver them to Captain Plank just to make sure it gets done in a timely way as you suggest," Eric says.

"Great idea," Commander Hicks says. "This shouldn't take but a minute." Commander Hicks looks at Commander Claggett with an expression that says, *Just sign the paperwork.* He can, because he outranks him. Commander Claggett's rank when written out fully is actually *lieutenant* commander, one step below commander—the XO's rank.

As Commander Claggett scrawls his signature four times and hands the paperwork to Commander Hicks, who adds his, I realize that Eric has done it again. Had I given these to Commander Claggett, who knows what would have happened to them? Delayed perhaps, for oh, two days? Now we're off the *Lake Champlain,* out of sight, out of mind, award problem solved.

But Eric has put Commander Claggett exactly where he wants him once again—and there's nothing he can do or say to get out of it.

Ben and Stuart are right. I'm not sure how he does it. And I'm not sure if I'm happy or irritated all the more.

"Thank you, sirs," Eric says. "Have a good evening."

We leave and now it's my turn to give Eric the look.

He grins, a little too proud of himself. "Here, let me show you to Brian's room and then I'll get these delivered."

Stepping into Brian's room is like stepping into a broom closet. Yes, it's a single-man room, but geez. No couch and extra furniture in here like Commander Claggett enjoys on the *Kansas City.*

"I'll be back," he says. "If you need anything in the meantime, you know where the guys are."

"I'll be fine."

I squeeze into the small chair that's wedged between the micro desk and bunk, put my elbows on the table and my head in my hands. I think I've had more stimuli today than my twenty-six-year-old brain can handle. Commander Claggett. Eric. The in-flight emergency. The restless water . . .

I decide to close it out for a moment. I fold my arms on the desk, rest my head there, and close my eyes.

7

Ian is whooping with delight and I'm hovering in that magical realm between sheer terror and unchecked exhilaration, running Big Smokey Falls with a scary fast flow.

The thunderous roar of water and Ian's laughing fill my ears. He's thrilled with his new electric-red kayak.

Too late, I realize we've drifted too far left. A torrent of white water crashes around me.

The world flips.

Pummeled by the river, my upside-down kayak crashes into boulders, twisting and jerking, pinning me underwater. The current rips the paddle from my hand.

And then, the violent thrashing abruptly halts.

I've stopped and I don't know why.

I can't move. My brain is blank. I flail wildly. The kayak isn't budging.

I'm out of air! Oh god! Involuntarily, I start to breathe in. My chest tightens like a vise around my lungs.

A far-distant voice tells me I know what to do, that I know the procedures to extricate myself from the kayak skirt that holds me in place. But I'm deaf with panic. My mouth opens and my body convulses.

My head snaps up, my heart thrumming against my chest. I wipe my face, wet with perspiration, trying to register where I am. I look blankly at the door.

"Sara?" Eric calls. I hear the knock on the door again. "Sara?"

It's okay. It's okay. You're all right.

I take a deep breath. Okay.

"Come in."

Eric moves through the door, but stops when he takes in my expression. "Are you okay?"

"Yeah . . . yes. I just nodded off for a moment."

"Oh, okay," he says, placing a neatly stacked pile on the desk. "I got you some things."

I lift a gray zippered pouch from the top and open it to find an entire stash of toiletries—shampoo, conditioner, soap, razor, toothbrush, toothpaste, deodorant, lotion, and a brush.

"How did you . . . ?"

"Ship's store."

"But it's almost twenty-one hundred. Surely it's not open now."

He grins.

Next on the pile, a T-shirt, a pair of gym shorts, and some flip-flops. And towels underneath those.

I lift up the T-shirt on top, plain maroon in color, size large. I raise my eyebrows.

"The store doesn't carry clothing, so I hope you don't mind. That's mine. So are the shorts. I figure you can roll them up at the waist or something. They do sell the flip-flops and I bought the smallest size they had."

"You bought all this? Eric, I don't have any money with me, but I'll pay you back. I feel terrible. I didn't think you were going to buy stuff."

"Sara, it's nothing."

"And you're lending me your clothes. Are you sure?"

"Of course. I'm just worried you'll be freaked out about wearing my gym stuff. They're clean. I mean they're washed and everything."

"No, no, it's not that. I just hate that I'm putting you out. You're giving me your clothes. Spending your money. You gave up your evening to write stupid award nominations."

"They weren't stupid and I haven't given up anything tonight."

His gaze doesn't waver and I'm held there, stunned by the current that just shot through my body.

"I . . . well, thanks . . . for all this."

"You're welcome," he says.

I pry my eyes away. "So, where are the showers?"

"I'll show you. I'll have to stand guard, though. There's only one place to take showers in Officer Country."

"Oh. Well, I'll be quick about it."

I take my pile and follow him down the passageway. When he checks the shower room, it's being used, so we stand outside and wait. Two guys walk out, towels around their waists, but I don't dwell on it. Eric then gives the okay.

I'm in, shampooed, conditioned, soaped, and washed in about three minutes. And I am *so* glad he brought me some flip-flops. The shower floor was just . . . well, I'm not going to dwell on that either.

I look at my rumpled, sweaty flight suit on the floor. Along with it lie sweaty shorts, a sweaty T-shirt, sweaty underwear, a sweaty bra, and sweaty socks. I wonder if they have the ability to do their laundry individually on this ship like we do on the *Kansas City*.

Well, there's no way I'm putting on my gross underwear. I know Eric probably won't appreciate it, but then again, he'll never know. I put on his shorts without underwear. But the bra, shoot. I'm going to have to endure that one. Yuck. It's still damp. His maroon shirt goes on after that. I do a super-quick brush of the hair and I'm done. If I were timing, I'd bet six minutes, tops.

I thought I was pretty fast. I mean, I *was* really fast. But when I emerge from the shower room, there's a line of three guys waiting to go in. I hate that I've made them wait.

"I feel a thousand times better," I say as we duck back into Brian's room. "Thank you."

I busy myself putting things away, but then, I realize he hasn't responded. I turn and find him leaning against the doorway, arms crossed, just watching.

I grab my hair and self-consciously twist it up, securing it into a pony-tail with the rubber band he gave me earlier.

"It's longer than I thought," he says, inclining his head slightly, indicating my hair.

"Oh, I, um . . . yeah," I say.

When it's wet, I guess my hair is pretty long, falling mid-back.

"So, uh . . . how about your dirty stuff?" he says. "Did you want to throw that in the laundry?"

"You have one?"

"Yeah. It's down two decks."

"Oh." I'm imagining myself running belowdecks in flip-flops.

"I'll take it for you. That's not a problem. I have detergent, too."

I so desperately want to wash my bra and underwear, but oh man. This guy is entirely too good-looking to wash my underwear.

"Really, I'm okay with it."

"Okay, just a second." Before I've really thought it through, I'm taking off my bra the clandestine way. It's easy in a big, draped shirt like I'm wearing now. Hands behind back to unhook clasp, pull arm toward body and out of sleeve, pull strap off shoulder and slide down arm while under shirt, reinsert arm in sleeve, repeat on other side, pull out from below. All with the shirt on and nothing showing. It's off in about ten seconds.

"Is that something all girls know?" he says. "My sisters used to do that."

"I cannot believe I just did that in front of you. What the hell was I thinking?"

"Hey, you've had a long day."

I try unsuccessfully to stifle a yawn as I hand him my disgusting pile. "I'm not quite sure how I'm going to repay you for this, but I owe you big time."

"You should get some sleep," he says. "Will you be okay? Do you need anything else?"

"No, I'm good, thanks."

When he leaves, I sit back in the desk chair and pull my knees to my chest. His shirt slides easily over my legs, so I'm covered completely in a blanket of maroon.

I cannot believe I just did that. Did I really just take off my bra in front of him? Oh my god. I can never tell Emily. I'd never hear the end of it.

I stretch my arms above my head, allowing the yawn in force, this time. But as my arms settle back to the chair, my lungs expelling a rush of air, I'm left with a distinct heaviness as the emergency landing materializes into conscious thought.

I stand, flicking off the overhead light, and crawl into the rack. I pull the covers over my head, close my eyes, and wait for the smoke, the ocean, and the nightmares to take me.

8

I stand in a tiny structure, sunken into the flight deck itself, designed for the pilots who remain on the ship to communicate with their counterparts in the air. The space is topped with slanted windows that protrude just above the steel surface of the deck. It's crowded with four people—Commander Claggett, Brian, Eric, and me. I rise on my tiptoes, watching Sabercat 54 hovering over the flight deck and lowering parts by hoist.

The ship continues to toss and dip in the heavy seas, the water muted to a predictable ashen gray under a stormy sunrise. The flight deck remains unsteady, as it was yesterday, and Zack is having a rough go of it. I can see him clearly, wrestling with the controls to keep it steady. But then, it does take some time for a pilot to settle into a groove in a situation like this.

I'm glad I have two other pilots—neutral observers—watching, so I don't have to question my sanity when Commander Claggett begins to speak.

"Now *that's* some aggressive flying," he says, leaning over to Brian. "Zack's an animal in the cockpit. Goes after it! Love it!"

To his credit, Brian turns and gives me a quizzical raise of the eyebrows.

I shift my attention back to an aircraft that's bobbing and weaving in what looks like a helicopter prize fight. Now I understand the holes in the ramp, which from this vantage point appear to have been mended.

"I'm going to maintenance to get this show on the road," Commander Claggett announces, brushing past me. "Come on, I want you involved with this."

Once the work begins, I think about Commander Claggett's presence here. In my opinion, it's a hindrance. The guys know what they have to do. They know there's a time crunch. Having someone standing over them who is not contributing to the maintenance effort, a person only interested in hurrying the process along, is detrimental to the evolution as a whole.

But I'm just here to observe and learn. I sit on a work stand near the hangar door for the next four hours, watching the Sabercat and Shadow Hunter maintenance teams shine as they join forces to bring our aircraft back to a working status.

As always, Lego and Messy lead the maintenance effort. They know the aircraft inside and out, one specializing in aircraft engines, the other in avionics and electronics. Between the two of them, they've saved us on numerous occasions when we've broken down without the resources we'd normally need to get ourselves flying again.

Their southern ingenuity is legend. Just like they can open the hood of any car, take the engine apart, and put it back together, so can they dissect the innards of an H-46 helicopter. Sometimes, I don't want to know how they fix things. They've pulled out the duct tape or its equivalent too many times to count, and yet somehow, always find a way to get us home.

Add their skills as aircrewmen to their maintenance prowess, and they are, simply put, the all-around best aircrew team I've ever flown with.

They look to me now, expressions of relief on their faces, as Commander Claggett finally takes his leave to update Captain Plank.

"How are you guys holding up?" I ask, jumping down from my seat.

"Decent, ma'am," Messy answers. "Although Kyle's not too happy."

"Why's that, Lego?" I ask.

"Because my wife sent a care package and it's sittin' on my rack on the *Kansas City*. Never got a chance to open it since we had to leave so fast."

"Oh, man," I say.

"Yeah, Michelle said in her last e-mail that the kids were sending along some art projects."

"More art projects?" Messy asks. "Dude, there's no more wall space." Messy looks to me. "He's got more damn art projects plastered over the walls in our berthing. I don't know how he passes inspection."

"Remind me not to share any of my homemade cookies with you," Lego says.

"Ah, dude, them's fightin' words. You know I'm only jokin'."

"Besides, you'll understand soon enough," Lego says.

"What's this?" I ask.

"You haven't told her?" Lego says.

"Haven't had a chance," Messy says, turning to me. "When we were in Pearl Harbor, I found out that Leah's pregnant."

"Congratulations!" I say. "Messy, that's great news. I'm so happy for you."

"Thanks, ma'am," Messy says. "She's due the week we're scheduled to get back."

"Sounds like a perfect homecoming to me," I say.

"Yeah," he says, sweetly.

"All right," I say. "I've bothered you two enough. I'll get out of your way."

I return to the work stand, but as I move to sit, I hear a now-familiar voice.

"Hi," Eric says, walking delicately through the maze of aircraft parts that litter his path.

Funny. The current thing. It just happened again.

"I wanted to check on your *involvement* in the maintenance effort," he says. "I can see you're adequately involved, Lieutenant, however, it's still inadequate."

A smile escapes.

"I'd say we need some more aggressiveness here. You know, grab a wrench. Go after it."

"Thanks a lot," I say, grimacing. "So what's up?"

"I came by to get you for training."

"Is it eleven hundred already?"

"Yeah, I know. Time flies when you're watching a transmission change." I'm smiling again. What the heck?

"Guys," I say to Lego and Messy. "I'll be back in about an hour or so."

"Okay, ma'am," Lego says.

Balance is a challenge as I attempt to weave my way as Eric did through the assorted helicopter parts on the flight deck—tied down or stored in secured containers to keep them from rolling. Although, based on what I've seen both yesterday and this morning, I think balance has been difficult for everyone. Members of ship's company notoriously razz the air detachment for not having their "sea legs." But even for these salty sailors, no matter how long they've been at sea, if the waves are big enough, they're going to find their gaits challenged, as well.

It makes me feel better when Eric has to brace himself against the open hangar door before stepping through. "I need to stop by Captain Plank's office on the way," he says over his shoulder.

"Okay," I say. And it is okay. Like really okay. The sensation couldn't be stranger, but walking with him, I feel lifted or . . . or something.

We stumble through several passageways as we make our way forward, leaning sideways and reaching out to the bulkheads for support.

"Geez!" he says, with a chuckle, accelerating forward as the ship pitches down, reaching for the handle of an open hatchway to steady himself.

"Guess Brian was right about the weather getting worse," I say, catching up.

"People would probably *pay* for a ride like this," he says.

"No kidding," I say, my legs planted wide, hands gripping the hatch opening. The bow begins to rise again, and I regain stability for a moment.

"After you," he says, standing aside. I step through the hatch into the ladder well that leads one deck up to the commanding officer's stateroom.

I reach for the ladder rail to begin climbing, and the ship lurches, pitching steeply downward once more.

"Ho—!" Eric blurts out before slamming into me from behind.

We stumble sideways and my hands fly out to grab something, anything. The next thing I know, we're righting ourselves, our hands latched onto the arms of the other.

"Sorry about that," he says with a laugh.

"No worries," I say.

"Wait, hang on," he says. We remain braced, hands to each other's upper arms, as the ship rolls through another monstrous swell. "There we go," he says, as the ship somewhat steadies. "You all right?"

"Yeah," I say, looking up to meet his eyes. "You?"

"Yeah," he says.

We stand like this a few seconds longer than necessary, before reacting like we've each touched a hot stove, abruptly letting go.

"Uh, right then," I say, turning to climb the ladder.

I shake my head to clear it, stepping off the last rung, pressing myself into the corner of the ladder well to wait for Eric.

"I think this ship puts the roller coaster at the Mall of America to shame," I say when he arrives.

"I don't doubt it," he says. "Although I've never been to the Mall of America, just heard about it." He turns right, down the last, even narrower, passageway that leads to Captain Plank's stateroom. "You're from Minnesota, then?" he asks.

"Sort of," I say, grasping the rails on either side, advancing hand by hand. "We moved around a lot, but that was the last place I lived before entering the navy, so I call it home. And my parents still live there, so yeah, I guess that's home."

"Well, it looks like you're going to have a lot to write home to your friends about. I doubt they've ever experienced anything like this."

Friends . . . What do I say to this? I've never really had too many friends. All along, I've blamed it on the fact that my military family had to move so much when I was growing up. But I know it's more me than anything— ever the introvert. Besides, I never felt the pressing need to make friends since I always had my brother. . . .

I don't realize Eric has stopped in front of Captain Plank's door until I nearly run into him.

"Sara?" he asks.

"Sorry?"

"You okay?"

I blink, my brother's face disappearing from my imaginings, and return my focus to Eric. "Um, yes. Yes."

He furrows his brow slightly as he turns to knock on the door.

"Sir, it's Lieutenant Marxen and Lieutenant Denning."

"Come in," Captain Plank answers.

Eric holds the door open for me to walk through, and while it's not a big deal, it sort of is. He's done it for me several times in the space of twenty-four hours, which just happens to be several times more than anyone else combined since I first donned a uniform eight years ago.

Nobody opens doors for me anymore. But I don't expect them to. I mean, I can open my own doors. It used to happen for me, when I was younger, in high school. But it was one of those things that became ancient history the instant I stepped foot in the Naval Academy. In that moment, I surrendered my "getting treated like a lady" card and was given the "you're in the military now so you can do it yourself" card. And I've always thought I wouldn't have it any other way.

So two things shock me here. One, he's holding doors open for me, and two, I like that he's doing so. I shouldn't like it, but I do.

My eyes shift discreetly to Captain Plank, who commands attention merely by his stillness. He sits ramrod straight at his conspicuously clean desk, pulling his eyes from his computer monitor only briefly to glance at us before swiveling in his chair. He leans over, punching in the key code to a safe located in the corner.

In the meantime, Eric and I stand next to each other at attention, the captain not having put us at ease. Every captain is different, some stricter than others, but on a bad weather day like today, it would be quite helpful to be able to stand normally for balance rather than legs and feet locked together.

Technically, if you're standing at attention, you're supposed to look straight ahead, not meeting the eyes of the superior who put you there. But since Captain Plank's back is turned, I have a moment to focus on the only item, save his computer screen, that holds real estate on his desk—his Beretta M9 pistol. Distinct due to its custom wood grip, the sidearm that he wore at his waist yesterday now rests in an elegantly carved, hardwood display stand, shiny with a furniture-grade satin finish.

My time for scrutiny is cut short as he swivels back to us, holding what looks like a large bank deposit pouch, colored dark blue and unmarked. From inside, he removes a smaller brown envelope, the words TOP SECRET printed across the front. He opens the envelope and hands the one-sheet message to Eric without comment or emotion.

He's giving a Top Secret message to a lieutenant . . . which means Eric would only be allowed to read it if he held a Top Secret clearance. It's not unheard of for a lieutenant to have one, depending on the job, but strange that a pilot in his capacity would. Strange, too, that Captain Plank would have had me come in with Eric if this was to be the nature of their meeting.

I take a chance, shifting my eyes to the left, watching as Eric scans the contents of the message. His face tightens as he reads.

"The Australians?" Eric asks, looking up. "Is this a done deal then, sir?"

"It is," Captain Plank states.

Eric exhales, a long exhale.

Each stares, unblinking, into the other's eyes as something is silently communicated between them. "Sir—"

"Your reservations are noted," Captain Plank says, acutely blunt.

He shifts his laser-sharp gaze to me. I can't see it directly, but I feel it. Like a missile that's acquired its target and locks on, his focus remains here for several long, uncomfortable seconds before he speaks.

"That is all," he says finally, issuing our dismissal.

Eric and I execute an about face and a crisp exit. Once outside, Eric puts his hands on his hips and stares down the passageway, firmly setting his jaw. He breathes in well, his chest rising, holding here for a long moment before finally exhaling. The passageway is empty, but something in his mind's eye holds his undivided attention.

"Eric?" I ask.

He drops his eyes to me, his expression serious, worried, frustrated—a host of emotions playing on his face. "Come on," he says, finally. "We're going to be late."

9

"About time you two showed," Stuart calls out as we walk into the wardroom.

"Sorry, my fault, Grady," Eric says, using what I now gather is the preferred way for the group to address Stuart—by his last name.

We pull out chairs to sit when Brian leans into Eric's ear. "Did you get the word that the skipper wanted to see you?" he asks.

Eric nods grimly. "I just came from there."

"What is it?" Brian says worriedly.

Eric lets out a resigned sigh. "It's confirmed."

"Confirmed . . . ?" Brian looks at Eric for some time with a questioning expression, but I see it in his eyes when he figures it out—whatever "it" is. They share a long and knowing look before taking their seats and turning their attention to Grady, who has started . . . singing?

Stuart Grady can't be more than five foot five, but it's sixty-five inches of spunk and madness. The episode with Captain Plank and the brief exchange between Brian and Eric are soon forgotten as Grady leads one of the funniest, most dynamic training lectures I can remember, launching into an extended rap about Russian submarines, the backbeat provided by Ben, Rob, and Ken.

Over the course of the hour, Eric's mood lightens, not only because of Stuart's hilarity, but also because of the easygoing chemistry of this pilot group. Even after the song ends, the guys keep it fun, jokes flying nonstop, one snappy witticism after another.

Through it all, I'm lulled into a false sense of security. I sit next to Eric, who now laughs alongside me. We joke. We smile. The defenses that are normally up and shored well have slackened. I don't need them here.

So I'm totally unprepared for what Commander Claggett has waiting when I return to the hangar to check in prior to lunch. I walk into the maintenance office and he's standing there, red. Make that purple.

"Come with me," he says.

He leads me out of the hangar to the far end of the flight deck behind our aircraft so we're hidden from view. And then he explodes.

"Where have you been?" he shouts.

"I—"

"How long did you wait after I left before you took off?"

"What—"

"This isn't a fucking vacation! The men need to see you here and you need to learn this shit! It's called professionalism!"

Professionalism? How dare he accuse—

"I want your ass in front of this bird until the transmission is in!"

He starts to march away and I think he's finished.

"And you sure as hell better be in the fuckin' aircraft the very second we're cleared for functional checks!" he says, turning.

I grit my teeth, fists clenched. *Hold your tongue, Sara. Hold your tongue.*

He stomps away. But he's still not finished. He wheels back, his body rigid.

"And you haven't once come to me to debrief the flight. Fuck, I have no idea where you've been hiding! I had to search you out for the god-damn Hazard Report. And has there been any follow-up on your part for that? Let me answer that. No. Has there been any initiative shown on your part whatsoever to ask me what's needed or what you can do to help this process along? No. But hey, you got your shower in. That was high on the priority list. I saw the guys waiting in line for you. I saw that! And then you had your fucking clothes washed? Are you fucking kidding me? And *you* were supposed to write the award nominations! Not Marxen! You're treating this whole thing like a goddamn slumber party when this is fuckin' serious shit!"

"But I was there!" I shout, pointing. "I was right there! All morning!"

"Save it!" he says, and storms off before I can get in another word.

I look across the aft end of the ship to the turbulent sea beyond, my blood roiling.

I hate this. I hate that man. I hate that I'm out here. I hate it all . . . and there's nothing to do about it.

I turn where I stand, a full 360 degrees, seeing nothing but an endless expanse of water. Weeks away from landfall, I can't pack up, leave work early, and go home. No. I must live with Commander Claggett within the confines of this tiny footprint of a navy cruiser in an ocean that spans sixty-four million square miles. Even the seabirds are absent. I haven't seen one in over a week.

I take several, deliberate, deep breaths. Behind me, the sounds of the maintenance guys returning from lunch increase in volume. They're going to be all over the aircraft here in a second, so I have to get myself together. Quickly.

I close my eyes and begin the mental transition.

I think about something neutral—dry, unemotional, and preciously neutral—and try to regurgitate it from memory. *Transmission oil hot caution light. Location—master caution panel. Power—battery bus. Oil temperature thermal switches—two forward transmission, one aft transmission. Light illumination—110 degrees.*

I repeat the facts, but say them aloud this time. "Transmission oil hot caution light. Location—master caution panel. Power—battery bus. Oil temperature thermal switches—two forward transmission, one aft transmission. Light illumination—one hundred ten degrees."

Wearing an expression that's as neutral as the facts that churn in my head, I pull my shoulders back and walk to the far side of the flight deck. I find my corner perch and there I sit, unmoving, until 2000 when the maintenance chief declares that 55 is ready for ground turns.

My helmet is on and I'm on top of the bird preflighting by the time Commander Claggett arrives. I don't care that the ship is rocking so badly my helmet visor is spotted from the salt spray. Or that I'm doing a balancing act with a flashlight because I preflight on a near moonless night. I hang on tight as I traverse the narrow sliver of non-skid across the top of the helicopter, over eleven feet above the deck, but there's no worry or fear. I'm just getting it done.

Without emotion, I climb into the cockpit, complete the necessary checklists, respond when spoken to, and endure over three hours of on-deck turning sitting next to a disrespectful, foul-mouthed powder keg.

Thankfully, we're not allowed to do airborne functional checks at night,

so we shut down just prior to midnight. Official sunrise is 0700 and therefore, so is our takeoff time. We can complete the first checks in the air en
route to the *Kansas City,* so there will be no need to land on the *Lake Champlain* again once we lift.

I wait until Commander Claggett steps out before I remove my helmet. Lego and Messy go about securing the aircraft for the night, folding
the rotors, tying them down, and covering the engine intakes.

I remain in the aircraft, looking up through the cockpit window. Breaks
in the clouds showcase hundreds of thousands of stars. The night sky in
the open sea is a treasure to behold. I suppose it's one of the few good
memories I'll take away from this deployment.

"Ma'am," Lego says.

"Hmm," I say, turning.

"We're gonna button up the doors now. You wanna get out?"

I leave my seat, climb into the cabin, and trudge down the steps of the
main cabin door.

"Are you all right?" he asks.

"Sort of. I'll see you in the morning."

I pass by the maintenance office to ensure I'm not needed for anything
else. The maintenance officer assures me I'm not, even though Commander
Claggett isn't here anymore to verify.

I drag myself back to Officer Country and Brian's room, taking a seat
on the rack. I have less than six hours before I see Commander Claggett
again. Better make the most of it.

I remove my flight suit and boots and proceed with a sponge bath.
Brian has a sink and mirror in his room, so I use a hand towel and do it
that way. And what the heck? Eric brought me a razor, so I'll use that,
too. I shave my legs standing up and use the lotion he provided, as well.
It actually doesn't smell too bad, even having been purchased from the
ship's store.

I wash my face and brush my teeth before donning my "pajamas," which
are Eric's maroon shirt and gray shorts. Removing the rubber band that
secures my hair, I scratch my head so it falls free. The brush Eric bought
for me is lying on Brian's desk, so I stand in front of the small mirror to
brush it out.

*See what happens when you let your guard down? You just open yourself
up. Normally, you would have shrugged this off, like water sliding over a rain-*

coat. But it hurt this time, didn't it? Stupid. You can't be stupid, Sara. You'll never make it.

It's almost thirty minutes after midnight when I hear the knock.

"Sara? It's Eric. Are you up?"

I open the door, but can't manage a smile. I notice that Eric's gym shorts and T-shirt ensemble is the same as mine, which shouldn't be a surprise since I'm wearing his clothes. His shirt is just a different color—olive green, like his eyes.

"We match," I say.

"That we do."

Our eyes hold . . . for a long time, they hold.

Sara, stop it. Enough!

"I know it's late," he says, "but I just came by to see if you needed any-thing."

"I'm fine, thanks. You thought of everything earlier," I say, motioning to the towels and toiletries on Brian's desk.

"All right. I'll just, uh . . . well, I'll see you tomorrow."

He starts to turn away, but stops.

"Is everything okay?" he asks.

"It's fine," I say too quickly. "I'm fine."

"Claggett?" he says.

"It's nothing, okay? Just . . ."

"It's *not* nothing. What happened?"

I look down at my hands that have been wadding up my shirt—his shirt—as I've been talking. I spread it out with my fingers before looking up.

"He sort of exploded earlier. Right after training."

"Oh, no."

"He got on me for not watching the tranny change this morning."

"But you did. You were there until we began training."

"I guess he forgot about the training."

Eric shakes his head. "I'll go talk to him—"

"No. He doesn't want to hear it. And besides, I can speak for myself."

"But—"

"Please. I said I'm fine, okay? I'll handle it."

He searches my eyes for a moment longer. "Okay. I guess I'll see you around, then." He turns and walks away without looking back.

I close the door and lean against it, nursing a queer, awful ache in the pit of my stomach.

10

"So then what?" Em says.

I'm giving her the play-by-play of my stay on the *Lake Champlain* following a torturously long day. The check flight for Sabercat 55 took a full thirteen hours to complete, all sitting next to a live wire in Commander Claggett.

"Hold that thought," I say. "I have *got* to get something in my stomach or I'm going to pass out."

Entering the empty wardroom, I make a beeline to the counter that supplies bread, peanut butter, and jelly. I put together a sandwich, fill a glass with lemonade, and drop into a wide, stainless steel chair—one of thirty or so positioned on either side of seven long, rectangular tables.

Having just departed the *Lake Champlain*, I gain a new appreciation for the ample size of our wardroom. Our tables are arranged end-to-end to form a U shape, filling the middle of the space. A lounge area with couches and a TV occupies the far corner. There's even room for a sizeable salad bar.

Steel blue-gray dominates—the color of the heavy-duty plastic table coverings. The chairs are a lighter shade of gray and this all contrasts not so nicely with bulkheads painted a stale yellow-cream, just like our stateroom.

I stare ahead at nothing as I eat, my mind crowded with images from my stay on the *Lake Champlain*. I'm so wholly engrossed in my thoughts that I don't notice the arrival of the ship's operations officer.

"Hey, Sara," he says in his slimy way. "Imagine finding you here."

"Yeah, imagine that, sir."

Oh, no. I don't want to be here—not alone with him. One of the most uncomfortable things about living and working on this ship is doing so with this man, Lieutenant Commander Doug Egan. During the six weeks I was onboard the *Kansas City* for work-ups, it was a nightmare because he wouldn't leave me alone, always "finding" me wherever I happened to be on the ship.

I'm in a delicate situation with him because he outranks me.

"What's this? You know you don't have to call me sir. It's Doug for you."

Oh, boy . . .

I keep him at arm's length and beyond, and I'm professional all the way with him. I've given him every subtle hint I can think of without actually saying, "Stay the hell away from me," but he just doesn't understand subtle.

"Let me grab some coffee and I'll join you," he says.

"Actually, I was just leaving."

"Leaving? But you've still got half a sandwich left."

"I'm really not that hungry."

I grab a napkin and begin wrapping my sandwich.

"So I was already thinking ahead to Hong Kong," he says. "I know this great place to eat that has an incredible view of Victoria Peak."

"I have duty in Hong Kong, sir."

"Well, lucky for you I sign off on the duty schedule. I can change that, no problem," he says with a wink.

"No, sir. You don't need to do that," I say, rising from the table. "I want to pull my weight with the duty schedule."

I make a hasty getaway to our stateroom, kicking the door closed once inside.

"What's going on with you?" Em says.

"Commander Egan."

"Oh, no."

"He found me in the wardroom."

"God, he is the creepiest creep. Seriously, you should say something to someone."

"But that's exactly what everyone wants to see happen—you know, another reason women shouldn't be here at sea. They just cause trouble."

"But you're not the one causing trouble. He is."

"I know. But it won't be perceived that way. You know that."

"Yeah, I know," Em says. "If women weren't here, this wouldn't happen in the first place. Blah, blah, blah."

"But you know what sucks about that? There are plenty of guys on this ship who don't treat me like this, who are decent. But I'd bet you ten to one that no matter where Commander Egan is stationed, like if he's on shore duty somewhere, he's going to be harassing the civilian secretary or a coworker or someone else. He's going to behave the same way whether out here or at home."

"Hey, you're preachin' to the choir, honey," Em says. "Well, it's up to you, but I would say something, because this is one fucking long cruise to be dealing with shit like that."

I drop my sandwich on my desk and change into my new pajamas— Eric's maroon shirt. I can't explain why I brought this with me. I brought his shorts, as well. Items I should have left on the *Lake Champlain*. I didn't see Eric before we took off this morning, so not only did I take his clothes, I didn't ask his permission. And now I'm going beyond that and wearing them.

My senses have officially taken their leave.

"What, no Vikings jersey?" Em says.

I stare, a deer-in-the-headlights stare. "I, uh . . . no . . . I mean, not tonight . . . that is, well, no."

"Have I seen that shirt before?"

"No . . . I, uh, I got it on the *Lake Champlain*. I didn't have any clean clothes, so . . ."

"And you're wearing that instead of your Vikings jersey? Wow, I never thought I'd see the day."

"This shirt's just . . . softer."

"Suit yourself," she says, raising her arms so her nightgown slides over them.

I wipe the faint bit of perspiration that has just surfaced at my hairline.

"By the way, they moved the Operation Low Level brief to tomorrow afternoon," she says.

"Wait, they didn't go ahead with the brief the day I left?"

"Nah. I guess the folks on the *Lake Champlain* are big players in the exercise, so it was postponed until they could be here."

"Oh, I see."

"And you've been assigned a training lecture," she says. "Automatic flight control system. It's due tomorrow."

"Great. Just what I need."

I watch as she searches through her stacks of books to select a new one. "Care for some reading material before bedtime?" she says, waving a dog-eared, tattered Harlequin in the air.

"No, absolutely not."

"Whatever, sappy pants," she says, crawling under her covers. "Looks like the sweet dreams will be mine tonight."

I climb into my rack, curl up sideways, and pull Eric's shirt over my knees, conflicted.

I switched shirts. My brother Ian's favorite Minnesota Vikings jersey for Eric's.

Ian's Vikings jersey has held up surprisingly well over the last nine years that I've worn it, and I've never imagined not wearing it. So it worries me how quickly I was able to fold it away to wear something else. To wear *someone* else.

I stretch out my legs, smoothing Eric's shirt so it lies flat across my torso, worrying also about the depth of feeling I would have to carry for some-one, conscious or not, to allow this to happen. The thought is mind-blowing. No, that can't be. It just can't be.

11

Em and I arrive early for the Operation Low Level brief, which we've learned is a counterterrorism training exercise, and take our seats in the wardroom. We're awaiting the arrival of Rear Admiral Robert Carlson, the carrier strike group commander, and his party. This exercise involves multiple players—the entire battle group will be participating—so we're joined by representatives from each ship, most of whom crowd the wardroom now.

Every pilot in our detachment is required to attend because the exercise will employ several helicopters, including both of ours. We're going to act as high-speed, low-level threats to the battle group. Each ship will then coordinate the tracking and simulated destruction of each threat.

I'm happy for the diversion. It will help me get my mind off my latest run-in with Commander Egan and distance myself from the emotion-twisting experiences of the *Lake Champlain*.

"Attention on deck!"

We rise and stand at attention as Admiral Carlson enters the wardroom, followed by the *Kansas City*'s commanding officer, Captain Scott Magruder. Behind him, a parade of commanding officers from every ship in the strike group.

At the end of the line? My heart stops. One Lieutenant Eric Marxen.

"Holy mother of god," Em whispers in my ear. "Look what just walked into our wardroom!"

"At ease," Admiral Carlson says. "Please take your seats."

As we sit, Em is drooling. "He looks like he just stepped out of fuckin' *GQ* magazine! Why can't they grow 'em like that on our ship?"

I motion with my head that she should pay attention to the admiral now that he has started speaking. But I'm not listening either. Eric stands to the side with his hands behind his back. He's wearing a khaki uniform, no ribbons or awards on his chest, just gold pilot wings above the left breast pocket. I wonder why he remains standing while the others in the arrival party have seated themselves.

I tune in to Admiral Carlson. Silver-haired, tall, and trim, he possesses a commanding voice that surprises. "We've completed almost three weeks of this cruise with the prime objective of making good transit time," he says. "Because we've made good progress, and because circumstances in the Middle Eastern theater currently allow it, our port call in Hong Kong is still a go on the schedule."

The news is met with smiles and audible sighs of relief. Ever since we cruised out of San Francisco Bay—what seems like years ago, not weeks—the rumor mill has been rife with speculation that all port calls were going to be canceled en route to the Gulf. Tidings from the Middle East have not been good. The aircraft carrier we're relieving, USS *Kitty Hawk,* has sent numerous messages saying we would be needed on station sooner rather than later. Everyone in the room knows we have to be ready at a moment's notice to drop everything, port calls included, to get there ahead of schedule, if necessary.

"This also means we have time for larger-scale exercises during our transit—critical training, in my opinion, if we're to carry out our mission once on station." He pauses briefly to survey the room, conveying the seriousness of the statement. In other words, time to leave thoughts of liberty behind and get on with the real business of training. "Operation Low Level is one such exercise that demands your undivided attention and focus. So without further ado, I'll give the floor to Lieutenant Eric Marxen, who will be acting as lead for the exercise. Lieutenant Marxen," he says, motioning to Eric.

As he steps forward, Emily nudges me. "Why is he giving the brief?" she whispers. "He's just a lieutenant."

"I have no idea."

"Not that I'm complaining," Em says. "I'd rather watch him than a wrinkled old admiral any day."

"Shhh," I say with a discreet shove on her arm.

"Thank you, sir," Eric says.

He begins to speak, and he owns the room. Some people are natural leaders and Eric's one of them. As I listen, I tick down a laundry list of character traits—smart, quick on his feet, engaging, articulate . . . and strong. Not just strong physically—it's clear he's lean and fit—but a confident strength brews on the inside, too. He's no different now than he was on the *Lake Champlain*. If anything, just more impressive.

Shut it down, Sara. Just shut it down. You know you can't go there.

But still. An exercise of this scope isn't normally run by someone of my pay grade.

". . . following the fifth high-speed, low-level run, the Sabercats will have the fast rope," Eric says. "That'll be a squad from SEAL Team One. Target is to be determined."

I glance at Em. She has her elbows on the table, chin propped in her hands, and is wearing a dreamy expression that's not exactly the most appropriate for a counterterrorism exercise brief. But how can I judge her? It's not like I'm walking the walk at the moment, either.

Well, you'd better start! How about now, shall we?

There. I've scolded myself. I listen as Eric fields questions from the admiral and several commanding officers with finesse. They seem particularly interested in the fast roping portion of the exercise.

When SEALs need to board a vessel quickly for hostile takeover, fast roping is one method to deliver them. The rope can be positioned in several places—over the aft ramp, out the main cabin door, or over a square cutout section in the underbelly of the aircraft we call the "hell hole." SEALs slide down the rope, or ropes, one after another, until the entire squad is dispatched in a matter of seconds.

"How long would I need my flight deck open for that if we're the target?" asks Commander Eichorn, commanding officer of the destroyer USS *Leftwich*.

"No more than five minutes, sir."

"And what about pickup?"

"That won't be necessary," Eric says. Light chuckles spread through the wardroom.

If SEALs don't require a helicopter pickup, they can depart via other means—by an inflatable, motorized raft called a Zodiac, or they can swim out. Zodiacs haven't received a mention in the brief today.

". . . and the commencement of the exercise is scheduled for zero four hundred tomorrow morning, weather permitting."

Eric answers a few more questions before wrapping up the brief, but then we're not given the standard dismissal. Normally, we'd be called to attention again and the group that arrived together would leave together. But the executive officer stands and announces the meeting has been concluded.

I know I shouldn't be watching this, but it's interesting to observe Eric interact with our skipper. They're shaking hands now and laughing like old friends. Interesting . . . It's the first time I've ever seen Captain Magruder smile.

I look down at Em, who hasn't moved. "Everyone's leaving," I say. "You're starting to look a little obvious."

"Oh, all right. Spoil my fun."

Emily rises and we're almost to the door when we're corralled by Commander Claggett and the rest of our pilots in the lounge area.

We have three aircraft commanders in our detachment. Commander Claggett is one, of course. His protégé, Lieutenant Chad Henkel, is another, and acts as the assistant officer in charge. Unfortunately, he follows Commander Claggett's lead on most everything, including his attitude toward Emily and me.

Matt Zemekis completes the aircraft commander trio. He has trouble keeping his hair cut to regulation and is currently experimenting with extra-long sideburns for some reason I can't fathom. He does treat me decently most of the time and isn't too bad to fly with.

Zack Taylor is the final member of our pilot group. He's a helicopter second pilot like Em and me. All three of us are hoping to earn our aircraft commander designations by the end of cruise. Even though he's a second pilot, he leads the aircraft commander group socially, attracting women in droves. Like Matt, fortunately, he tolerates Em and me pretty well.

"Captain Magruder wants to see those of us who are flying tomorrow," Commander Claggett says. "We're meeting in his office in five minutes. That'll be me, Chad, Matt, and Lace."

"But I thought Zack had the flight," I say.

"That's what I thought, too," Commander Claggett says. It's hard not to notice the disappointment in his voice.

"So what gives?" Zack asks.

"Fuck if I know," Commander Claggett says. "Captain Magruder's orders."

As the group breaks up, Emily starts hitting me on the arm. "Oh my god, he's walking over here. He's walking over here!"

Eric approaches with a guarded smile.

"Hi, Sara."

"Hi, Eric."

Emily loses all decorum. "You *know* him?" She gives me a look like I've been keeping a big secret from her.

"Well, actually, we just met," I say. "When I was stuck on the *Lake Champlain*."

"Eric Marxen," he says, putting out his hand to Emily. "Nice to meet you."

She shakes it, but carries the oddest look on her face. I don't think I would have believed it unless I'd witnessed it myself, but Emily is speechless.

"Captain Magruder invited us to stay for dinner," Eric says, turning to me. "But I need to stop by the maintenance office first. I was hoping you could direct me there."

"Oh, I'll show you!" Emily pipes up, suddenly finding her voice.

"Thanks," he says. "And Sara, I trust you've been told you're flying to-morrow."

"I just found out, yeah."

"Captain Magruder will go over the details with you when you meet."

"You know we're meeting?"

"I *am* in charge of the exercise."

"But—"

"I don't want to keep you," he says. "Emily?"

"Here, come on," she says. "The office is this way."

As I watch him walk away, I realize I'm bothered by our interaction. While polite, he was all business. Although, should I really expect his behavior to be any different after the way I dismissed him on the *Lake Champlain*?

But this is good. This is what I want.

Right?

Entering the commanding officer's quarters, I find Captain Magruder in a huddle with our three aircraft commanders. He motions for me to join them.

"For the exercise tomorrow," Captain Magruder says, "Nick, I want you flying with Lieutenant Denning. Lieutenant Henkel, you'll fly with Lieutenant Zemekis."

This is highly irregular. The captain of the ship doesn't assign flight crews.

"I want to reiterate the importance of executing clean flights with exacting scrutiny on the gauges," Captain Magruder says. He hands Commander Claggett and Chad briefing cards that detail the headings, altitudes, and speeds required. "Five runs each. No deviation from the altitudes or speeds listed."

We all nod, but I wonder why he's so keen on the details for this flight. Normally, we'd just execute our mission and be done with it.

"As you heard in the brief, this training exercise has Admiral Carlson's full attention, mostly due to the fact that every ship in the group has some role in the tracking and simulated destruction of the low-level threats," Captain Magruder says. "Keep to the timeline and the established holding patterns since we'll have the Shadow Hunters and Nighthawks in the air, too."

The Nighthawks are a squadron of H-60 Seahawk helicopters deployed aboard the *Nimitz*.

"The Shadow Hunters will take the lead, acting as airborne command. Their word is final," he says. "Following the low-level runs, you have a zero seven hundred overhead at *Nimitz* to pick up a squad from SEAL Team One for a fast rope to simulate hostile boarding. You'll be given the target name then. The overhead to target is scheduled for zero seven fifteen. You need to be in, out, and gone over the target deck."

Captain Magruder looks directly at Commander Claggett. "Nick, that's going to be your bird, and Lieutenant Denning will be at the controls for that."

What . . . ?

I do a quick scan of the faces of Commander Claggett, Matt, and Chad, and see that I'm not the only one surprised.

"Yes, sir," Commander Claggett says.

"That's all I have," Captain Magruder says.

Very odd. Exceedingly odd. No, make that unheard of. The captain of the ship dictating who will be at the controls on a flight? Never.

What the hell is going on?

12

As we enter the wardroom for dinner, it's far louder than normal because of our visitors from the Operation Low Level brief. Admiral Carlson is already seated with Captain Magruder and the other commanding officers. I notice that Eric sits with them.

Captain Magruder motions Em and me over, and he and Admiral Carlson rise.

"Sir, this is Lieutenant Sara Denning and Lieutenant Emily Wyatt," Captain Magruder says.

"Nice to meet you both," Admiral Carlson says, extending his hand. "I want you to know we're happy to have you with us in the strike group."

"Thank you, sir," Emily says.

That was weird. I wonder why we were singled out like that. Well, no matter. I turn to find a seat, surreptitiously glancing in Eric's direction as I do so. Shoot. He catches me peeking because he's looking right at me.

But that's not what gives me pause.

"Is she the one?" Admiral Carlson whispers.

"Yeah, that's her," Captain Magruder says.

I bring my eyes to theirs, but they don't look away. I wonder if they know that I heard them. Scanning to the left, I see that Eric's eyes haven't left my position.

Emily heads to the open seat next to Eric, while I turn, finding two free chairs at the far end of our U-shaped table arrangement. Petty Officer Sampson, our lead mess crank, hurriedly approaches with lemon water and a larger-than-normal menu. I glance up to see that Eric is giving his full attention to Emily.

Switching my gaze to Admiral Carlson, I think about the comment I just overheard. "Is she the one?" *What on earth?*

I don't have a chance to consider the question, though, because Commander Egan shatters my concentration with his arrival. He sits next to me, adjusting his chair until it touches mine, and I recoil. When he gets close, my skin gets prickly. I swear, I'm going to break out in a rash as this cruise progresses, with him around.

"Sara, Sara, Sara," he says. "Talkin' it up with the admiral, I see."

Maybe he's trying to be funny? I don't even look at him. "Yes, sir."

I had planned to order something off the menu because Petty Officer Sampson has pulled out all the stops for Admiral Carlson. But I don't want to sit here waiting for my food, drawn into a conversation I don't want to have with Commander Egan. I can give myself space by selecting from the salad bar instead. I push my chair back, and as I walk away from him, every inch I put between us allows me to breathe easier.

I pick up a plate from the storage well and begin piling it with lettuce. The salad on the ship isn't great by most people's standards, but for me, I'm eating better now than I normally do. I inherited little—actually, make that none—of my mother's legendary culinary skills, so having a mess hall has always been one of the perks of military life for me.

"You guys are lucky," Eric says, silently appearing at my side.

The current is a jolt this time.

"We're lucky?"

"To have a salad bar," he says, picking up a plate. "This would never fit in our wardroom."

"Oh, yeah. This is really a great thing."

I add spinach and cucumbers to my lettuce bed, and out of the corner of my eye, I see that he's filling his plate, too. Maybe he's extra hungry. When I watched Emily take her seat next to him earlier, he had already been served a full plate of food, which included a salad.

The ship takes a heavy roll and the cherry tomato I'm trying to harness with the salad tongs slips and accelerates across the grooved railings in front of the vegetable bins. I quickly grab the side of the bar to keep my balance as the tomato goes airborne at the end of the rails. Eric's hand shoots out, snatching it in midair.

I raise my eyebrows. "Nice save."

He turns to me, latches onto my gaze, and holds it. Uncanny, how he does that. And his all-business demeanor from earlier evaporates.

"I wanted to ask how you were doing," he says in a low voice. "I didn't have a chance to talk with you before you left yesterday morning."

"The flight went fine. We did the maintenance checks and—"

"I wasn't asking about the aircraft," he says. "I was asking about you."

"Oh." The effort required to pull my eyes away is a monumental one. I focus on the construction of my salad, stalling, adding items that under normal circumstances would never find their way onto my plate. Olives, anchovies . . .

"I'm doing all right," I say, looking resolutely at the salad bins. "Thanks for asking."

Emily's half-baked Harlequins flash through my mind, expounding on the heated magnetic pull between two people. Nonsensical nonsense, I call it. And that is *not* what's happening here. Not onboard a navy ship. Not in a wardroom. And most definitely not in uniform.

I continue mindlessly adding ingredients, my head spinning.

I will not succumb to this. I won't. Besides, there's nothing to succumb to. It's the rolling of the ship. That's it. My stomach hasn't been feeling right today anyway.

"You know, I wouldn't have taken you for the jalapeño type," he says.

"Jalapeño . . . what?"

He points to my plate and I cringe. The jalapeño slices awkwardly outnumber the tomatoes and cucumbers combined, creating a dull green boundary layer of way-too-hot-for-me peppers that nearly covers the entire salad.

Holy hell, Sara. Where is your dignity?

I straighten and look at him directly, preparing to say my good-byes, but notice for the first time a scar that traces across his upper lip. It only makes him more handsome—in a rugged, no-nonsense sort of way.

Okay, that's it. I'm done. This is getting out of control.

I need to get away from here. Now.

I move to turn back to my seat, but a hand on my arm stops me; that and a shot of something that just rocketed through my body the moment he touched me.

"Can I ask you something?" His eyes shift to look behind me for a moment before he speaks again. The tone is not at all playful as it just was. "Commander Egan . . . Is everything all right there?"

I hesitate, deciding he doesn't need to know. "Yes, why wouldn't it be?"

"You flinched when he sat next to you," he says, removing his hand from my arm.

How did he notice that? I was sitting at the far end of the table.

"It's fine," I say.

"It's *not* fine." His eyes hold mine, daring me to say otherwise.

This is altogether new to me—someone needling into my feelings like this. And he's right on the mark, too, which is even more disconcerting.

"I need to go," I say, and turn back to my seat.

"Soooo, do you know Lieutenant Marxen or something?" Commander Egan says. "You took forever getting your salad."

"No . . . no, not really," I say.

I pretend to scoot my chair in closer to the table while actually moving it farther away from him. The supply officer who sits next to me has got to be wondering why my chair is now rammed up next to his.

Eric watches all of this, his jaw set. He then crosses the room to Admiral Carlson and leans into his ear before returning to his seat.

"Commander Egan!" Admiral Carlson calls from across the table.

"Yes, sir."

"I need to speak with you."

"Yes, sir." Commander Egan pushes back his chair and walks to the admiral's side.

It's difficult to make out what they're discussing. Something related to Operation Low Level, I think.

"You know, sir," Eric says, addressing Commander Egan loudly. "You can just have my seat. It would probably be easier than having to stand there."

"That's a great idea," Admiral Carlson says.

Eric pushes his dinner plate aside and rises. He has a quick word with Petty Officer Sampson, who comes to my side, collects Commander Egan's plate, and takes it to his new seat.

Commander Egan doesn't look happy with the new seating arrangement, and neither does Em, for that matter.

I share a quick look with Eric as he exits the wardroom. *So there,* his expression reads.

* * *

I swore to myself I'd go back to Ian's Vikings jersey, but here I am, second night in a row, slipping into Eric's maroon shirt. He never asked about it today in the wardroom and I wonder if he realizes I have it. I rub the spot on my arm where he placed his hand, trying to get my head around the still-tingling sensation.

Em roars into the room like a tornado. "Okay, so tell me this!" she says, the door slamming behind her. "How is it that you can describe a full two days spent on the *Lake Champlain* and fail to mention a certain Lieutenant Marxen?"

I turn and busy myself in my closet, hanging my khakis with extra care. "Easy. He's just another guy," I say, speaking to my clothing.

"Just another guy? Just another guy? He's a fucking Greek god! You don't omit details like that!"

"There were almost four hundred men on that ship," I say, turning to face her. "Sorry I didn't mention every one."

"But you did," she says, plopping into her desk chair. She holds up her fingers to count. "Let's see, Brian Wilcox, Stuart Grady, Ben Holcomb, Rob LeGrand, Ken Watkins. Hell, you even mentioned Seaman Ogilvy, who served you coffee. So it's highly improbable that you would have missed—"

She straightens, her eyes widening. "Wait a minute. Wait one fucking minute!" Her eyes bore into mine, like she's a coldblooded dective on the hunt. "There's something going on between you two, isn't there?"

"No, of course not," I say.

"Yes . . . ," she says, drawing it out for effect. "Now it makes sense. I wondered why he went up to the salad bar when he'd already been served a salad."

"That doesn't mean anything," I say.

"And you talked. For a *long* time."

I shake my head.

"And he stared at you. I remember that. And you were looking back . . . with like, weird dreamy eyes."

"I was not!"

She nods, the facts stringing together in her head forming a neatly packaged conclusion—one that suits her romance-infected mind perfectly.

"You *like* him, don't you!"

"No, absolutely not."

She continues as if I haven't said a thing. "You purposely avoided telling me about him because you're *smitten* and you didn't want me to know!"

"Em, that's ridiculous! Stop it."

"Unfreakingbelievable!"

"You are *so* off base."

She crosses her arms. "Your heated denials only serve to clarify the truth of the matter."

"Besides," I say, "it's not allowed anyway . . . not that there's anything there . . . I mean, to be allowed . . ." What a stuttering mess.

"Ha! There *is* something there. And yes, it *is* allowed! You're of equal rank. You're in different squadrons. No conflict of interest. Boom! You're good! You are *so* good!"

"Enough, Em. Enough! I'm going to bed."

"Hold on . . . ," she says, rising, her mouth agape. "Hold on!"

"What now?"

I've never seen Em move so fast in my life. In less than a second, she has the back of my shirt collar in her fist, giving it a firm yank.

"I knew it!" she says.

"What the hell are you doing?" I say, spinning on her.

"Size large!"

Her hand goes to her heart and she staggers backward, her eyes furtively roving across my torso. "That's his shirt, isn't it?" she whispers.

I shrug.

"Oh my god, you're wearing his shirt!" She collapses on the bed, flopping backward, her hands gesturing to the overhead. "That's so fuckin' romantic, I can't stand it!"

"Em, wait, hang on! After we landed, I was a sweaty mess and I didn't have anything clean to wear. He just let me borrow it. That's all."

"That's all?" she says, shooting upright. "That's all? Do you have any idea what this means?"

"Em, it was just a clean shirt."

"AGHHH!" she shrieks, clutching her hair. "You suck at this, you know that? You don't even grasp the implications. His shirt. His shirt! On you! Part of him on you! He's claiming his territory, Sara!"

"Claiming his territory? Em, that's ridiculous." I point to her stack of Harlequins. "Too many of those in your head."

"No, no, no!" she says. "I *know* how this works and you don't!"

"Em, I can't handle this conversation."

I jump over her, launching from her mattress up to my bunk. But she stands and grips the railing, peering over the side.

"You can't hide," she says.

"Go away, Em."

"You are *so* busted."

I pull the covers over my head and turn away from her, but I can hear her breathing. And even though I can't see her, I know she's smiling. An I-got-you smile. I hate those kinds.

"This shirt is softer, my ass," she says. "Case closed."

13

I've remained at the controls since Operation Low Level commenced at 0400. We've had our hands full with the challenge of flying on a moonless night, an inky black moonless night. We're doing it the old-fashioned way, too—without night vision goggles. In typical military fashion, they were recalled by the manufacturer, but without replacements being offered. I have a throbbing headache because the concentration required during a flight like this is all-consuming.

On a night like tonight, without goggles, it's hard to know where the ocean ends and the sky begins. With no horizon reference, flight decks resemble little more than lighted postage stamps, floating in the middle of space. Everything seems to float—the stars, radio antennas, buoys, ships—in one vast, black, spherical void.

When you can't discern the water from the horizon, if you aren't sharply focused on your instruments, you can get disoriented in a heartbeat. Many pilots have flown their aircraft into the water at night, never realizing they were descending, until it was too late.

I breathe a relieved sigh when the sun finally makes its friendly appearance. We land on the deck of *Nimitz*, and I have to pull the dark visor of my helmet down to shield my eyes from the glare. But the security I felt upon landing quickly fades. You know the seas are bad when a mighty ship like this heaves with the waves, as it is now. The bow drops below the horizon and the pale new-morning sky that just filled my view is devoured by the leaden sea. Counting the seconds, I wait anxiously until the bow rises upward again, restoring my view of the heavens.

The cycle repeats. I inhale and exhale in time with the troughs and crests. A living ocean. It breathes. It waits.

I take a sip from my water bottle, pulling my gaze into my lap, forcing myself to think of something else. Anything else.

So far, Operation Low Level has proceeded without a hitch, and just as Captain Magruder said, the Shadow Hunters have run the whole thing. Actually, Eric has run the whole thing. His voice has been a constant on the radios, calm as you please, directing one of the most complicated exercises I can remember. In fact, this has been one of the most well-run large-scale operations I've ever been involved in.

While the H-46 platform offers unmatched maneuverability for its lifting capacity, the H-60 helicopter is unrivaled for its command and control capabilities. The Shadow Hunter aircraft contains sophisticated, powerful radar equipment, which, when linked to the Aegis weapons system aboard the *Lake Champlain*, further extends its already considerable operational range, allowing Eric to direct us just as an air traffic controller would.

I've had plenty on my plate tonight, but it didn't stop my brain from internalizing the charge I felt the moment I heard his voice. But that electric feeling has paved the way for a nice helping of guilt for the way I've treated him. He was absolutely right. The situation wasn't fine with Commander Egan on the *Kansas City*, nor was it fine with Commander Claggett on the *Lake Champlain*. He was only trying to help and I pushed him away. . . .

When I look up, Messy leads an eight-man SEAL squad to our aircraft. Because their faces aren't camouflaged, I recognize most of them from my last cruise. We worked with the same group.

The man who boards last hooks his helmet to our internal radio system. "This is Lieutenant Mike Shallow," he says. "I'm the squad leader for the exercise today."

I remember Mike. We had several flights together when we worked off the coast of Oahu this winter.

"I was briefed that Lieutenant Denning would be at the controls for today's evolution," Mike says.

I'm really getting uncomfortable now. This is so highly irregular, I don't know what to make of it. And by the look in Commander Claggett's eyes, he doesn't either.

"Lieutenant Shallow, what the fuck is going on here exactly?" Commander Claggett says. "I signed for this aircraft, and as such, I decide who is at the controls. I let it slide when Captain Magruder brought it up, but what the hell do you know about it, and why do you care?"

I cannot believe he's treating another officer like this. Although, wait. Yes, I can.

"Sir, what was your name again?" Mike says.

"That has nothing to do with this. Now answer my question, Lieutenant."

"Sir, orders from Admiral Carlson."

"Admiral Carlson? Since when does an admiral, or anyone else for that matter, dictate who flies my aircraft?"

"Sir, we have seven minutes to be overhead *Leftwich,* and I need to finish our brief."

I guess the surprise target is the destroyer USS *Leftwich.*

Commander Claggett's silence is enough of a response for Mike, who moves into the passageway that leads from the cabin to the cockpit. He leans in to look, and I face him.

"Hey, good to see you again," he says.

"Thanks," I say.

"No Animal tonight, huh?" he remarks. "Shame."

I shake my head. Commander Max Amicus, nicknamed Animal, served as the officer in charge on my last cruise, the one where Mike and I flew together in Hawaii. The two of them got on exceptionally well, probably because they were both Auburn University alum. I also got along with Animal—so much so that he sort of took me under his wing on that cruise. And I agree with Mike's sentiment. I'd give any number of paychecks to have Animal flying in the seat next to me now instead of Commander Claggett.

"Today's exercise is pretty straightforward, just like our last two off Kaneohe," Mike says. He resolutely ignores Commander Claggett, looking only at me.

"Straight approach up the wake, ten feet, although lower would be better, one hundred twenty knots, but faster would be better, too," he says. "We have eight men to deploy."

Mike turns to look behind him. "All set on the rigging, Lego?"

"We're good to go, sir."

"You're gonna drop the rope to the deck when we're finished, since we're not doing multiples."

"Roger that, sir," Lego says.

He turns back to me. "Oh, and only the *Leftwich*'s skipper knows we're coming. No radio calls on this one."

"Okay, no radio," I say. "And it will be like before. We won't be single-engine capable with you guys, so if I start sliding over and descending, I'm doing an emergency landing."

In the world of fast roping, an engine failure is one of the worst things that can happen. Descending without the power to control the rate of descent, knowing there is no other option but to land, and with SEALs sliding on a rope underneath the aircraft, it's bad news all the way around.

"Copy that," Mike says. "Any questions for me?"

I can't help it. I have to ask. "Mike, really, why were you briefed that I would be at the controls today?"

He pulls a notepad from his pocket and scratches an answer, then holds it up so only I can read it.

Because we requested it, he has written. He grins before disappearing into the cabin.

Well, I can't think about it now. We have five minutes and we're going to need to bust tail to get there on time. *Nimitz* gives us an immediate takeoff clearance, and I head straight west to find *Leftwich,* who is cruising two miles off the bow.

I push it to 130 knots and ten feet of altitude. Actually, I'm doing the altitude part by feel. All I know is that we're oh, so close to the water. Too close. A sweaty sheen coats my skin. *Focus on the target, Sara.*

When we arrive, *Leftwich*'s safety nets are pushed up around the flight deck. They have no idea we're coming. I slow, simultaneously spinning sideways to arrive perpendicular to the ship. I briefly glimpse Eric's helicopter, hovering just to the north of us, watching.

"Rope's away!" Lego calls. "First man out!"

It's only fifteen seconds after that when he gives his final call.

"Last man out. On deck. Dropping the rope. Clear to go!"

I nose over and we're away. I bet we weren't over that deck more than twenty seconds, which for a SEAL is everything. Time spent waffling to stabilize in a hover could not only get them killed, but get us killed, too, if it were an actual hostile boarding.

It's a fast trip home. After shutdown, I exit through the passageway into the main cabin, where Lego and Messy are stowing the gear.

"So what was Lieutenant Shallow's answer?" Lego asks.

"He wrote, *Because we requested it.* I don't get it, Lego. I don't get it at all."

"That's because you don't hear what we do in the back, ma'am. You'd know why then."

Not only can I not see our passengers—in this case, a SEAL squad—but I can't hear them either, not unless they're hooked into the aircraft's intercommunications system, or ICS. Most passengers are not hooked in when they fly with us, but Lego and Messy can still walk up and down the cabin engaging in conversations, albeit shouted ones, with anyone not plugged into the radio system.

"Think about it, ma'am," Messy says. "How much fast roping did we do in Hawaii? More than usual, right? It had to be twenty-some-odd exercises. And who was at the controls for those?"

True, we did do an inordinate amount of fast roping. And now that I think about it . . . I was at the controls . . . on every one. And Animal was the aircraft commander on every one. I wasn't writing the flight schedule, so I had no control over this, but we flew together a lot. I even remember mulling it over at the time, wondering why I was always paired with him. Not that I minded. He was an outstanding teacher—the best, really.

Funny. I could say the same for Lego and Messy. They were on every one of those flights. Normally, the aircrew are rotated. At home in San Diego, I might fly with five different copilots and ten separate aircrewmen in the course of a week. But on that short deployment to Hawaii, and now on this detachment, I've flown the majority of my missions with the same two guys. I certainly haven't questioned it, because they're a dream to fly with, but yeah . . . unusual.

14

Because we requested it. The phrase turns in my mind as I walk to the ship's weight room, a space enclosed in a metal, cagelike structure tucked behind apartment-sized freezers in the cargo area. It houses several cardio machines, including a stair climber, a stationary bike, and a treadmill—never operable at the same time, by the way—two universal machines, benches, a squat rack, and a full set of free weights.

Probably a bit risky for the ship to keep it open in heavy seas like this, but I'm glad of it. I need a place to think. Not only about the pilot-at-the-controls thing, but Em's convictions about my feelings for Eric. All of it has my head in a tangle, but it's nothing some exercising won't cure.

I hear a familiar "S'up, ma'am?" from the far corner as I enter. It's Petty Officer Jefferson, known to all as T-Bear. His given name is Torbjorn, which means "thunder bear" in Danish, even though he's African American. T-Bear is mammoth-sized, standing six foot six and weighing close to three hundred pounds. It's all muscle, too.

He's a weight room mainstay, along with his lifting partner, Petty Officer Diggins, known as Diggs. Standing next to T-Bear, Diggs looks "small," but he still wields a frame that's six foot four and he's probably pushing 270.

"Hey T-Bear, hey Diggs."

"Runnin' or bikin' today, ma'am?" T-Bear asks.

"Biking," I say, pointing to the aerodyne bike.

"Tell me you're gonna stop before an hour this time."

"I don't know. I've got a lot on my mind today, so I'm thinking it's going to be a long one."

"Damn. I don't know how you do it," he says before turning back to the squat rack.

I watch in humbled awe as he ducks underneath the bar and hoists it onto his shoulders. It bends with the weight of 520 pounds. With Diggs standing behind him to spot, he methodically cranks out ten reps. And the ship is rolling. Unbelievable. And he says he doesn't know how I do it.

I climb onto the bike and set it to level six, holding tight to the handles so I don't fall off as the ship rocks. Within minutes, I've got a good sweat going, my heart, lungs, and legs in a rhythm, thinking I'm going to try to sort out why Admiral Carlson and the SEAL team would request me specifically to pilot one of their training exercises. But my heart has other ideas. Instead, I begin to replay my conversations with Eric.

The longer I pedal, the more I downplay it. This is nothing. How many times have I interacted with other pilots? Hundreds. Other officers? Thousands. How many were nice guys? Lots. How many treated me with respect? Still, lots. But have I ever been affected like this? Never.

I keep thinking about it. I keep thinking about him. And I shouldn't. That's not what I'm out here for.

That's right, Sara, remember why you're here. Why you're in the navy. All of it.

"To Ian Denning!" my father said. "When you take your oath next week, you'll begin a new journey, continuing the long and illustrious Denning family legacy of Naval Academy graduates and proudly serving U.S. Naval officers."

"And navy pilots!" my Uncle Paul chimed in.

Because our send-off party included almost one hundred family members and friends, my hugs for Ian had to wait until the end. I remember we shared a long embrace.

"Congratulations, Ian," I said. "I'm so proud of you."

Our compulsory brother-sister banter proved strangely absent that evening. Our lives were headed in different directions and it was the first time we had actually faced this new reality.

"Thanks." His eyes started watering. "I'm stoked to get started," he said, quickly gathering himself.

"Well, you're going to do the Denning family proud. No doubt about it," I said.

He looked at me thoughtfully, his tall, lanky frame supporting the suit and tie he wore like he was a coat hanger. Looking at Ian was like looking at myself—that always awkward slender build, the blond hair, the crystal-blue eyes—twins in every way.

"I'm gonna miss you," he said.

The tears welled. "Me, too."

He cleared his throat. "Still up for tomorrow?" he asked with a gleam in his eye.

I smiled, happy for the topic change. "You know I am!"

His brilliant blue eyes sparkled with anticipation and excitement.

I vaguely notice when T-Bear and Diggs leave the weight room, my breaths coming fast and heavy as I stand on the pedals, climbing the last of two artificial hills.

I can't shake the memories. It always happens this way—my subconscious ensuring that I remember the details. That I will never forget.

"This is gonna be epic!" I said as we slid our white-water kayaks into the calm stretch of flat water at the Otter Slide put-in—starting point for the most challenging six-mile segment of white water on the Wolf River. It was a four-hour drive from our Minneapolis home to our favorite Wisconsin river, but worth it. At the time, I carried one wild indulgence in my life, white-water kayaking. "And we've gotta hit Big Smokey Falls!"

"I don't know," he said. "We've never had a flow like this. It's awfully high."

"But we've run it before. And think about it. It'll be the perfect send-off. You're not going to get to do this for a long time once you start at Navy."

My enthusiasm, unbridled, was contagious.

"All right," he said.

I remember the white water, roiling and careening over a minefield of boulders . . . and underwater, bright blue eyes.

When I return to our stateroom, Em sits up in her rack. "Hey," she says, removing her headphones. "Look what the cat dragged in. You're soaked."

"Aerodyne bike."

"And you wonder why I don't work out."

I kick off my boots and remove my socks. "Nothing a shower won't fix."

"Nope," she says, popping the *p* at the end of the word. "No showers."

"What do you mean, no showers?"

"We're on water hours. Some issue with the evaporators. They're not producing enough fresh water. And since the boilers are a higher priority than we are . . ."

I drop into my chair. Great. "Is it like the normal water hours thing? Will they give us thirty minutes or something later?"

"Yeah. I think three o'clock is the next window."

Oh, man. I'll have to wait four more hours. I am so gross. I open my desk and spy my water bottle—and it's full.

Sweet. I peel off my workout gear, strip naked, squirt my water bottle on my towel, and do the best I can. A sponge bath is better than nothing.

"Besides the fact that we don't have water, has anything else come up I should know about?"

"You're flying a pax transfer with Commander Claggett tomorrow."

"You've got to be kidding." *How many flights have I had with him lately? Ughh.* "Any chance you'd like to take that?" I ask.

"Uh, let me think about that. No."

"You know, I never thought I'd see the day when you'd pass on flight hours, no matter how you could get them."

"I think everyone has a limit, and I've reached mine with him. You can have the flight hours. Even turning buttonhooks all day wouldn't be worth it."

You know it's bad when . . .

Not all H-46 pilots can do a buttonhook, nor do many even attempt it. Em and I had the good fortune of training with Commander Amicus, who taught us how. There's not much better in terms of H-46 maneuvering. It's a high-speed approach followed by 180 degrees of turn to a stop, the deceleration so rapid, you move from over one hundred knots to less than twenty in just a few seconds. You're effectively hooking around a spot on the ground, and they're a blast—if you do them right.

There's a lot that can go wrong with a buttonhook—swinging wildly off direction, both sideways and up, hard landings you might not fly away from, and dropping the engines offline, to name a few.

But assuming all goes right, at the end of the day, it's just great precision flying and so much fun. So if Em would really pass on buttonhooks so she wouldn't have to fly with Commander Claggett . . .

"I have to run by Zack's room and then I'm grabbing a coffee," Emily says, rolling out of her rack. "Want one?"

"Please."

"Oh, and don't forget your training lecture. You have that at eighteen hundred, remember?"

Crap. I had totally forgotten.

"Now I do."

"Gee, I wonder if a certain Lieutenant Marxen had anything to do with that?"

"Shut up, Em."

"You know I'm right!" she says, skipping out the door.

I throw on my khakis, sit at my desk, and open the manual for the automatic flight control system. On my laptop, I create a new document, typing the acronym "AFCS" across the top of the page.

Five minutes later, I stare at the still-blank page, my mind where it was an hour ago on the exercise bike—*him*. I close the manual and sit back in my chair, rubbing my eyes. Sorting out my feelings for Eric is one thing. Figuring out Eric, in general, is another. A lieutenant, a pilot like me, privy to Top Secret messages, giving an exercise brief that had an admiral and several ships' captains on the edges of their seats, and running a large-scale, multiple-threat counterterrorism exercise, which, oh by the way, he did extraordinarily well. It doesn't make sense. . . .

I sit up, scooch my chair in, and bring up my e-mail. As my fingers move across the keyboard, I'm appalled with myself, acting like someone who Googles the guy who just asked her out, to check up on him.

I type anyway, composing my question to an old Academy friend, Tom Jenkins, who flies F/A-18 jets aboard *Nimitz*. I ran into Tom in San Diego prior to leaving, and we had talked about meeting up in Hong Kong to catch up on old times.

After signing my name, I read through the message once more.

Hi Tom,

How are you? Hope cruise is treating you okay so far. I know this question comes a bit out of the blue, but I was wondering if you might know or have ever worked with Eric Marxen. He's an Academy grad flying H-60s off the *Lake Champlain*. His name came up the other day in the wardroom. Things are fine here. Looking forward to Hong Kong.

Sara

I cringe as I hit SEND, then jump in my seat, startled when I hear knocking on the door.

"Yes?"

"Sara, it's Doug."

Oh, no. Not Commander Egan again. I stand up and open the door just a crack. "Yes, sir?"

"Well, can I come in?"

I open the door wider, he walks in, and seats himself in Emily's chair.

"I thought you'd like to know about the Hong Kong shore patrol rotation," he says.

"Yes, sir, I know."

"Well, you're scheduled for Sunday after we pull in."

"Yes, I know, sir. Is that everything, then?"

"Well, no." He stops for a moment, I think realizing for the first time that I'm still standing by the door. "Aren't you going to sit down?"

"No, sir. I'm fine right here."

"Sara, really, I'd prefer it if you'd call me Doug. There's no need to be so formal."

"I know, sir."

"Well, anyway, the shore patrol office is going to be located at the Harbourview Hotel. They've arranged a banquet room for us. I wanted to let you know that I've reserved a room there, so if you need anything—"

Emily saves me, walking in at just the right moment. "Em, you're back! I know you wanted to change, so sir, would you mind?"

"Yeah, this flight suit stinks to high heaven," Em says. "Thanks for stopping by, sir."

Commander Egan rises. "Well, just remember, I'll be there if you need anything."

Em closes the door behind him.

"He'll be there if you need anything?" she says, her face screwing up.

"Shore patrol is going to be headquartered at the Harbourview Hotel. He was telling me he reserved a room there and if I needed anything . . ."

Em winces.

"No kidding."

"And you're going to bring this up with the skipper when?"

"Drop it, Em."

"I'm just saying."

15

We spin up the rotors, the blades whipping the diamond-filled sky into a blurry sheen. The water is calm, illuminated by a waning crescent moon that hangs low on the horizon. Still waters. Finally. Four days from Hong Kong.

The seas quieted two days ago, and in those two days, I've flown four flights with Mike's SEAL squad. For each one, Captain Magruder came personally to the aircrew briefing space to relay Admiral Carlson's orders that I was to be at the controls. The aircraft commanders are miffed and I don't blame them. It's their aircraft. If I was in their shoes, I'd be pissed, too.

And to make it worse, no one is giving the detachment any answers. This many SEAL flights? Why? Sara at the controls for all of them? Why? We've received the "need to know" response, which is downright annoying. If anyone has a "need to know," I would think it would be the aircrew who are conducting the flights.

The most distressing thing, though, is how this is affecting me and Em. The comments were good-natured at first. "You're really racking up the hours." "Maybe you'd like to share?" "Just gives me more time to read." But as I left the room for tonight's flight, the tone changed. "Remember when you asked if I'd like to fly that pax transfer with Commander Claggett? Well, I've changed my mind. Apparently, I have to take what I can get."

I breathe a heavy sigh as we lift, flight number five in three days, another fast rope exercise. Chad and I fly loops around the *Kansas City*, while Mike's team makes ready in the back for a practice run before heading to the cruiser, USS *Reeves*, a late addition to our carrier strike group.

"Okay, sir, we're all set aft," Lego says.

"Roger," Chad says.

No Commander Claggett tonight, thank god. Although, flying with Chad lately hasn't been much better. I'm expecting him to transfer the controls, but he shakes me off.

"Chad?"

"I've got it," comes his blunt reply.

I guess Mike isn't connected to the ICS, because I suspect he'd be throwing a fit if he'd just heard that. Or maybe not. Maybe practice runs don't count in terms of who's at the controls.

I confirm the landing checks and Chad begins his approach. We gain airspeed, and just shy of the aft end of the ship, he begins his flare.

And we're coming in hot. Way too hot. It's ugly as he tries to stabilize, and I'm thankful we didn't just plow it into the hangar. Boy, we're spending a long time over the deck. . . .

Lego finally calls last man out and we circle to land to pick up the team so we can continue on to *Reeves*. Once on deck, the squad stands by, ready to board the aircraft, but only Mike approaches. He walks to Lego and Messy's position in front of the aircraft and taps Messy on the shoulder.

Mike signals for Messy to give him his ICS cord. Messy pulls the cord from his helmet and hands it to Mike, who plugs it into the back of his own helmet. Mike then motions to Lego to disconnect his cord. . . . Mike doesn't want our aircrewmen to hear what he has to say. This can't be good.

"What the fuck was that!" Mike says. "Why wasn't Sara at the controls?"

"Who says she wasn't at the controls?" Chad says.

"I'd say it's pretty fuckin' obvious who was at the controls."

"Hey listen, asshole, this is my aircraft and nobody tells me how to run it."

Mike walks forward to stand directly in front of Chad, glaring. The Mike who is always friendly to me, who always has an encouraging word, has turned to ice.

"Do *not* fuck with us," he says. "She had better be at the goddamn controls on the next approach or you can kiss this cruise good-bye! Admiral Carlson's sort of a stickler for having his direct orders followed." He doesn't wait for a response, but yanks out the ICS cord and hands it back to Messy.

I wish I hadn't heard that. Crap. Chad has been backed into a corner, summarily told off, and I was witness to the whole thing. Not good.

As Mike's squad boards the aircraft, Chad says, "Take the fuckin' controls."

We're en route to *Reeves* when Eric's voice breaks through the radio to guide us. For every one of these SEAL flights, he's had the call. It's always briefed that the Shadow Hunters will run the operations, but it's always him. And, of course, it was the same for Operation Low Level. I think about the e-mail I sent to Tom. I haven't heard back yet, so my mind has been free to roam, imagining all sorts of possible reasons that Eric does what he does, but none of it adds up. At the same time, I berate myself for my schoolgirl behavior. Why so much energy on this? Maybe he's just one of those superstar lieutenants that comes along once in a blue moon and the higher-ups are taking full advantage, letting him run the show. I don't know.

Since *Reeves* has gone silent, turning off all navigational aids, lights, and anything to help us find her, I follow Eric's directions to close on her position. Before I see the ship, I spot Eric's helicopter, visible by its running lights, hovering, as he observes from a distance. Once again, he directs our movements to find an invisible target.

"Okay, ma'am, deck in sight," Lego says. "Thirty yards, let's slow it up."

"We have it," I report to Eric.

"Five, four, three, rope's away. Steady. First man out . . ." Lego says.

My only visual reference is an antenna array, silhouetted against a starry backdrop. And I've no sooner processed this than Lego begins to give his final calls.

". . . last man out. Pulling in the rope. Steady. Rope's in. Steady. Clear to go," Lego says.

It's painfully obvious that my approach and stabilization to a hover were far smoother and over twice as fast as Chad's. And I did so without the benefit of a lighted ship.

The cockpit remains quiet as I fly to a holding pattern that Eric dictates, while we wait for the pickup. I imagine the SEALs, weighted with all their gear, jumping into the blackened ocean. My stomach churns at the thought. They used Zodiacs for their boarding runs last night and for their exits at the end. Not so tonight. They're swimming to the extraction point.

Twenty minutes later, we hover, wheels on the water, for pickup, and the nauseated feeling is almost overwhelming. I swallow hard. The water is everywhere, kicked up from the rotor wash, dripping from the windshield, splashing against the clear cockpit bubble beneath my feet, and swirling in black rings that radiate away from the aircraft. I shift in my seat, biting my lip. *Come on. Come on. Get those guys in, Lego. Get them in.*

"Last man is in," Lego says. "We're closed up in back. Clear to lift."

I tighten my grip on the controls, pulling up too quickly.

"Easy, ma'am," Lego says gently.

Relax, Sara. Relax.

We land on *Nimitz* just as the sun begins to peek over the horizon, and I'm panting like I've just finished running an all-out sprint.

It takes me a minute, but I've got my breathing under control when Mike crawls between the cockpit seats. He looks like a dripping wet rat, but an excited dripping wet rat. He loves what he does. That's obvious.

"Hey, Sara," he says. He never looks at Chad, nor does he address him. "You flew awesome. Better than last night even, and I thought that was pretty damn fine."

"Thanks, Mike."

He disconnects his ICS cord and retreats into the main cabin before exiting the aircraft.

"Shit, I'm soaked," Messy says. "Let's get outta here."

"I've got the controls," Chad reports.

"You've got 'em," I say, thankfully handing them over.

As Chad picks up and slides left, the scene could be out of some rah-rah military movie. An eight-man SEAL squad marching across the flight deck, dressed in dark camouflage, seawater rolling off their weapons and packs, silhouetted by the rising sun.

The reality is that there is no glamour in this, but I'm proud to the core to be a part of it. In moments like these, I smile inwardly, knowing I've just competently completed a mission and that anyone viewing the cockpit from the outside wouldn't realize who is looking back at them from behind the helmet visor. It's also in these moments, I don't feel alone or isolated, but rather, respected and appreciated, a pilot working just like any other.

16

I sit at my desk, adjusting to the strange stillness of the ship now at anchor in Hong Kong's famous Victoria Harbour. Tom's e-mail response glows on my computer screen.

> Hey Sara!
>
> Great to hear from you. Sorry, I can't help you with Eric Marxen. I've asked around and no one here knows him. Do you know what year he graduated? I'll be at the Hail and Farewell tomorrow. Maybe I'll see you there?
>
> Tom

I shake my head, embarrassed that I sent the e-mail in the first place. *This is just sad, Sara. Really sad.*

I turn off my computer as the call for liberty comes through the 1MC, the ship's intercom system, and I suspect it looks like a dam breaking on the quarterdeck as sailors flee the ship.

"Finally!" Emily squeals, bursting through the door.

She rips off her uniform and flings open the doors to her closet, searching for something to wear. My mouth drops as I watch her slip into a spaghetti-strapped fuchsia-colored top, a denim mini-skirt, and sandals. Never in a million years could I imagine walking off the ship in something like this. She sees it in my expression, too.

"There is absolutely no commentary allowed for how I dress to leave the ship," she says.

I chew on the inside of my cheek to keep from saying something.

"Man, what did they do to you at the Academy, anyway? How is this so disturbing to you?"

What did they do . . . ? Expect excellence? Demand professionalism? Require the utmost in dedication to duty? Of course. But there was always that extra bit for me. Don't let them see a woman, only a naval officer.

"It's just not professional, that's all."

"Did I not just say to leave the commentary at the door? You know, Sara, I love you, but fuck you. I say that endearingly, of course."

She pulls clothes out of her metal drawers and shoves them in her back-pack.

"But it's like you're no longer Lieutenant Wyatt, a respected officer and pilot. Instead, you're Emily, the hot chick."

"You think the guys would call me hot? I would actually find that flat-tering."

I sink my head in my hands.

"And Sara, think about it. Does it really matter? They're going to think what they're going to think no matter what we're wearing."

"I hope not."

"Oh, please. You cannot be that naïve. I mean, look at you. You can try to hide all you want in your baggy flight suit and crumpled khakis, but the fact you're tall, thin, and blond sorta stands out, know what I mean?"

"I don't stand out."

"Uh . . . right."

"But you will," I say, pointing to her outfit.

"Your senses are so skewed about civilian clothes. Surely they let you wear them at the Academy?"

"Well, no, not really."

"Excuse me? That was a joke."

"We wore uniforms pretty much all the time."

"Well, at Lehigh, we wore regular clothes, these kinds of clothes," she says, moving her arms up and down her body. "Then for NROTC, we threw on our uniforms once a week and called it good. And guess what? Everyone was okay with that. No one was any less respected for what they were wearing."

"But how do you want these guys to see you? I mean, spaghetti straps?"

"Sara, if you can't even fathom wearing a sleeveless shirt, you've got issues."

"I've got plenty. I know."

"I'll say it again. You need lace underwear."

She ignores my roll of the eyes.

"So are you getting dressed or what?" Em says. "I want to get outta here!"

We stand in a long and unusually slow-moving line of sailors waiting to cross the quarterdeck—access point to the narrow gangplank that runs diagonally down the hull, leading to the liberty launch that waits below in Victoria Harbour.

"Can you believe this?" Emily says, looking across the harbor-scape. "Just look at this place!"

"I know," I say. "It's so busy. You can read about Hong Kong all you want, but man."

Hong Kong is one of the busiest container ports in the world—the amount of goods that move through the shipping channels, staggering. Cargo ships, container ships, Chinese sailing junks, yachts—you name the seagoing vessel and it's here. The shipping lanes are crammed with traffic, even where we're located, a full hour out of port. I'm sure it's even busier closer in.

"If we could just get off this fucking ship!" Em says.

Many minutes later, as we approach the head of the line, we see the reason for our slow progress.

Are those . . . ?

Sailors are busily unloading thousands of tiny packages from a pallet-sized crate.

"Ma'ams, you have to take three of these in order to leave the ship," the petty officer of the watch says, holding out a handful of packaged condoms.

"Excuse me?" I say.

"XO's orders, ma'am."

"But we don't need these," I say.

"I'm sorry, ma'am, but no one is allowed to leave the ship without them."

"Hey, hey, Miss Equality," Em says. "We should take them like everybody else."

"But this is ridiculous."

"Look, Sara, I want to get off this fuckin' ship and so do all these other guys." She motions to the increasingly long line behind us. "They're going to get pissed if you delay them any longer, just like I'm getting pissed."

"But—"

"Sara, just take the goddamn condoms and let's go!"

I can't believe this.

I put out my hand and the petty officer drops three Trojan six-packs into my waiting palm.

"There are eighteen condoms here, Em."

"Well, we're scheduled to be in port for four days, so yeah . . . I guess I could see that."

My eyes widen.

"Go," she says, giving me a push.

As she receives her requisite eighteen layers of protection, I slip my backpack off my shoulder and stuff mine inside.

One hour later, we've made it through the chop of Victoria Harbour and onto Fenwick Pier. It's only one o'clock in the afternoon, and Em is ecstatic about our impending shopping excursion.

The conversation we had last night went something like this:

"Think about it, Sara. It's an *all-officer* Hail and Farewell. Eric might be there. And if he's there, you need to dress . . . well, not like you dress."

"Listen, the only reason I'm going to this affair is that it's mandatory. I plan to find Captain Magruder, ensure he sees me, and then I'm leaving. And my clothes are fine."

"They are not fine. There is no way you can wear your frumpy clothes to a liaison like this!"

"A liaison? Who said anything about a liaison?"

She barreled on. "You're going to screw this up if you don't get help. So wardrobe, yes, wardrobe!"

So here I am in Hong Kong, foregoing sightseeing opportunities galore to go shopping with Emily for clothes I don't need for a *liaison* that is not going to happen.

"Come on," she says. "First stop, the MTR so we can get subway tickets. We need to get over to the Kowloon side."

Hong Kong is divided into several parts due to the number of islands that make up the Hong Kong territory. All are divided by waterways, crossable only by ferry or underground train. We have landed on Hong Kong Island, but Em's shopping plans, and also the Hyatt Regency where we'll be staying tonight, reside on the Kowloon side.

Em quickly figures out the transportation logistics, and within thirty minutes, we're strolling down Nathan Road's famous Golden Mile. The concentration of signage here alone gives pause—like Times Square on steroids. I crane my neck upward, to neon signs stacked one above the other twenty stories high. This is repeated down the length of the boulevard for as far as the eye can see, layers upon layers of light and color.

The streets and sidewalks underneath share this congestion, choked with cars and pedestrians. Old World meets New World, the traffic stopping—barely—for the man pulling a hand cart, a full pig carcass strapped across the top. The modern grocery store, nestled among other high-end shops, sits catty-corner to the farmer's market where squid and seaweed hang from tattered awnings.

And the shops . . . hundreds of them. Em is in her glory. She pulls me into the first boutique she sees.

A pattern develops quickly. She picks out clothes, I try them on, I say no to everything, she pouts, we move on. And it continues like this for the next three hours. Fleetingly, I remember myself in high school, the girl who used to shop for new clothing as a matter of course. But now, I can't for the life of me remember why I thought it was so important.

My mom was never one for shopping, dressing up, or participating in any other such "frippery." Ironically, I found my mother's manner horrifying in high school. While the other girls' moms dressed to the latest season's fashion, mine stubbornly refused to participate, content to arrive at any school function in her favorite well-worn jeans and vintage tees. So at the time, I made it a point to remain well-heeled and scrupulously up to date, but whether due to my true nature or teenage rebellion, I don't know.

After graduation—after Ian—fashion forwardness plummeted on my list of priorities. But more importantly, I started to understand my mother—a woman who stood on her own, not fazed by the trivial, the trends, or the gossip. She is the woman I most admire, a woman who knows what's important and stays true to herself, and I love her all the more for it.

We're now working our way back to the hotel, and I'm sort of feeling sorry for Em. She actually looks depressed, like she's failed in her mission to buy me clothes.

But at least she's acting more normally and the tension between us has subsided. Because of the SEAL flights and the Sara-has-to-be-at-the-controls thing, it's just been a little weird, lately. So the bantering we're enjoying now is really great—just like normal. I think we just needed some time away from the ship.

Emily gives me a pitiful look as we walk into a store crammed with women's casual wear. As she's done all afternoon, she selects several tops and skirts and pushes me into the fitting room.

"Please, Sara, for me. Just please, have an open mind here." She hands me a short-sleeved, royal blue wrap shirt—something I never would have picked for myself. She helps me into it and pulls the wrap at the waist to tie it on the side. It's instantly flattering. The resulting V-shaped neckline sits flat on my chest and, while nice-looking, is still quite conservative, which is good for me.

I stare in the mirror and then shift my gaze to Em's pleading expression. I look back to my reflection. I'm wearing jeans and running shoes now, but if I replaced the running shoes with sandals, this might actually work. I know Em will scoff if I stay in jeans, but at this point, if I concede to wear anything new at all, she'll jump for joy.

"Okay, Em, I'll do it."

Before I have a chance to change my mind, the blouse is off my body and in Em's hands at the cash register.

After paying, I put my foot down. "Okay, Em, that's it. I'm done. I've *got* to get off my feet."

All I want is to be horizontal in our hotel room.

"You're kidding! *You're* tired?"

"I could run a marathon and it would be easier than this. Aren't your feet killing you?"

"I never thought I'd live to see the day when I outlasted you physically."

"Well, the day has come. Can we please go check in now?"

Em adjusts the shopping bags on her arms, distributing the weight equally, as she considers this. "Okay, we can check in—"

She stops when she sees the smile on my face. "That does *not* mean you're lying in bed all afternoon."

I pretend I have no idea what she's talking about.

"I know exactly what you're thinking, Denning, and the answer is no. If we check in, you're hanging with me."

"Hanging . . . where?"

17

My legs *hang* stiffly at the end of the Hyatt's twenty-five-meter pool, located on the eighth-floor terrace. Lined with mother-of-pearl tiles across the bottom, the pool shimmers in topaz blues and emerald greens. Emily dragged me here, and as always, it's a struggle. On several levels.

The liberty spirit is alive and well poolside, battle group officers strutting and peacocking while ogling the bikini-clad guests. Like Em and me, many of these men are staying here because of the Hail and Farewell tonight, and I suspect they're drinking the place dry based on the nonstop comings and goings of the waitstaff. The last time alcohol touched their lips was in Pearl Harbor over three weeks ago, so apparently, they're making up for lost time.

"You do realize you're the only one here not wearing a suit," Em says, surfacing in front of me after having swum the length of the pool underwater.

I look down at my rolled-up jeans. "But I don't intend on swimming."

"You don't have to swim, knucklehead. Besides, suits are for lounge chairs anyway."

"An even greater reason for not wearing one! I mean, here? With this group? Look how these guys are acting! No way."

She rolls her eyes before ducking underwater to wet her hair again, smoothing it with her hands after standing.

"Besides, just the *thought* of swimming makes me queasy," I say.

She moves to the side and crosses her arms over the deck, floating her legs behind her. "You know, it is totally beyond me how someone so deathly afraid of water would think it's a great idea to join the navy."

"I'm not afraid of water."

"Yeah . . . right."

"*Under*water. I'm not particularly fond of being *under*water."

"Whatever. But even so, what in god's name were you thinking? I mean, the navy? Really?"

"You know . . . Ian . . ."

"Surely you could have found another way to honor his memory."

"Hey, I'm working on it, all right?"

Em closes her eyes with a happy sigh, resting her head on her arms. I used to do this, too, once upon a time. When my dad was stationed in Virginia Beach, flying jets out of Naval Air Station Oceana, our family vacationed at the beautifully secluded Lake Anna in Northern Virginia, just outside of Fredericksburg. I could while away an entire afternoon floating on the edge of a raft, head resting on my arms, just like Em's, legs rising and falling with the waves as Ian paddled me around. When he got bored, he would jump off, dunking me in the process. We'd chase each other underwater, beneath and around the raft, giggling as we shot through the surface for air, and then we'd dive right back under again—for hours, day after day, and it never got old.

This would be an impossibility for me now, of course, since . . . well, since Ian. At the time—I was only eleven—I had thought I'd bring my own kids back to Lake Anna. But now, a vacation like this would hold little appeal. Even the notion of having kids—a given for my eleven-year-old self—has deserted me. I was so young, and yet my life's path was so clear then—college, husband, kids. . . . It's just what girls were supposed to do.

"Ahh! Stop it!" I screech, holding my hands in front of my face, as Emily splashes me.

"Hello, in there," she says.

"What?"

"Denning, you're completely zoning on me."

"Oh," I say, trying in vain to brush the water off my shirt before it soaks through.

Em pushes against the deck, straightening her arms and pulling her feet up underneath her. She pops to a stand in a single movement. I follow as she walks to our lounge chairs and grabs the Coppertone out of her bag.

"Can you help me out with the sunscreen?" she asks.

Emily confounds me. This pool is teeming with men, ones we serve in uniform with every day, and yet, I watch as she casually unclasps the back of her bikini top, lies facedown, and picks up the latest issue of *Cosmo*.

"Em, you can't . . ." I wave my hand up and down the length of the lounge chair, at a loss for words.

"Can't *what*?"

"Just . . . just this! It's not—"

"Don't tell me it's not professional!" she snaps. She reaches behind her, hooks her bikini top back together, and sits up to face me. "You know, Sara, I've had it with this! Listen to you! 'My way is the only way!' 'I'm professional and you're not!' If you think you're the only woman trying to prove herself on this deployment, I've got news for you. Just because I wear short skirts and swim in a bikini doesn't make me any less of a naval officer than you. Nor does it have anything remotely to do with my ability as a pilot. I mean, where the hell do you get off? You're the one who always screams about equality, that it shouldn't matter who's flying as long as they get the job done."

"But—"

"But nothing! You can't have it both ways!"

I cross my arms, pursing my lips. I force the air in and out of my nose as I grapple with the guiding tenet that has influenced every thought, action, and behavior since I earned my wings. *If you're competent, it shouldn't matter who's behind the visor.*

"And here's a news flash," she continues. "Femininity and professionalism aren't mutually exclusive! So stop looking down your nose and turn that condescending stare somewhere else!"

I open my mouth to argue, but she cuts me off.

"And while we're at it, for someone who thinks men and women should be equal, you sure do a damn fine job of telling me I'm not. I don't know who's worse, you or Claggett!"

She pulls up the back to the lounge chair, leans against it, and cracks her magazine open, blocking her face from view.

"You need to take a good, hard look at yourself, Sara Denning," she says from behind the magazine, "because only one of us is being true to herself."

I stand, stock-still, reeling from the assault. Emily and I have had our moments, to be sure, and our relationship has been a bit strained on the ship lately, but she's never unloaded like this, not in all the years I've known her.

I raise my eyes, scanning the pool deck, where people are laughing, splashing, joking, drinking . . . enjoying. And it strikes me that I stand very alone in this. What am I missing . . . ?

"I, um, I'll see you in the room," I mumble.

"Hey, it's your liberty," she says. With a flick of the hand, she shoos me away.

Crimson comforters with crisscrossed gold stitching adorn the two queen-size beds in our hotel room. I lie on the one closest to the curtained window, staring at the trompe l'oeil ceiling. As intended, its gilded panels appear to float, pulling my eyes up and up, into an illusory three-dimensional heaven. I hover here, studying the figure on the bed far below, wondering why she appears so sad. So I ask her. *Why?*

She tells me this is the only way she knows how. That she must remain focused and concentrated in order to live up to her family's expectations. To prove to her father, a decorated navy pilot, that she is up to task. That she can do whatever her brother would have done. Should have done.

But you can still be you. Look at Emily. Does she not meet expectations? Is she not one of the most outstanding naval officers and pilots you know?

The forlorn figure on the bed shifts uncomfortably. *Yes,* she answers. *But Emily is . . . is . . .*

What? True to herself? Happy?

The figure hesitates, but finally answers. *Yes.*

Are you *happy?*

The figure is still. Silent.

I float like a leaf, swirling, spinning, light, dropping until I join the figure, and become heavily weighted once more.

I'm not sure how much time has passed, but when Emily finally returns to our room, it's been long enough to realize that I owe her an apology. Try as I might, though, I can't seem to say it right. I stumble. I start over. I say it again. "Em, really, I just—"

"Sara, stop," Emily says, turning from the mirror. "Listen, you've apologized. I've apologized. We're good, okay? So can we just put this behind us and try to enjoy our liberty? Please?"

And that's it. Em moves on. She's good that way. No brooding or sulking. Besides, she has more pressing things on her mind. For the next two hours, she remains in constant motion, trying on various outfits, experimenting with umpteen clothing combinations, attempting to decide what to wear tonight. She's downright giddy, and this has lifted my spirits considerably.

If only it would help with the nerves.

The Hail and Farewell begins at seven o'clock, and the closer we draw to the hour, the more nervous I become. Nervously excited, I should say, which is a strange feeling for me. I hate getting "up" for anything. But after I decided I was going to enjoy my liberty just like Emily, I've allowed a thought that I had shut out earlier. Eric might be here. Since then, I've secretly buzzed, unable to shut off the anticipation.

"Okay, how about this?" Em says, flaunting an extremely mini miniskirt.

She turns a slow circle, ensuring I have a comprehensive view and adequate time to form my appraisal.

"They've all looked great. Too short, in my opinion, but you don't really care about my opinion, so I'd say you're safe with any of them."

She rolls her eyes. "Okay, I think I'm going with this."

She does a quick spin in front of the long closet mirror, pink chiffon layers levitating around her. She wears a form-fitting black sleeveless top, holds her head high, and radiates confidence.

As I watch her, I wonder for the thousandth time how she can stand hanging out with me. I'm so much more comfortable in my uniform, which is lame, I know. But at a function like this, I'm naked—approached by men with drinks in their hands who only see the woman before them. Not the officer. I've spent so much time learning how to be the always-professional, gender-neutral officer that I don't know how to act otherwise. It's social awkwardness at the highest level.

And like two worlds colliding, everything will be ratcheted up a notch tonight if Eric is here.

Em adds layers of jewelry and I marvel at her. She doesn't have this problem. Completely at ease, uniform or no.

"Em, how do you do it?"

"How do I do what?" she says defensively. She's prepping for another one of my lectures, I can tell.

"That," I say, motioning up and down her body, from perfect hair and makeup to miniskirt and heels. "You're just so . . . comfortable."

She stops, turning to face me, realizing I've asked her an honest question, no barbs attached.

I receive a long, pointed look before she speaks. "I'm not trying to be something I'm not," she says.

I stare back.

I stare back some more.

Growing up, I had never considered a career in the navy, despite being raised by my father, a pilot and twenty-four-year Navy veteran. He would regale Ian and me with tales of his around-the-world adventures, and while we were both enthralled, it was only Ian who wanted to follow in our father's footsteps. I had set my sights elsewhere until that fateful day nine years ago, when life as I knew it ended. When I made Ian's dream my own.

I was woefully ill-prepared for what lay ahead. Even though my father treated Ian and me equally, imparting lessons learned from his time in the navy to both of us, my teenage self lingered in the Mall of America, devoured the latest issues of *Vogue*, and even donned a white lace gown with elbow-length gloves for the Minneapolis Honors Cotillion.

The grief from losing Ian overwhelmed my carefree soul, but entering the Naval Academy crushed it altogether. I was irrevocably changed through that experience, withdrawing into myself to survive, knowing I couldn't quit because Ian wouldn't have quit. To succeed at the Academy, you *really* have to want to be there. And as a woman, immersed in an invisible, insidiously misogynistic culture, it's doubly true.

Somehow, I managed. Somehow, I graduated. And then, a strange thing happened. I did well in flight school. Really well. And one day, it dawned on me that I was enjoying what I was doing. The training, the missions, the stick and rudder skills. I was growing and melding and succeeding in the navy without even realizing it. I wasn't just doing this for Ian anymore. His dream had truly become mine. I had found what I was meant to do.

"But I *know* who I am," I say. "I'm a pilot. I'm—"

She holds up a hand. "I'm not talking about being a pilot."

She gives me a knowing look, pausing well before continuing. "Sometimes I get glimpses of the real Sara, like when we're at home. But I tell you what, at the squadron and out here, you're different. I mean, *really* different."

The real Sara . . . Em is right. Even though I've found something I do well, something I enjoy, it has come at a steep price. In the deepest depths of my damaged soul, I know that the real Sara is lost. She has been for a long time, hidden behind so many defensive layers, I can't find her anymore.

I deny it anyway. "No, it—"

The hand goes up again. "I'm not saying that this *different* you is a *bad* you. But you don't have to suffocate all that's Sara. Like now. We're going to a party and it's fun to dress up. So why not?"

"I don't know, Em. I just . . . I don't know."

She reaches into one of several shopping bags lined under the bathroom counter, and I throw my arms up in front of my face as she draws something back like a rubber band and flings it toward me. A pair of lacy black underwear lands on my extended fingers. I look up as a black bra follows, landing on my shoulder.

"What the—"

"I'm telling you," she says, her playful tone returning. "You need these."

"When did you—"

"While you were in one of the fitting rooms. Come on, Sara. No one will know."

"*I'll* know. I just can't do this. Not yet, anyway."

"Suit yourself," she says, turning her attention back to the mirror.

"I'm sorry, Em. But thanks anyway."

"Hey, you're a work in progress, but I'm patient."

I climb out of bed and don my new blue blouse, tying the wrap myself. It doesn't look as good as when Em did it, but close enough. After brushing my hair, I'm about to pull it into a ponytail when I feel a hand on my arm.

"Please," she begs. "Don't ruin it."

"Ruin what?"

"Your hair. Keep it long."

"I don't know. I don't like it in my face, and with who we'll be seeing tonight . . . I mean, just wearing something like this is on the edge for me."

"Okay, just humor me for a second." She turns to the dressing area counter and rummages through her toiletries bag. "Here, stand still and let me see how this looks."

She slides a brown, wooden headband over my head, pulling my hair back on the sides in the process. "What do you think?"

I look in the mirror. At least my hair would be out of my eyes.

"It's sort of not too bad," I admit.

"Oh, thank fuckin' god."

She makes a few last-minute additions to her makeup and final touch-ups to her hair.

"Okay, let's get outta here," she says. "I need a drink."

18

Emily has timed our arrival to be exactly forty-five minutes late. We walk into the Crystal Ballroom, just off the lobby, into a sizeable crowd. The strike group officers here number in the hundreds when you include the pilots from the carrier air wing. And the women? Like moths to flame. They're everywhere. And they're gorgeous, too. I don't know where they came from, but they all look like they've just stepped off a runway. I don't think I could look or feel any more plain.

Emily fits in perfectly with this group of women who wear bright colors, strapless dresses, and perfect makeup. And if they were looking to meet up with someone, they picked the perfect place. The men outnumber the women easily five to one.

Just like the scene at the pool, it's obvious that this group has been imbibing for hours prior to our arrival, probably hitting several pubs en route to this event. The conversation is loud, the laughter excessive. I stealthily scan the room for Eric as I follow Em, who makes a beeline for the bar.

It's not long before she twirls a half-emptied drink in her hand, holding court with two male admirers—officers from another ship. Soon, several more men join our little gathering. Emily gives them all a grand hello, happy drunk style.

I feel so out of place. My hands are shoved in my pockets and I stare at the ground while Emily buzzes in animated conversation. In addition to the extremely uncomfortable no-uniform thing, I'm just plain introverted. It's always been this way, but now it's getting worse. And in this single evening, it's getting way worse. The more people that cluster around to join our group, the more withdrawn I become. Emily seems intent on introducing me to everyone who arrives, and I'm offered enough drinks over the next thirty minutes that had I accepted them all, I'd be lying unconscious by now.

But standing here does give me a chance to observe Emily. Sure, she's tipsy, but boy does she shine in an environment like this. Her personality flows unrestrained—loudly amusing, uncannily clever—and she draws a crowd, a big one. She seems to extract energy from a gathering like this, glowing brighter by the minute.

Me? There's no glowing here. I start chuckling as I stare at my feet, the image of a supernova and a black hole, side by side, coming to mind.

"What are you laughing at?" Em says.

"Nothing."

"Come on. What is it?"

"You're, um . . . well, you're just sort of amazing, that's all."

"Yes, I am rather amazing, aren't I," she declares, pointing her nose up.

"I'm going to see if I can find Captain Magruder and maybe get something to eat," I say.

"Fine," she says, but then quickly grabs my arm. "Just come back."

I squeeze through the crowd, wondering why she would want me to come back. I don't exactly bring much to the conversation. But she's always been like this. Even at home in San Diego. Always sticking close. The best friend thing, I guess.

I head for the buffet and spot Commander Claggett, who stands with Chad, Matt, and Zack, all with drinks in their hands. They're in deep discussion with three, no, make it four women. Doesn't look like they're going to notice much else tonight. No Captain Magruder, though, which is secretly good because it means I can't leave yet, raising the chances I might bump into Eric.

Once at the food table, I walk back and forth, checking the selection. I'm approached by a group of men wearing civilian clothes topped with navy-issue brown leather flight jackets. Out of the group of six, five busy themselves at the table while one strikes up a conversation. His name tag has only his call sign embroidered on it—Bull. He never gives me his name, nor does he ask mine. He's a bit heavyset, his jacket straining at the zippers.

He talks. I listen. All I need to do is nod my head a few times because he has a lot to say, mostly about himself. But there are moments when I have to speak up or else it would be completely awkward. So I offer questions here and there.

"So you fly what again?" I ask.

"Jets. F-14s, F-18s. You know."

"Wow, you fly both."

"Yeah, we switch around."

He's lying. On several counts. First, F-14s were decommissioned years ago. Second, his squadron patch says E-2 Hawkeye, which means he's not a jet pilot at all, but flies turboprops.

"So what does your patch mean? E-2?"

"Oh, it's just another aircraft. I fly those, too."

"Three aircraft . . ."

"And—not that this is a big deal—but I also fly with the Blue Angels."

"Really? You're a Blue Angel?"

He nods.

I can't believe this. He must be awfully desperate. Even a civilian wouldn't believe this. Or would they? The more I think about it, he would probably only employ a known tactic, one he knows works. Yikes.

"So how do you do the airshows and all that when you're out here?"

"Oh, I just fly back and forth. It's no big deal. We all do it."

"Your resume is impressive, definitely."

"Yeah, well, when I graduated from the Naval Academy, I set some high goals for myself."

"An Academy grad, too?"

If he is, I'll be surprised.

"You know, I had a friend who went there," I say. "He said you all stayed in some huge dormitory, thousands of people in one building. The name began with a B but I can't remember what it was."

"Oh, Bingham Hall, yeah. We all stayed there. But that was a long time ago."

He didn't go to the Academy either. We lived in Bancroft Hall. No such thing as Bingham Hall, and no Academy grad anywhere, no matter how far removed or however drunk they might be, would ever forget the name Bancroft Hall.

He laughs. "I'm sorry, I feel like I've been talking this entire time."

You have.

"Do you want—" he starts.

We're interrupted, fortunately, by a welcome voice. "Hey, Sara, is that you?"

It's Tom Jenkins.

"Tom!" I say.

Bull looks at me in surprise and then at Tom. "You know her?"

"Yeah, we were classmates at the Academy."

Bull's drunken smile turns to a scowl. "Bitch," he says, before marching away.

"What the hell was that?" Tom says.

"I don't know. Well, actually, I do know. He's embarrassed because he told me he was a Blue Angel, among other things."

"Really? What an idiot."

"Well, maybe it wasn't nice of me to play along when I knew he was lying."

"Hey, that's on him. He was the one lying. Anyway, just forget that guy."

Good ol' Tom Jenkins. I could always count on him to back me up. I had many classmates like Tom—forward thinking, open, and firmly seated on the tolerant end of the women-in-the-military thought continuum. Always respectful, always inclusive, a true friend in every sense of the word, and a dream for a squad mate.

But while Tom fell on one end of the continuum, there were a few who fell on the other . . . and it was an extreme end—the women-haters. An aberrant group who acted as if they were afraid of us, like we were contagious. Mutant humanoids to be kept at arm's length and more. They would even go so far as to ignore you. *If I don't acknowledge you, then you're really not here.*

Next to them on the continuum, a slightly less extreme cadre. Those who were okay with women as a member of the species, but only if they behaved, and stayed in their rightful place—in the kitchen, the nursery, that sort of thing. They firmly believed women shouldn't serve in the military or attend the service academies. The women who did were abdicating their responsibilities to family while engaged in more selfish pursuits.

In the middle somewhere, many male midshipmen believed that yes, women *could* attend the Naval Academy, but most weren't qualified, ushered in by quota only, and not up to standards. Certainly not the standards *they* had met.

Beyond them came those who begrudgingly accepted that women were indeed up to task and could meet the standards, but who were just plain pissed, damn it, that women had infiltrated the fraternity.

And then, finally, you could exhale as you slid into Tom's space. Where women deserved to be there just like him, well qualified, equally devoted, and serving their country just like anyone else.

A roving waiter, tray in hand, passes next to us, proffering glasses of red wine. Tom takes a glass, while I politely decline.

"Hey, sorry I took so long in answering your e-mail. The op tempo has been insane," he says.

"That's all right. It wasn't really important, anyway."

"So do you have plans for later?" Tom asks, taking a sip from his glass. "A bunch of us are gonna grab some dinner and you're welcome to come."

I discreetly look behind and around Tom, doing a quick scan for Eric.

"Um, yeah, maybe. Thanks for asking."

"We're meeting in the lobby at twenty-one hundred, so if you want to join us, just show up."

Tom's squadron mates begin to trickle over and he makes introductions. He's with a nice group. No Blue Angel stories here.

"I thought you were going to get food," Emily says. She sidles up next to me with a fresh drink in her hand.

"I was but then I ran into Tom here—"

She leans over and whispers in my ear. "So, come on, girl. Introductions! ASAP!"

I introduce the group to Emily and then excuse myself. She smiles as I leave, mouthing, "You're the best!"

"Happy hunting," I say.

I turn away and run smack into Commander Egan.

"Heyyy, Sara," he says. He must be sweating alcohol, the smell is so strong. He looks me up and down, nodding approvingly. Just cue the nausea.

"Can I get you a drink?" he asks.

"No thank you, sir."

"Are you sure?"

"Quite sure, sir."

And then I see him. From over Commander Egan's shoulder, a herd of stumbling partygoers moves past, revealing a small group standing just behind. Eric has just joined them—three of his detachment pilots, Stuart, Rob, and Ken; and three women who look like they've spent the entire day in a beauty salon. Talk about faces lighting up when Eric arrives. He smiles, talking easily, and I grow sicker inside as I watch.

One woman in a royal blue halter leans over to whisper in Eric's ear. He responds with a quiet laugh, at which point she slides her arm around him and one of her friends takes a photo.

I look down at my own blouse, the same bright blue, the color that Em raved about because she said it matched my eyes. It's not even close to being filled out like that woman's. And below that? Stupid faded jeans and sandals I've owned since high school.

"How 'bout a stroll?" Commander Egan says. "Why don't you and me take a stroll outside?"

"What?"

Like an annoying fly, he pesters. I swat at the air, shooing him away while my eyes remain riveted on the scene in front of me. The woman in blue squeezes Eric closer to her as the group laughs. This is so devastatingly hard to watch.

Honestly, Sara, did you really think he'd be looking for you? And why are you upset? He can talk with whomever he wants. It doesn't mean anything. And besides, there's nothing between you two, anyway, so this is just silly.

My reaction to this situation is almost more upsetting than the situation itself.

I look down again at my blouse, awkwardly tied, and my headband slides forward, reminding me I've worn my hair long.

You were trying to look nice for him. Admit it.

I chance one more torturous glance at the scene, and the woman in blue throws her head back, laughing. Her hair cascades in perfectly highlighted waves across her shoulders as she reaches for Eric's arm for balance.

Like you ever had a chance, Sara.

"Hey, this is a party," Commander Egan says. "You need to relax." His voice echoes somewhere in the background, but I'm not listening. I'm backing away.

In less than thirty seconds, I'm slapping the elevator button for the twenty-seventh floor. I wait until the doors close before slamming my palm into the side paneling.

"You can fly a helicopter with a failing transmission and not waver," I say out loud. "You can stand tall while Commander Claggett throws daggers and not flinch. But you compare yourself to another woman based on what you're wearing and you slink away like a frightened puppy? You've gotta be fucking kidding me!" I give the side of the elevator one more good whack before the doors open, then shuffle to my room, defeated.

19

It's approaching six o'clock in the evening in the makeshift shore patrol office housed in the Harbourview Hotel's banquet hall on the ground floor. Scores of round dinner tables, stripped bare of their coverings, crowd the room. Couches and wide-cushioned chairs line the sides. Petty officers and chiefs representing each ship in the battle group, all dressed in the uniform of the day, summer whites, lounge, play cards, eat, or watch TV as they await their turn on roving patrol.

We have over one hundred men assigned to shore patrol and just one shore patrol officer—me. Our job is to aid in the security for our sailors while they're ashore, but also to act as a liaison for any matters involving the local police or other civilian authorities.

I woke up this morning at the Hyatt Regency in Kowloon, took the subway to Hong Kong Island, checked into the Harbourview Hotel, changed into my uniform, and reported for shore patrol duty at 0700. Now, back in my element, I'm regaining a bit of dignity. I'm secure here. Confident. I know how to do this.

For some naïve reason, I thought we would enjoy a light day today, being that it's Sunday. I couldn't have been more off the mark. Most of the people we've seen this morning and throughout the afternoon never went to sleep last night. We've already sent close to forty-five men back to their ships under the escort of MPs for their drunken or lewd behavior.

I've thanked the shore patrol gods several times for assigning Senior Chief Makovich to my watch. He's the oldest H-46 aircrewman in the fleet and has notoriously survived three Class A mishaps during his long, salt-and-peppered career. Class A mishaps are the biggies—total aircraft destruction, a million dollars or more of damage to the aircraft, or loss of life. Heavy stuff.

His experience shines in a situation like this. He has tamed even the most unruly sailors as we arrange for the appropriate escort back to their ships. It probably doesn't hurt that T-Bear and Diggs are here to assist him, either—easily the two largest and most intimidating-looking sailors in the battle group.

I sit at one of the back tables, catching my breath, dreaming of a hot bath and putting my feet up, when it finally dawns on me that I can sit in my room just as easily as here, and if anyone needs me, they can call.

I'm about to rise when I hear greetings in the background. "Hey, sir. What are you doing here?"

"Just visiting a friend," Eric says.

My head snaps up, my body electric. Eric walks toward me wearing faded jeans, running shoes, and an untucked T-shirt. Damn it. Why does he affect me like this?

I spent most of last night pondering that question, right after shifting the blame for my behavior at the Hail and Farewell. It was Eric. It was the woman in blue. It was the navy. Commander Egan. Around and around I went until the spinner finally, truthfully, landed on me.

I let him in. I lowered my guard. The most frustrating thing is that I thought I'd learned my lesson on the *Lake Champlain*. I told myself not to be stupid. Not to let down my defenses. It's how you get hurt, plain and simple. But then, I did it again last night.

So in the wee hours, I made a deal with myself. The next time you see Eric, you are neutral. Cool as a cucumber. You are friendly, but will open yourself no further. Period.

Blast it when he approaches with an easy smile. "May I?" he asks, indicating the chair across from me.

Keep it on the surface, Sara. You can do this.

"Of course," I say. "Just passing by or . . ."

"No. Actually, I came to find you."

Damn it.

I look up as T-Bear and Diggs approach.

"Everything good here, ma'am?" T-Bear asks.

If I didn't know better, I'd say T-Bear wants to know if this guy who's just wandered in isn't bothering me or anything.

"It's fine, yes," I say.

Good. This is helpful. This is your chance to go casual.

"Guys, I'd like you to meet Eric Marxen. He flies off the *Lake Champlain*. Eric, this is Petty Officer Jefferson, better known as T-Bear, and Petty Officer Diggins, known to all as Diggs."

Eric stands and shakes their hands. "Nice to meet you both."

"Likewise, sir," T-Bear says.

"T-Bear and Diggs are my weight room buddies," I say. "You cannot believe what these guys can lift. It blows my mind."

"I *can* believe it," Eric says.

"Sir, that's nothing. You should see the lieutenant. She's an animal. Spends way too much time on the cardio equipment."

"I can believe that, too."

"Well, it was nice to meet you, sir," T-Bear says.

"Yeah, you too, guys."

As T-Bear and Diggs walk away, Eric turns to me. "How's it been today?"

Well, at least he's keeping it casual, too. This is good.

"Pretty busy, actually."

We turn in unison to the small commotion at the banquet room entry. Three shore patrolmen escort a hopping mad sailor in civilian clothes, and they're followed by an older Asian woman who holds the hand of a younger one—one who is clearly a lady of the evening.

Everyone is speaking at once, the sailor in filth-ridden English and the two women in a whip-quick language I don't understand.

"See what I mean?" I rise to cross the room and Eric follows.

"Whoa, whoa, whoa," I say, gesturing for everyone to calm down.

I look quickly for our translator, but I don't see him. I spy Senior Chief Makovich instead.

"Senior?" I say. "Have you seen Kong-sang Chan?"

He takes a quick survey of the room. "No, ma'am. Let me see if I can round him up."

The quiet doesn't last for more than about twenty seconds when the two women start going at it again. I hear Eric laughing and turn as he walks up next to me.

"What's so funny?" I say.

"They're claiming they haven't been paid."

"I'm not paying them a goddamn thing!" the sailor says.

"Wait. You understand them?"

He nods.

"What are they speaking?"

"Mandarin."

The women point at the sailor and begin speaking over each other once more. I put up my hands again to urge everyone to calm down, but I stop, stunned, when Eric begins to address them in what appears to be seamless, fluent Mandarin.

My head moves back and forth as they converse, until Eric finally turns to me. "This young woman here was approached by—" He looks at the sailor. "What's your name, sailor?"

"Jason Williams," he says.

"And your rate?" Eric asks.

"Machinist's mate second class."

Eric shifts to me. "This woman was approached by Petty Officer Williams for her services. The price was agreed upon by her mamasan here," he says, indicating the older woman, "and she performed said services in an upstairs room at the New Makati Pub and Disco, but then he refused payment."

"She didn't perform anything, goddamn it!" Petty Officer Williams says.

"Petty Officer Williams, can you give us your side of the story?" I say.

"She's a fuckin' he/she!" He's shouting now and has the attention of everyone in the room. "I didn't agree to anything with any fuckin' shemale! Makes me fuckin' sick to my stomach!"

I look more closely at the young woman. Holy cow. She has an Adam's apple.

As shore patrol officer, you are judge and jury for cases like this. I glance down at Petty Officer Williams's hand. He wears a wedding ring. Inwardly, I'm thinking, *If you hadn't been messing around on your wife, you wouldn't have gotten yourself into this mess.* But I don't say that.

"I know you feel you've been wronged," I say. "But I want you to think about this. If you refuse to pay, I'm going to have to call the MPs and they're going to detain you in the brig while an investigation is conducted into this matter. You'll lose your remaining liberty in Hong Kong, and because these investigations take so long, you'll probably lose your liberty in Singapore, too."

I can already see I'm talking his language.

"In addition, if charges are filed, we're going to have a bit of an embarrassing international incident on our hands."

I can see the wheels turning, although he's probably only thinking about the losing liberty part.

"And finally, these two are citizens of our host country. And as guests in this country, we should strive to maintain the best possible relations so that the U.S. Navy is asked to return."

His eyes make it clear that I should have just stuck with the losing liberty argument.

"I think it would be a lot easier, personally, to just give them their money, and then you'll be free to go on your way and enjoy the rest of your time in Hong Kong a free and happy man."

"This is fuckin' bullshit," he says, shoving his hand down his front pocket and pulling out a wad of Hong Kong dollars. He counts out the money and throws it on the ground in protest.

I motion to the shore patrolmen to let him go and he runs off as the two women scramble forward and scoop up their earnings.

They speak animatedly to Eric, offering their thanks, I hope, and scurry away.

Eric and I share a look as we walk back to the table. "I cannot believe we just had that conversation," I say.

"You handled that like a pro," he says.

"Well, he shouldn't have been messing around on his wife. Serves him right."

Eric laughs.

"But Mandarin? You speak Mandarin?"

He nods.

"Any other languages I should know about, just in case the need arises?"

"Just Arabic . . . and well, Pashto and Farsi."

I stop. "Four languages? Are you serious or are you just pulling my leg?"

"Actually, I'm serious."

"But why—?"

"I'll tell you about it when we have more time someday."

We start walking again toward the back of the room and a loud growling noise from my stomach sends an embarrassed blush to my face. "I guess I need to find something to eat," I say.

"Say nothing more. I've got it covered."

Oh, wait. No. No. No. This wasn't supposed to happen. This is already heading somewhere I swore I wouldn't go. Too easy. Too familiar.

"Um, no, that's okay. You don't have to—"

"Let me guess," he says, turning to face me. "You're *fine*?"

The question hangs there, ringed with accusation.

I look down to the floor, guilt clawing at my throat. "I'm sorry," I say, looking up.

"I just want to do something nice for you, that's all. It's just dinner. I'll bring it. I'll leave. That's it."

I consider this for several moments, looking well into his soulful eyes. "Okay," I say, relenting.

He turns, but I call out after him. "We can eat together." *That's only considerate, right? He's going to get you food. The least you can do is eat with him.* "What I mean is, you don't have to leave right away."

"Sure. If that's what you want."

"We could eat in my room." *What did I just say? Good god, Sara. What are you doing?*

He raises his eyebrows slightly.

"It would just be a lot quieter and I was going to head up there anyway," I rationalize. "The guys can call me if they need me."

"Whatever you say. What's the number?"

"Eight oh eight."

"Copy, eight oh eight," he says. "I should be back within the hour."

20

Once in my room, I cast off my uniform and run a hot bath. I slide into the tub, resting my head against the rounded rim, and close my eyes, shutting out the experiences of the day. I got far more than I bargained for on this round of duty, and I sincerely doubt it's over yet, because for most sailors, the night is young. But it's hard to stop thinking about that last incident. I don't think I ever could have anticipated that one.

And did I really just invite Eric up to my room? I can't even begin to explain this one to myself.

You called yourself stupid before, Sara, but this is getting ridiculous.

While toweling off, I decide to dress comfortably for now, even though I'll most certainly be donning my uniform again tonight. I pull on Eric's maroon shirt and gray shorts—

Wait. He's going to see me in these. He'll know I took his clothes.

You have not put yourself in a good place here.

I do have my blue wrap blouse and jeans that I wore to the Hail and Farewell. When I left the ship, I had no intention of returning until my duty day, the last day. When we pull into port, not only do we stand shore patrol duty, but also ship duty. Every department must keep a minimum number of personnel on the ship, enough that you could get the ship under way, if necessary. So I brought everything with me for both the party at the Hyatt and for my time on shore patrol, attempting to stay away from the ship for as long as possible before I had to return.

Or I could put on my uniform again . . .

The knock on the door forces the decision. Shoot. Uniform? Jeans? Shirt? I don't want to keep him waiting. *Okay, just go with what you have.*

I finish rolling the shorts at the waist and bound for the door. I open it wide . . . and gasp.

"Sssara," Commander Egan says, stumbling through the door.

He's a disheveled drunken mess, his plaid shirt only half tucked in, with stains running down the front as if he's spilled a time or two. Bloodshot eyes stare awkwardly into mine. He carries a six-pack of beer in one hand and clumsily pulls one can out.

"Where've you been?" he slurs.

"Sir, I was in the shore patrol office. I was just getting dressed to go back there now."

"You don't have to do that. The chiefs can handle *everything*." He waves his beer can grandiosely in the air. "What you need is some time to relax."

"No, sir, it's my job to report down there, so I need to ask you to leave so I can get dressed."

"Always soooo professional," he says, stepping toward me. "Here, this'll help."

He thrusts the can forward, just in front of my face.

"No, sir, I don't want anything."

"Well, all right," he says. He tucks the remaining five cans under one arm and opens the other. Tipping his head back, he takes several long gulps.

"You know what the rumor going 'round is, don't you?" he says, stepping forward once more.

I shake my head, taking a step back, while looking beyond him to the partially open door.

"Everyone thinks we're doin' it. Can you believe that? People think we're doin' it."

God, how revolting.

"I don't know why they'd think that," he says, moving toward me.

"I don't know either, sir," I say, retreating once more.

"It's Doug, remember. Why is it so hard for you to call me Doug?"

"Sir, you're drunk. You need to leave."

"Of all the rumors. You and me . . . together," he suggests.

The tone of his voice and the look in his drunken eyes has changed. I back up, the open door moving farther away.

You've let this go too far. Shit.

I glance around quickly. I'm hedged between the foot of the bed and the desk and there's no room to go around him. I look again at the bed. Maybe I can jump and run over it to get to the door.

While my eyes are on the bed, a hand grabs my arm. Reflexively, I yank to get it clear, but his grasp is firm. *What the hell?*

"Sir, what are you doing?"

"Sara, Sara, Sara . . ."

"Sir, let go of me."

"But why? Isn't this what you want?"

"No, sir, I don't want this."

He hastily sets his beer can on the desk and grabs my other arm. *Shit! This is getting out of control fast!*

Like a movie reel, frames from my self-defense classes at the Academy start clicking through my head. Kick him between the legs? Jab at his eyes? Scream?

"Let go of me," I say. "You're drunk."

"Maybe so, but I'm havin' a good time."

His grip is getting tighter and it's starting to hurt.

"Let go of me!" I back up, pulling my arms, but it only makes him grab on harder.

Sara, you need to do something and do it right now!

I deliver the strongest kick I have between his legs and he doubles over with a howl. I follow with a hard kick behind the knees and they buckle, dropping him to the floor. Shoving him forward to his stomach, I drive my knee into the small of his back, grabbing his arms and wrenching them behind him.

"What . . . ?" Eric says, materializing in the doorway. He completes a hyperfast assessment. "Did he . . . ?"

I nod, but at the same time, Commander Egan jerks his head around, directing a scathing look at Eric. "This is none of your business, asshole!" He almost knocks me off balance with an unexpected lurch, but I lean my weight forward, tightening my grip.

"The hell it isn't!" Eric moves so fast, I can barely discern what's happening. In seconds, he has Commander Egan pulled to his feet, holding his arms in a viselike grip behind his back, a look so cold on his face, it borders on frightening. He hauls him from the room and I hear it when he says in a low, menacing tone, "You touch her again, I'll break your face, motherfucker!"

* * *

Footsteps recede down the hallway and I push up to stand, shaking, my body coursing with adrenaline. I pace back and forth at the foot of the bed, focusing on deep inhalations and long, slow exhalations, berating myself for allowing the situation to have gotten that far.

I hear the door close, and instantly, Eric is at my side. He places his hands lightly on my shoulders, looking me squarely in the eyes.

"Are you okay?" he asks.

I nod.

"Are you sure?"

"I'm sure. I just need a minute."

"Do you want to sit down?"

The bed would be the obvious choice for seating, but I slump to the ground where I stand, and lean back against the wall. Eric sits next to me.

"Everything happened so fast," I say.

"May I look at your arms?"

I extend them and he holds my forearms in his hands, rolling them back and forth, inspecting them. "That son of a bitch," he says through gritted teeth.

My eyes widen as I view the bruises swelling on my arms. I knew he was squeezing hard, but . . .

I look back to Eric and he's trying desperately to control something. He's distraught, worried, but he's angry, too. It looks like he's going to jump out of his skin.

"I'm okay," I say, but he shakes his head, unconvinced. "Really."

He lowers his eyes, looking at my arms, gently sliding his fingers across the bruising.

When he finally looks up again, his eyes hold mine as he rubs his thumbs against the backs of my hands. If he's trying to soothe me, it's working. If he's trying to whip my insides to buttercream, it's also working. I wonder if it's possible for someone's eyes to reach into yours, find the heartstrings beyond, and grab them tight. Because that's how I feel. Eric is holding me from the inside.

"I screwed up," I say. "I should have stopped it sooner. But I kept thinking, this can't be happening. I mean, I knew what to do, but at the same time, I just wasn't prepared. . . ."

"I wasn't prepared for what I saw either," he says.

"What you did . . . your reaction. You were so fast. How did you—?"

"I wish I could explain how that made me feel. I'm sorry. That must have looked—"

He lets go of my hands and leans back against the wall, his shoulder to my shoulder.

As soon as he lets go, I feel like I'm falling, and the sensation is a horrible one. "Can I ask a favor?"

"Anything," he says.

"Can I . . . ?" I tentatively reach for his left hand with my right.

He grabs it quickly, pulling our forearms together.

"Is this okay?" he asks.

"Yes. Thank you."

We sit in silence and I feel the gentle pressure of his fingers against my hand. I close my eyes and lean my head against the wall, responding to his touch with a light pressure of my own.

I keep my eyes closed as I talk. "Thanks. This is helping."

He moves a hand to my head and I feel his fingers lightly combing my hair away from my face. I open my eyes to watch. He's so careful, like he's making everything right again.

"Okay?" he says.

"Better. Thanks. And thanks for what you did."

"I didn't do anything," he says. "I think you had it pretty well in hand." He tries to smile, but it doesn't turn out quite right. I'd almost say this has affected him worse than it has me.

Maybe I can help get us to a lighter place. "Did you bring something to eat?"

He holds my eyes for a moment longer, then rises and walks to the door, where he dropped a bag when he first walked in.

"I'll get some water," I say.

I return to the table with bottled water from the mini-fridge and he lays out our meal—steamed rice and roast pork. He splits it onto two paper plates before handing me a pair of chopsticks.

"This is perfect," I say, hoping to elicit a response.

He offers a tight-lipped nod only.

We eat in silence, and the longer we go, the more worried I become.

"Eric, are you okay?"

He looks at me carefully before answering. "No."

His gaze shifts to my arm that rests above the table, his eyes roving up and down the bruising. "What are you going to do?" he asks.

"I don't know."

"Report it to Captain Magruder, of course."

I consider this for several long moments. "I don't know. I don't want to make this a bigger deal than it is. He was drunk—"

"What? You can't dismiss this—"

"He was stupid, he was drunk, I handled it."

He stares at me, incomprehension written across his face.

"I handled it," I say, glad when the phone rings so I can escape his admonishing stare. I cross the room to answer.

"Ma'am, we need you back down here," T-Bear says. I press the phone well to my ear to hear him through the noise in the background—barked orders, chaotic shouts, muffled grunts.

"No problem. I'll be right there."

I hang up the phone and Eric is already standing.

"You don't have to do this," he says. "I'll run to the ship, grab my uniform—"

"I'm fine."

He shoots me a sharp look at the word "fine."

"Eric, I can do this."

I don't wait for an answer, grabbing my uniform from the bed and changing in the bathroom. But when I look in the mirror, I'm shocked. The bruising is glaringly obvious against the stark white of my short-sleeved shirt.

I walk out, Eric takes one look, and his mouth hardens into a tight line. I spy my backpack on the bed and think of a solution, not a navy-regulation solution, but it'll have to do. I fish out a thin black sweater that I threw in at the last minute and hastily put it on.

"Can I walk down with you?" he asks, opening the door.

I nod my assent and we move through a corridor of red and gold to reach the elevators—red and gold carpeting, red and gold wallpaper, red and gold fixtures and frames. Eric stares intently ahead.

It's not until we enter the elevator that he finally speaks. "I need to run to the ship for a minute, but I'd like to come back. It's going to be busy for you tonight, and I don't care if I sit in the shore patrol office the entire time. I'd just feel better that way."

I'm about to disagree. I don't need help. I can do my job just fine by myself. But wait. *He backed off on taking your duty, so you should probably give a little, too, Sara.*

"Okay," I say.

His shoulders visibly relax.

The elevator doors open and we enter the banquet room, now teeming with dozens of inebriated sailors under escort from dozens more shore patrolmen. I spot a group of chiefs, including the translator, clustered in the corner and decide that's where I need to be.

But I stop short. *Wait a second. Is that—?*

"What is it?" Eric asks, following my gaze to the opposite side of the room.

"I know that man. That's Animal, I mean, Commander Amicus, a pilot in our squadron. I just never expected to see him here."

When I look back to Eric, he wears a slightly changed expression, one that's hard to read.

"Yeah, I suppose this isn't the likeliest place to bump into someone," he says. "I'll see you in a bit, okay?"

Eric walks away, and beyond him, Commander Amicus presses through the crowded group of sailors. Both disappear into the lobby.

Strange. I could have sworn I just saw a nod of acknowledgment between the two.

21

I walk back to my table in the far corner of the banquet room, breathing a tired sigh as I drop heavily into my chair. It took over three hours to clear up that mess—a barroom brawl, complete with property damage, injuries to civilians, and over twenty sailors sent back to their ships. Ugly. We arranged for reparations to the bar owner, and the translator had his work cut out for him. But in the end, I think we smoothed it the best a situation like this could be smoothed.

Eric times his return perfectly. As he walks toward me, I notice his demeanor has changed. He's more relaxed, at ease. Maybe he just needed some time.

"Hey," he says, pulling out a seat. "How are you holding up?"

"I'm good, thanks."

"How did that last brouhaha turn out?"

"It was a tad on the crazy side, but we got it settled."

I'm so glad he's back. And that reaction surprises me.

"How are *you* doing?" I say.

"Better. Thanks—"

His response is cut short due to high-pitched Mandarin wailing. A large family, a contingent over twenty strong—by the looks of it, grandparents, uncles, aunts, kids—enters the room along with a single American sailor sporting a fresh crew cut and Levis.

"Can you make out what's happening?" I ask.

Eric listens as the group talks animatedly over each other, pointing and gesticulating to the sailor.

"Boy, you're getting all the good ones," he says.

"What is it?"

"The short story is that this kid is responsible for taking the virginity of that man's daughter and now they're insisting he marry her."

"You're not serious."

"Serious as a heart attack."

I look across the room. Our translator is already en route. "Wanna come?" I ask.

"I'll just watch from here, thanks."

And so it goes, one crisis after another, Eric sitting in the back monitoring it all. He doesn't seem bothered by any of it. He's not bothered that he's not sleeping. Or that he's spending his night in the shore patrol office. He seems content, even. And though I hate to admit it, it's been nice to finish with each little incident and have him there waiting for me.

By the time we turn over with the new shift at 0700, I'm exhausted. It's been a long night in many respects. After retrieving my backpack from my room, I turn in my room key to the registration desk, and plod to one of the lobby couches to await van transportation back to the pier.

Eric is waiting. He motions me to the side and I practically sleepwalk to get there.

"I know how this is going to sound, but just bear with me for a second," he says. "You've been up all night, you're dead on your feet, and I thought you might like to sleep in a real bed and not have to go back to the ship. I got a room here and I'd like to offer it to you so you can sleep."

I furrow my brow in a bone-weary effort at concentration. He has a room. . . .

"It's not what you're thinking," he says, putting his hands up. "Please, don't read into this. It's a straight-up offer of a nice bed, that's all."

"I'm way too tired to argue," I say. "Just lead the way."

My eyes draw open with effort, my body heavy from a dead sleep. Paisley wallpaper—red and gold—fills my vision. I stare at it and I remember. I'm in the Harbourview Hotel . . . with Eric.

I roll over to find him. He sits in a chair in the far corner, his crossed legs resting on an ottoman. The blackout curtains are drawn, the only light coming from a small reading lamp on the end table.

"What time is it?" I ask.

"It's four in the afternoon."

"Four o'clock." I rub my eyes. "Are you serious?"

"You were *out*."

My brain circuits flicker.

"Nine hours . . ."

"Yep."

I roll onto my back and rest my hands on my forehead.

"Wait," I say, rolling my head back to him. "You watched me sleep?"

"I didn't have anything better to do," he says, lips upturned.

He watched me sleep . . . for nine hours.

"I'm sorry," I say. "I had no idea I was that tired."

"Hey, you needed it."

I raise my arms above my head and point my toes in an all-body stretch. My muscles vibrate to life with a rush of oxygen, then settle, relaxed, as I curl myself toward Eric again.

He looks so comfortable in his observation spot.

And I have a mortifying thought. "I didn't snore, did I?"

"Well . . ."

My hands fly to cover my mouth. "Oh, god!"

"Joking! I'm joking!"

I shoot him an expression of mock indignation and retreat under the covers. Glancing under the blankets, I realize I'm wearing his maroon shirt and gray shorts. Uh-oh. He never mentioned the fact that I wore these clothes—his clothes—last night. Stands to reason, I suppose, considering the circumstances. But now, well, he's been staring at the evidence for nine hours.

I lick my lips, chalky with sleep. Pushing the comforter away, I swing my feet to the carpet, grab my backpack, and shuffle to the bathroom. I note my uniform hanging in the closet. He must have put it there, because the last I remember, I had thrown it in a heap at the foot of the bed.

I indulge in a non-navy shower, which is to say, a long one—a rare treat during a ship-based deployment. I tip my head back, close my eyes, and let the hot water do its magic, my muscles going limp in the tranquilizing steam. My pores open, my skin breathes, and after several minutes, I start to sway, dizzyingly free of tension.

I step out, grabbing a towel, thinking how nice it would be to crawl back under the covers.

I wipe the mirror, creating a momentary steam-free circle, and comb my hair before gathering it into its requisite ponytail. Twisting the last loop of the rubber band around my hair, I stare at my naked self.

I'm naked . . . and Eric is sitting in a chair less than twenty feet away.

They say the spinal cord transmits information at a speed of one hundred meters per second at a capacity of one gigabyte per second. . . .

My body reacts, blood rushing, face flushing, and I lean on the swirling granite countertop, gripping the sides. I told myself *no more,* and yet . . .

This is too much. Way too much. You need to stop this absurdity, get dressed, and get out of here.

I re-dress in his shirt and shorts, add sandals, check myself in the still-foggy mirror, face clear of makeup, as always, and breathe in a lungful of resolve.

I open the bathroom door, tugging on the strap of my backpack, and peek around the corner. Eric remains where I left him, sitting with his feet up.

"I, um, I'd better go," I say.

"Okay."

I'm not sure what I expected to hear, but it wasn't that.

"Thank you. For all of this," I say with a sweep of my hand around the room. "It was really thoughtful of you to do this for me."

"Anytime," he says, unmoving.

What are you waiting for, Sara?

"Well, okay," I say. I lift my uniform from where it hangs in the closet and turn for the door. Flipping the latch for the deadbolt, I push down on the handle, opening it partway. I step forward, one foot out, one foot in . . . and here I stay. My backpack grows inexplicably heavy and I can't seem to find the energy to continue forward.

I linger, facing the hallway, sensing him before I see him. He approaches from behind, his hand rising above my head, holding the door.

"I'll see you around, okay?" he says softly.

With his chest to my back, his breath wafts across my neck. He doesn't wear cologne, just aftershave. And nothing over the top, just him.

My eyes lose focus, the sound of his breathing amplified, my backpack growing heavier still. And though it defies the laws of physics, the air is charged here, pulling me in only one direction.

"I don't want to go," I whisper. I'm not sure if I've just said that to myself or to him. I step back.

With his arm still high on the door frame, he gently pushes the door closed. The space around me becomes very small, my back to the wall, and his eyes search mine like he's going to crawl inside. His breathing is the only sound that registers in the stillness, which is when I become aware of the absence of mine.

He reaches to my face, brushing his hand lightly against it, his lips turning upward when I finally exhale. His fingers trace a delicate line under my chin, along my jawline, and through my hair, his hand coming to rest there. His thumb caresses my cheek, my nerves alight, the yearning overwhelming.

I lean forward and he presses his lips to mine.

Something cracks. Invisible and intangible, it breaks and crumbles. Shuddering, I shake away the pieces, released into an unknown lightness, floating free, untethered, my arms slackening. My backpack quietly drops to the floor and the clothes hanger slips from my fingers. His lips move gently, his other hand reaching to cradle my face.

I raise my hands to rest against his abdomen, which feels startlingly like a hardened set of wooden shutters. My body hums, blindsided with a swelling need.

I wrap my arms around his neck, pulling him toward me, and my mouth opens. He responds immediately, lips parting, pressing his body to mine, pressing us both against the wall. Our chests now flush, my heart pounds. I curl my fingers into his skin as his kiss becomes increasingly urgent. His hands move down the length of my neck, his fingers slipping under my shirt, skimming across my collarbones—

He abruptly straightens, pushing back. Holding my shoulders, his breathing heavy, he looks into my eyes. As I try to find my own breath, I realize he's asking my permission.

"We should . . . over there," I mumble.

He takes a calming breath—several, actually—before lacing his fingers through mine and leading me toward the bed. Looking back, he speaks with surprising clarity. "You're wearing my shirt."

Guilty.

He pulls me toward him, his hands lightly gathering the maroon material at the bottom. "May I have it back?"

His hands slide underneath, and in one smooth motion, it's off. It strikes me that he doesn't look me over, but keeps his focus on my eyes.

I point to his shirt. "May I?"

Without waiting for a response, I gather the edges and pull up. His chest now bare, he pulls me toward him, eagerly forming his mouth around mine. His hand smooths across my back, unhooking my bra and sliding the straps off my shoulders. I look down, past gray shorts rolled at the waist, to the sheer material bunched at my feet.

"I guess you'll be needing your shorts back, too, then," I say.

"Yeah, I think that would be a good idea," he rasps.

I slide them down, underwear and all, as he rids himself of his jeans. I've barely straightened when he finds my mouth, opening it once more. He places his hand on my stomach, smoothing it over my skin, moving upward. I shiver when his fingers move across my breast. He takes it fully in his hand, and I let out a gasp, a moan, maybe both. But the goose bumps soon subside, my skin warming with his kiss, his lips melting hungrily into mine.

I cling to a single strand of coherent thought. "Do you . . . do you have protection?" I manage, pulling away just enough to speak.

"I do," he says, his breathing labored.

"You do?"

"Well, yes, I—"

My face falls slightly.

"Wait, it's not like that," he says, reading my reaction perfectly. He brings his hands to either side of my head, smoothing his fingers across my temples. "I wasn't planning this, if that's what you're thinking. When you leave the ship, you have to take—"

"I know, Eric," I say, swallowing with unexpected relief. "I know."

He bends down, rummages in his jeans, and removes a tiny packet. I recognize the brand because I have eighteen in my backpack just like it.

I reach for his hand, guiding him to the bed, and lay back, pulling him toward me. His eyes hold mine as he presses his body along my length, his weight settling, our features melding, wholly perfect, and overwhelmingly wonderful. I swallow, a steady burn eating its way through my insides.

"Is this okay?" he asks.

Desire has swallowed my left brain whole. I offer a non-thinking, well-programmed response. "It's fine."

"What kind of fine?" he asks, trailing kisses from my lips to my ear, hovering there now. His breath, warm and moist, echoes loudly. He is all I hear, all I feel.

"The real kind."

22

My head fits neatly in the crook of his shoulder, my cheek resting on his chest. We've lain here for some time, air-drying after a not-so-quick rinse in the shower. His fingers absently comb through my still-wet hair, neither of us speaking.

Rather, I've been content to observe, afforded a close-up view of abdominal muscles ripped from here to tomorrow. Although, that's not what holds my focus.

It's the scars.

So many. I trace my fingers along one and then another, knowing they each have a tale to tell. But one in particular stands out. It's raised and circular and I keep coming back to this one. I scooch away from him slightly, scanning his body from the side. I find the circular scar's twin residing on his lower back, almost directly opposite. I touch it, feeling the raised tissue, and slide my hand up and over to his abdomen again. Now, I'm no expert in ballistics. . . .

"Are these . . . ?"

I look up to him, but his expression doesn't change. Nor does he answer.

"Entrance and exit wounds?" I finish.

He continues to stroke my hair, deliberating.

"Yeah," he says.

I give both scars equal attention in my explorations, running my fingers over each. As I study them, my mind races to a hundred different horrific scenarios to explain how he came by these. He watches me intently, his mouth evenly set.

"Are you going to tell me about this?" I ask.

He thinks on this for a moment. "Maybe someday, when we have more time."

I glance at the circular scar again before returning my gaze to him.

"Is that the same day you're going to explain why you speak so many languages?"

A hint of a grin escapes. "Yeah. That day."

"I see."

"Speaking of injuries," he says, touching my arms lightly where the bruising is heaviest. "Are you feeling okay?"

"It looks a lot worse than it feels."

I scooch myself close again, nuzzling my head against him. He caresses the skin across my back, my head rising and falling with his breathing. His heartbeat echoes slowly, rhythmically in my ear, and my eyes close in response, my breathing slowing to match his. This settles me, trying as I am to wrap my head around what just happened. Talk about letting your guard down. But god, it felt right.

I'll admit, I don't have much in the way of comparison. Yeah, there was that first time in high school. Feeling awkward and scared, I closed my eyes the entire time. I can't bring myself to say I made love, which would imply it was somehow a good experience. Even saying I had sex would be a stretch. The "act" was more along the lines of some farcical science experiment, figuring out how the parts and the plumbing worked. But even after that initial round of awful, it never got much better.

Unfortunately, I never had the chance to make it right. To feel like you're supposed to feel when you make love. That period during college and after, when most people start to figure it out, was wiped clean for me. After Ian, I shut down on so many levels, a relationship was the very last thing I wanted or felt like I deserved. Of course, what I wanted or deserved became radically moot points upon entering the navy, as I shifted into survival mode.

Over time, one by one, my emotional systems clicked back on line, most running quietly in the background behind multiple layers of defenses. With one notable exception.

I run my fingers across Eric's chest, feeling the strength of his heartbeat beneath my palm. He brings his hand up, running it over mine, curling his fingers around it. My heart swells.

This part of me has remained steadfastly under lock and key. I think back to the day when I first wore Eric's shirt instead of Ian's Vikings jersey, at a loss as to how that could have happened.

But this? To open myself to Eric like this? And for it to have been as wonderful as Emily's Harlequin romances would lead you to believe?

"I have an idea," he says, shaking me from my contemplations. "I'd love to show you something—I guess you'd call it sightseeing—if you're up for it."

"Sure," I say, thankful for the opportunity to step back a moment.

We rise to dress and I pull out my jeans and the blue blouse I wore to the Hail and Farewell. The images, the feelings, that the clothes conjure, slice like a knife. The woman in blue. Who was she?

He holds up his maroon shirt, scooped from where it lay strewn on the floor. "You're not going to wear my shirt?" His tone is so playful, so sweet.

There was one more thing I missed during that figure-it-out time in college—the vulnerability attached to opening yourself to someone like this. Like a rogue wave, it crashes over me. He wouldn't act like this with someone else . . . would he? This had to have meant more to him than just . . .

"What's wrong?" he says, placing a steadying hand on the side of my face. His eyes are clear.

There can't be anything wrong. There can't be.

"Nothing," I say. "The wrap on this shirt just gives me fits to tie. Besides, I thought you wanted that back." I motion to the shirt in his hand.

"That was just temporary. You can have it, if you want."

"Yes, I want it!"

"What you're wearing is better, though," he says, indicating my blouse.

"You think so? Em made me buy it."

"She has great taste," he says.

I slip on my sandals and put my arms through the sleeves of my black sweater. "Where are we going?"

"You'll see," he says.

He leads me to the MTR ticket stall to buy a pass, and we move through the turnstile, descending several flights of stairs until he finds the train he wants. It's the blue line and the train we board is headed west, along the northern edge of Hong Kong Island.

Debarking at Central Station, we walk hand in hand down Garden Road, and I finally see where he's leading me. The sign says PEAK TRAM STATION.

"Victoria Peak?"

"The view from up there is incredible. Just wait."

We board the tram and, 1,500 vertical feet later, debark in front of Peak Tower, a seven-storied boat-shaped building that sits atop the mountain. From here, we ride an elevator to the Peak Tower viewing deck. My pulse quickens as Eric leads me to the railing.

Hong Kong is laid out before us in all its breathtaking nighttime glory, treating us to a shimmering light show from uncountable millions of neon bulbs that reflect in the waters surrounding us.

But this million-dollar view is competing with something else for my attention—a hand that holds mine, a strong hand, calloused in places. He applies gentle pressure to my fingers, rubbing his thumb softly across my palm.

"Eric, this is spectacular, truly."

He shifts to face me. "It's never looked better."

Taking my other hand in his, he sweeps my arms behind my back, pinning them there.

"So beautiful . . . ," he whispers, looking into my eyes.

"I'm not. I'm—"

"You have no idea." The exclamation point to his sentiment is provided with a lingering kiss.

In his embrace, I sense a wholeness, a wellness, that I've never before experienced. And these thoughts collide with my previous discussions with Em. I've always insisted I was fine, but now I'm presented with evidence to the contrary. I've never felt more *fine* in my life than right here, right now. And this definition of fine is so far removed from my old definition, I now realize "fine" wasn't the correct word at all. "Existing" would be more appropriate.

But my ruminations begin to flounder, replaced by an urgency that wells from out of nowhere. His hands glide down my waist, landing on the grooves of my hips. Our mouths open, tongues melding, our breathing heavy—

It's a jolt when he pulls away.

"You know, I'm thinking this was a bad idea," he says, struggling for air.

"No," I say, panting. "Good idea, wrong place."

He smiles. "It's not going to make saying good-bye very easy."

"Good-bye?" I say, still recovering my breath.

"Sara, this is so ridiculously hard, but I have to go back to the ship tonight. Before we left Hawaii, I offered to take Ben's duty here, so he could meet his wife, who's flown over to see him."

My shoulders slump.

"I know. But I'd hate to renege on a promise like that."

"No, I understand. You have to follow through."

"I'm sorry," he says, glancing at his watch. "Ben will be pacing the quarterdeck, guaranteed."

"Really, it's okay."

Caressing the side of my face, he leans down and kisses me gently—a lighter kiss, the aching kind of lighter.

"Come on," he says.

We ride the elevator to ground level and stroll toward the entrance of the tram station. Normally, my eyes would have been drawn to the magical cityscape, or certainly to Eric, his arm now wrapped securely around my shoulders. But I can't help noticing the man who has been watching us. He stands in the shadows about twenty yards away, his back leaned against the station building. Even in the dark, his eyes shine a brilliant blue. I don't think I would have given him nor anyone else a second look tonight, except that this man has Ian's eyes.

I tell myself I'm imagining things. But I swivel my head several times to check. The man is definitely following our progress in line. I shift my feet uneasily.

"What is it?" Eric says.

"That man over there. He's watching us."

A dark expression crosses Eric's face as he locks eyes with the man, who appears to smirk in the dark.

"Do you know him?" I ask.

"Yes," he answers tersely, the distaste in his voice clear. "We've worked together before."

"Are you okay?" I ask, alarmed as Eric's body tenses.

"Come on. They're boarding." He keeps his arm around me, pulling me tight, as he ushers me forward.

23

Stepping into my stateroom, I only have eyes for my rack. No surprise after another all-nighter, this time standing duty on the ship. After I said good-bye to Eric, I slept alone at the Harbourview, then reported yesterday morning for duty aboard the ship. And now, twenty-four hours later, I'm asleep on my feet once more.

Today is our last day in Hong Kong and liberty doesn't expire until noon, but I have no interest in leaving the ship. I crawl into bed, not bothering to remove my khakis and non-regulation sweater, and fall into a heavy sleep.

I hear shuffling and wake with a start. My heart skitters for a moment until I confirm the source of the noise. It's Em.

"I feel like shit," she says, letting the door slam behind her.

I rub my eyes. She's in her khakis. How did she get in her uniform? She's just coming off liberty, right?

"Em, what time is it?"

"It's eighteen hundred."

"What!" I check my watch. "I slept all day?"

"Sure as hell did. I came off liberty at noon and you haven't moved. Hell, we've been under way for three hours already."

"Oh, man." I sit up groggily. I did it again, sleeping another day away.

"They're still serving in the wardroom if you want to run in there," she says.

I lower myself from my bunk. "Nah, I'll get something later."

Em lies on her rack with her hands over her head and closes her eyes. I'm about to take my sweater off when I remember the bruises on my arms. Do I want to tell her what happened? Do I want to receive the "I told you so"? Pulling the chair out at my desk, I decide to leave the sweater on for now.

Oh, man. And then Eric. What the heck do I admit to there? That would be "I told you so" times a hundred.

Emily's schedule and mine ran totally opposite this port call. With the exception of the first day, one of us was either on duty or on shore patrol while the other was on liberty. So we haven't spoken to each other since the Hail and Farewell.

"I gather you had a long night on duty," she says, eyes still closed.

"Yeah. I never went to sleep last night."

"That sucks. I figured it must have been something like that for you to sleep so long."

"I didn't miss anything, did I?"

"Nope. Everyone's been sleeping the day away like you, so you're good."

"Thank goodness," I say.

"Oh, crap!" Em says, bolting up. "You did miss one thing. You're not going to fuckin' believe this! Captain Magruder fired Commander Egan!"

"What!"

"He is fuckin' gone! Like his stateroom has been cleared out and he is no longer on this ship. I heard they were sending him back on a flight from Hong Kong."

No way. Eric couldn't have . . . or could he? He said he had to leave to go back to the ship for a minute. . . . How . . . ?

"Can you fuckin' believe that?"

"Does anyone know why?" I ask, holding my breath. Crap. I don't want anyone to know what happened. But at the same time, relief washes over me. He's no longer on the ship.

"That's the thing. No one had any idea this was coming and no one knows why. But hey, that asshole isn't going to be around to harass you anymore!"

No, he won't be around to harass me anymore. Eric made sure of that.

"God, my head hurts," Em says. "Please tell me you have some Advil."

"Comin' up." I walk to the tiny sink we share in the corner and rummage through the medicine cabinet.

"Even though I have a splitting headache," Em says, "I need to hear about your liberty. Please tell me you found Eric, and fork over the details."

I am so not ready for this conversation. I bring her the Advil along with a cup of water.

"Thanks," she says.

"Yes, I found him, but why don't you tell me about your liberty first?" I say, stalling. "You never came back to the room after the Hail and Farewell."

"I wish I could remember," she says, tipping her head back to swallow.

"Are you serious? You can't remember?"

"I haven't consumed that much alcohol since . . . oh, fuck, I don't even know." She hands the cup back to me. "So, no, I don't remember a fuckin' thing and I only have a wicked hangover to show for it." She grimaces. "Ow, that was loud."

"Maybe I should let you get some sleep," I suggest. "I can turn down the lights. It'll be quiet."

"It'll be quiet?" Em says incredulously. "It'll be quiet? Who the hell do you think you're dealing with here? If you think that'll get you out of telling me you slept with Eric, I've got news for you."

"What! How did you know!"

She smiles proudly. "I didn't."

I shake my head. "Emily . . . so help me . . ."

"But now that you've confirmed it," she sniggers, "I want every juicy morsel, every delectable detail of your rendezvous."

"I'm not giving you anything! I was tricked!"

"Oh, come on! You can't deny me this! You know I'm an addict," she says, pointing to the paperback volumes spilling out of her desk.

I think about this, swayed by her pleading expression. "Okay," I say. "I'll give you one thing."

"Anything."

I walk to her stack of books and rifle through them, selecting one. The guy on the cover has light brown hair, worn close to the head. He stands on a rocky outcrop, one foot raised, hands resting on the hips of his faded, low-rise jeans, a border patrol agent's badge clipped to the waist. Wearing boots, no shirt, and sporting a ten-pack, he looks thoughtfully across the desertscape with olive-green eyes, soft like melted glass.

I toss her the book. She studies it briefly before looking up. "So?"

"So, he looks like that, only when I saw him, he wasn't wearing jeans," I say, trying—but failing—to keep the smile from spreading across my face.

She flops back on her bed. "Oh dear god. I have died and gone to fuckin' heaven."

24

Eric is onboard the *Kansas City*. He never mentioned a need to come to our ship when we were in Hong Kong, but Shadow Hunter 67 landed earlier this morning and delivered not only him, but Brian Wilcox and Captain Plank, too.

Em gave me the lowdown on the morning's events because I was trapped in a maintenance meeting. She said a Nighthawk helicopter from *Nimitz* arrived next, carrying Admiral Carlson and two other men she didn't recognize. And finally, a contingent of Australians stepped off their Squirrel helicopter, which is still parked on our flight deck.

Em is in a meeting with the group now. She said her attendance and that of Commander Claggett had been requested. The only thing that bugs me about this is that I'm down here in the hangar, knee-deep in an aircraft inspection, while Eric is in the wardroom. I'm trying to figure a way to steal a moment with him. Maybe I can just loiter here in the hangar until the Shadow Hunters come to pick him up.

I clutch a pencil-thin flashlight between my teeth, peering into one of the aircraft's engine inspection panels, when I feel a tap on the shoulder.

"Jus' a sec," I say.

I finish twisting on the oil cap, pull my hands from the engine bay, and spit out the flashlight. It's Em.

"What's up?" I say, pulling down on the visor of my ball cap. The navy-issue ball cap is big, boxy, and ugly as sin. When you deploy on a ship, you're issued a cap with the ship's logo embroidered on the front. The cap is far too large for my head—they always are—so I tuck my hair underneath to make it fit better. I work at loose strands now, shoving them under the headband, when I take in Em's expression.

"Wait. What's the matter?"

She lets out a disheartened sigh. "Your presence is requested in the wardroom."

"What?"

"They want the aircrew that's scheduled for the fast rope tonight."

"But that's you, Em."

There was no one more relieved than I when I saw the flight schedule. Finally, I thought. No more Sara-at-the-controls rubbish. The other pilots are just as qualified as I am to fly these SEAL exercises and it doesn't make a lick of sense as to why they haven't been scheduled. So when Em found out she was flying the fast rope tonight, she was in a great mood.

"Not anymore," she says, the hurt clear in her voice. "They specifically requested you."

"But that's crazy."

"The only good thing was that Claggett got chewed out in front of the whole group for not doing as he was told. He was supposed to schedule you, not me."

"I'm sorry, Em. Really—"

"Just go," she says, her eyes downcast.

My steps are heavy as I leave the hangar. I don't want these stupid flights to come between Em and me, but here we go again. I mean, last night was perfect. Yes, she found out about Eric, but I was able to keep the whole thing on the surface and we joked and laughed about it and had fun.

It won't be fun anymore after this rigmarole.

I turn down a darkened passageway en route to the wardroom. The overhead lights are out *again* and emergency lighting provides the scant illumination available. Men mill about outside, some in flight suits, some in khakis, some in camouflage gear. It probably went dark in the wardroom and that's why this group stands in the passageway now.

I squint in the low light to find my way, spotting Eric in the process. He's talking to Brian and Captain Magruder.

Admittedly, my heart leaps when I see him. I don't want to disturb them, however, so I walk past, planning to just mouth "hello."

I look in his direction, hoping to catch his eye. He doesn't see me.

I stop. And wait.

I adjust my ball cap, tugging on it. This should grab his attention.

He looks up. Yes, he's finally noticed me! I'm about to open my mouth when he gives me a curt nod and continues his conversation without a second glance.

A cold needle of uncertainty inserts itself into my heart.

He just looked at me. He *saw* me. And yet he reacted as if I wasn't there. And his expression. So remote. So disengaged. So . . .

I look at him again, hoping for . . . something, but receiving . . . nothing.

Wait a minute. . . .

I am resolutely ignored as he continues his conversation with Brian and Captain Magruder.

But I'm standing right here. I'm right—

It hits me with the force of a punch thrown straight to the gut. He played me.

My arms reflexively wrap around my middle and I can't seem to work it right to draw in breath.

This can't be. It can't.

My legs move forward and I reach for the wardroom door.

"It's not going to make saying good-bye very easy." He was telling you good-bye, you moron. That was his way. Thanks. It was great. You're beautiful. Good-bye.

I grasp at the door handle, squeezing it to steady myself. *No.* I take one more chance, peering over my shoulder. He gives no hint whatever that I stand mere feet from him.

My eyes drop to the floor. Visions of the woman in blue at the Hail and Farewell threaten to drown me. Her beauty, his smile, her arm around him.

How many else have there been? Are there?

I don't know whether to cry, shout, or take off running.

"Okay, sirs," Petty Officer Sampson announces. "You're cleared to come back in. We've got the power back on inside."

I'm forced to step inside the wardroom when those behind me start to jostle in that direction. I walk straight to the lounge area, taking shallow bird breaths, the ones that hitch in your throat.

You are so stupid. How could you ever think . . . ? A guy like him? Some-one like you? Look at you. Stupid ball cap. A flight suit that hangs on you like a tent. No makeup. Grease on your hands. Beautiful . . . Right.

Eric, Brian, Captain Magruder, and the rest begin to straggle in. Eric looks at me with disinterest before continuing forward.

My heart, cleaved in two, plunges to the floor.

But then, Eric does a lightning-fast double-take.

A luminous smile breaks across his face. Glowing, even. He walks immediately toward me.

"Hey!" he says. "You know, I didn't even recognize you there for a minute." He ducks to look under my hat.

"You didn't . . . ," I choke.

"All this bumping around in the dark, you know."

"You didn't . . . the dark . . ."

"It's good to see you," he says in a low voice, his eyes speaking the truth as clearly as the sun rises in the morning.

I sway, stepping back to brace myself. "It is?"

He looks quickly to the other side of the wardroom. "I'd better get going. We need to start. Maybe I can catch you after?"

I recover. Sort of. "Yeah . . . after."

He whisks away to the front of the room while I stumble forward, weak-kneed, taking a place in back. I slump in my seat, stretched beyond all emotional limits. My arms and legs, loose like spaghetti, spill over the chair.

What in god's name just happened to you, Sara? You are so not in a good place if he can cause a reaction like that.

I look down as everyone takes their seats, and then, one long face swipe later, I sit back and turn my attention to the front of the room, where Eric stands, just as he did for the Operation Low Level brief. He gives me an almost imperceptible nod before beginning.

We're okay. This is okay.

I think.

I scan the room, recognizing only half of the people in attendance—Admiral Carlson, Captain Magruder, Captain Plank, Commander Claggett, Brian Wilcox, and Mike Shallow.

I learn that we'll be working with the Australian Special Forces—the

Special Air Service Regiment, or SAS. I glance across the table to the four men wearing Australian insignia. They're lean and tanned and one in particular grabs my attention.

I sit up. It's the man with blue eyes. The man who watched Eric and me atop Victoria Peak. The man with Ian's eyes. Were Em to describe this person, she would say he had stepped out of the same issue of *GQ* magazine as Eric. But I can only see the eyes, which pop so brightly against his dark brown hair. Ian's eyes . . . I forget myself for a moment as Ian's face replaces the man's.

In the far reaches of my awareness, Eric clears his throat. I refocus and find that the man is smiling. Oh no. I've been staring and I hadn't meant to. I swiftly return my attention to Eric. But an interesting thing is happening. Eric's demeanor has changed. Completely.

The brief takes on a different tone than the last time he spoke here. Before, he was lighthearted, made jokes, all the while conveying the seriousness of the exercise. But there's no joking now.

We'll be fast roping three teams tonight, the Aussie squad and two of ours, one led by Mike Shallow and the other by Lieutenant Peter Gage. I've never met Peter, but he sits next to Mike now, members of the same platoon. They could be brothers, these two, with their sandy brown hair and blue eyes. Even sitting, they appear to be tall, like Eric, though slightly larger in build.

Our targets include the *Lake Champlain* and the HMAS *Melbourne*, a Royal Australian Navy guided-missile frigate. And the brief that Eric is giving sounds like something that should be coming from Captain Magruder or even Admiral Carlson, given the scope. But he's got it wired. Every single angle. Every contingency plan. No matter the question or the concern, he's able to address it.

And this has me wondering once again. Why a *lieutenant* in charge? Why the same person coordinating every SEAL flight? Eric just briefed that the Shadow Hunters would be running the exercises tonight, but will it be them or *him*? My mind flashes back to a man speaking fluent Mandarin in Hong Kong. And the other languages . . . *"I'll tell you about it when we have more time someday."*

My friend Tom didn't know anything, but maybe I could ask someone else. But who? Captain Magruder? They seem like friends . . . which in itself doesn't make sense.

I study Captain Magruder and Admiral Carlson, the strain written across their faces mirroring Eric's. It's clear this exercise with the Australians signals a change. Operation Low Level involved many of the same high-ranking players, but Admiral Carlson and company acted differently then. Yes, it was a large-scale exercise, but the SEAL team's role in it was relatively small. It seemed to me that their concern rated a "normal" level. But the demeanor of the group today is decidedly different. An underlying tension permeates just about everything.

As Eric wraps up, everyone begins to push their chairs back and stand. Eric is surrounded by Admiral Carlson, Captain Magruder, and Captain Plank—another high-level, spur-of-the-moment conference. I won't be able to speak with him like this. I decide to move to the lounge area and wait there, hopefully without anyone taking undue notice.

I turn to walk that way, but I'm stopped, my path blocked by three of the Aussies. The blue-eyed one stands front and center.

"Do you make it a habit of staring?" he says with a thick Australian lilt.

I look up, as he stands at Eric's height. It's not hard to imagine what Em would be doing if she were here. Frothing at the mouth, probably.

"I'm sorry. I'm not sure what you're talking about."

"You were staring earlier."

"Oh," I say, putting my hands to my face. "Oh, that. I'm sorry. You just remind me of someone. That's all."

"And who would that be?"

"My brother," I say.

"I see." As he regards me, a peculiar undercurrent of energy stirs between us.

"My name is Jonas," he says, offering his hand. "It looks like we're going to be working together."

The eyes that initially reminded me of Ian . . . something about them.

I realize I'm staring again and I've waited a bit too long to shake his hand. I finally offer mine. "Sara. It's nice to meet you."

"Likewise. And these are my mates, Collin and Bartholomew," he says, motioning to the two chiseled men standing next to him. They offer only tough nods in response.

He folds his arms across his chest, giving me a long look.

"What is it?" I say.

"It's nothing . . . although now I see what all the ruckus is about." His eyes dart briefly to where Eric stands at the front of the room.

"What are you talking about?" I say.

I don't get to hear the explanation because Eric has just moved to my side, and I'm not sure how he could have covered the distance so quickly. And not just Eric, but Brian, Mike, and Peter, too.

A strange, suffocating thickness settles on the group.

"Sara, we need to finish your brief," Eric says, jaw clenched.

Jonas looks between Eric and me several times. "Interesting," he says, taking his time with each syllable.

Jonas's eyes finally rest on me. "Well, I don't want to keep you from your brief, but I'll see you tonight . . . without Mr. Marxen."

Eric has gone rigid. What is going on here?

"He won't be there, but we will," Mike says, motioning with his head to Peter, who stands next to him.

This is so uncomfortable. It's a staredown and I don't want to be here anymore.

"Let's go finish up, shall we?" Brian says. He places his hands on my back and on Eric's and ushers us away.

Just then, the call for flight quarters rings out over the 1MC, which means it's time for the Aussies to leave. They file out of the wardroom as I'm corralled by Eric, Brian, Mike, and Peter.

"Eric, what was that?"

"Is there someplace we can talk?" he asks. "We don't have long. Our guys are supposed to pick us up right after the deck is clear."

"Well, Em is manning the tower, so we could go to my stateroom."

"Perfect," he says. And then turning to the others, "Guys, thanks. And tonight . . ."

"We've got it covered, man," Mike says. "Don't worry."

"Brian, I'll meet you in the hangar," Eric says.

"Okay, see you in a few."

I lead Eric to my room, but once we're inside, it's like watching a caged animal. He paces back and forth without saying a word. I put my hand on his shoulder to stop him and he looks at me with an intensity that . . . well, if light started shining out of his eyes, it wouldn't surprise me right now.

"I don't understand," I say. "What just happened?"

"Jonas is . . . well, he's not to be trusted," he says. "The reasoning behind that statement is for another time because I'm only going to be here for a few minutes. But in the meantime, just . . . well, be careful. Mike and Pete will be there tonight. . . ."

"But we're just going to brief and fly. He can't do anything. Although I'm not sure why I would need to be careful in the first place."

His lips tighten as he tries to contain whatever it is that's threatening to come out.

"Eric, what am I dealing with here? What should I be careful about?"

"Just . . ." He takes a big inhale before letting the air rush out in a huff. "Just everything."

He looks at his watch. "I have to go," he says. "Singapore . . . we'll be there in five days. I'll see you in five days. When we pull in. Okay?"

"But how—"

"I'll find you. Don't worry."

He puts his lips to my forehead before rushing out the door.

25

"All navigational aids and running lights will be off. The Shadow Hunters will have the call," Mike says.

It's 0100 and Mike and Peter have joined Commander Claggett, Lego, Messy, and me in our small briefing space on the *Kansas City*. They sit next to me, like protective bookends, directly across from the Australian captain, Jonas. He wears a name tag now. His last name reads MARTIN.

Mike's voice is strained. No joking or smiling like I'm used to. And Jonas is, well, staring. I suppose turnabout is fair play, but it's not easy being on the receiving end of a gaze like his. I force myself to focus on Mike or Peter or whoever is speaking, all the while wishing for a quick end to the brief.

"Exactly forty minutes after the last drop, you'll meet us one point five miles to the east for pickup," Mike continues. "Again, the Shadow Hunters will call you into our posit."

"The Shadow Hunters or Lieutenant Marxen?" I blurt out.

"Why?" Jonas asks, his eyes boring into mine. "Does it matter?"

"No. No, I, uh . . . no," I say, looking to the ground, wishing I had never asked.

"I don't know," Mike answers quickly. He turns to Lego. "Lego, just like we did in the exercise outside of Hong Kong, have the ramp at the water."

"Will do, sir."

Another wheels-on-the-water pickup. At night. I haven't even stepped foot in the aircraft, and my stomach has already turned over.

"Okay, any questions?" Mike says, looking at me directly.

"An in-the-water pickup?" I ask. The entire evening has been briefed as a dedicated fast rope night, so I thought the SEALs would stay dry.

"Night swim training," Mike says, a slow, conspiratorial smile spreading across his face.

"I see," I whisper.

Mike registers my discomfort and his expression shifts to an understanding one. "Ready for some fresh air?"

"Definitely."

"No questions for me," Jonas says, although he's not looking at Mike when he says it, his eyes trained on me. Mike's gentle visage disappears. And for the first time in as long as I can remember, I'm actually looking forward to a night preflight. I need some space.

Mike, Peter, and Jonas rise and enter the hangar to brief their squads while Commander Claggett, Lego, Messy, and I head to the flight deck.

Commander Claggett is in a foul mood and I can understand why. I've always been taught "praise in public, reprimand in private." But he was called out in front of the entire group today for the flight schedule snafu.

Just in case, I decide to steer clear, moving immediately aft through the aircraft cabin to the back of the bird to begin my preflight. I step off the ramp, only a few feet from the end of the flight deck, the ocean curling and roiling in our wake. Tendrils of water lick and smack as they roll inward, emitting a shower of phosphorescent green sparks. The water is utterly black beyond this tunnel of churning white foam. The blackest black. The message is clear, issued in a whispered roar. *I'm waiting. . . .*

I shiver, no longer looking forward to a night preflight.

"Beautiful, isn't it?" Jonas says.

My sharp intake of breath is audible, my hand flying to my heart.

"Sorry, love. I didn't mean to startle you."

"No . . . no, I'm fine," I say. "I just didn't expect to see you there." I never heard him approach. With a composing breath, I bring my hand back to my side. "I'm sorry, you were saying what?"

"The ocean," he says, inclining his head. "Beautiful tonight, isn't it?"

"Oh . . . um, no, actually," I say.

He raises his eyebrows.

He's just being conversational, Sara. This is not the time to delve into your irrational issues with water.

"I just . . . never mind," I say.

"What would you call it, then?"

I look up to meet his eyes, more black than blue on this dark night, and surprise myself with another truthful response. "Dangerous, maybe. But not beautiful."

He glances at the wake before moving his gaze to the blackness beyond. "I think it can be both," he says, turning to me. "But I prefer to focus on the beautiful." He regards me earnestly, his features softening with the smile that spreads across his face.

This man is a walking contradiction—an imposing force, without question, and yet polite and friendly, to me, anyway.

"You know, I wasn't sure when I'd get a chance to speak with you again," he says, his voice lowering. "We were somewhat rudely interrupted this afternoon."

I nod, at a strange loss for words.

"I must have startled you more than I realized," he says lightheartedly. "You're all tensed, love."

"Oh, I . . . it's nothing."

He stiffens, the ease in his demeanor vanishing. His lips crease into an intimidating hard line as Mike and Peter round the corner of the aircraft.

Mike's expression is notably even more daunting. "What are you doing?" Mike asks.

"Just getting reacquainted," Jonas says breezily.

"You need to get back to your squad where you belong," Mike says.

"You know, I rather like it *here*," Jonas replies.

Mike and Peter respond as Eric did earlier—shoulders back and tensing.

"But let's not get our dander up," Jonas says, raising his hands and backing away. Looking to me, he softens his voice. "I'm sure we'll talk later." He issues a baleful glare to Mike and Peter before turning on his heel.

I wait until he disappears around the front of the aircraft.

"Guys, what . . . ?"

"Holy crap, Sara," Mike says, dropping the hardened expression. "I'm so sorry. We didn't see him leave the hangar."

Mike speaks as if he just lost control of the prisoner he was escorting to trial or something.

"It's okay, Mike, really," I say. "He was just saying hello."

Mike and Peter share a disgusted look.

"What did Eric tell you about him?" Peter asks.

"Well, not much. He didn't have time. The only thing he said was that he's not to be trusted."

"He's right," Peter says. "Dead right."

"Remember back to your bedtime stories—the wolf in sheep's clothing," Mike says. "Don't ever forget that with him."

This situation couldn't get any more bizarre. This is an ally we're supposed to be working with, right? But everyone's acting like he's a threat.

"I need to get up and preflight," I say.

I climb atop the aircraft, and the fact that they've slipped up in their watch is evident now because one of them remains duly attached to me, observing my every move. It's not until I'm seated in the aircraft and the bird is turning that they return to the hangar.

We perform multiple approaches to the *Lake Champlain* and the *Melbourne,* Eric—no surprise—coordinating all of it. His voice is a constant reminder that Mike and Peter aren't the only ones on alert.

"Forward forty, forward thirty," Lego says as we approach the stern of the *Melbourne.* "Forward ten, five, rope's away!"

I hold a steady hover while the Australians take their turn sliding down the rope, wondering about the speed of their transitions to the deck. As the night has progressed, and as they've gotten more slides under their belts, I assumed they would get faster. But there's a noticeable difference in speed when measured against their SEAL counterparts.

". . . last man out. Pulling in the rope. Steady. Rope's in. Clear to go," Lego reports.

"Lego," I say after transitioning clear of the flight deck, "is it just me or are they moving slower than our guys?"

"It's not just you, ma'am," Lego says.

Our thoughts are verified when we land and the Australians reenter the aircraft.

Jonas hooks into the ICS, his voice fraught with angry frustration. "One more," he says sharply.

"Sir, do you need us to position any differently?" Lego asks delicately.

"No," he says. "The positioning is fine. It's my team that's not."

Oh. Awkward.

"The price you pay for five greenies," Jonas continues.

Five new men. The SEAL squads here don't have this problem. Seasoned members all, they stand near the edge of the flight deck, patiently waiting their turn as we rotate the teams through.

"But I must say," Jonas says in a turn of tone, "the delivery is spot on. Well done up front."

I'm about to acknowledge the compliment when I look to my left, noting the tight expression on Commander Claggett's face. Probably best to let it go.

"Ma'am, we're ready to lift in back," Lego says.

I take off while thinking about Jonas's comments, wondering once again what it is that Eric, Mike, and the others would find so disturbing about him. My mind spins with that question for the next four hours until Jonas and his team exit the aircraft for the last time, fanning out across the deck of the *Melbourne* and slipping away into the dark.

26

"Clear on the left! Clear on the right! Clear on the firing line!" bellows Senior Chief Messenger, the chief master-at-arms.

I stand at the end of a row of five people on our "shooting range," which is actually the flight deck. Next to me, Zack, Matt, and Chad have just completed the donning of their safety goggles while Emily fidgets with her ear protection. We're shooting for marksmanship ribbons with the standard-issue Beretta M9, a semiautomatic 9mm pistol. Even though I already carry an Expert pistol medal, if the opportunity for target practice arises, I take it. I don't get to practice too often and it's something I enjoy. Like precision flying, accurate shooting requires steady hands, sharp eyes, and a gentle touch.

There are fifty of us today and we've fired in prone, kneeling, and standing positions at ranges of fifteen and now twenty-five yards. In this last round, we'll fire a standard magazine, fifteen rounds, in forty-five seconds—seven kneeling and eight standing.

Once the range is declared clear, I take aim. I fire one round every three seconds, creating a nice cluster in the center of my target. The shooting holes for Em, Matt, and Zack form starburst patterns over their targets, the entry points spreading far and wide. I doubt they'll even get the minimum score for Marksman. Chad's shots look better, probably in the Sharpshooter range, and he's receiving high fives for his efforts.

Senior Chief Messenger and his men from the master-at-arms division walk forward with us to tally our hits.

"Highest score of anybody today, ma'am," he says, writing my point total, 292, on the target sheet. "Impressive."

"Thanks, Senior."

I glance over to Emily. She's joking and laughing with Chad, Zack, and Matt, and I'm noticeably excluded from whatever they're finding humorous. The subtle shift in the dynamics of our group is happening once more, just like it was prior to Hong Kong. First, the flight with the SAS, then two more SEAL flights in the two subsequent nights, all with me at the controls and all without explanation.

"I said, you wanna keep this as a souvenir?" Senior Chief Messenger asks.

"Excuse me. What?"

"The target sheet, ma'am. Would you like to keep it as a souvenir?"

I look down at the paper he holds, ripped from the target backing and rolled into a tight cylinder.

"Oh, um, sure," I say, catching Emily's eye for a quick moment, an accusatory look, before she whips her head around, returning her attention to her boisterous group.

That look . . . That's not fair.

I march straight over to her and tap her on the shoulder.

"Em, what is this?" I ask, the anger simmering.

"What is what?" she asks, mirroring my tone.

Chad, Matt, and Zack scuttle away as Emily turns toward me.

"This," I say, motioning to the three that hurry across the flight deck. "And that look and getting ignored and all of it. You know this flying thing isn't my fault. I have no control over any of it."

"Don't you?" she asks sharply.

"What? No!"

"I don't see you complaining," she says, crossing her arms.

"Complaining? I'm just doing what they're telling me to do," I say.

"While Zack and I are sitting on our asses!"

"What?" I say in a volume just shy of shouting. "What do you want, Em? What do you want me to do? You know this bothers me! You know I don't like it!"

"Yeah, I'm sure this is really difficult for you," she says, turning on her heel and leaving me standing alone, mouth agape.

What the hell just happened?

* * *

I climb up to my rack, thinking I'm going to nap, but knowing it's going to be darn near impossible based on what just happened with Em. I need the sleep, though. These middle-of-the-night briefs are taking their toll, and we have another one tonight. The aircraft commanders are rotating through on these, but the one pilot constant is me.

Should I complain like Emily said? I've asked questions, but never outright disagreed or protested my scheduling. Maybe she's right. Maybe I should. Zack and Emily are my squadron mates, both attempting to qualify as a helicopter aircraft commander, just as I am. They need the hours. They need the experience.

And the same is true on the aircrewman side. We have six aircrewmen in this detachment, but on these SEAL exercises, when we assign a different crew, it comes back from the skipper with red marks crossed through it and notes to assign Lego and Messy instead.

But we haven't put our foot down. We haven't complained. We just do it. And we'll do it again tonight. To a submarine.

We fast roped to a sub several times while working in Hawaii this winter and we've done it once in daytime hours on this cruise prior to pulling into Hong Kong. We practiced with the USS *Birmingham,* the fast-attack submarine that's traveling with our task group.

It's actually not so bad working with submarines—in the daytime, anyway. The sails are large enough that you still have a hover reference. But at night with no goggles . . . black sail, black water, black sky. Lego has been a champ for me on these, fine-tuning my positioning, but I really do seem to do these kinds of flights by feel.

As I close my eyes, I try to put the flight hours discrepancy issue out of my mind, thinking about the flight instead, wondering what I'll reference tonight when no one anywhere is running any lights. Moonlight has helped the previous two nights, and I can normally rely on the canvas of stars against the horizon. Too bad I can't talk with Em about this. I mean, I guess I could, but it would be like rubbing salt in the wound. And for the same reason, it would be just as uncomfortable to bring it up with the aircraft commanders.

With a small sigh, miraculously, I drift to sleep.

"Sara, wake up," Em says.

"What?" I say, blinking. "What time is it?"

"It's seventeen hundred. Our meeting's about to start," she says stiffly. I watch, saddened, as she walks out the door without me.

I tug down on the long-sleeved running shirt I'm wearing—the one I donned for our shooting exercise earlier. Somehow, I've managed to keep my arms covered since I returned from shore patrol and have delayed the need to outright lie for how I received these bruises, ones that have only grown darker and harsher looking.

Entering Commander Claggett's stateroom, I move toward an open spot on the couch and I'd swear I was a ghost. No acknowledgment. No eye contact. Nothing. From anyone. Commander Claggett, who obviously didn't wait for me to begin the meeting, continues speaking without missing a beat.

"And on to marksmanship trials . . . Let's see, we need to congratulate Chad on his Sharpshooter qual," he says. "Nice job, man."

The group claps lightly as Commander Claggett's finger moves down the agenda.

"Singapore duty schedule? Chad?"

No acknowledgment whatsoever for my Expert marks. *Forget it, Sara. It doesn't matter anyway.*

"Zack will have it when we pull in," Chad says. "Lace has it the following day, Emily, you're next, me, and Matt. So we each have a day."

"And, yes, we have confirmation. Drum roll, Chad," Commander Claggett says.

Chad drums his fingers on his chair.

"Wog Day is a go!" Commander Claggett announces.

"Sweet!" "Excellent!" Chad and Matt say at once, accompanied with exuberant high fives.

"Day after tomorrow, the day before we pull into Sing!" Commander Claggett says.

Zack, Em, and I look at each other, letting out a collective heavy sigh. And I'm included again.

Wog Day. In the navy, you're considered a Pollywog until you've crossed the equator aboard ship. Assuming you participate in the Wog Day ritual, if you successfully complete all the trials of the day, you earn the coveted title, Shellback.

The rumors have been flying ever since we left Hong Kong that the captain might deviate from our course to Singapore and travel the extra eighty-five miles south to the equator so we could have the ceremony. I guess the folks from strike group operations are cooperating and he must have gotten the go-ahead.

In anticipation of this, the Shellbacks have been preparing. Oh, have they been preparing. All Pollywogs must navigate an obstacle course that, from what I understand, includes weeks' worth of the ship's food garbage. I've heard tell that the mess cranks have been saving up the garbage, even putting it in the ovens to ensure it's extra "ripe" for us on Wog Day.

Our aircraft commanders are Shellbacks, so they can't wait.

"The festivities will commence tomorrow evening at twenty hundred with the Wog Queen Beauty Contest," Commander Claggett continues.

"Zack, you're all over that, man!" Matt says.

"Ah, dude, no way!"

"Dude, you're gonna own it!" Matt says.

The men dress like women in the Wog Queen Beauty Contest, walk a "runway," the whole thing. They do it with gusto, too, because if they win, they don't have to go through the Wog ceremony the next day. But it's not as easy as it sounds. You have to be good—really good—to win. Like the shave-your-legs kind of good.

"All right, that's all I have. Anything else?"

"Nick, you're briefing at twenty hundred for a twenty-one thirty take-off, right?" Chad asks.

"Yep, briefing to sit on my hands," he says.

For the first time since I entered Commander Claggett's room, the others turn their heads to look at me. Their glances are brief, but disapproving, and the fun mood disappears.

27

We've shut down on *Nimitz* because we're briefing with the entire cast of this special ops exercise—two squads of SEALs, one SAS crew, the Shadow Hunters, and the Sabercats. When I arrive in the briefing space, the majority of SEAL and SAS team members are present. I don't see Eric, but then again, the last time I was with him, he said he'd see me in Singapore. Maybe he's not flying this time around. Although, this would be a marked departure from the flight schedule over the past weeks.

Which is ironic. The fact that he's directed every SEAL flight so far has gnawed at me because it's so out of the norm on so many levels. But suddenly, it seems stranger still that he *wouldn't* be here. That he wouldn't direct this exercise.

Commander Claggett divests himself of me, retreating to a far corner. Lego and Messy jump into conversations with team members, and I find a seat to the side and wait alone for the arrival of the Shadow Hunter crew.

I'm not alone for long.

"Hello, love," Jonas says, sliding into the seat next to me.

I flinch. Another noiseless approach.

He responds with a laugh. "You're a tightly wound one, aren't you?"

"You just surprised me, that's all."

"You know, this is unfortunate, really. I think Mr. Marxen's overblown reaction has affected how you view me."

"No, it's not that. You're just—"

"Strong? Handsome? Worth your while?"

I smile in spite of myself, a small laugh escaping in the process.

"There, that's more like it," he says. "You're a tough nut, but I knew you had a smile in there somewhere."

In the fluorescent lighting, his blue eyes sparkle. So different from the black eyes two nights ago.

"You know, I'm thinking you need a strong bit of liberty in Singapore," he says. "You're far too tense."

"Yeah," I say with a laugh, "I've been told that before—"

My head snaps up in surprise at the sound of Eric's voice. "Would you like me to find you another seat?" Eric says between gritted teeth.

"No, actually—" I start.

Jonas shoots to a stand opposite him, and the discord swirls, thick enough to taste.

He aims his piercing gaze at Eric. "So tell me, how is the evaluation coming?" Jonas says, motioning to me.

"What?" I ask.

Eric's eyes don't leave Jonas's. "Leave it," Eric threatens.

"I don't recall date nights being included in the metrics," Jonas says.

Metrics? Evaluation?

"Eric, what is he talking about?"

"You're crossing the line," Eric says, fully ignoring my question.

"I'm only following you," Jonas says. "Isn't that what I'm supposed to do? Isn't that what everyone always tells me to do? Follow the leader?"

Eric and Jonas move toward each other as I look up, squeezed between their towering forms.

"That's enough," Eric warns.

"But you know, this time I *should* follow your lead." Jonas purposefully shifts his eyes to me before bringing his laser focus back to Eric. "Whatever it takes to complete the mission, eh?"

Jonas slowly steps backward, moving away from Eric, whose fists are clenched, the veins in his arms bulging. Jonas begins to turn, then hesitates, looking down to me. "If I were you, love . . ." He straightens, turning to Eric, his eyes cold and threatening. "I'd watch my back."

Eric erupts, snatching Jonas by the collar with viperlike quickness, and shoving him backward against the bulkhead.

I thought I had seen a cold look on Eric's face when he restrained Commander Egan. But compared to his expression now, he could have been whispering sweet nothings in Commander Egan's ear.

The air is electric. Chairs screech and feet scuffle as men mobilize. Mike is the first to get here. He puts his body between Eric and Jonas, grabbing Eric's arm, the one with the hand clenched around Jonas's collar.

"This is not the time," Mike says in a low voice. "This is *not* the time."

Peter is next. He grabs Eric's shoulders while Collin and Bartholomew do the same with Jonas. Eric still has Jonas in his grip.

"Let go," Mike orders.

Eric releases his hold, one deliberate finger at a time.

"Is Martin stirring up trouble again?" a gruff, familiar voice asks.

My mouth drops as I watch Commander Amicus—Commander Amicus?—step in front of Jonas. What is Animal doing here?

"Of course it would be me," Jonas says. "It could never be Marxen. "

Animal's steel-gray eyes stare into Jonas's without flinching. "Go on, get outta here."

Jonas moves sideways, his eyes locked with Eric's in challenge until Bartholomew and Collin steer him away.

Mike pulls Eric around, pinning him to the bulkhead, hand on his chest. Animal quickly joins them.

"You all right?" Animal asks.

Eric doesn't respond, his jaw muscles working furiously, his teeth clenched.

Mike has moved away slightly to let Animal stand directly in front of Eric, the deference clear. In all the while I've known Animal, he's maintained a calm demeanor. Nothing fazes the man and it's no different now as he silently communicates with Eric, standing him down in a way I hadn't thought possible.

I look closely now at Animal, his black hair lying in a tangle over his broad, yet angular, face. His nickname suits him perfectly. His routinely unkempt hair, his well-muscled burly appearance—like a lean, mean grizzly bear. He's like Eric in that way—that quiet strength underneath.

"You need to brief," Animal says. He inclines his head to the front of the room, sending Eric forward.

Only now do I notice the hum of background conversation is absent. Quickly replaying the events in my head, I realize the room has been silent ever since Eric grabbed Jonas.

"Take your seats," Animal instructs those in the room. He looks down to me for the first time. "May I?" he asks, indicating the seat next to me.

"Animal? What are you doing here?"

"I'm here to fly with you."

"But—"

"You know me. Always making the training rounds."

True, Animal's job has him traveling to helicopter squadrons across the country to conduct training. "But, sir? Now? In the South China Sea?"

He motions to Eric, who has begun to speak. "The brief is starting," he says.

I decide I can ask him after, but when Eric finishes, he whisks me from the room without comment, intent on getting the bird turned up quickly with no extraneous conversation.

I suppose this is a good thing. It doesn't allow me to dwell on the splinters that now pick at my conscience. Training rounds . . . Evaluation . . . Metrics . . .

Animal and I take off en route to the submarine, *Birmingham,* and I've no sooner gotten the ops normal call out of my mouth when the caution panel glows orange. At the same time, I feel a shift in the controls. The automatic flight control system, or AFCS, has switched off.

"Sir, did you . . . ?" I ask.

"Of course I switched it off," Animal says.

I should have expected this.

"Okay, let me hear it," he says.

I let out a practiced exhale. "AFCS is for pussies," I say, repeating Animal's mantra, something he has forced me to say a thousand times.

"Damn straight!"

When the AFCS is on, it makes the aircraft easier to fly. For most pilots, if the system switches off, you would feel the aircraft wobble and yaw immediately, the aircraft instantly squirrely. The degradation in controllability is normally so great, the rules state you can't transport passengers or fly at night without the system on.

"But sir—"

"The aircraft doesn't feel any different to me," he says. "Lego, how 'bout you?"

"Smooth as a pig's belly, sir."

Flying without noticeable interruption when switching the AFCS off has always been my goal. And it's because of Animal that I'm able to do it. When he was the officer in charge on my last cruise, after my first shipboard landing, he declared I no longer required the AFCS, and for every flight thereafter, he turned it off. He never made an exception, either.

And those rules about not transporting passengers or not flying at night? Animal scoffed at those and we did it anyway. Routinely.

I feel I need to do my due diligence, however, and remind him of the rules. "But sir, it's night and we're carrying pax."

"What do you think they did before they invented AFCS?" he asks. "They had passengers then. They still had to deliver 'em. And they still had to fly at night. No reason we shouldn't be able to do that now."

Not a lot's changed with Animal since I last flew with him. I smile. "Aye, aye, sir."

We start the exercise by dropping Peter's and Jonas's squads to the *Birmingham,* followed by Mike's squad to the frigate, *Melbourne.* The *Lake Champlain* is also included in the rotation, the teams taking turns between each ship and submarine. Over and over, we repeat the sequence, rotating crews from platform to platform.

Our final run will be to the *Birmingham,* and we wait now on the deck of *Nimitz* to pick up Mike's team. I count eleven men walking toward the aircraft for this last go-round. Odd. The SEALs have been working in teams of eight or sixteen throughout this cruise, including this evening—no deviation.

Mike is usually last in the aircraft, but now, three others follow. Because everyone's faces are camouflaged tonight, I only recognize one of the extra men—Jonas. Even through the black face paint, those eyes shine through. Strange that he's with Mike's squad.

As Eric calls us in, I wonder if he can actually see us, make out the form of our helicopter in the night sky when we're working without lights. I know my night vision has improved, catching shapes as I hadn't before—like now, when the sail of the *Birmingham* emerges seemingly from the air itself.

As Lego directs me in, I find the faint demarcation between ocean and sky, a sky of diamonds. The diamonds are up and the black nothing is down. Keep the diamonds up and the black nothing down and the heli-copter will remain airborne.

Lego keeps me steady and on target with his calls; however, the amount of time spent over the sub's deck is definitely longer than over the ship's. Having any kind of visual reference to a ship's superstructure allows my inputs to the controls to happen far more quickly, because I can already sense that we're moving off target. But now I'm referencing an only semi-visible sail and relying almost exclusively on Lego for positioning. As a result, my corrections come just that microsecond later than normal.

It's not horrible—we're in and out in less than thirty seconds—but I've gotten used to some awfully fast transitions over a ship. As Lego gives the clearance to go, I nose over and gain altitude, arcing around the aft end of the *Birmingham*. For a brief moment, I can discern eleven black shad-ows slinking across a solid obsidian surface, but just like that, they've dis-appeared into the night.

28

"Cock-a-doodle-doo!" I flap my wings and crow reveille once more. "Cock-a-doodle-doo!"

Em and I share a look that says it all. Are we really doing this? Are we really standing on the bow, drenched in maple syrup, covered in feathers, and crowing reveille as the sun rises? Because it's Wog Day, the answer is yes.

And as weird as this is, I'll take it any day over arguing with Em. Without consciously agreeing to do so, we put our flight-hours spat aside so we could join forces to conquer the challenges of Wog Day.

Underneath our feathers, we wear our khaki uniforms inside out and backward as all Pollywogs are required to do. We've also donned knee pads underneath our pants, and gloves on our hands, because on Wog Day, crawling is the only acceptable mode of transport. And just for me, long sleeves under everything to cover the bruises on my arms that are doing anything but fading.

After we finish crowing, our handlers determine that it's time for Wog Breakfast. So we crawl along the main deck, passing through a gauntlet of fire hoses that spray hundreds of gallons of seawater on the two hundred or so Pollywogs that crawl in line with us.

It's the shillelaghs that make this crawl so torturous. Shellbacks line the main deck, armed with two-foot-long strips of fire hose, fashioned with duct-taped handles. I steel myself for the next blow as they aim for the butt and back of the legs. The Shellbacks are motivated in part by the T-shirts that Em and I wear, worn inside out and backward, of course, that our air detachment Shellbacks were so careful to stencil. In clear, bold, black lettering, our T-shirts read, AIR DET WOG—SHIP'S COMPANY CAN'T BREAK US. Great.

But they're also motivated—even gleeful—because we're officers. On this day, hundreds of enlisted Shellbacks get to have a go at the nine Pollywogs in the officers' wardroom who scrabble on hands and knees, at their mercy for several humiliation-inducing hours.

By the end of the crawl through the main deck, my backside is a bruised, welted, stinging, achy mess. I thought I would be thankful to reach the mezzanine deck for Wog Breakfast. To find relief from the beatings of the shillelaghs.

I am wrong.

Wog Breakfast is served in a long trough filled with noodles, cottage cheese, oysters, fish parts, and who knows what else. The whole rotten mixture is purple in color and I get a close-up view, just prior to dunking my head in it. We're required to blow bubbles. . . . And it's not the breakfast mixture itself that's the worst part. It's the vomit from the Wogs before us.

I lift my head to breathe, but I dare not use my nose, because if I smell this, I'm just going to add to the vomit pile. Which means . . . if I want air, I'm going to have to open my mouth. The slimy, chunky ick that floats in the trough now leaks and oozes into my mouth. I breathe. I spit. I scooch down the line. I dunk my head once more.

I declare a mini victory when I make it to the end of the trough without throwing up. Next to me, poor Em. She lost it before we even started.

After "breakfast," the Shellbacks herd us to the flight deck, shillelaghs flying. You're not allowed to speak when you're a Wog, nor look anywhere but down as you crawl. Em moves in front of me, but that's all I really know. Just that she's there.

Zack is not here. He won the Wog Queen Beauty Contest last night with a lacy red bra and underwear supplied by Emily. He shaved his legs and Emily and I did his hair and makeup. It was scary, truth be told, how good he looked when we got through with him. Music blared on the 1MC, the contestants strutted across the catwalk on the flight deck, and just when I thought it couldn't get any more hilarious, they started dancing—the naked-stripper-against-a-pole kind of dancing. I actually peed my pants I laughed so hard.

A good laugh is hard to come by for me, so I took it, wet pants and all. But I'm not laughing now as we're ushered to face King Neptune's Royal

Court at the far end of the flight deck. The Court consists of King Neptune, his wife Amphitrite, the Royal Baby, the Royal Police, and even Davy Jones—all played by crew members. Pollywogs are summoned before the Court to undergo trial for their offenses to the God of the Sea.

Em and I are brought up together and the powers that be read the "charges" against us. Em screws up and pleads not guilty. Crap. She's sent to the back of the line and I can hear the slap of the shillelaghs that accompany her. I'm right behind her. I know the right answer. But I don't want to get separated, so I plead not guilty as well. Back to the end of the Royal Court line I go. More waiting. More whacking.

The next time we reach the Royal Court, we plead guilty to our nebulous crimes and are sent to the stockade. Our hands and heads are inserted into a giant wooden contraption and I wonder who on earth built it and where they've been keeping it. Once we're positioned, the top is closed over us. We take a chance, turning our heads slightly to look at each other. Oh, my. If I look like Emily, and I'm sure I do, it's not pretty. Her face is green and purple and her hair . . . strands of slimy I don't know what. I turn away.

I turn away not only from Emily, but from the sight of what is coming next. It is foul. In fact, I'm seriously wondering if I can do this next bit. How bad do I want to be a Shellback? I don't know if I want it this bad.

The sight that makes me nauseated for the first time today is the Royal Baby. They've picked the fattest guy on the ship with the biggest, ugliest, hairiest stomach to sit in a throne in nothing but his underwear. Fellow Shellbacks have greased his furry gut and ever-so-delicately placed a cherry in his belly button.

I watch in horror as the Pollywogs in line on their hands and knees are forced to pick the cherry out of his belly button with their teeth.

I finally throw up. I'm not even in front of the Baby yet.

The Shellbacks whoop with delight as they release us from the stockade and whack us from behind en route to the Baby. I'm in front of Em this time, crawling with my head down, not wanting to look at or think about what's coming next. Without warning, someone lifts my shoulders from behind so that my torso moves upright while I'm still on my knees. My vision is filled with black, curly, greasy stomach hair on a gut that is outright offensive.

There's no time to deliberate, because it's done for me. The Baby pulls my head into his stomach and rolls it around in the grease. God only knows how I do it, but when I'm released, I clutch a cherry in my teeth. The dry heaves start in earnest now, because there's nothing left to throw up.

Next stop—garbage chute. Haven't we been crawling through what has effectively been a garbage chute all morning? So the fact that the Shell-backs are chanting that it's time to crawl through the "garbage chute" has me wondering . . . in a very bad way.

The chute looks like a play toy that preschoolers use—a long, plastic tube, colored in bright pinks and yellows, that runs about thirty feet in length. And the rumors are true. All the chatter about saving up the ship's garbage for weeks and roasting it in the ovens is true. They've filled the chute with it and we're slithering through on our stomachs, army crawl style. I'm not sure how anyone has anything left to throw up at this point, but I'm sludging through vomitus from the word go.

Surely this is the end. Surely this obstacle course from hell is complete. I envision breaking through this torture tube to sunlight on the other side and having it over. Done and over.

Right. Next stop—the coffin. The coffin reminds me of my time in S.E.R.E. School—Survival, Evasion, Rescue, Escape—POW training for anyone who might find themselves in a combat position. All pilots have to attend, and when we were in the prisoner phase, the guards locked us in small boxes without room to lift our heads. We sat, curled in the dark, for hours.

At least with this "coffin," we get to lie flat. So I shimmy into the elon-gated box, filled with muck much the same as I have just crawled through, and the lid is closed. They've created a peephole on the top, so when they order you to roll around in the garbage, they can ensure you're doing it *properly*.

I'm starting to think this isn't worth it. Everyone was given the option to sit in the library and not participate if they didn't care to. But the stigma. And especially for me. I really want to show that I can do this. That women can do this. I think most sailors on the ship felt that Em and I were going to sit this one out. Surprise, surprise when they found out we were game.

I squint when sunlight floods the coffin as the lid is pulled back. I'm then led to a giant tank filled with something green. I climb in and am ordered to submerge. It takes every ounce of willpower I possess to dunk myself. How can it be that with everything I've been through this morning, the simple act of dunking my head would garner more stress than all the other obstacles combined? I do it quickly, and when I surface, I hear the shouts of those in front of me, including Emily.

The sailors yell, "What are you?"

"A fuckin' Shellback!" she shouts.

I exhale in relief. "Yeah, what she said."

29

The sailors at the end of the Pollywog obstacle course shake my hand and send me straight to the makeshift shower rigged on the flight deck. I meet up with Emily and we strip on the spot. We've worn our swimsuits underneath, so we take our T-shirts and khakis off—clothing that will never be worn again—and dump them in the trash pile with everyone else's.

We're able to get the worst of the muck off our bodies before trudging to our stateroom and the showers that await.

We flip for it. Em wins and jumps in first.

She's a long time in the shower and when I finally get my turn, I realize why. I shampoo and re-shampoo my hair at least five times and it still feels like the ick of a lake bottom. It's going to take several more washings to make it fully right again.

When I exit the shower, Em gapes as she looks at the backs of my legs. I peek over. I'm black and blue and covered in welts. Lovely.

"They got your arms, too," she says.

Oops. I had completely forgotten. But, hey, I'll take it. An excuse gift from the sky.

"I guess so," I say.

Em slips into a light pink stretch camisole and form-fitting black shorts and reaches into her closet for a pair of flip-flops. "Going to the steel beach picnic?" she asks.

All newly christened Shellbacks are being rewarded with a steel beach picnic—the first of the cruise. For these "picnics," barbeque grills are set up on the flight deck—made of steel, and thus the name—and it's a chance for the crew to eat and relax on a good weather day.

"I'll wait if you're coming," she adds.

What's this? Maybe our flight hours truce is going to last longer than I thought. Thank heavens. I so want it to be normal between us.

"Yeah, give me just a second."

I throw on my running shorts, a moisture-wicking technical T-shirt, and lace up my running shoes.

"This is a picnic, not a workout," she says.

"This is all I have," I say, making for the door and stepping into the passageway. "Besides, it's too hot to wear anything else."

"Good thing we're pulling into Singapore tomorrow. Looks like another shopping trip's in order."

"It's not that bad—"

"It's that bad."

I roll my eyes, but there's a skip in my step. Please let Em and me be back to normal.

When we emerge onto the flight deck, smoke and a delicious barbeque smell fill the air. Hamburgers, hot dogs, and rows of chicken breasts vie for space between giant vats of baked beans, all of it spread across three extra-long barbeque grills. Mess cranks cook, ladle, and serve it all with marked efficiency to sailors formed in three makeshift lines behind each grill, paper plates and cutlery in their hands.

All evidence of the Wog Day obstacle course has been cleared and the decks have been hosed down and cleaned. The sounds of Jimmy Buffett play through the ship's intercom system and crewmembers sprawl over the deck, some sitting with their legs dangling over the side, and some, like our male pilots, resting on lounge chairs, shirts off, tanning in the equatorial sun.

After we receive our food, it hurts to sit, so I stand instead. As I look around, it occurs to me that I've never seen the ship's crew this happy. The laughs, the jokes, the smiles. The activities both last night and today were a definite morale-builder.

But I'm exhausted. I can't believe they've scheduled night flight ops after a day like today. It kind of puts a damper on the steel beach picnic for me. I'm imagining sitting in the cockpit for hours when I don't want to put my bum on anything. But the operational tempo of the strike group never slows. No SEAL ops tonight—we'll just be moving cargo—but damn, I could use a break.

"What are you huffing about?" Em says.

"Um, nothing," I say. *Tell me I wasn't just talking out loud.*

"Damn? Damn what?" she asks.

Crap.

"I just . . . I have to fly again tonight—"

"Of course you do," she says, not hiding the sarcasm.

"Oh, no . . . I didn't mean—"

"Christ, it's not even a SEAL flight."

"No, Em," I say. "Please don't do this."

"Whatever," she says.

"No! I talked with Chad. I asked him why I had to fly and he said because I've been a regular on nights, he was just keeping me there. That's the only—"

"Hey, Em!" Zack calls from his lounge chair. He and the other pilots are waving her over.

She waves back, before turning to me. "Wouldn't want to keep you from resting up before your flight." She moves toward the group. "Later," she says over her shoulder.

By the time I'm in the aircraft, Wog Day is a distant memory, save for my derrière, which is a constant, painful reminder. It's also hard to shell the image of Emily walking away from me, which is why I've decided I need to put my foot down about the scheduling. It's not fair to Emily or Zack and it's putting a wedge between Em and me that doesn't need to be there.

I keep telling myself, if I can just get through this flight, I'll be in Singapore tomorrow. Eric will be there and I know he'll lend an open ear and maybe even have some suggestions for what to do with the SEAL flight bunk. I don't have any idea yet how we're going to meet, but he said he'd find me, so I'm not going to worry about it.

I'm flying with Matt tonight, and it's close to midnight when the radios erupt in chatter. All airborne helicopters are told to switch up to SAR common, which is usually not a good thing. The search-and-rescue frequency is exactly that—used for coordination of SAR efforts.

The H-60s have already been listening to this frequency. *Nimitz* is calling all of its Nighthawk aircraft to land on her deck.

"Shadow Hunter six six, *Lake Champlain* Tower, confirm your position, over."

"*Lake Champlain* Tower, Shadow Hunter six six, four miles due east, one hundred feet. We've begun our search pattern based on last known position, over."

It's Brian Wilcox. And they're starting a search pattern. A search for what? Man overboard? Aircraft?

"All airborne helicopters check in with *Lake Champlain* Tower for search coordination, over."

I quickly dial in the *Lake Champlain* navigational aid.

"*Lake Champlain* Tower, Sabercat five five, three miles to the south, three hundred feet, over," Matt says.

"Sabercat five five, *Lake Champlain* Tower, proceed northeast, establish holding three miles east of our posit, maintain three hundred feet, over."

"What the hell's goin' on?" Lego asks.

"Lace, switch up Nuts," Matt says. "Let's see if the Shadow Hunters know anything."

I switch up the discreet frequency we call Nuts, saying a silent prayer that it will be Eric who answers.

"Shadow Hunter six six, Sabercat five five, on Nuts, over," Matt says.

"Sabercat five five, Shadow Hunter six six, go ahead." I think it's Rob LeGrand.

"Six six, five five, what's goin' on?" Matt asks.

"We think one of our sixties is in the water," Rob says. "They disappeared from radar four minutes after their ops normal call."

Holy crap. A 60 in the water. *One of our 60s . . . Our 60s . . .*

One of the Shadow Hunter 60s? Is that what he meant? One of theirs? Or is he referring collectively to the H-60 aircraft? Three ships carry them— the *Nimitz,* the *Leftwich* . . . and the *Lake Champlain.*

"Fuck . . ." Lego says.

"No shit," Matt says. "Mess, better get your gear on."

"Already on, sir. I'm ready to go."

Lego and Messy are both rescue swimmers. If necessary, we can drop Messy in the water and pull anyone out via hoist.

"*Lake Champlain* Tower, Sabercat five five, entering holding, due east, three hundred feet, over," Matt says.

From our position, I see the Shadow Hunter's search light scanning the ocean. They're low to the water, probably closer to fifty feet than one hundred now.

And I'm staring at my worst nightmare realized—an aircraft down in the water, aircrew trapped inside. The mouth of the blackened sea has opened.

The cockpit gauges blur and I'm transported. . . .

I shiver in a watery tomb, consumed in blackness, struggling to free myself—drowning, in gut-wrenching clarity. The water presses in without mercy, long fingers slithering around my throat, squeezing. Watery tentacles coil through the airframe, dragging it downward. I'm being swallowed.

And then, something I haven't felt in over nine years—a panic that threatens my hold on the now.

My fingers claw at the nylon webbing that holds me down. I press my feet against the cockpit floor, straightening to lift myself from the seat. *Out! Get me out!*

Trapped, I grab at the shoulder straps, my heart racing.

Don't do this, Sara! Don't do this! Stay here!

My hands go to the harness release. I fumble, unable to find the lever. *No! Stop!* I pinch my eyes shut. *Hold on! Stay here!*

I freeze, gripping the straps with all my strength, every muscle contracted to the point I feel I might snap.

Say the facts. Say them! Transmission oil hot caution light. Location— master caution panel. Power—battery bus. Oil temperature thermal switches— two forward transmission, one aft transmission. Light illumination—110 degrees. Good. Say it out loud!

Without pressing my radio switch, I say the facts aloud. Over and over I repeat them—thank god, Matt is flying—while I attempt to pull myself together.

Let go of the straps. Breathe. Breathe. You've got this. You've got this.

My mouth is powder, my throat scratched. I lick my lips. *Your legs. Relax. Let the tension go. You've got this.*

As I regain my hold on reality, I'm already asking the question. Why? I've controlled my fear of flying over the water for years. Maybe it's that an actual aircrew is down. Far too easy to project myself into this scenario . . . to project someone else.

Which 60? Damn it, why didn't they say which one?

The panic subsides, replaced with a growing anger. For me. For behaving this way. *You swore you'd never let this happen again.*

"*Lake Champlain* Tower, Shadow Hunter six seven, ops normal, four souls, four plus zero zero fuel." Like I've received a shot of adrenaline straight to the heart, my body snaps to alertness at the sound of Eric's voice.

Thank god.

I look to the west. They've just taken off from the deck of the *Lake Champlain*.

"Shadow Hunter six seven, Shadow Hunter six six," Brian says. "Take over on station. We're departing for fuel."

"Copy, six six, we're there in three," Eric says.

Shadow Hunter 67 closes 66's position and takes over the search. The battle group converges. Like spiders scurrying to the middle of a giant web, ships move in from every direction.

"Shadow Hunter six seven, Sabercat five five, on Nuts, over," Matt says.

"Five five, six seven, go ahead," Eric says.

"Who are we looking for?"

"Knight Rider four five. Stand by—"

Leftwich's bird. They have only one aircraft.

"*Lake Champlain* Tower, Shadow Hunter six seven, we have a visual, over."

Please let the next call be a rescue call—an aircrew that needs pickup.

"Six seven, five five, we have our rescue swimmer standing by, if necessary, over."

"Five five, six seven, stand by," Eric says.

Their searchlight scans a small area now. What do they see? Debris? Strobe lights atop the crewmen's helmets?

My stomach is churning. It's too close. Too real.

"Shadow Hunter six seven, *Lake Champlain* Tower, we have safety boats en route, over."

"Copy, in sight," Eric says.

Smaller craft close Eric's position. They carry rescue swimmers and could affect a pickup, as well.

The lack of reporting from Eric has me worried. Signal flares burst in the distance, the smoke rising like shimmering orange ghosts. This eerie, glowing cloud alternately brightens and dims as searchlights from several surface craft pass through it.

A flicker of orange catches my eye.

"Matt, low fuel," I say.

"Crap," he says, before keying his radio. "*Lake Champlain* Tower, Sabercat five five, we need to depart holding for fuel."

"Sabercat five five, *Lake Champlain* Tower, roger, cleared to depart holding. Cleared to shut down."

Oh. We won't be needed. That can be good and bad.

Once we land, our pilots and maintenance crew come out in force to meet us, wanting to know what we saw.

"One of our boats is out there," Commander Claggett says.

"Anything on ship's radio?" Matt asks.

"Not yet."

There's nothing more sobering. As a result, the Sara-at-the-controls nonsense, the flight hours complaints, the snide looks, the flippant remarks— all absent.

"Flight ops have been canceled," Commander Claggett says. "Probably best for us to call it a night."

As the group disperses, I remain on the flight deck, where the air reverberates with the solemn, steady beat of Shadow Hunter 67's helicopter blades. In the far distance, I see the water awash in silver from probing searchlights, a crowding of ships, orange smoke hovering thickly over it all . . . and a satisfied sea.

30

I thrash, my movements frantic, animalistic. Upside down, I grapple with the kayak's rubber skirt at my waist, twisting and jerking. I wrestle with my life vest, clawing at the straps. Every procedure I've memorized and practiced for a wet exit has left me.

Involuntarily, I suck inward, clamping my mouth shut at the last moment. The water just finds another way. Through my nose, it scours my sinuses until my mouth explodes open. The water consumes me.

In a surreal moment of clarity, I realize that "drowning" is a horrifically inadequate word for what is, in truth, a violent death—long, excruciating, and suffused with raw, primal terror.

Before I succumb to oblivion, I see Ian. His eyes look reassuringly into mine, calm beyond reason, as he pulls me free of the kayak. He holds me close as the water snatches us into its current, tossing us like toothpicks. With superhuman effort, he reaches his hand upward, grabbing an overhanging willow branch, pulling me toward the shore.

The water arcs over us, yanking our bodies straight like stiff pennants in a gale wind, Ian's hand the sole anchor point for our safety.

"Grab on!" he yells, indicating a rocky outcropping.

I try to do the action, but fail. Using his last reserves of strength, Ian pulls my arm up and over the rock, hooking it there. I turn my head just in time to see Ian's hand slipping from the willow branch.

My brother. My twin. The one I loved most in the world. Whose kindergarten construction paper Valentines still hung in my bedroom. Who snuggled with me at night in our tree house. Who held my hand on our first day of school. If I hadn't panicked, he wouldn't have had to come for me. He would still be alive today.

I stand on the pedals, cranking hard, the lactic acid searing, using this pain to mask the other. My heavy breaths echo loudly in the empty weight room, the ship unnaturally quiet and eerily still, having pulled into Singapore a day late. The strike group's delay is due to the deaths of the four aircrew of Knight Rider 45. We've only heard bits and pieces of the story—the detailed version won't come out for weeks—but supposedly they found their helmets floating among the wreckage. Every time I picture it, my eyes start watering.

My thoughts move to Eric as I pedal faster. I need to see him. For many reasons. One of which is the need for a sounding board, wrestling as I am with how I reacted during the search for Knight Rider. I almost succumbed to panic . . . just like nine years ago.

I spin faster, breathing in hitches. And while I can never change what happened, I've been on a mission since that day to do right by Ian's memory, to finish what he would have started.

Following in his footsteps to the Naval Academy was an easy decision. So was flying. I knew good and well it would always occur over the water. I knew I would have to face what I feared the most every time I strapped into the cockpit. Many would call it an *irrational* fear of drowning and maybe that's true.

But after all these years, I thought I had learned to control it.

Until now. And this scares me more than what I feared in the first place.

Dressed in my maroon pajama top and gray running shorts, emotionally and physically drained, I drop into my desk chair and pull out my hydraulic systems book, desperate for a distraction. I remember Em's comment—that I need to put away my aircraft systems manuals and let go of myself. I'd never admit it to her, but I can probably add this to the list of things she's right about . . . a rather lengthy list.

The knock on the door doesn't bother me anymore, now that Commander Egan is no longer on the ship. I suspect it's Trey Perkins, the communications officer, coming by to shoot the breeze as he often does when we're on duty together. He has taken over as the interim operations officer until Commander Egan's replacement arrives.

I open the door and my heart surges.

"Hey," Eric says.

I step back, he follows, the door closes, and I'm in his arms.

He squeezes so hard, it's difficult to breathe.

"God, I missed you," he whispers in my ear.

He pulls away slightly, looking me over.

"How are you?" he asks, his eyes drifting downward and stopping on my arms, now yellowed with the aging bruises.

"I'm good," I say, holding them up for inspection.

"They're healing," he says.

"But I have new ones." I turn and show him the backs of my legs, raising my shorts slightly so the welts are clear.

"What the hell?"

"Wog Day."

"No way! Was I just hugging a newly minted Shellback?"

"A genuine, bona fide Shellback, and with the scars to prove it."

I take his hand, leading him to a seat on Em's bunk. I cross my legs and turn to face him.

"Did you get sick?" he asks with devilish curiosity. He seems intent on ignoring the elephant in the room—Knight Rider. But for now, I'm glad of it. I don't want anything to spoil this time between us.

"Yep."

"Wog Breakfast?"

"No, Royal Baby."

"You threw up on the Royal Baby?"

"No, I threw up before I ever got there. Just looking at what was coming . . . god."

I make a face as my stomach turns a mild queasy twist at the memory.

"But it's just a big fat guy with grease on his stomach," he says, chuckling lightly at my sour expression.

"Yeah and that guys pulls your head into his stomach and rolls it around. Yuck!"

"Did you get the cherry?" He cringes.

"I did, and by that time, I didn't have anything left to throw up. I was just dry heaving after that."

He laughs. So good to hear him laugh.

"So you're already a Shellback then, I take it?"

He nods while looking at my arms again. "Did anyone ask questions?"

"No. I was able to hide them. And then Wog Day came along and they assumed my arms fell victim to a few errant shillelagh whacks."

"Good cover."

But then, thinking about my bruised arms, I remember something.

"Commander Egan is no longer on this ship," I say.

"Is that so?" he says, feigning ignorance.

"And you don't know anything about that?"

"Has it been better for you?"

"Seriously, how did you—"

"You didn't answer my question. Has it been better?"

"In that regard, certainly."

"In that regard?"

"Well—" I stop myself. I don't want to complain. "Are you hungry?"

I walk down the deserted passageway to the wardroom, proceeding to the counter that reliably supplies the makings for peanut-butter-and-jelly sandwiches. I prepare two of them before spying the apple pie that Petty Officer Sampson has left out from lunch—two slices remain.

When I return to the room, I remove the comforter from my bunk and lay it on the floor.

"Picnic?" I ask.

"Absolutely," he says, seating himself.

I lay out our food, two plastic forks, and grab the water bottle from my desk. We begin eating, but Eric doesn't miss a beat. "So what's not better?" he asks.

I put down my sandwich. "I don't want to complain. I mean, I normally don't, and yet it seems every time I'm with you, you're hearing about something."

"What's not better?" he asks again.

"Persistent, aren't you?" I say.

"When it concerns you, yes," he says with a look to melt the heart.

I realize that what I'm about to say has been rendered trivial by the incident with Knight Rider. But I'm sure we'll speak about that soon enough.

"Okay," I say. "It's the SEAL flights."

A shadow crosses his face, just briefly.

"You know I've been flying these, but what you probably don't know is that for some reason, I always have to be the pilot at the controls. It's being dictated by Captain Magruder and Admiral Carlson."

His expression doesn't change.

"Don't you find that unusual?" I say, finding his reaction unusual. "How can someone who is not the aircraft commander demand something like this? It's unheard of."

"They must have their reasons," he says matter-of-factly.

I think back to the smiles and light conversation he shared with Captain Magruder and Admiral Carlson that day in our wardroom for the Operation Low Level brief, so unusual given the differences in rank. And how Admiral Carlson responded so quickly to Eric's suggestion to speak with Commander Egan.

"You talk like you know them," I say.

"I do. They were the O-reps for the crew team at Navy. We go back a long way."

Officer representatives are assigned to each sports team at the Naval Academy, acting as liaisons for their athletes. The relationship between midshipmen and O-reps is often a close one.

"Ah, now it makes sense. I'd never seen Captain Magruder smile before I saw him talking with you that day in our wardroom."

"Yeah, he's not too outwardly friendly, but a great man. He and the admiral both. I'm confident they have valid reasons for wanting you to fly."

"Well, it sucks," I say.

He raises his eyebrows.

"Not the flying," I say, reaching for my water bottle. "It's the other pilots."

I sigh, taking a long drink, feeling silly for making such a big deal out of this. But now that I've brought it up, I might as well finish.

"There's a flight hours imbalance, me taking most of them lately. That and the fact I have to be the one at the controls. They resent what's happening. They talk behind my back. They don't include me anymore. I even had a fight about it with Em. And I can't rationalize that it's worth it or necessary or anything because no one will give me any answers. I don't know why I'm doing what I'm doing and no one else does either."

I stare at the water bottle in my hand, turning it around and around,

each SEAL flight playing in super-fast-forward in my head, trying to remember, attempting to string something together to give me an answer.
"I even asked Mike once why I had to be at the controls and he wrote me
a note saying, *We requested it.*"

"He did?"

"Yeah, but that's all he'd say. You know, maybe you could ask him some-
time. You guys seem like friends."

Eric motions to the water bottle I hold. "May I?" I hand it to him and
he takes a long sip before answering. "I suppose I could."

"How do you know each other, anyway? You're in completely different
specialties."

"We went to school together. And he's a good one to have around. Always has my back. Just like the other night—"

He stops. I'm not sure I want to bring up Jonas now, either.

But at the same time, what did he just say? They went to school together? Mike went to Auburn, not Navy.

"So anyway, you're not liking the pilot-at-the-controls attention," he
says, moving on.

"Well, ever since I entered the Navy, I've subscribed to the small dot
theory. I just want to be one of the small dots, not standing out. I certainly don't want to be the big dot, but that's what this is turning into."

I reach with my fork, trying a bit of apple pie.

"I don't know that you've ever been a small dot, despite what you might
think. The cream sort of rises," he says.

I shake him off, picking up my water bottle, which is almost empty. I
rise to refill it, but when I return, Eric is resting his back against the metal
cabinetry, the majority of his sandwich left on the napkin, uneaten. I sit
next to him and he takes my hand.

"So how about you?" I say. "Is everything okay?"

"It's all right," he says, but his tone has changed. I know what he's
thinking because I'm thinking it, too. He looks down at our interlaced
hands, having pulled them into his lap. My hand is now surrounded by
both of his.

"Knight Rider?" I say.

He looks up to meet my eyes. "We flew to *Leftwich* yesterday to return their helmets."

31

Eric squeezes my hand and it's a long time before he speaks. His eyes shift focus to something just beyond me, his mind most likely lost in the events of the last two days. Like me and like most, we try, yet fail, to make sense of it all.

Of course, I could take the easy route, using that insufferably horrendous, yet neatly packaged quip, *Everything happens for a reason.* One of the mourners at Ian's funeral actually had the nerve to say this to me. But I can't do it. I can't subscribe to this sophomoric explanation for events that clearly fall outside of reason.

No. There is no reason. Not for Ian's death. And not for something like this.

Finally, Eric returns his eyes to me. "I'll never forget the looks on the faces of the men in their detachment," he says, his voice dull with ache. "They were like ghosts. Thirty guys stood there with absolutely nothing to do. Their bird was gone, they'd lost four guys, and they just stood there. And the wreckage . . . just pieces of soundproofing floating in the water, that's all, and four helmets. Empty helmets . . ."

"I wondered what you were seeing down there," I say. "I followed the path of your searchlight, trying to imagine what was happening."

"Wait, you were there?"

"Well, yeah. I was in five five. We were orbiting above you."

"You were there. . . . I didn't know."

"I don't think I was ever up on radios."

He searches my eyes, swallowing.

"When the call first went out that a bird was down, I thought—" He lowers his eyes.

"I know. I thought it, too."

I take time to study him in the ensuing silence. His angular face that's set in the jaw at the moment is at once handsome and intimidating. When he smiles, when he's at ease, I don't see the intimidating part. But I've seen glimpses of this other side of him—when he coldly glared at Commander Claggett, or wrapped up a drunk Commander Egan, or when he faced off against a threatening Jonas.

But no matter the situation, no matter the personality facet shown, he models competency—always. Even after the incident with Jonas on *Nimitz*, he pulled himself together, delivered a perfect brief, and executed the stellar coordination of the exercises that followed. He was calm, in control, and he got it done.

During the search for Knight Rider, I failed on every count. The fact that I faltered is a bitter pill to swallow. I doubt I would ever admit to a failing like this to anyone, but if that loss of situational awareness ever happens again, it's my crew that would pay. I need to find a solution and I need help. Normally, Em would be my go-to person, but it would be awkward now. Since our squabble at the marksmanship quals, we haven't had a chance to talk anything through. And then the flight hours thing flared up again after Wog Day at the steel beach picnic. But even so, this is something so personal, I know there's only one person I want to confide in.

"May I talk to you about something?" I ask.

He looks up. "Of course."

"Remember what you said about me, right after the emergency landing on your ship? You said I was a pressure player."

"I remember."

"Well, I was anything but during the search."

He turns his body toward mine and I lower my head. "I don't even know where to start," I say.

I stare at my lap, already second-guessing my decision to disclose this. *The cream rises. A pressure player.* Do I squander that? Do I let him know I almost checked out in the middle of a flight?

"What happened?" he asks.

Just tell him.

I look up, hesitating. And then I force it out. "I don't know exactly. I mean, I do know. I just . . . well, nine years ago I almost drowned."

His eyes, steady as ever, encourage me to continue.

"I was pinned underwater in a kayak and I couldn't get out." I stop, shaking my head. "No, that's not right. I *could* have gotten out. I knew the procedures for a wet exit. I'd practiced it. I knew how to release myself from the skirt and I could have. I just needed to execute the steps. So simple . . ."

I look away, ashamed. So simple. How many times had I performed this maneuver in practice?

Eric squeezes my hand. "Go on."

I bring my eyes back to meet his. "Eric, I panicked. I jerked and flailed and thrashed, about as useful as a wicker canoe. My brother had to come for me. He had to get me out. He pulled me to safety before the river took him."

"Oh, no."

"It was my fault—all of it. Insisting we run our kayaks on a day we shouldn't have. Ian paying with his life for my inaction. I'll never forgive myself. Not ever."

His steady gaze holds mine. I want to look away, but his calm green eyes communicate only concern and understanding.

"Since then, the thought of being underwater terrifies me. I can't seem to make peace with it. So day to day, like when we're out here, it's a struggle, to put it mildly. But I've learned how to shut out my fear and focus. I've managed. Not great, but I've managed. But while searching for Knight Rider, I don't know, something triggered the panic. I was this close to losing it. My brain froze, everything blurred. I still don't know how I pulled back from that. But then I think, what about next time? That was an easy flight. What if—"

"Sara," he says. "You pulled it together. You handled it. Don't *what if* yourself."

"But—"

"You handled it," he says. "And I'm confident you'll handle it again." His eyes . . . strong, convincing. "And I'm so sorry about your brother."

I look at him—for a long time I look—realizing what I've just said.

It's the first time I've ever told anyone the truth about what happened that day. Emily doesn't know. I couldn't even bring myself to tell my parents. That it was my fault that Ian drowned? How could I possibly tell them?

This was Ian Denning. The all-American, blond-haired, blue-eyed star football player and student council president, who was slightly wild but adorably sweet and always humble. And most importantly, the boy who would carry the mantle. Who would continue the Denning family legacy, something so profoundly important to my father. He glowed when he spoke of Ian entering the service. He knew the legacy would continue and flourish in Ian's hands.

Sweet, sweet Ian . . . My fault. My father had lost his only son and so much more. For days after Ian's death, he trod a path between Ian's bedroom and the living room, pacing like a caged tiger. He would stop in front of the eleven-by-twenty framed photo of Ian and him and his father, retired Rear Admiral Stuart Denning, standing proudly in Tecumseh Court on the grounds of the Naval Academy, and shake his head before returning to Ian's room. I'd never heard my father cry before, but he did then. He'd lock himself in Ian's room and sob.

My mother almost ceased to function, refusing to leave her bedroom. So I took over, shopping for food my parents never touched, cooking dinners they didn't eat, restocking the tissue boxes and ensuring my uncle delivered the whiskey they drank like water. And all the while, I wondered how I could remain standing when my other half had been taken.

What could I do when this tragedy couldn't be undone? I did the only thing I could do. I tried to live Ian's life for him, the one I had taken. I knew I would never compare to him nor achieve what he would have achieved. And taking Ian's place would never satisfy my father or grandfather. But I had to do something.

In addition to honoring Ian, this would serve as my penance. At the Naval Academy, this was certainly the case. But then I rode a new wave of guilt when I started doing well in flight school. When I realized I liked flying—no, loved flying. I shouldn't be allowed a gift like this, so the walls I had erected to protect myself also became the means for me to hide my shame.

I blink, suddenly realizing how long I've been staring at Eric, the man who started breaking down those walls. But then the guilt comes again. Why should I be allowed something so special when I took everything from Ian?

My hands nervously roll over his. "Eric, I've never told anyone that be-fore. My parents, Emily, they know that Ian drowned, but I never told them he had to rescue me first. That it was my—"

"Don't say it was your fault." He holds my eyes, not blinking, until I can't stand it anymore.

"But it was—"

"Tell me," he says. "Would you have done the same for Ian? Would you have rescued him?"

"Well, of course, but—"

"Would you have blamed him for being trapped, regardless of the cir-cumstances?"

"Of course not. Never."

Eric reaches a hand to my face, sliding his fingers through my hair. His thumb softly brushes my temple, his olive-green eyes softening. "Then don't blame yourself," he says gently.

Like floodwaters from a broken dam, his words flow through my con-sciousness, chipping away at firmly held beliefs—my very notions of self—and previously impermeable walls of guilt. His gaze remains fixed firmly on mine, communicating the force of his conviction with alarming strength and sincerity.

I lean back slightly and Eric gathers my hands in his. I stare into his eyes, alight with scattered specks of gold, and for one very small moment, for the first time in nine long years, I wonder if I might be able to forgive myself.

He rises, pulling me up with him and into a tight embrace. "Are you going to be all right?" he asks.

"I think so. And thanks. For listening. For understanding."

"Anytime," he says.

He pulls back, and takes my face in his hands, brushing my hair back as he searches my eyes. "You're so strong," he whispers. "So strong . . . and yet . . ." His voice trails, his eyes drifting away from mine.

"What?" I ask, not sure I heard those last, almost imperceptible words correctly. "What did you just say?"

He returns his focus to me, but his eyes are distracted, strange. "Did I . . . what?" he says. "I'm sorry. It's just been a long day. So are you sure? You'll be okay?"

"Um, yeah . . . yes, I'll be fine."

With a soft kiss on the lips, he leaves me.

I drop into my desk chair, realizing only then that he never answered my question.

After a fitful night of sleep, I spend what should have been my first liberty day in Singapore assisting in the emergency recall of all ship's personnel. Why? Just this morning, the battle group was ordered to get under way immediately. As we've feared all along, our rendezvous with the Persian Gulf needs to happen sooner than planned.

We were supposed to have had six full days in Singapore. Even if Eric and I both stood duty, I was fully counting on four whole days together. There's so much more we need to talk about. While I feel far better about coming clean with what happened during the search for Knight Rider and disclosing what really happened with Ian, we still haven't discussed Jonas. Why the animosity? What evaluation was Jonas talking about? And why would that provoke such a harsh reaction?

But by 1800, we are under way and Singapore is but a blur in my memory. Check that. I don't have a memory of Singapore because I never left the ship.

32

Improvement areas for Lt. Denning include being more assertive on the radios . . .

I stop right there. I can't read any more. My progress report is in full view on the computer screen in Chad's room. The aircraft commanders have written my evaluation, along with Emily's and Zack's, and were having trouble saving them, so they asked me to help.

How can you have trouble saving a document, number one? And number two, why am I helping them save something that won't be worth the paper it's going to be printed on?

To make it worse, I'm privy to bits of Zack's progress report as I bring it up. *Leading the second pilots on the way to aircraft commander . . . has a thirst for knowledge . . . confident and aggressive . . .*

I'm still bitching about it when Em and I walk into the wardroom for breakfast.

"How much more assertive can I be, for god's sake? I mean, there are only so many ways to ask for a green deck for landing."

Thinking back to flight school, I now realize how lucky I was. The instructors stationed there during the time I went through didn't have any hang-ups about women in the cockpit, so I was given a fair shot. I made the standard radio calls, just like every other student, and was graded accordingly. And the curriculum, in general, was more objectively measured. If you took a systems test, you either knew the material or you didn't. As a result, I excelled there.

But leaving school and entering the fleet was an altogether different experience. Biases thrive onboard ships and in seagoing aircraft squadrons, and earning respect in environments like these is often managed one teeth-grinding day at a time. But I've never endured a more difficult experience than the one I'm living through now in my current assignment under Commander Claggett.

"At least you're not tentative anymore," Em says.

"Yeah, thanks a lot."

Things have been good with Em lately. We're only three days from crossing the Strait of Hormuz to enter the Persian Gulf, and since we pulled out of Singapore a week ago, I haven't flown a single SEAL mission. Every day without a SEAL flight is a day our relations improve, and I have to say, it's nice to have my commiserator back in my corner.

"You know, I'm not even hungry," I say as we seat ourselves.

"I realize your *thirst for knowledge* is overwhelming your need to eat, but if you *aggressively and confidently* order an omelet this morning, you should be able to get something in your stomach. And you need food, missy. Seriously, you're wasting away here."

It's true. I haven't been eating well. Since we left Singapore, I haven't flown much, Zack and Em taking most of the flight hours. And while this has helped things between me and Em, it's what's happening in the cockpit when I *have* been scheduled that's not so good. I've flown seven times, thirty-five hours, and can probably count thirty minutes total as the pilot at the controls—usually holding them on deck while the aircraft commanders left for bathroom breaks.

They've staged a silent protest to my SEAL mission flying and it includes not just time on the controls, but everything. I don't talk on the radios, I don't brief, and they answer for me if an aircrewman asks me a question. The winds and weather have been such that they've been able to get away with it, but I wonder how much longer this will go on.

In the meantime, I thought I could take comfort in listening to Eric's voice on the radios. We usually hear our helicopter counterparts at some point during the day since we share the airspace around the battle group. Even without the SEAL missions, I thought I'd hear his voice, but it has proved strangely absent. I've looked for him on the deck of the *Lake Champlain* and seen the other Shadow Hunters there, but not him. Not once.

No e-mail either, since the servers onboard that allow for personal e-mails have been down due to a massive security software upgrade. And no cell phones—they usually don't work while under way. Bottom line, no communication of any kind with Eric in seven days.

I pick through the omelet that Em forces me to order, thinking about my flight later today that's scheduled with Chad. I recall the comment that Commander Claggett made about *briefing to sit on my hands*. Now I know what it feels like . . . and it sucks. It really does. But I'd like to think they've made their point and we can move on now.

Although, apparently, today is not the day for moving on. Chad has been at the controls for over six hours by the time we touch down on *Nimitz*.

"Sabercat five five, *Nimitz* Tower, we need you to shut down present position, over."

"*Nimitz* Tower, Sabercat five five, say again, over?" Chad says.

"Sabercat five five, *Nimitz* Tower, shut down present position."

Chad and I look at each other. "What the hell?" he says.

"Okay, sir, we're exiting the aircraft for shutdown," Lego says.

"Any idea what's goin' on, sir?" Messy asks.

"Fuck if I know," Chad says.

As the rotors slow to a stop, a lieutenant dressed in summer whites with gold epaulets attached to his shoulders approaches the aircraft. He leans in to say something to Lego.

"Sir, he said we need to come with him."

"All right. Cutting power."

We follow the lieutenant into the superstructure and, once inside, he introduces himself. "I'm Greg Baskin, Admiral Carlson's aide."

I remember Greg. He accompanied the admiral to the *Kansas City* for the Operation Low Level brief so many weeks ago.

Chad puts out his hand. "Chad Henkel."

"Sara Denning," I say, shaking his hand. "And this is Petty Officer Legossi and Petty Officer Messina."

While Greg is shaking their hands, Chad and I are shaking our heads.

"So, Greg, what's going on here?" Chad says.

Greg begins walking and talking at the same time.

"Chad, you and Petty Officers Messina and Legossi need to wait here," he says, directing us into a ready room of sorts—a passenger ready room. Several rows of chairs occupy the small, gray space and a closed-circuit

TV hanging in the corner runs the movie of the day. It looks like *The Hunt for Red October*.

"Sara, you'll be coming with me," he says.

I look at Chad. "Chad, what's going on?"

"Ask Greg. I have no idea."

"Make yourselves comfortable," he says to Chad, Lego, and Messy. "We have boxed lunches on order for you."

"So, this goes in the highly fucking unusual category," Chad says. He's obviously not in the mood for this, especially having spent the last six hours sitting next to me. "Does our ship know about this? What about our flight? We have overheads."

"Everything's been taken care of," he says. "You just need to wait here until we get back."

"How long are we talking?" Chad asks.

"Just get comfortable."

That answer certainly isn't making *me* comfortable.

"Well, I'm gonna follow orders and set myself right heah," Messy says. He plops in a seat, grabs the chair located in front of him, turns it around, and puts up his feet.

"And I'm joinin' ya," Lego says.

Chad, not bothering to disguise his irriation, turns to take a seat.

"This way, Sara," Greg says.

We begin a long carrier trek, winding through an endless labyrinth of narrow gray corridors toward an unknown destination. I have no idea what to think. Wait. Actually, I do. This must be about Commander Egan. It has to be. But to have us shut down in the middle of a logistics run, interrupting a flight? It doesn't make sense.

"Greg, excuse me, but should I be worried here? Am I in trouble or something?"

"No, you're not in trouble. I'm taking you to a meeting."

"A meeting?"

"I'm sorry, that's all I know."

We finally arrive in Officer Country and Greg directs me to a broad stateroom door with Admiral Carlson's name on the identification plate. He opens the door without knocking and we enter what looks like the foyer to someone's home. It's a shock to see carpeting and normal furniture. A coffee table is surrounded by leather couches, all of it decorated in a nautical theme.

Three separate doors are accessed from this room—his sleeping quarters, a conference room, and the admiral's mess, where he eats.

"Wait here just one second," Greg says.

He knocks on the far right door, opening it a crack. "Sir, Lieutenant Denning is here."

"Send her in," comes the response.

I look to Greg, but he doesn't say anything. He opens the door wider and ushers me through. Rather than follow, he closes the door behind me.

I stop, doing a hyper-fast survey of the room. I recognize the majority of the ten men assembled here, and based on who's in attendance, this is not going to be a meeting about Commander Egan. Quickly scanning the faces, I realize that most would call this an intimidating group, but I've been around high-ranking officers since I was small, and their bearing was always a comfortable reminder of my father. I know how to act, how to speak, how to be taken seriously, but even so, my heart beats faster.

At least Eric is here. My heart flies when I see him. In the last seven days, I've dreamed of our reunion—a warm embrace, happy conversation. . . .

But then I really look at him.

He holds a neutral expression, removed, distant. I search his eyes, and they're not right. Something's not right. But I can't let my gaze linger. I've already stayed here too long.

Next to him, Commander Amicus—Animal. My survey of the room stops cold right here. My eyes zero in on the polished gold SEAL insignia that shines from his khaki uniform. SEAL insignia? Animal isn't a SEAL.

The man to his right, another commander whom I don't recognize, also wears a SEAL pin. Chiseled from top to bottom, he has dark brown eyes that narrow as he observes me. His name tag reads STEVE KENNAN.

Captain Plank, the *Lake Champlain* skipper, sits erect between Commander Kennan and Admiral Carlson, who presides at the head of the long, rectangular conference table. Captain Magruder sits to Admiral Carlson's right and opposite Captain Plank.

Commander Eichorn, commanding officer of the *Leftwich,* is next, followed by an Australian lieutenant colonel, one of the SAS members on the *Kansas City* that day . . . that bizarre day when I met Jonas. He sits next to the lieutenant colonel now, with a cocksure expression.

Mike Shallow is the final member of this gathering, sitting to Jonas's right and to my immediate left.

"Lieutenant Denning, have a seat, please," Admiral Carlson says, gesturing to the empty seat at the end of the table, directly opposite him.

I lower myself and glance quickly at Eric, who is now seated to my immediate right. I was hoping for an encouraging nod . . . something. His expression remains impassive.

"You know everyone at this table with the exception of three, I believe," Admiral Carlson says. He motions first to the man sitting next to Animal. "This is Commander Kennan. He leads SEAL Team One in San Diego."

Commander Kennan's scrutinizing gaze hasn't changed. His black hair matches Animal's, but is worn short and close to the head.

"Lieutenant Colonel Tyson," he continues, pointing to the Australian seated across the table from Commander Kennan, "leads the SAS Regiment."

The Australian, a more darkly tanned version of Commander Kennan, regards me with a cool expression.

"And finally, Commander Eichorn," Admiral Carlson says. "Commanding officer of the *Leftwich.*"

Although I've never met him personally, I certainly remember Commander Eichorn from the Operation Low Level brief. He's a hard one to forget—completely bald, with a permanent scowl etched on his face.

"I know this is confusing for you, but you'll understand why we're meeting here in just a moment. I need to let you know right up front that the information presented here today is classified Top Secret. Absolutely nothing that is said here will leave this room. Do you understand?"

"Yes, sir, I do. But, sir, I only hold a Secret clearance."

"Not anymore. Your new security clearance has already been approved."

My eyes shift again quickly to Eric, who maintains his neutral expression.

"I'm going to let Commander Amicus give you a brief overview of our purpose here," Admiral Carlson says.

I turn my head to the right to look at Animal, but I can't take my eyes off of the SEAL insignia he wears.

He points to his pin. "You're looking at this. . . ."

And suddenly, every question I've ever had about the SEAL flights—the scheduling, my role as the pilot at the controls, the flight hours discrepancies, Eric's involvement, the high-level interest in training missions, the tension with the arrival of the Aussies, evaluations, metrics, all of it—comes to a head. My stomach drops because I realize I'm about to learn the answers, and I'm not really sure I want to.

33

The unique design of the Navy SEAL trident makes it one of the most recognizable insignia found in all branches of U.S. military service. Comprising four symbols—an eagle, an anchor, a trident, and a pistol—the gold pin is also one of the largest insignia, just under the size of a standard business card.

Animal is right. I *am* looking at his pin, my brain turning a thousand miles an hour as I attempt to reconcile what I'm seeing.

"I was sent to evaluate you for flying our missions," Animal says. "Not training, but actual missions."

The air strains from the awkward silence, while I remain staring. Maybe it's that I'm trying to digest the fact that Animal is in fact a SEAL, because a silly question leaves my mouth. "You mean you're not a pilot, sir?"

"You think my flying's that bad? Thanks a lot." He laughs, thankfully relieving some of the oppressive tension I feel. "Yes, I'm a pilot. I'm part of an experimental program that puts SEALs in a position to fly, and evaluate potential pilot candidates for our missions. Due to the highly classified nature of what we do, we don't wear the insignia and only our squadron skippers know our primary designation."

He stops for a moment, while I look at his pin again and then back to his face.

"Normally, every aspect of a SEAL mission is covered in-house. Demolition, parachuting, diving, everything," he says. "The only thing that falls outside our purview is air transport. And you've heard it too many times—the aircraft that goes down, taking the entire SEAL squad with it. Sometimes it's mechanical failure, sometimes it's due to enemy fire, but we realized that in all cases, we were at the mercy of whoever happened to be on the flight schedule. So we decided we needed to be proactive. Pick the best pilots for the job to ensure our teams have the greatest chance of success.

"We take the selection of our pilots very seriously, now hand-picking each of them. Once I realized you were the best-qualified West Coast candidate, we began your training in Hawaii. It was no accident that you were the pilot at the controls on the fast roping missions we completed together, nor that you've worked with Mike's team so often. Mike and his squad needed to feel confident that you were the one for the job. They've given you the highest marks, just as I have. And now, Captain Martin has added his highest recommendation."

I glance at Mike first, who gives a small nod of approval. And then beyond him, to Jonas. His blue eyes are bright with energy, victorious almost. And the smile that goes with it, just as bright . . . yet so out of place among the serious faces here.

"Commander Kennan is here because your selection would impact every member of his team, including Mike and his platoon. The same is true for Lieutenant Colonel Tyson and, in this case, Second Squadron."

My eyes shift to Commander Kennan and then to Lieutenant Colonel Tyson. Their keen eyes regard me so sharply, I feel as if they're looking straight through me. Maybe they're not so sure about me. That's what it feels like.

"But one thing stands out uniquely in your case and that's why we have so much high-level interest at this table. You're a helicopter second pilot. Normally, the flying skills we require are those of a seasoned aircraft commander with far more hours under his belt."

Captain Magruder, Admiral Carlson, Captain Plank, and Commander Eichorn wear the same serious, yet undecided expressions as Commander Kennan and Lieutenant Colonel Tyson. It's then that I realize that Mike, Jonas, and Animal have given these six their recommendation for a pilot and they're not sure if they agree.

"In my opinion, skills are skills. If you're one of the few, regardless of flight hours, who can get one of our teams transitioned to a hostile deck within a matter of seconds, then you're the pilot I want."

He takes a purposeful look around the room.

"But there are some in this room who wanted to meet you and get to know you better, before they gave their approval. You might think of this as a bit of an interview."

An interview?

Wait a minute . . .

An unexpected anger flares from somewhere, because I know what this is.

So they're evaluating me right now. Evaluating how I'm sitting, responding, reacting. I take consolation in the fact that Animal thinks a pilot is a pilot. He's gotten past the female part, saying he thought I was the best qualified candidate. Mike and Jonas are okay with it, too. And Eric has been unfailingly supportive since the first time I met him. There's a comfort in this, in having Eric by my side in this meeting.

Animal looks to the others at the table, inviting them to speak.

Captain Plank, so still, glances briefly at a sheet of paper in front of him and then returns his gaze to me. "Tell me about your experience working with GMG2 Franklin," he says in the same no-nonsense way I remember from the *Lake Champlain*.

Gunners Mate Guns Second Class Franklin. He must have some sort of background sheet about my previous naval experience. I look around quickly. Every man here has this same sheet.

"Sir, Petty Officer Franklin served as my running mate on Third Class Midshipman Cruise aboard the ammunition ship USS *Flint*. We cleaned and maintained the weaponry stored in the *Flint*'s arsenal. Forgive me, sir, but there isn't much to report. We just stripped and cleaned guns for hours on end that summer."

"What guns?" he asks.

What guns . . . ? He's asking me what guns?

"M9s, M16s, .50 cals, M60s . . ." I say.

"It says here you have an Expert marksmanship rating in both pistol and rifle."

"Yes, sir."

"In the most recent marksmanship quals on the *Kansas City*," and he briefly glances at Captain Magruder before turning his attention back to me, "you achieved the highest scores of any shooter on the ship. And by a good margin."

"Yes, sir."

"Is this something you practiced during your time on the *Flint*?"

"Yes, sir, we did get to shoot quite a bit during my time onboard."

"According to Captain Magruder, after the completion of the pistol quals, the chief master-at-arms reported that he was surprised with your familiarity with the weapon."

"Well, sir, I am. I could field strip those weapons in my sleep, I did it so often. Petty Officer Franklin always tested me, too. How fast could I strip the M9? How fast could I do it blindfolded? We played games like that all the time. So I don't know, sir. I suppose it's like riding a bike. All the muscle memory is still there."

"Could you do it now?" Captain Plank asks.

Could I do what now? I wonder silently.

"Field strip an M9, sir?" I ask to make sure.

"Yes," he says.

"I don't know, sir. It's been years."

"Why don't you try?" he says sternly.

I turn my head slightly as I glance around the table, meeting the eyes of each man present. What the hell is going on here?

I watch as Captain Plank produces the Beretta M9 he wears at his side from underneath the table and hands it to Animal.

Animal rises, walks to where I'm sitting, engages the manual safety, removes the empty magazine, pulls back the slide to show me the chamber is empty, and lays it on the table before me.

I turn to Eric, trying to hide the shock I feel. I just wish I was getting something back. What's wrong with him? But I obviously can't think about that now. I look briefly at the other nine expectant faces. I can't believe this.

I pick up the weapon with the custom wood grip, noting for the first time the carved initials, RP, on the side. Everything about the sidearm is intimately familiar. My mind drifts back to a broad wooden worktable in the weapons hold seven decks below the weather decks, the one you had to ride a special elevator to reach. Guns in piles on the floor, on workbenches, stacked in the corner. Lightbulbs dangling in midair, hung from ten-foot-long cords to light the space. A dented old CD player supplying Petty Officer Franklin's favorite eighties pop music. Bore brushes and toothbrushes scattered across the table. The smell of gunpowder, the black on my hands, and Petty Officer Franklin joking that I looked like a chimney sweep because of the soot on my face.

I'm remembering and my hands are moving, automatic movements so ingrained, it's like watching someone else performing the actions—depressing the disassembly latch button, rotating the latch lever, pulling the slide forward and off the frame, setting the frame aside, removing the recoil spring and guide rod, sliding them apart and setting them aside, and finally, pressing down on the locking block button and removing the barrel. The reassembly happens just as quickly, just as automatically. When finished, I release the slide and it cracks back into place. I lay the gun on the table, just as I did at the end of my timing games with Petty Officer Franklin.

When I look up, there has been a change. The expressions shown are different now.

"Sara, I'm curious," Animal says. "Is that something you practice? That took you twenty-two seconds."

"No, sir, I don't practice. The time is slow, I realize. When I did it with Petty Officer Franklin, I could do it blindfolded at that speed. I could normally hit fifteen seconds with my eyes open. But I didn't know I was going to have to do this today. I would have practiced, had I known."

I'm not sure, but it almost seems like the men at the table are amused. All of them, including the SEALs and the members of the SAS, shake their heads slightly. I suppose compared to them, my performance isn't that impressive.

"That wasn't a criticism," Animal says. "Not even close."

"But sir, why . . . ?" I ask, motioning to the gun with my hand.

"If you're given the go-ahead to fly these missions, you'll need to wear one on your person," he says. "It's good that you're familiar with it and know how to use it."

I'm thinking I really *don't* know how to use it. I can hit a target in practice, but that's not going to be the case in any real-life scenario. And how would I end up in a position to use it anyway? I mean, it's hard to shoot when your hands are on the controls.

I shift my attention to Commander Kennan, who speaks for the first time. "Lieutenant Denning, I observed your flying firsthand two weeks ago. Quite frankly, I was shocked at your speed of delivery over *Birmingham*."

"But I've never flown with—Wait. Was that you? That night? There were eleven."

"I needed to see it for myself and so did Lieutenant Colonel Tyson," he says, nodding to the Australian commander.

I'm sort of glad I didn't know I was undergoing an in-flight evaluation. But he thought I was fast, so I guess that goes in the *good* column. I bite the inside of my cheek, though, as Commander Kennan scans the paperwork in front of him, wondering what he's going to hit me with next.

"You're obviously a talented aviator," he says. "But while your exceptional piloting skills are a great strength, I'd be curious to know what you consider your greatest weakness."

Interesting. It's just like Animal said—a "job" interview. I just wish I'd had some heads up so I could have prepared to field a question like this. But who am I kidding? I already know the answer. I've worked on that weakness every day since that horrible day nine years ago.

In my hesitation to answer, he adds, "We understand you nearly drowned once."

A shiver runs through me.

"You were with your brother," Commander Kennan prompts.

Wait. How could they know this? My gaze shifts to Eric, whose remains expressionless.

No . . . He wouldn't . . .

I look again at the sheets on the table. Maybe this information is in my background file. I rub my palms on my flight suit, the shiver long forgotten, replaced by a prickling sweat. They would probably know Ian had died. They might even know it was by drowning. But how could they possibly know I was there? Or that I'd nearly drowned? Maybe they assumed . . .

But Commander Kennan just asked about my greatest weakness, which they've obviously tied to the incident with my brother.

"Lieutenant?" he says.

I snap my head back to Commander Kennan. "I'm sorry, sir. Yes, sir. It was nine years ago. And yes, my brother was there."

"Your brother, Ian, he died that day. Is that right?" Commander Kennan asks.

There can be only one reason they're so interested in this. I turn to Eric, who only holds my gaze for a short second before averting his eyes.

He has never averted his eyes. Ever.

"Is that right?" Commander Kennan repeats.

I stare, uncomprehendingly, as Eric looks steadfastly at his lap. *What did you tell them?*

"Lieutenant?"

I turn to Commander Kennan, staring blankly.

"Sara, I'm sure this is difficult to talk about," Animal says. "But we'd just like to hear it from you."

He nods encouragingly and I return my attention to Commander Kennan. "I'm sorry, sir."

I brace myself with a deep, steadying breath. "Nine years ago, Ian and I ran our kayaks on a day that we shouldn't have. The water was too high, too fast. I flipped and became pinned underwater."

I could lie now. I could tell them the skirt release was inoperative or that I was jammed in such a way that I couldn't reach it. Only one person knows the truth. . . .

"Sir, I knew the procedures. I knew what to do. How to get out. But I panicked, and Ian had to come for me."

Pressing my lips together, I take a long blink.

"He dove down, pulled my skirt release—something I knew how to do, should have done—and lifted me to the surface. He pulled me to safety before the water swept him away."

I glance to the other faces in the room, their expressions neutral, before returning to Commander Kennan. "Ever since that day, I've worked on it. I've learned how to focus better. To shut out what's happening around me and wall off what I'm feeling inside so I can keep my head about me when it matters."

He doesn't respond right away, looking studiously at me. Certainly, if there was a showstopper, this would be it. How could they possibly allow me to fly a mission if they thought I might freeze or crack under the pressure?

But they would never have known in the first place unless . . .

"And have you been successful?" Colonel Tyson asks pointedly.

Oh god. Did he tell them about that, too? About what happened during the search for Knight Rider?

"Lieutenant Denning," Captain Plank interjects. "I watched you with my own eyes as you landed an aircraft on my deck in sea state seven in a cockpit completely consumed in smoke as your transmission was failing. You couldn't have done that had you not kept your head."

What's this? Did Captain Plank just stick up for me?

"Sir?"

"In response to Colonel Tyson's question," Captain Plank says, "I would answer yes, you *have* been successful."

Colonel Tyson turns a scrutinizing gaze on me and it's some time before he speaks. "I would agree," he says finally.

I search the faces at the table, recognizing another subtle shift in posture and countenance by each. Animal looks as well, ensuring no one else wishes to "get to know" me.

I sense they have just silently given him the go-ahead.

34

"Sara," Animal says. "I initially said I was evaluating you for flying our missions, and I said that in the plural. We expect to use you many times in the future. But you're also meeting with us today because of intelligence pointing to an assassination plot by the Iraqi government, targeting former president James MacIntyre."

Whoa. Whoa. Whoa.

"He's traveling to Kuwait with his wife and two of his sons to commemorate the allied victory in the first Gulf War."

A former president? A former president of the United States?

Animal continues speaking, but I'm stuck here. This is so big. I suppose the SEALs and SAS members are used to this kind of thing, but me . . .

"We've learned through ASIS—"

"Forgive me, sir. ASIS?"

"Australian Secret Intelligence Service. The Aussie equivalent of the CIA."

I shift my gaze to Colonel Tyson.

"Yes," Animal says. "Their intelligence service discovered the plot, so the Australian government has offered their assistance. That's why we're conducting a joint mission."

"Thank you, sir."

"We've learned from ASIS that weapons and personnel to carry out this plan will arrive by sea via two surface units, which I will refer to as Surface Unit One and Surface Unit Two, and one submarine. The planners have been extremely thorough, because they've devised two separate transfers, each as backup for the other."

Two surface units and a submarine. Our last flight . . . This is exactly what we practiced on our last flight.

"It's an educated guess at this point, but we think Surface Unit One will off-load at the Port of Shuwaikh in southern Kuwait. The intel folks believe she's a civilian ship, a luxury yacht. They don't have a positive ID yet, so depending on when this whole thing goes down, we may or may not have surveillance photos ahead of time. Bottom line, you may be flying toward your target without knowing what it looks like. The Shadow Hunters will direct you in, but you may have to assess the drop zone almost instantaneously. The plan is to drop a team on their deck before they enter port."

This is why Eric is here. Now it makes sense why he's had the call for every SEAL training flight.

"The second transfer involves a submarine and Surface Unit Two," he says. "The submarine is from the Iraqi fleet. We believe it will transfer the personnel and weapons it carries to Surface Unit Two—once again, a ship from the civilian sector. The plan is to stop the submarine before it makes the transfer to Surface Unit Two."

And that must be why Commander Eichorn is here. Anti-submarine warfare for the strike group falls under his purview.

"The sub is a Russian-built Kilo class," Commander Eichorn says. His deep bass voice resonates in the low-ceilinged conference room. "What can you tell me about the Kilo class?"

I recall the facts, ones learned by rote at the Naval Academy, but rendered fresh by Stuart Grady, who stood in front of the *Lake Champlain* wardroom and launched into a Russian-submarine-fleet rap that ended with the profile for the Kilo class.

"Sir, the Kilo class is approximately two hundred and thirty feet in length, uses diesel-electric propulsion, has a max depth of three hundred meters, a surface speed from ten to twelve knots—"

"Okay," he says, holding up his hand. "Just checking." I notice Captain Magruder and Captain Plank nodding their heads.

Just checking what? That question had an awfully patronizing feel. I imagine the thoughts moving through Commander Eichorn's head. *She might be able to fly, but surely she doesn't know anything else. . . .* That's what it sounded like.

But I can't dwell here because Animal is speaking again. ". . . the Shadow Hunters will call you into the sub's position."

I turn my head to Eric and hold there. He raises his eyes, finally, to meet mine.

"Yeah, Lightning will coordinate and oversee the whole operation from his platform," Animal says, following the movement of my head.

Lightning?

"Although it would be nice to have him back on the ground with us where he belongs," Mike says, looking knowingly at Eric.

"Hey, our asses have been saved on more than one occasion because he's been in the air," Animal says.

"Yeah, yeah," Mike says. "But I've lost count of the number of times he's saved us on the ground. We need him back, that's all I'm saying." He glances once at Commander Kennan before returning to Animal. "And yes, I know I sound like a broken record on this, but it's true."

I look to Eric again, who meets my eyes, and my focus stays here. He doesn't waver as he watches the realization dawn on my face.

I finally drag my gaze back to Animal. "Sir, is Eric like . . . like you?"

"He wishes!" Animal laughs, and I notice the first hint of a smile from Commander Kennan.

Eric fidgets in his seat, not sharing Animal's enthusiasm.

"Sir, you wore your wings when I flew with you, but you were really . . ."

"A SEAL. Like him."

I turn my head slowly back to Eric. *Why didn't you tell me?*

"There are only a few who carry dual insignia like this," Animal says. "Remember, this whole program is still in the experimental stage. But yeah, he evaluates just like I do in addition to all the in-air coordination he does via the H-60."

Coordinating and evaluating. Evaluating . . . *"How's the evaluation coming?"* Jonas asked. *"I don't recall date nights being included in the metrics."*

This whole time . . . was he . . . ?

"You're not what I expected." That's what he said on the *Lake Champlain.* He knew I was his assignment.

Oh my god.

"Sir, speaking of evaluation," Jonas says, directing his comment to Animal. "I think it's clear to all of us here, especially after meeting with her today, that Lieutenant Denning has exceeded our expectations in terms of qualifications and gained our confidence to carry out this mission. So

I'm having trouble with the fact that Lieutenant Marxen has argued so vehemently against her selection for this role."

What?

I turn to Eric. This can't be true.

"Lieutenant Marxen, I know this meeting has convinced several of us who have been on the fence," Admiral Carlson says. "Has your decision changed based on what you've learned today?"

Our eyes lock and I wait for him to come forward with his support as he has always come forward.

But did he really argue *against* my selection?

Admiral Carlson just verified what Jonas stated, though.

He knew about Ian. He knew I panicked. He knew about my trouble during the search for Knight Rider. And he obviously shared his reservations with everyone at the table.

Which means I really *was* being evaluated by him. The entire time. And he never told me.

And he never told me he was a SEAL.

What else hasn't he told me?

And what about us? What was that? Was it real? My throat burns as my eyes search his in vain, searching for the man I thought I knew. The one I thought I could trust.

And Jonas? He's been painted as the bad guy. *"He's not to be trusted,"* Eric had said.

"Eric?" Admiral Carlson asks again. "Has your decision changed?"

Eric looks at me directly when he answers. "No."

I recoil as if he's slapped me in the face.

"She's not the one for this mission," he says.

My insides turn to glue, my head moving side to side in disbelief at his betrayal.

She's not the one for this mission. . . . How could he stoop to this? Like *tentative* flying. Is that what this is? It's so wrong. And it's so not him. But how do I know it's not him? Do I really know him at all?

I swallow hard. *Keep it together, Sara.* Not a soul at the table realizes I'm breaking apart inside.

"Eric, I'm afraid I'm going to have to pull rank on this one," Admiral Carlson says. "She's our man . . . I mean, person."

I turn my head to Admiral Carlson, who looks slightly embarrassed.

And then my eyes move to the person who really did champion my selection. Jonas gives me a small, apologetic smile. But then something occurs to me.

"Excuse me, sir?" I say, turning to Animal. My voice is shaky and I have to pause, taking a full breath to steady myself. "What about the second pilot dilemma? I'm not allowed to sign for the aircraft."

"*That* was never an issue," he says, confirming my earlier suspicions. "I'll fly with you when it's time. These missions are need-to-know only, so until you're an aircraft commander, I'll sign for the aircraft. But it should only be a couple of months until you have that designation, so I don't expect we'll have to do this but once."

"Sir, what's the time frame for this mission?" I ask, my voice still not as stable as I would like.

"Still trying to nail that down. It could be weeks."

"How will I know?"

"You'll need to keep this for starters, just as all of us here at the table will," he says, passing a cell phone down the table for me. Sleek and silver, it looks more like a credit card holder than a phone. "And this is a twenty-four/seven thing. We have to be able to reach you no matter where you are. The text will read all ones when it's time. Obviously, if we're at sea, it won't be an issue. But if not, wherever you are when you get the message, you need to hightail it to the *KC*."

"And you'll be there?"

"I'll probably be delivered by yours truly here," he says, motioning to Eric. "We'll brief and fly from the *Kansas City*."

Yours truly. Yours truly. Nothing true about him. My eyes squeeze shut for just a moment, my hands gripping the sides of my seat.

"But, couldn't you just fly it then, sir?" I ask, returning my gaze to him. "You could do all of these missions."

"Because first, I'm not always going to be on the West Coast and second, you're the better stick."

Most guys would never admit that. Not ever. But I doubt SEALs lack much in the way of self-esteem, and Animal's job is to evaluate. He has just given his honest opinion and I doubt he would have said it if he didn't mean it.

I'm floored and flattered at the same time.

I think this through for a moment. "Sir, what about aircrew?"

"I think you already know the answer to that."

Lego and Messy, of course.

Animal turns to Admiral Carlson. "Sir, that's all I have unless you or anyone else needs to add anything."

Admiral Carlson looks to everyone at the table before answering. "No, that's all we have." He then turns to me. "Lieutenant, any further questions for us?"

"No, sir."

The voice I hear next is Eric's and it cuts like—

Lightning . . . He never told me . . .

"Sir," Eric says, "I'll escort her to the flight deck."

I look at him directly. Why would he want to do that? What more could he possibly need to say to me? Or is it that he thinks I'm incapable of finding my way back to the flight deck . . . just as I'm incapable of completing this mission?

"That won't be necessary," I say sharply. "I can find it myself."

I hurriedly push my chair back and storm out to the passageway, nearly crashing into Greg in the process.

"Are you ready to head back?" he asks.

"Yes, yes," I say, stammering, my mind pummeled from the hurt and anger that spar for top emotion.

I thought he'd played me once, that day in a dark passageway under a dirty ball cap. Until he convinced me otherwise.

But there can be no pretense of mistaken identity this time. Now I know.

35

"Sara, please come to dinner," Em says. She stands next to my bunk, gently squeezing my shoulder.

"My stomach's still not right," I say.

"I don't buy it. What the hell is wrong? I mean, what is *really* wrong?"

I can't tell Em about the meeting, but I've been brushing her off for two days now. She's worried and it's easy to see why. I haven't left my bunk and have had no interest in eating. I've lied and told our detachment I've been sick—weak excuse, I know. Weak, in general. My eyes sting; I'm beyond upset with myself for reacting like this. For allowing myself to be reduced to this state.

I owe her more than this, though. I owe *myself* more. *You can't let him do this to you.*

With budding resolve, I turn my head to Em, thinking how strong I'm going to be, how I'm going to play it off. But those mothering eyes of hers turn on, the ones that know I'm struggling, and I crumble.

"Eric . . ." It's all I can manage.

"Oh, no. But how? You haven't seen him, have you?"

"I did—on a flight two days ago."

"But I thought . . . how can anything be wrong?"

I have to look away, focusing on the overhead instead. "He's just not who I thought he was."

"Well, crap, Sara. That fuckin' sucks."

I put my hands over my eyes, like this will make it all go away.

"Hold on just a moment," she says. I hear our stateroom door open and close. She returns in less than a minute.

"Here; the alcohol will have to wait until we pull in." I roll over and she's standing next to our bunk with a steaming cup of hot chocolate.

I'm so screwed up emotionally, this brings tears to my eyes.

I lower myself to the floor, drop to my desk chair, and accept the sturdy mug. "Thanks." I take a long sip and it helps. "You're awesome, by the way."

"So—" she starts.

I'm saved from further questioning by Captain Magruder. His voice booms over the 1MC to address ship's company before we begin our transit through the Strait of Hormuz this evening. My ears perk up when he gets to the meat of his talk.

"Gentlemen, we are entering a combat zone. Practice time is over. From now on, missiles will be loaded in the launchers. We'll have real bullets in the Phalanx. The .50 cals will be manned and ready on the ship as well as in our aircraft. This is what we've been training for."

Em rolls her eyes as he signs off. "He's so ate up."

Normally, I would have replied with some smart-aleck comment, but it's been a sobering two days since my meeting on *Nimitz*. This is the no shit real deal. If we're dropping SEALs to a ship and a submarine to disrupt a weapons transfer and prevent would-be assassins from entering Kuwait, those guys are going to defend themselves.

Just this transit through the Strait of Hormuz is dicey. We'll run a gauntlet of Silkworm missile batteries entrenched in Iran, pointed across a channel only thirty-five miles wide.

And then, the Persian Gulf itself is extremely small, relatively speaking, for a U.S. Navy carrier strike group. At just six hundred miles long and two hundred miles across, there's not a lot of room to maneuver. And in this small space, crude oil tankers carrying 40 percent of all the world's seaborne traded oil move through tight shipping lanes amidst a bevy of potential terrorist threats in the form of light patrol boats, submarines, and even one-man rafts.

I stare at the curling wisp of steam that rises from my mug, wondering if I'm making too much of this. Emily is dismissive, but I hear the worry in the captain's voice.

And now, the worry rings clearly in my head, as well.

"So, what happened?" she asks.

"Em, I'm sorry. I'll tell you what happened one day, it's just not today, that's all."

"Is that why you said you'd cover Chad's duty when we pull in tomor-row?"

"Yeah. I just need some time by myself."

"Well, okay. Just let me know if you need anything, all right?"

The softer side of Emily always comes through when it matters. I shouldn't say soft, though. It's just the loyal friend side. We've had our moments, certainly, but when it counts, she has my back.

"If I were you, love, I'd watch my back," Jonas said. I wipe my hands against my face. He was right.

36

"Ma'am, you have a visitor on the quarterdeck," the petty officer of the watch tells me on the telephone.

We pulled into the port of Jebel Ali in the United Arab Emirates in the wee hours this morning, a facility that sits smack in the middle of nowhere. Our ship stands as the only terrain feature for miles in what looks like the world's largest flat dirt parking lot.

And he's come to see me.

I don't know what to think. Actually, I take that back. I don't *want* to think. It hurts too much.

But that part of me that clings to any semblance of respectability wants him to look me in the eye and own up—tell me to my face that he lied to me.

"I'll be right down," I say finally.

I don my black leather boots, adjust my khaki uniform, and walk as straight and tall as I can to the weather decks. Opening the hatch, I step outside into a blazing Middle Eastern sun, one that is thankfully poised to drop below the horizon. As I turn toward the large awning that acts as the entry and exit point to the gangplank, my eyes move to the lone empty road that leads away from the ship, a black strip of asphalt cutting a razor-sharp line through multicolored shipping containers, sprawling cranes, and finally, endless miles of bleak desert landscape.

As I round the corner, an unexpected, accented voice calls to me.

"G'day, Sara," Jonas says.

"Jonas?" My brain wasn't ready for this. I stare at him as I recalibrate.

He's dressed casually in jeans and a collared polo shirt and stands with his hands in his front pockets.

"Expecting someone else?" he asks.

"I don't know," I say, moving forward slowly.

"I just came to check on you. You didn't look too happy when you left *Nimitz.*"

I move off to the side a bit, away from listening ears on the quarter-deck, and stand next to the ship's railing. He follows, casually leaning back against the edge.

"It's fine . . . I'm fine," I say, pinching my eyes shut. *Why those words, Sara? Why those?*

"Would you like to talk about it?"

"No . . . I'd rather not." I look down at my hands, each rolling over the other.

"Let me guess, he said you shouldn't trust me, or something to that effect."

I offer a slight nod, but continue looking down.

"That's interesting coming from someone who was obviously less than forthcoming. Wouldn't you say?"

I finally look up to crystalline blue eyes, ones curiously without a hint of warmth, only truth.

"Why doesn't he trust you?" I ask. "Why the animosity?"

"Professional jealousy, I suspect." He turns toward me, one elbow leaning on the railing now. "We've worked together before."

"I know. He told me."

"Did he, now?"

"Just in passing."

"I see." In the light of the blinding setting sun, his eyes are the bluest I've ever seen, and they hold mine for several long moments. "But the jealousy, well, I think it's more than just professional, quite honestly."

I pivot slightly to face him, the inference floating there.

"Perhaps," I say. "But Mike and Peter react the same way around you."

"True enough. But the brother band of SEALs is a tight one. They're going to support him no matter what. Even someone who lured you into trusting them so they could get the information they needed."

I don't want this to be true. But I know he's right, damn it. I turn away from him and lean my forearms on the railing.

"Anyhow," he says, "I just thought you could use some support right now, from someone who's in your corner."

I clasp my fingers together, staring intently at them, as I try to think of a way to escape this conversation.

"You know, I was trying to put myself in your shoes during that meeting," he continues. "Having someone turn on you like that—"

A shift in movement on the gangplank catches my attention. Eric is almost halfway up the steps when he abruptly stops and grasps the railings. Looking at me and then to Jonas, who now wears a glib expression, his eyes erupt. He makes no move toward us, but I start to wonder how the railings are holding up against the crushing pressure of his grip.

But what am I feeling? Like a magnet, I only want to go in one direction. And it's not for the explanation I was seeking earlier, either.

Don't you move, Sara. Don't you dare.

He holds my gaze as he backs down the gangplank, all the way until he reaches the ground. I watch him as he turns and walks stiffly down the pier until he's lost from my sight.

"Hey," Jonas says, lightly touching my arm. "Do you want to get off the ship? Maybe get something to eat?"

I step back. "No . . . thanks," I say. "I'm on duty."

"I see. Well, maybe some other time then?"

"I have to get back," I say, walking backward toward the hatch.

"Are you going to be okay?"

"Yes . . . yes, I'll be fine." Wince.

"G'day then, love." He gives me a small salute before turning and casually sauntering down the gangplank.

I'm about to open the hatch when the petty officer of the watch calls over to me. "Ma'am, Senior Chief Makovich on the phone for you."

I return to the quarterdeck awning to take the call. "Ma'am, we need you down at the pier entrance," Senior says.

Senior is on duty like I am, although I wonder what he's doing at the pier entrance.

"What's wrong?" I ask.

"It's Commander Claggett. He's drunk and raising holy fuckin' hell down here."

37

The pier where we're moored is several hundred yards long, so I do an easy jog to get to the gate more quickly. I hear Commander Claggett's raised voice, cursing up a storm, from at least fifty yards away. He's wasted, and it's only late afternoon, the sun just now dropping below the horizon.

"Fuck!" Commander Claggett shouts. "I'd pay you if you hadn't lifted my goddamn wallet!"

I approach, slowing my jog to a walk, and look to Senior Chief Makovich for an explanation.

"He thinks the taxi driver stole his wallet," Senior says. "And the driver's pissed because he isn't getting paid."

"Sir," I say, trying to gain Commander Claggett's attention. "Sir, I'm going to find your wallet. I need you to sit here while I do that."

"The driver has my fuckin' wallet! That's the only place you need to look!"

"Sir, please, sit here," I say.

I grab his arm, maneuver him behind the small guard shack, and somewhat forcibly push him to sit. He's so inebriated, he's wobbly, so it isn't too difficult.

I turn my attention then to the driver. "Sir, excuse me, but this man seems to have misplaced his wallet," I say, indicating Commander Claggett. "Would you have any idea where that might be?"

The driver looks right past me.

"Sir?"

Nothing.

Hmm. "Senior, could you come here for a minute?"

Senior walks to my side and I act on a hunch. "Did you hear what I just asked this gentleman?"

He nods.

"Could you repeat it, please?"

"I don't speak Arabic, ma'am," Senior says.

I don't think that's the problem.

"In English, Senior," I say.

He gives me a strange look, but repeats my question in English, just the way I asked it, receiving an immediate response.

Son of a . . .

In broken English, the driver says he hasn't seen it.

I bet he lost his wallet well before he got into this taxi or—and I'm crossing my fingers here—he may have dropped it in the taxi itself.

"Can you ask the driver if I can look for it? Tell him I'd like to check the floorboards."

The driver already understands what I'm asking, but pretends to listen again. He gives Senior an immediate no.

"Could you tell the driver that if he has any hope of getting paid, I'm going to need to check his taxi."

After Senior explains, we get a begrudging yes.

I open the back door and start patting my hands along the floor mats. *Please be here. . . .*

I breathe a thankful sigh when my hand lands on leather. I pull out a wallet, but flip it open first to make sure it is indeed Commander Claggett's. I spy his military ID, but my eyes are drawn to the photo that's partially hidden behind it, probably loosened when the wallet fell.

But this can't be what I think it is.

I gently pull out the photo to confirm what I'm seeing, blinking to focus well on the young woman who stares back at me. She is probably my age and wears a flight suit. Strands of light blond hair blow across her cheeks, partially hiding her sky-blue eyes. She's laughing as she stands in the main cabin door of an H-46 helicopter.

"Did you find the wall—?" Senior says, looking over my shoulder.

"Senior . . . ?" I ask, motioning to the photo. "Who . . . ?"

A cloud passes over his face. "Um . . ." He looks back to Commander

Claggett, who is still seated behind the guard shack. After several long moments, he returns his gaze to me. "I'll tell you once we get him onboard."

I push the photo back behind his ID, then rifle through the wallet and find a one-hundred-dirham note. "Is this okay?" I ask the driver.

At least he decides to acknowledge me now that I'm waving money in his face. Well, not really acknowledge. He just reaches out, takes the money, jumps in his taxi, and screams away.

Senior and I escort Commander Claggett back to the ship and deposit him in his rack. He's snoring before we close the door.

My mind races as I follow Senior to the maintenance office. The woman . . . A woman in uniform. An expression of lighthearted joy on her face. How did this photo find its way into Commander Claggett's wallet?

Entering the maintenance office, Senior closes the door behind me. He motions for me to sit, then finds his own seat opposite, at his desk. With a heavy sigh, he leans back in his chair.

"Her name was Kara Hughes. She was assigned to the Sabercats."

I nod, encouraging him to go on.

"The commander, well, he was a lieutenant at the time, fell hard for her. They were engaged when that photo was taken."

My mouth opens wide . . . and stays open. No. I can't imagine it. Not in my wildest dreams can I imagine it. It's hard for me to picture him with a woman period, but a woman in uniform? Never.

"Impossible. That's impossible."

"She had blond hair . . . like you."

I shake my head.

"They didn't tell anyone about their status as a couple because they wouldn't have been allowed to fly together."

I'm still shaking my head. A couple? Commander Claggett? No. Not possible.

"You know I've survived three Class A mishaps," he says soberly.

My head stops moving and I feel a slow, squeezing sensation in my stomach. A sensation that moves toward a deep-rooted ache as my brain fast-forwards to an outcome I don't want to hear.

"We were flying cargo from Home Guard in San Diego to a frigate— hoist only—and she was pitchin' up a storm that day. He was at the controls. . . ." Senior stops and breathes deeply. "He was one of the best sticks in the squadron at the time. But it happened so fast. The right main mount snagged in the safety netting and we were pulled into one of the ship's stanchions. It ripped a hole in the airframe before we flipped over. One second I was giving hoisting calls, and the next, we were in the drink."

Senior stares ahead as he remembers, his voice pained and distant. "The bird only stayed on the surface for about thirty seconds before she went down. Lieutenant Hughes never got out."

"Oh, Senior . . ."

He takes another heavy breath, laced with grief.

"Believe it or not, Commander Claggett used to be a good guy, easy-going even, but he hasn't been the same since."

"Is that why—"

"Why he treats you like he does? I'd bet my life on it. You're the worst possible person he could have on this detachment."

"The worst?"

"Well, your resemblance to her is a bit uncanny, first of all. And then the names? Sara? Kara? I'll never forget when he first saw you at the squadron back home with a detachment roster in his hands. He looked at the name, looked at you, and it was like he'd seen a ghost."

I'm back to shaking my head. That's probably why he latched onto the nickname Lace so quickly. It had to be so much easier than spitting out the name Sara.

"And to make it worse, you're a great pilot, like he was. Although truthfully, I think he knows you're the better stick, just like we do. He's blamed himself for the accident, for killing her, and I can't help but wonder if in the back of his mind he thinks that if he'd had your skills, she'd still be alive."

"The holes in the ramp . . . that day . . . he didn't want to talk about it."

"That cut way too close to home."

"I had no idea. . . ."

My eyes lose their focus as I try to imagine Commander Claggett with a smile on his face, laughing with the woman who laughs in the photo. My eyes glass up and I blink quickly, but not in time for Senior not to notice.

"But Senior, that still doesn't explain why he treats me so badly."

"He can't let you in, Lieutenant. Don't you see? That grief is so raw, even three years removed, that if he did, he wouldn't be able to function. The further he can push you away by learning how to 'hate' you," and Senior puts his fingers in quotes here, "the further removed he can remain from his grief. He doesn't want to face it. Can't face it. And every day, you're front and center, reminding him of her, so he's doing the only thing he can to survive, I think."

"The drinking . . ."

"Excessive, right? There's a reason."

I put my elbows on Senior's desk and drop my head in my hands. Every horrible thought I've ever had about Commander Claggett disappears into the realm of fresh understanding. And the thing is, I understand the grief from which Commander Claggett is trying to hide far better than Senior realizes.

When I finally raise my head, Senior regards me, his arms folded in front of his chest. "I hope I was right in telling you that. With the squadron turnover, there's no one around who knows except me. But then, I figure, it's probably good for you to know. Like I said, I remember when he was just friendly Nick Claggett. He's in there somewhere."

I give Senior a long look. For a salty navy chief, he possesses a far bigger heart than I ever would have imagined.

38

"Sara, please," Em says. "Please come with me tonight. You need to get out. You need to get off this ship."

Most of the officers on the *Kansas City* are headed to Pancho Villa's, a Tex-Mex restaurant and nightclub housed in the Astoria Hotel in Dubai. This restaurant is a popular hangout with British and Australian expats, and therefore, just as popular with visiting U.S. Navy ships' personnel.

I haven't been inclined to do anything since we arrived in port and I certainly haven't wanted to leave the ship. Since I saw Eric two days ago, I've run for hours on the treadmill, climbed thousands of electronic feet on the stair climber, and pedaled far too many miles on the aerodyne bike.

I can't let it go—the hurt, the humiliation, the betrayal. But worst of all, I can't let go of him.

I've approached the problem by trying to sweat it out of my system. Sweat *him* out. But it's not working and I'm miserable.

I finally realize that I'm going to go stir crazy if I stay on this ship. Nothing is going to get accomplished here. And at the very least, if I go, it will make Em feel better.

"Okay, I'll go," I say, acquiescing. "I just need to run by Commander Claggett's room first to get the flight schedule approved for tomorrow."

"We're starting the runs to Fujairah, aren't we?" she asks.

"Yep. You're up for the first one."

"Sweet."

Fujairah, a coastal city in the United Arab Emirates, sits on the Gulf of Oman, about sixty miles east of us. We've been briefed that we'll be flying logistics runs and training hops to their airport throughout the next five months.

These flights are supposedly a great deal. The aircraft commanders who have flown them in the past say they often require overnight stays at the Hilton Hotel, complete with a swimming pool and buffet breakfasts. Em has been talking my ear off about these flights, how she can't wait to go, yadda, yadda, yadda.

This will be good for her, though. With all she's had to endure with me and the SEAL flights, she deserves this. And even though she and Zack have been flying far more than me over the last couple weeks, for some reason, Em is still falling far short on the flight hours as compared to Zack. Yeah, this will be good for her.

"Okay, give me a minute. I'll be right back."

When I enter Commander Claggett's room this time, I see a person sitting at his desk who ironically has erected more defensive layers than I have. Who used to be friendly and easygoing. Who laughed and joked. Who loved a woman.

It's bewildering for me to think of him like this after we've spent so much abrasive time together. So bewildering, I forget myself and just stand, gawking.

"So you're here for what?" he says.

"I . . ."

I have the flight schedule in my hand, yet I've forgotten completely it's the reason I'm here.

"Still sick?" He smirks.

"Uh, no . . . no, I'm not sick."

"What do you need then?"

"The flight schedule," I say, remembering. "I need you to sign the schedule, sir."

I hand it to him, he looks down, but snaps his head up almost immediately.

"This is not what we discussed. Zack takes this flight."

"But Emily's lower in flight hours."

"I know perfectly well where every pilot in this detachment stands on flight hours."

"But, sir—"

"Why are you arguing? I said who I want on the flight and that's it, end of story."

Em is going to be so disappointed. She was really looking forward to this. And she should be the one flying. The discrepancy in flight hours between her and Zack is glaringly obvious.

"I'm just trying to understand your reasoning, sir."

"What the fuck, Lieutenant!"

Why did I push it? *Damn it. Damn it. Damn it.*

But then, a normal officer in charge like Brian Wilcox would have explained his reasoning. Maybe cross-country navigation is a deficiency for Zack so he needs this particular flight more than Emily. I would get that. It would make sense.

"This is so goddamn simple! I tell you who goes on the schedule. You say, 'Yes, sir.' You type exactly what I tell you. You give it to me for signature. Period. Do you think you can handle that?"

Several thoughts cross my mind at once. I think of Emily's disappointment. She's put up with so much crap so far this cruise, always on the short end with flight hours and dealing with the embarrassment of being pulled from flights so I can take her place. And then Commander Claggett's treatment of me, as though I was less than everyone else, and playing that damned female card—*tentative, lacking assertiveness.* It makes me want to scream. And finally, I know as well as anyone how hard it is to lose someone. And not just that, but to feel responsible for it. God, I know. But this has to stop. The treatment of Emily. Of me. And it has to stop before he drinks himself to death.

I straighten and pull my shoulders back. "You didn't used to be like this," I say.

"What?" he says.

I have a choice now. I can say, "Never mind," and be on my way. But I don't.

"You weren't like this before."

"Before what? What the hell are you talking about?"

"I know about her. I know about Kara. And I'm so sorry, sir. Truly. But you can't treat other—"

I stop mid-sentence, watching the blood drain from his face, realizing what I've just done. I've plunged a dagger in his heart, and I instantly regret it. Because for a brief moment, I have direct access to his soul. I see it in his eyes. The love is there. The agony. And I've just intruded on something so intensely private, I have to look away.

"Get out," he says so quietly that it's worse than if he had yelled it.

"Sir, I'm sorry—"

"Get out," he says sharply.

I start to step backward. "Sir, really, I didn't mean—"

"Get the fuck out of my room! Get out now!" he shouts.

Oh god. Oh god. Oh god. What have I done?

I turn and grapple with the door handle. *Come on, come on!* The door finally opens and I stumble into the passageway, the door slamming behind me.

I stand with my back against the bulkhead, my breath stuck in my throat. What the hell did I just do? I went so far out of bounds with him. So far. Nothing he's ever said or done to me comes even close to what I just did to him. What was I thinking?

And then I hear it. Soft at first, but eventually loud enough that there's no mistaking it. The sounds of a grown man crying.

Oh, god . . .

I flee to my room.

"What the hell?" Em asks.

I move right by her and rush into the head, locking the door behind me. Dropping to the ground, I cover my eyes and let the tears come. For many reasons they come. Commander Claggett's tragic loss is just the straw.

To cry is to admit I made a grievous error in judgment, erroneously lowering my guard. But ultimately, despite four days and nights of denial, it's an admission that my heart is, in fact, broken.

39

Em waits for me. I thought she'd be long gone by the time I finally returned to the room, utterly spent.

Using the intuition of a best friend, she doesn't ask me a thing. Instead, she acts like nothing happened and we're still going out. She knows she needs to get me off this ship. *I* know I need to get me off this ship. Walking into a packed nightclub wouldn't normally be my first choice in a case like this, but I really don't have a say in the matter.

Once we arrive, Emily only has eyes for the bar. Although, she does pause at the entrance. "Are you going to be okay?" she asks.

"I think so."

We step inside and enter another world—music pulsing, dance floor thumping, disco lights flashing. She leads me through the throng, which includes the majority of our ship's company and many officers I recognize from the Hail and Farewell in Hong Kong.

While we wait at the bar for her margarita, I take in the very Western attire of most of the female patrons. These Aussies and Brits flaunt miniskirts, sleeveless tops, and plunging necklines. Em was right about that. . . .

When we first pulled into Jebel Ali, the executive officer personally spoke with us—just us, not the men—about the importance of wearing conservative attire when leaving the ship for liberty. He *highly recommended* long pants and long sleeves.

Em complied, kicking and screaming the whole way as she left the ship the first night. To her chagrin, she departed wearing one of my long-sleeved blouses.

I remember the eruption when she returned. "The XO can kiss my ass on the conservative dress!" she shouted. "Oh, my fuckin' god. You should have seen the Aussies and the Brits. I don't think they got the fuckin' memo!"

I was surprised she didn't rip the buttons out of my shirt in her haste to remove it.

Of course, conservative attire isn't an issue for me, so I'm comfortable as a clam tonight in my jeans and long-sleeved white oxford.

"You need to eat," Em says, shouting to be heard above the fray. She lifts her margarita glass from the granite countertop. "Let's get a table."

My eyes burn. From the bathroom floor to a crowded nightclub in the space of an hour. I'm starting to think I might have to join Em with the margaritas.

We've taken two steps away from the bar when I run into Rob Legrand and Brian Wilcox.

"Hey, Sara," Rob says, leaning into my ear so he can be heard.

Brian chooses to wave instead of shouting.

I say hello in return, but I doubt they heard me. Behind us, the crowd on the dance floor moves as a singular gyrating organism to music that makes my lungs vibrate.

"This is my roommate, Emily."

While Brian and Rob shake Emily's hand, I begin a slow scan to find open seating. My dead heart lurches when my eyes settle on Eric. He sits with his detachment pilots in a booth in the far corner.

"Hey, Em!" a man shouts, approaching her from behind. "Fancy seeing you here!"

She turns and gives him a hug, and they begin a loud conversation as if they've known each other for years. I'm guessing they met last night.

I can't turn away from Eric, though. He doesn't look good.

Brian and Rob have followed my gaze.

"So what did you do to him?" Rob asks. "Did you kick him or something?" He laughs at his joke until he sees my expression.

"No, he kicked me," I say flatly.

"Ah," he says, retreating.

It's an awkward moment and I'm not even going to try to cover it up.

Brian steps closer, leaning into me. "He told me about the two of you."

I shift to face him. "What?"

"In confidence, of course."

I try to appear indifferent, unaffected, but Brian sees right through it.

"I know it's none of my business, but whatever happened between you two . . . well, he's devastated."

Devastated? *Devastated? I'm* the one he betrayed! I opened my soul to him! I shared my deepest secret and he used it against me! And *he's* devastated? Why, because he lost his go-to girl for sex on this deployment? Damn him. . . .

I peer over Brian's shoulder. Eric stares absently at a water glass he twirls on the table, his demeanor a far cry from what it was in the meeting. The pilots seated with him are engaged in animated conversation, but Eric remains isolated and withdrawn, clearly detached from anything happening around him, looking . . . devastated.

I turn back to Brian, leaning close to his ear. "Brian, have you known him long?"

"Since I taught him to fly the H-60 so many years ago. I was an instructor pilot then."

"Did you just teach him or did you really know him?"

Brian steps away to let a group of three squeeze behind him on their way to the bar.

"We became great friends," he says, leaning in again. "So much so that I know his background—all of it." He looks at me knowingly.

"But I thought—"

"Just the squadron skippers, right? Normally, that's the case. But we're close, so he confided in me about that, even before I was selected as one of their pilots."

"You were . . . ?"

"Yeah. We've been through a lot together, and I'll be flying with Eric again whenever this mission gets called," he says, pointing to the silver cell phone at his waist.

I look down at mine, the one I've worn dutifully 24/7 just as Animal ordered. Running my thumb along the smooth, thin edge, I think of Eric confiding in Brian, considering him a close friend. It doesn't match with a person who could deceive.

"Do you trust him?" I ask finally, looking up.

He responds without hesitation. "Absolutely."

I put my fingers to my temples and squeeze. I'm going to fly apart if I don't.

Em waves her arms over her head to gain my attention. While Brian and I were talking, she has moved away and found a table.

"I, uh, I need to go," I say.

Brian nods. "You take care, okay?"

As I walk toward Em, the energy ratchets higher. She's speaking animatedly with two men I've never seen before and motions for me to sit while continuing her conversation.

But they beat a hasty departure when Jonas trumpets his arrival. "Hello, ladies!" He's accompanied by Bartholomew and Collin. Admittedly, this trio is an intimidating one.

"Mind if we join you?" Jonas asks.

"Are you kidding?" Emily says. She hurriedly sits, adjusting her position to make room.

Bartholomew and Collin take seats next to her and Jonas moves in next to me. I slide over until I'm pinned against the wall.

"Nice that you're finally off the ship, eh?" he says.

"Oh my god, Sara. They have accents!" Emily giggles.

"Em, this is Bartholomew, Collin, and Jonas," I say. "Guys, this is my roommate, Emily."

"How do, love?" Collin asks.

"I do fine," she says, starstruck. Emily is melting in her chair. How embarrassing.

"So how are you?" Jonas says.

He has just drawn a demarcation line between those on the other side of the table and us. With a turn of the head and a hush of the voice, he has transformed what was just a horribly loud, overcrowded pub into a small, intimate, private space. He speaks to me now as if we're the only two present. I feel myself backing into the wall, though.

"What's the matter, love?" he says. "You look uncomfortable."

"I . . . I need to leave."

"Shall we slip outside?" he asks, sliding over and standing.

I rush to escape the seat, instantly feeling better as I stand. But now, a rock-and-a-hard-place conundrum. I don't want to leave the "security" of a crowded room, but I'd do almost anything to gain a little space between me and Jonas—the space that collapses as his hand wraps around mine.

"You'd do well with some fresh air," he says.

"No, I think I'd rather go by myself, thanks," I say, trying to pull my hand away.

He holds it firmly. "Are you sure, love? You oughtn't be wandering alone outside."

"I'm sure—"

"Let go of her," Eric says, appearing out of nowhere. The command is growled.

"Well now, I don't believe this is any of your business," Jonas says.

"I said let her go." It's a tone that brooks no argument—except from me.

"I don't need your help," I say, looking at Eric in defiance.

I turn to Jonas. "Let go of me."

"Of course, love," he says, releasing his hand. "Anything you ask."

"Sara—" Eric says.

"I have nothing to say to you."

I turn, needing a quick exit. Through the horde on the dance floor, I spy the lobby doors and hurry toward them, dodging, pushing and shoving partygoers en route.

Once outside, I stare up at the large, concrete barrier that surrounds the hotel, creating a buffer between it and the bustling streets that form the heart of Dubai's shopping district. Within the barrier, large potted palms provide the only texture and relief to the otherwise stark masonry that forms the hotel's outer facade.

I decide to stay within the hotel borders, moving hastily around the oblong-shaped high rise. As I do, I adjust to the relative silence, the concrete walls muting the sound of the city just beyond. I pass no one as I walk, the path eerily deserted, and Jonas's comment about wandering outside alone begins to gain a bit of leverage.

Reaching the rear of the hotel, I dismiss the thought, pacing in frustration, stomping on shadows. And then . . . a recognizable shadow. Eric's crosses mine as he moves toward me.

"Go away," I say.

"Please, let me—"

"I don't want to hear it."

I turn away, trapped. Hemmed in by the high walls.

"Let me explain."

"There's nothing to explain!" I say, rounding on him. "You've lied to me from the beginning!"

"I haven't—"

"Tell me, how did I fare in your evaluation after we made love? What were the metrics for that!"

He steps forward, but I raise my hands in warning. "Don't . . . just . . . don't."

"I haven't lied," he says calmly.

"How can you possibly say that? Shall I make a list? You aren't a pilot—"

"I am a pilot. I went through flight training just like you. I belong to the Shadow Hunter squadron. I do their mission. All of it."

"And you never told me you were a SEAL, which is the same as lying in my book."

"I wanted to tell you. I did. I just wasn't ready."

"Not ready? Why not? It's part of who you are. A big part. Why wouldn't you tell me something like that?"

"Because there's so much. There's so much about me . . ." He stops, pressing his lips together. "Look, I thought I'd have more time because I didn't think they were going to call you into that meeting. I didn't think they were going to pick you, which means you wouldn't have found out about me, and I could have waited for the right time to tell you everything."

"Why didn't you think they'd pick me?"

"Because I argued against it. I argued against it and I can usually get people to see my way."

"Using information I gave you in confidence!" My hands go to my hips, furious. "Eric, I trusted you! I'd never told anyone what happened with Ian and you just—"

"They knew Ian had drowned; I only confirmed that you'd come close."

"But why bring it up in the first place?

"Because I needed something concrete. I was grasping—"

"For a reason to keep me off the mission? But I can do this!"

"I didn't say you couldn't do it."

"Well then what? You think I might panic? Is that it?"

"No. I know you can keep your head. That was never a problem."

"But you tried to keep me off! Why?"

He looks to the heavens before returning his gaze to me. "There's so much about this mission . . . so much you can't see."

"Then enlighten me," I say, crossing my arms.

He sets his mouth and his eyes close briefly. But when he opens them, it's clear he's not going to give me an answer.

"Then what? My flying?"

"No."

"My systems knowledge?"

"No."

He wipes his face, looking to the sky again.

"My pub knowledge? What?"

"None of the above. You were by far and away the best candidate."

"But then—"

"In fact," he says, "I spent so long arguing in your favor that when I changed my mind, they'd already been convinced. There was no going back."

"But why wouldn't you support me?" I say, moving my hands emphatically. "Why would you change your mind?"

My voice has risen and I'm not sure how it got so loud.

"Why would the others agree and you not? And—"

"Because they're not sending the woman they've fallen in love with on a mission that could get her killed!" Eric has to raise his voice to be heard over me.

I step back, my ranting stopped cold.

"What did you say?" I whisper.

His arms drop to his sides, his palms outturned. "Sara, I love you."

I stand, dazed, like a boxer on the receiving end of a swift uppercut. My brain churns, processing the words. But it's not the words themselves that have rendered me mute. It's the incredulity at my reaction—I *want* to believe him.

No, you can't, Sara. Fool me once . . . Fool me twice . . . You know the saying.

But time-tested adage or not, I want to believe him so badly, it hurts. With effort, I move my head side to side, but he stands unmoving, his gaze steady.

"Are you trying to shred my heart now for good measure?" I say, my voice strained. "Well, congratulations. Well done."

"No, I—"

"Please go." I pull my eyes from his and stare at the ground. It's a struggle to keep my head down, not to look. The wait is agonizing.

I hear shuffling. In my peripheral vision, his shadow recedes. And with it, he takes my heart, pulling it like the loose end on a skein of yarn, while I watch it unravel.

"Just one thing," he says, turning.

I look up to see him removing his hand from his pocket. "Please do this one thing for me." He extends his arm, something clutched in his fist. "You can hate me all you want, but—"

"Hate you?" My head moves of its own accord this time, shaking side to side. "I don't hate you." And then, the words pour out. The ones I never intended to say, but have felt all along. "Eric, I love you. I know it like I know to breathe. That's why this hurts so much."

His hand moves back to his pocket. "What?" he says.

He walks toward me and I have nowhere to go, my back pressed to the wall. I look down at my feet, his legs moving into my field of view.

"You love me?" he asks.

My eyes rise to meet his and I lift my hand. "Ever since you gave me this," I say, indicating the rubber band I've worn on my wrist, the one I haven't taken off since I left the *Lake Champlain*.

He moves closer still, his breath whispering across my cheeks, his body radiating a welcoming warmth. For a long time we stand, our eyes fixed, while my defenses melt into an ignominious puddle at my feet. That mythical magnetic force swells between us, the pull indescribable . . . and inescapable. And then, my lips are on his. Our mouths move together and I breathe him in. Strong hands slide across my back, pulling me toward him, and I wrap my arms tightly around his neck.

I revel in the exquisite pressure of his chest pressed solidly against mine and delight in the hands that move firmly around my waist. I savor his taste, his touch, his kiss. His kiss . . . something so achingly poignant about his kiss.

He leans back just slightly, looking directly into my watering eyes. "I love you so much," he whispers. "Please know this."

I swallow. *Fool me once . . . Fool me twice . . .*

Well, call me a fool, then, because if this isn't true love, I don't know what is.

"I know," I say.

I really do.

40

A steady cricket hum, the soft rustling of palms in the mild evening breeze—the perfect accompaniment to a long, languorous kiss. A kiss of reacquaintance. A sensual exploration of our lips and mouths, his fingers gently skimming my cheek, and slipping through my hair.

Because of the length of this silent interplay, his voice, though soft, startles.

"I'm so sorry," he says, drawing back. "For everything."

He wraps his arms loosely around my shoulders, but keeps me close.

"I acted out of turn," he continues. "I hope you can forgive me."

I reach up, taking both of his hands in mine, and pull them low between us, lacing my fingers through his.

"I forgive you," I say with a squeeze to his hands.

His lips turn upward ever so slightly.

"But will you promise me something?" I ask.

I step back just a bit so I can better look him in the eyes, which are well dilated in the low light. "You have to let me do my job," I say.

He remains utterly still, but for the movement of his eyes, which rapidly search mine. I know something bothers him, something about this mission in particular. But I see it in his expression when he closes the door on whatever reservation it was he carried.

"I promise," he says.

I exhale.

"Actually, I owe you more than just one apology," he says. "I wasn't allowed to say anything about the evaluation, but I should have told you the rest. My job . . ."

He looks down at our hands, lacing and relacing his fingers through mine, and in the background, I'm putting the pieces together. "The languages," I say. "Arabic, Pashto, Farsi . . ."

"I was sent to language school. Several, actually."

"The scars . . ."

He nods.

"I still don't understand, though. Why not tell me?"

He looks down at our hands for some time before raising his head again.

"Tell me honestly," he says. "That night with Commander Egan, did I frighten you?"

I hesitate, which tells him all he needs to know.

"And the run-in with Jonas on *Nimitz*?"

I nod this time.

"I hated that you had to see that. It's a side of me that . . . well, I'm struggling with that side. It helps me do my job as a SEAL, do it very well in fact, but . . ."

"But what?"

"I was worried"—and the worry is absolutely there in his expression—"that this part of me would drive you away." He pauses, looking away, as if seeking the solace of the shadows. "Sara, when I do my job, it doesn't take me to a good place."

"But—"

"No, just hear me out. On my last mission . . . eleven people . . . we entered a room with eleven people . . . and when we left, they were dead. They were dead . . . all of them. And I don't remember how it happened. I can't let myself remember. And then I get awards for this and I'm praised for it. And no one understands that it wasn't me. Ask Mike. Ask Pete. They have to do the debriefs because I can't recall it. I can't recall anything. I read the after-action reports and I don't know who they're talking about. I become . . . I don't know . . . someone else . . . something else. I don't know."

He releases my hands, wiping his face, perspiration running down his hairline.

"I've worked so hard to control this person . . . this thing . . . whatever it is . . . and I was just barely getting a handle on it. Barely. So when I was offered the flying job, I jumped at it. I needed to get away, to bring myself back to . . . well, me. And I was finally finding that with Brian and

Rob and the guys. I could just let go and be easy. Be me. And when I met you, I was in that place. A good place."

He scans my eyes, and I imagine him cataloging every fleck of color in them, ordering them just so.

"But that's the thing," he says. "Just when I was getting a handle on it, learning how to control this, along you come—the catalyst for everything that wants to explode inside me. You've only seen a glimpse."

He takes my hands again. "I've put off this talk with you because for you to really know me, I'm going to have to open that side to you. So you know what you're getting into. So you know what I'm capable of. And I'm terrified that once you see it—"

"Stop," I say, putting a finger over his lips. "Don't say any more."

I lower my hand, placing it over his heart, the beat so very strong. "Eric, when I said I loved you, I meant all of you."

His hands curl around mine, pulling them close to his chest, his eyes glistening. He leans in, a delicate kiss, sending an exhilarating charge surging through me. And this feeling of "electricity" causes me to laugh—something I couldn't have imagined just twenty minutes ago.

"What is it?" he asks.

I look up to him, raising my eyebrows. "Lightning?"

"Yeah," he says. "I got that in BUD/S."

Basic Underwater Demolition/SEAL training. School for SEALs. *Now* his comment about Mike makes sense. "You said you went to school with Mike. I didn't understand it at the time."

"Oh, you caught that. Impressive."

"So why Lightning?"

"Well, like I mentioned earlier, I tend to go to the extreme a lot of the time. I guess I should say there's a lot of energy inside for me to control. It was the guys' not-so-subtle way of telling me I need to lighten up."

"Are you serious?"

"Yeah, why?"

"That's why I was christened with my name."

"Lace?"

"Yeah. Em is always on me about lightening up. She thought if I wore lace underwear, that would do the trick."

He laughs, the sound ringing preciously sweet.

"So she started calling me Lace and when she figured out I hated it, well, it was game over. She told the other pilots, who told the aircrew, and the rest is history."

"So we make quite the intense pair, I guess," he says, reaching his hand to my face, holding it there.

But then something flits through my memory. We're standing here, breaking down walls, but a brick remains, probably a stupid, irrational brick, but it weighs just the same.

"What is it?" he asks.

So perceptive . . .

"I just . . . this is so stupid."

"Please, I want to hear it, whatever it is. I don't want anything between us."

I clear my throat, already embarrassed about what I'm about to say. "Well, I saw you at the Hail and Farewell—"

"You were there?"

I nod.

"I was hoping to see you there," he says. "I was looking for you."

"Really?" My question is delivered with a frown as I remember who I saw him with.

"What's this?" he says, touching my lips.

"Well, to be honest, I was looking for you, too. But when I found you . . . well, you were busy." My attempt at keeping the hurt out of my voice fails miserably.

"I don't recall being busy."

And then it all tumbles out. "You were standing with these women, three of them, and they were gorgeous, and you were talking and laughing and taking pictures and—"

"Hold on. Hold on," he says, raising his hands. "Wait a second. Three women . . ." He searches for it and then the light clicks. "Okay, I remember. But did you see Stuart, Rob, and Ken there, too?"

"I did."

"And yet you assumed I was the interested party in all of this?"

"Well . . . I . . . weren't you?"

"Sara," he says, his tone sounding like my mother when she would scold me. "Those women were Stuart, Rob, and Ken's wives. They flew in from California. It was planned months ago."

I blink, startled with the pronouncement.

"Remember how I had to leave to stand Ben's duty? His wife came, too. The four of the them."

"Their wives?" Sheepishly, I slink back against the wall, wallowing in embarrassment.

And he lets me, too.

"I just thought . . ."

"You thought wrong," he says with a forgiving smile. "I gather you were a little jealous?"

"A lot jealous, if you must know."

He smiles, taking my hands in his, and then it's my turn to notice something, a twitch in his expression.

"What is it?" I ask.

"You're fast surpassing me on the perceptive bit."

"What is it?" I say.

"I have to confess, you aren't the only one who's felt jealous."

"You felt jealous? Who—"

"Jonas." He almost chokes on the name. "I saw you on the ship with him that day and then tonight . . ."

I shake my head. "It's nothing."

He sounds relieved at first, but it doesn't last long.

"I didn't know if . . . or what that was or . . ."

"It was nothing. I think the attention I've been getting from him has more to do with you than me."

He nods in rigid acknowledgment. "We have a history, one I haven't told you about yet. And if he was looking for a way to get to me, he certainly found it. I kept trying to convince myself that that was the reason, but the way you looked at him that first time during the brief . . . you just stared."

"Oh, that," I say, remembering. "I hadn't had the chance to talk with you about Ian yet. Jonas's eyes remind me of Ian's. That's all. And when I was looking at him, all I could see was Ian's face. I just sort of forgot myself."

"But just the fact that he was alone with you. I was so worried. You have no idea."

"Why does he make you so nervous?"

I jump as a voice emerges from the shadows. "Why does who make you so nervous?" Jonas says.

I whip my head around to see him approaching with a swagger.

With two quick strides, Eric stands in front of me.

"This is a private conversation," Eric says.

"Ah, but I'm the topic of the moment, aren't I?"

Jonas moves forward and Eric tenses.

"Ah, look," Jonas says. "Lightning's ready to strike. Always a flair for the dramatic." He gives a *tsk-tsk* sort of look. "If I didn't know better, I'd think you were trying to scare her away from me."

"What do you want?" Eric says.

"Just checking on Sara. I was worried when she didn't return."

"She's fine. You can go now."

I had always reserved the image of a taut rubber band, stretched to the breaking point, for Commander Claggett. Not anymore. I reach for Eric's hand, which he cinches around mine as he takes a step back, pulling me closer to him in the process.

But then, all three of our heads move at once to look at the phones vibrating on our waist belts.

Unclipping mine, I see a straight row of 1s across the screen. Jonas shoots Eric a cold look, returns the phone to his belt strap, and sprints away.

"We need to go," Eric says.

"So this is it? Right now?"

"This is it."

His eyes are anxious.

"Eric, it'll be okay. I just need to go tell Emily."

"Okay." He looks at his watch. "But here, take this." He reaches into his pocket and produces . . . an earpiece?

"What's this?"

"It's a radio," he explains, unfurling a thin wire. "For you. To wear during the mission." He hands it to me—a tiny earbud, the wiring, and a push-to-talk switch.

I raise my eyebrows. "To talk to . . . ?"

"Just me."

"I see." I turn the radio over in my fingers. "And why . . . ?"

"Well . . . I'm sure everything's going to be fine, but just in case, I'd feel better if we had direct communication. If you need anything, I'm just a click away."

I hold the earbud and stretch the wiring until it goes taut, considering this.

"Okay," I say finally, bunching the radio into my fist again.

He takes my hand. "Oh, and no one can know you're wearing this," he adds.

"But why—"

"You'll know later . . . I think. I hope I'm wrong."

"What—"

"Come on, we have to go."

41

When I arrive on the flight deck, Animal is already here, perched on top of Sabercat 55 in the middle of his preflight inspection. He gives me a small salute before returning to the business of closing up an inspection panel.

I look across the hangar, not seeing any of our pilots, and I wonder who's going to man the tower for flight quarters. Em and I returned from Pancho Villa's together, but she's sound asleep right now. I shift my gaze up to the tower, and lo and behold, I see Commander Claggett. Strange. He never stands tower duty. Our eyes meet, but only for a moment because I turn when Lego approaches.

Both he and Messy have emerged from the aircraft cabin. They've been carrying the sleek silver phones, too.

"Hey, ma'am," Lego says. "Did you see who we're flyin' with?"

"Yeah."

"You don't sound surprised," he says, perplexed.

I shrug.

"So what's goin' on?"

"We'll get the brief here in a second, but I'm pretty sure we're fast roping tonight. It's the real deal, too. That's the reason for the phones and everything."

"Fuck," he says.

"Well, it shouldn't be any different than the training flights, so just go with it and we'll be in, out, and done."

"I'm all for in, out, and done," he says.

Although during the brief Lego and Messy realize immediately this isn't your average flight. Their eyes grow to the size of watermelons when Animal hands me an M9 pistol.

And not just any M9. I run my fingers over the polished wood grip, the one with the carved initials, RP.

"Sir, is this . . . ?"

"Captain Plank's?" Animal answers. "He sends it with his regards."

I stare at it, overwhelmed by the gesture. "Wow," I mouth.

"It's loaded, so handle with care," Animal says. "You can wear it here, in this pocket on your survival vest."

I unzip my pocket, slide the gun into place, and zip it closed, feeling unduly heavy on my left side. Animal tucks his gun away, but unlike me, he carries what most SEALs do, a Sig Sauer 9mm P226 model.

"And you two have the .50 cal ready like I asked, right?" he says, looking to Lego and Messy.

"Yes, sir, all set," Lego says.

"Okay, the meat of the brief is this," Animal says. "We're flying to *Nimitz* first to pick up the SAS crew." He points to the map spread on the maintenance officer's desk. "*Nimitz* is three hundred miles from here, eighty miles to the northeast of Bahrain."

"But, sir, I saw three members of the SAS team not even an hour ago in Dubai," I say. "How are they on *Nimitz*?"

"They're not yet. The Shadow Hunters are shuttling them there now. Mike's squad is already onboard." He turns to Lego. "We'll need the aux tank for this."

"Got it," Lego says. "We'll pull it on *Nimitz* then?"

"Yeah, we'll drop it there before we load the teams, and then fill the main tanks."

Our auxiliary fuel tank allows us to significantly extend our range, and it would definitely be needed if *Nimitz* is three hundred miles away.

"Then it's a fifty-mile transit west-southwest to our first target—a submarine—right about here," he says, moving his finger over the map. "No fast roping this one. We'll do a low hover and deliver the guys via Zodiac instead. The Shadow Hunters will have the call."

"Do they actually know where the sub is?" I ask.

"The intel guys know the approximate location of the rendezvous point. Due to time constraints, we'll have to drop the SAS team at that location, whether we've confirmed the sub's position or not. The Shadow Hunters will stay on site and direct the Zodiac from there."

When an H-60 aircrew searches for a submarine, they drop sonobuoys in the water to listen for their target. But to accurately pinpoint its location takes time. They must spread a pattern of buoys and triangulate positions from there. No easy task.

"But what about Surface Unit Two?" I ask.

"The plan is to engage the sub before Surface Unit Two gets there. The timetable from the intel guys has them arriving separately. But if she shows, the Shadow Hunters will still be on scene to provide cover."

"Got it."

"We'll then head back to *Nimitz,* refuel, pick up Mike's squad, and fly to Surface Unit One. She's a civilian superyacht, a nice one, complete with flight deck."

"A superyacht?" Lego says. "Like how big are we talkin'?"

"Four hundred and fifty feet."

Lego whistles.

"Her name's *Twister* and she's cruising about one hundred eighty miles northwest of *Nimitz,* right here." He points to a spot about twenty miles off the southern coast of Kuwait.

"The targets are so far apart," I say. "The sub is so far south."

"Yeah, the distance between them makes it more difficult, but what are you gonna do? Anyhow, we'll drop the team and we'll be outta there."

"What about Pete's squad?" I ask.

"They'll be standing by as backup on *Nimitz,*" Animal says.

"*Twister,* huh?" Messy says, his eyes still focused on the spot on the map indicating the coast of Kuwait.

"Long story, but that's where the baddies are," Animal says.

"Did they get any photos?" I ask.

"Not in time for us."

"Great," I say with a sigh. "Did they say where the flight deck was?"

"It should be aft."

"Should be?"

"Hey, we barely got her name, let alone a description."

"Oh, boy," I say. "So what about refueling?"

If we've just flown 180 miles without an auxiliary fuel tank, we won't have enough fuel to return to *Nimitz,* even if she closes our position.

"We'll get fuel at Kuwait International," Animal says. "Make sure you bring the freqs for that."

"Will do," I say.

Animal, Lego, and Messy walk out of the maintenance office, but I hang back after they leave, pulling Eric's radio from my flight suit pocket. I insert the tiny earpiece, run the wire down my flight suit sleeve, slip the push-to-talk switch over my finger, and don my gloves. With my hair pulled across my ears, it's hidden well.

Normally, I would do a radio check at this point, as with switching on any radio. I cast a quick glance outside the hangar. Lego and Messy are attaching their communication long cords for start-up and Animal is getting settled in the left seat. Another quick check around the hangar reveals it's clear.

I'm about to push the button when I realize I have no idea what to call Eric. Shadow Hunter? Eric? Lightning? I shake my head. Secret radios and code names? It's like being dropped into the middle of a Tom Clancy novel. Well, he said he would be the only one listening, but just in case, I leave the name out. "Radio check, over."

"I've got you loud and clear, Sara," Eric says.

Oh, does it feel good to hear his voice. And I guess we don't need call signs.

"Eric, I have you loud and clear. We're taking off in about five minutes."

"Copy. We're already en route."

I don my helmet and walk to the bird, surprisingly feeling okay about having Eric in my ear. I suspect I'll hear him over the aircraft radio, too, but having him with me personally isn't as off-putting as I thought it would be.

Although, as I walk to the aircraft, I wonder again why he wouldn't want anyone to know I was wearing this. Is he worried Animal and the guys would give him grief for being too overprotective? Of course, this would be completely true, and normally, just based on principle, I wouldn't have agreed to something like this. I mean, would he have given a hidden radio to a male pilot . . . just in case? Probably not. But given the lengths Eric pursued to keep me off the mission in the name of keeping me safe, this is actually a pretty small thing. But yeah, probably best to keep it to myself. They'd give him all sorts of hell if they knew.

* * *

It's a two-and-a-half-hour flight to *Nimitz*. By the time we arrive, at 0230, Eric has already landed his aircraft, the number "67" painted in bold white on the tail boom. Behind the aircraft, which sits at the far aft end of the flight deck, the Special Forces teams wait by the island super-structure.

"I'm headin' over to get the pax, sir," Messy says.

Animal unbuckles his harness. "I'm coming with you."

The group standing at the island is an agitated one. I recognize Eric, Brian, Mike, Pete, the Australian trio, and now Animal is there, too. There's an awful lot of finger pointing going on. Something's not right.

It's at least twenty minutes before Messy finally breaks away, leading a team of eight men to our bird. It looks like Mike's squad. Animal is still arguing in the distance. At least that's what it looks like.

"Hey, Sara, this is Mike," he says, now plugged in.

"What's going on?" I ask.

"Man, cluster from the word go. My squad was supposed to go with you on the second launch to *Twister* and the Aussies were supposed to do the sub boarding. But it got switched at the last minute."

"That's kind of a big change in plans."

"No shit. The Aussies were the only ones who knew about it, too, so it makes us look like fucking idiots. But we're on the clock now, so we just have to go."

"But what was the reasoning for the change?"

"It's totally political. Since we're using Aussie intelligence and the pri-mary target of the two is the yacht, the SAS gets first dibs. Fucking brag-ging rights."

"That's strange."

"Actually, it's not. Shit like this happens more often than you think."

When Animal returns, he is fuming. Eric walks with Brian back to their bird, and he's not happy either.

"Fuckin' politics," Animal grunts once seated. "All right, let's get this show on the road."

Eric gives us a heading that takes us almost due west, and I'm thank-ful for the half-moon that shines tonight. It sits just above the horizon, so for now, the sky is bright enough to give a reference to the water, yet dark enough to conceal our presence initially. I also add calm seas to the thank-you list. Most helpful for the precision work needed tonight.

As Eric takes off behind us, I think about how much he's going to have to juggle coordinating this part of the operation. First, he has to find a submarine. Intel has given him coordinates, but even so, he'll probably have to do some searching. But at least the odds are in his favor. Submarines have a distinct disadvantage when operating in the Gulf. It's a shallow body of water, relatively speaking, so subs can't dive deep to hide. Eric will also have help from *Leftwich,* whose sonar has a far greater range than the sonobuoys Eric would drop. And then, while prosecuting the submarine, he may or may not have to engage Surface Unit 2.

While we're en route to the first drop, Animal gives a quick review of what's about to go down. ". . . and Mike, you guys are supposed to be on the Zodiac before the sub surfaces, right?" he asks.

"That's the plan," Mike says, albeit a bit sarcastically. I even hear a small chuckle on the radio.

Animal responds with a small snicker of his own. "Yeah, and if it does go as planned, this should be a quiet drop. But be ready for anything."

"Roger that, sir," Lego says.

"Got anything else, Mike?" Animal asks.

"Nope. We're all set back here."

When we arrive at the drop point, now approaching 0330, there's nothing to see—no sail, no wake, no phosphorescence, no telltale sign of a submarine. Just as planned, I guess. So I fly an approach to arrive at a low hover with just a few knots of forward airspeed so the teams can push the Zodiac off the aft ramp.

As the SEALs exit out the back, we're inundated with water that has been kicked up from the rotor wash. I swallow what feels like acid in my throat.

Lego calls the last man out, and I lift and breathe a heavy sigh. Turning a small circle to check on our group in the water before departing, Mike gives a small salute.

"Shadow Hunter six seven, Sabercat five five, ops normal, four souls, one plus two zero fuel," I say, just able to make out the receding silhouette of Eric's helicopter as I fly away.

"Copy, ops normal," Eric says.

The return flight to *Nimitz* proceeds without event, and once we're on deck, Animal leaves the aircraft and jogs to the superstructure, where the SAS squad awaits. More heated discussion. Animal throws up his hands and turns, motioning to Lego and Messy to join him.

"What the hell?" Lego says.

"It's okay, Lego," I say. "Just go."

"All right. Disconnecting."

Once Lego and Messy join the group, Jonas sends out two of his men, rope in hand. As they get closer, I recognize Collin and Bartholomew. They walk toward the rear of the aircraft and will attach everything while this spur-of-the-moment conference continues near the superstructure.

Five minutes later, Lego and Messy return, Animal right behind them. They're shaking their heads.

"What's up?" I ask, once they're connected again.

"Just stupid shit," Lego says. "We just need to get outta here and get on with this."

"No doubt," Messy agrees.

The SAS squad, dressed in camouflage just like their SEAL counterparts, marches under the rotor arc, crossing in front of the cockpit. Jonas looks directly at Animal, who has just seated himself, and delivers an insolent wink.

"Fucking Australian psychopath . . . ," Animal mutters under his breath. But then again, he did just key his mic switch, so the whole aircrew just heard his sentiment.

Lego and Messy do a good job of hiding it, but I still detect the unease in their voices, and in Animal's, too, which serves to fuel my own trepidation. I breathe in deeply, trying in earnest to quell the sudden feeling that I'm in over my head.

42

By the time we finally refuel and everyone is seated, it's close to 0400. We have almost one and a half hours of flying time to get to *Twister,* but we should still arrive under cover of night.

My thoughts spin in circles for the next hour, about a number of things. The wink Animal received from Jonas, for one. Jonas's expression? Confident. Cocky. In a far better mood than Eric or Animal. All I know is that I'll be happy to get him off this aircraft and on his way.

I also think about the fact that I haven't spoken with Eric once through the radio he gave me. But then, there really hasn't been a need. We've been speaking as we normally would through our discreet aircraft frequency.

And right now, I don't know where his aircraft is physically. There's every chance he's still back at the first drop point, searching for a submarine, or even engaging Surface Unit 2. Amazing. He's coordinating two hostile boarding missions and handling all the complexities involved with prosecuting a submarine at the same time. This is multitasking in the extreme.

But you wouldn't know it based on Eric's voice. He continues to calmly supply our headings and this, in turn, calms me. I'm already envisioning the return to Jebel Ali and a visit on the quarterdeck from a different person this time.

"What are you smiling about?" Animal asks.

"Oh, nothing, sir. I'm just ready to have this night over with."

"You got that right."

Naturally, because I'm ready to be done with this flight, the transit proceeds as if we're trapped in molasses. Worse, it's dark now. Really dark. The half-moon that lighted our way since we departed Jebel Ali has just dropped below the horizon. There is absolutely nothing to see or refer to that gives any indication we are moving forward. For the SAS squad, the cover from a moonless night is exactly what they want. For the pilot— one without night vision goggles—it's not so great.

I occupy myself with the visualization of the approach. Just like shooting free throws with an invisible basketball, I see in my mind's eye the fast rope as I want it to occur, which usually leads to a rapid-fire transition over the deck.

When the time finally comes, the hour approaching 0530, the sky is just beginning its early-morning transformation. A veil of blue replaces the unforgiving black, although the sun has yet to make its appearance over the horizon.

"All right, guys," Animal says. "This is going to need all your focus. If anything's going to happen with this mission, it'll happen here. Mess, be ready on the .50 cal. There's a good chance we're gonna need it."

"Roger that, sir," Messy says.

"Set on the rope, Lego?"

"All set, sir."

"Martin, you set aft?"

"Standing by," Jonas says.

"Five five, six seven, you're one mile," Eric says. "Give me an ops normal when you're done and then buster out."

I hear the urgency in his voice. Get out of there, basically.

"Six seven, five five, wilco," I say.

"I've got the wake," Messy calls.

"Roger, I've got it," I say, picking up the whitewater trail that leads to the ship.

As we look ahead, the dark silhouette of a massive-sized, multi-deck yacht ekes into view.

"Holy smokes, will you look at that!" Messy says.

This ship looks almost as large as the frigate in our battle group—at least five stories high. But the details I need are lacking. She's not running any lights and I squint to find the flight deck.

"Sara, do you have the deck?" Animal asks.

"Not yet."

"Lucky day," Animal says. "It's smack on the back end, just like we've practiced."

"Yeah, lucky," I mumble. "Okay, I've got it now."

The external worries that I normally shut out begin to gain traction. Training is . . . well, training. I've done some pretty fancy flying at night and with not much in the way of references, but no one has ever shot at me in the process. Eric knew what I might face and was terrified at the prospect. I start to wonder for the first time ever, only thirty seconds from the drop, what will be waiting. Will they have gunmen standing at the ready, weapons aimed at the flight deck, or more accurately, at the pilots and crew hovering over it?

Since I left the worries until so late, I have only one thought to still them. *In, out, and done.* Just like training. If you can get in and out expeditiously, you minimize time spent presenting yourself as a target. Just do it. *In, out, and done.*

"Okay, ma'am, ease it up and begin your flare," Lego says.

We're about thirty yards from the ship when I begin to slow, simultaneously spinning to the left, bringing the helicopter perpendicular to the superstructure.

"Right thirty, right twenty . . . ," Lego calls as we begin to fly sideways.

I look to the right, out my side window, the hairs rising on the back of my neck. This flight deck is micro-sized, probably used for small corporate helicopters only. But then, I have to remind myself we're not landing here, so it doesn't matter. *Just stay smooth on the controls. You'll be done and gone in twenty seconds.*

"Right ten . . ."

Now that I'm sideways and slowing down, I pull up on the collective lever that allows me to stop my rate of descent.

The number-two engine spools up quickly, too quickly, emitting a loud whining noise.

"Right five, rope's out . . ."

I'm listening for the number-one engine, waiting for it to kick in and relieve number two.

"Over deck, first man out . . ."

Something's wrong. . . .

"We lost number one!" Animal shouts.

The rotors are slowing. The second engine is trying to take the load, but it doesn't have enough power to keep us up. We're sinking! *Holy crap!*

The low rpm warning horn blares in my helmet and there's nothing I can do except make a last-second positional correction, moving the aircraft a touch to the left. A sick queasiness spreads through me as I watch the tips of the rotor blades clear the superstructure by mere inches, dropping into a space never designed for an aircraft as large as ours.

"Last man out—pull up, pull up, we're dropping, shit, we're dropping!"

"Landing—" is all I can get out before we slam hard on the deck. The last members of the SAS squad run out from under the rotor arc and disappear into the dark recesses of the ship.

"Holy fuck!" Lego says.

I glance over to the engine gauges. The tachometer reads zero, but everything else reads good. No caution lights, either.

"Sara, keep it turning!" Animal shouts. "Mess, stay on the .50 cal! Lego, check the cowling, tell me what you see! I'll cover you!"

"On it!" Lego says.

Animal yanks out his radio cord and scrambles out of his seat, pulling the 9mm from his vest in the process. I'm left looking at the superstructure of the ship, realizing I'm probably the easiest target that has ever presented itself to a waiting gun. Holy shit.

"Ah, fuck!" Lego says. "We busted an oil line!"

"Can you fix it?" Animal says from one of the crewman's radio lines in the back.

"Yeah, but we're gonna need to shut down."

"Fuck!" Animal says.

"Give me ten minutes, sir."

"We don't have ten minutes! Can you do it in five?"

"If I have Mess to help me, then yeah, five minutes!"

"Okay, do it!" Animal orders. "But stay up on your long cords so I can talk to you."

"We're on it!" Lego says.

"Sara, shut down and get back here ASAP!"

I kill the remaining engine, stop the rotors, and crawl to the back, past the main cabin door. Animal has manned the .50 cal.

"Here, you take this," he says, swiveling the butt of the machine gun to me. "I'll cover from the rear."

He runs to the aft ramp, sidearm in hand, and peers out the back. I grab the machine gun and point it at the superstructure. The main cabin door is to my left, the gun protruding through the window that lies adjacent to it.

I've only fired a .50 cal a handful of times in my career and only at non-moving cardboard cutouts. But I've stripped and cleaned hundreds of these weapons. I'm hoping that will count for something now.

I quickly scan the ship structure in front of me. On navy ships, I'm used to looking at the metal doors of an aircraft hangar once we've landed. But here, I see a row of floor-to-ceiling glass windows. They span almost the width of the flight deck, leaving room for walkways on either side so passengers can move forward along the outside railings of the ship.

Just above the level of glass windows is a patio with . . . lounge chairs? I blink in the low light. Yep. Six lounge chairs with overstuffed cushions and an awning overhead. I'm unable to make out much more from this vantage point.

I take a chance and sneak a look behind me, peering through the windows to where Lego and Messy stand on the other side of the aircraft. They're covered in engine oil, their faces periodically illuminated by their flashlights that flicker through the engine compartment.

I turn back to face the windows, scanning across the deck and then up to the patio above. I don't see anyone.

And it's quiet.

Actually, it's too quiet.

"Sir, forgive me for asking a stupid question, but doesn't it seem awfully quiet to you? I mean, for landing on a hostile ship and all?"

"You've just read my mind," Animal says.

"What the . . . ," Lego says.

"What is it?" Animal asks.

"Sir, you're not gonna fuckin' believe this! The line's been cut! The oil line's been fuckin' cut!"

"What?"

"Holy crap, Kyle," Messy says. "Look at this!"

"Oh, my fuckin' god . . . ," Lego says.

"What now?" Animal says.

"Sir, did you ever get an oil pressure caution light?" Messy asks.

"No."

"How about the oil pressure gauge?"

"It read normal," he says.

"Wait, that's imposs—" I start.

"That's because someone cut the wires to the indicators," Messy says.

"That son of a bitch . . . ," Animal says in disbelief.

"What?" I say. "What's happening?"

"Lightning was right . . . ," Animal says, more to himself than any of us.

"Right about what?" I ask.

"Lego, Mess, get that oil line patched up as fast as you fuckin' can!" Animal says.

"We're almost there, sir!"

And then, like a slow-motion sequence in an action film, two shots ring out from the dark.

Animal jerks back and falls in a lump on the ramp. I swing the mount to the origin of the gunfire, but I'm yanked backward, my arms pulled behind me. The bracingly cold shaft of a gun barrel presses into my neck.

"That's a good girl," Jonas says. "Let's just stay nice and calm."

43

At the rear of the aircraft, Collin and Bartholomew usher Lego and Messy into the cabin at gunpoint.

"Now, before we proceed further, I believe Romeo is awaiting your ops normal call," Jonas says.

I hear a small moan. Animal is trying to move. He lies at the top of the ramp, in a crumpled heap near the side bulkhead.

"You are going to turn on the battery," Jonas says, "and you will give a proper ops normal call. If there is any deviation whatsoever, guaranteed you'll have a front-row seat as I finish off Mr. Amicus," he says, pointing to Animal's wounded form.

Oh my god. Animal . . .

Don't shake, Sara. Just do this. Stay calm.

I step into the passageway that leads to the cockpit and reach up to flip on the battery switch that's secured to the overhead console. But my hand is shaking so badly, I can't get the switch.

Breathe, Sara. Breathe.

I try again, supporting my right arm with my left, and finally turn it on. I reach over and key the mic on the cyclic control stick located in front of my seat.

"Shadow Hunter six seven, Sabercat five five, ops normal, four souls, zero plus three zero fuel, over."

"Five five, six seven, copy ops normal," Eric says. "State plans for fueling, over."

I look back at Jonas, and he shakes his head in warning.

"Six seven, five five, Kuwait International, over."

"Five five, six seven, copy," he says, sounding relieved.

Jonas reaches past me and flicks the battery switch off.

Pulling back into the main cabin, Jonas turns to Lego and Messy.

"Now, Mr. Legossi, Mr. Messina, you are going to finish the repair to the oil line and you will do so in a timely manner, as we have a schedule to keep. We need to be airborne in fifteen minutes."

He looks up, his attention turned to the men now entering the aircraft from the far aft ramp, all of Middle Eastern descent. They're carrying several crates between them that they begin loading into the aircraft. They walk right past Animal without a glance.

"Oil line?" I say. "But how would you know—"

"Because we cut it, lovely lady. That's how I know."

"But why?"

"I doubt you would have bothered to land otherwise," he states matter-of-factly.

"What if we can't repair it?" Lego says.

"Ah, your reputation precedes you. This is well within your capability to repair . . . and repair quickly."

Lego is about to protest.

"Ah, ah, ah," Jonas says, wagging a finger. "You *will* do this, unless of course . . ." and he points to Animal, who has now rolled over onto his back, blood seeping through his flight suit.

Jonas eyes Lego carefully.

"I already see the wheels turning, Mr. Legossi," Jonas says. "Not only will you fix it, but you will fix it *right,* because you and the pretty lieutenant here are going to fly us out. So fix it as if your own life and the lieutenant's depend on it. Because they do."

Lego switches his gaze to me and we share a long look. He's silently asking me for approval to finish the repair.

"Why do you need this aircraft?" I ask.

"We need transport to complete our mission," he says proudly.

"What mission? What are you doing?"

"Ensuring my retirement, love. Some mighty powerful people would like to see the demise of a certain former U.S. president, and they've paid handsomely to ensure it happens. They know we can get it done."

"What? The assassination . . . it's . . . it's you?"

He smiles wickedly, but the sick grin quickly disappears.

"Well, no, love, originally it was not me." He waves his hands at the men loading crates. "It was our Iraqi friends here. But the Aussie intel analysts are rather pesky and discovered their plan."

"But why are you—"

"I suppose you could call me a hired hand, which is unfortunate, really. Someone coming to a job like this with my qualifications should carry a far more elegant moniker."

This can't be happening. This can't—

Stop it, Sara! Think!

But I don't know what to do—

Well, keep him talking until you figure something out!

"But who . . . hired you?" I stutter.

"Ultimately, the Iraqis, and for a handsome sum, I might add."

"Ultimately . . . ?"

"Ah, you would be interested to know this," he says. "You have a high-ranking U.S. intelligence officer under the employ of the Iraqis. We go back a long way, he and I, so when he needed someone to disrupt this joint Australian-U.S. intervention and ensure the boats made it to harbor, he contacted me. Brilliant choice, wouldn't you say, mates?" he says, looking up to Collin and Bartholomew, who meet his gaze only momentarily before returning their focus to Lego and Messy.

I, too, glance at my aircrewmen, guns pointed at the backs of their heads, and my legs quaver, weakened when I think of Lego's kids and their artwork tacked around his bunk. And Messy's wife, Leah, and their baby, due just after we return.

You're responsible for them, Sara.

But I still don't know what to do—

Keep stalling! He likes to talk. He's arrogant. Use it!

"You said you needed our aircraft to complete the mission. Why would you need it if the plan was to take the ship to port?" I ask.

"A recent development, that. The Kuwaitis went and closed their ports and secured their borders. The airspace is restricted, too—that is, unless you're a U.S. Navy helicopter," he says, clearly proud of himself. "I came up with the solution—entering the country with our men, weapons, and equipment via this aircraft right here," he says, slapping the bulkhead.

"What about your squad? The other men on your team?" I say.

"Uh . . . tied up at the moment," Jonas says with an altogether unmirthful laugh. "Easy when you have a rookie crew, selected by myself, of course."

So it's just Jonas, Collin, and Bartholomew. I wonder fleetingly if he meant exactly what he just said—that he's tied up his teammates and left them somewhere on the ship.

"Where are we going?" I ask.

"Ah, that you don't need to know, because you won't be with us at that point."

"What do you mean?"

"We just need you to fly long enough to know that the engine has been repaired properly and then, how shall I say this? Well, you're expendable at that point. So the four of you will be going for a swim."

I look up to Lego and Messy and our eyes share the same anger.

"But who's going to fly then?"

"That, my dear, is why I'm receiving a kingly sum for this. Your Romeo isn't the only one with a dual designation."

The military rolodex file I carry in my head starts spinning. Australian Navy. Australian Navy aircraft. Australian Navy helicopters. They fly tail-rotor aircraft, not tandem-rotor. He hasn't flown a tandem-rotor aircraft.

"You can't fly an H-46," I say.

"Hey, if I can fly a tail-rotor bird, I can certainly handle this thing."

Interesting. Something in his voice . . . He said he needed us to fly to ensure the engine was repaired correctly, but I wonder if it's more than that. I wonder if he's worried about his own ability to execute the takeoff. The initial lift to a hover would be the most dangerous moment, when the aircraft is the most difficult to control. But once in level flight with eighty or ninety knots of airspeed, taking the controls and maintaining a somewhat smooth flight wouldn't be too difficult. And if he's flying to a runway somewhere, he can land at speed, just like an airplane would, avoiding the hover altogether. But I caught something in his voice—the worry. Worry he was trying to cover up with a bluster of bravado. To negotiate his price with the Iraqis, no doubt he played up his abilities as a pilot. But I think he needs us. He needs us to make this work.

My eyes shift to Animal. He's fumbling with his hands, trying to find the zipper of his survival vest. Oh god, this is ripping my heart out to watch him.

I make the boldest decision I've ever made in my life.

Turning to Jonas, I breathe in deeply, steeling my nerve, because I'm scared out of my mind. "We're not repairing anything until I can stop the bleeding on Commander Amicus."

"Excuse me?" Jonas says with a mixture of shock and anger. "You're not exactly in a position to be making demands."

"You need these two to repair the engine and you need me to fly. We're not going to do either until I can tend to him."

"Hey, I don't need you to fly," he says.

"Then just shoot me and get it over with." The words are out before I can stop them. But I can't bear to watch Animal struggling another second.

If he really needs me to fly, I should be okay. If not . . .

Jonas looks at Lego and Messy and then down to Animal. He hesitates before speaking again, and in that moment, I know I'm right. He does need us.

"No shooting in the aircraft now, love. Not with the explosives we've loaded." He points to the crates in the cabin. "No, I'm afraid your end will not be so tidy. Once we kick you out, it will be the sharks, I think. That is, if the sea snakes don't get you first."

I think back to Mike's comment about a wolf in sheep's clothing. But it's so much worse than that.

"But for the sake of speeding things along, since you're in a bit of a state over the condition of Mr. Amicus, you may tend to your leader and your boys can return to the business of repairing."

I nod slightly to Lego and he does the same in acknowledgment.

As he and Messy turn to go, Jonas adds, "And here." He walks forward and reaches into Collin's rucksack, pulling out a canister. "More oil."

"Thorough," I say disgustedly.

He pushes me forward. "Make it quick. You've got five minutes."

I grab the med bag and kneel next to Animal, who immediately tries to talk.

"Shhh," I whisper. "I'm going to stop the bleeding, okay?"

My hands are shaking as I undo the fasteners to the medical kit. I look at my right glove, the one hiding the push-to-talk switch. I hadn't considered using it earlier, when I was talking with Jonas. Maybe if I'd pushed it, Eric could have heard something, realized something was wrong. But I *can't* stop to press it now. Not with what I'm doing. Not if I want any chance of stanching the bleeding.

What else? I have a gun—Captain Plank's 9mm Beretta—tucked in the pocket of my survival vest. But as soon as the thought enters my head, I know it's a non-starter. Jonas has a gun aimed at my back and even if I could manage to unzip my vest, pull the gun out, turn, aim, and fire before he pulled the trigger, Bartholomew would probably just laugh as he watched the attempt. He stands now on the ship's deck just beyond the aft ramp of the helicopter, overseeing the loading operations, with a clear line of sight to me and all that I'm doing.

Stop it with the gun and radio, Sara! You need your mind on what you're doing!

I finally get the straps undone, laying the kit open, and turn to Animal. I unzip his survival vest, pulling his arms through the sleeves, which reveals a flight suit saturated in blood. *Okay.*

I pull on the zipper to his flight suit, opening it until I see the wound in his side, or maybe it's two. God, there's so much blood. Reaching for the ample supply of dressings from the med bag, I apply them directly over the site, holding them down to keep the pressure on.

"Three minutes!" Jonas announces.

I clumsily roll Animal's body to wrap the bandages around his torso and secure the dressings. I finish tying the first bandages in a tight knot, but the dressings are already soaked through. Oh, no . . .

"Two minutes!"

"Sara," Animal whispers with effort.

I look into his eyes. There is no fear in them whatsoever. If I had to describe the expression on his face, I'd say he looks pissed.

"What is it?"

"You're right," he says, wheezing. "He needs you."

I nod.

"Can't fly . . ." Animal's breaths are coming more rapidly and shallow now.

"I understand."

He moves his lips like he wants to say something else, but I touch them gently.

"I'm going to get you out of here," I whisper. "Just hang on, okay?"

The plan that's taking shape in my mind is a long shot. But Animal just reiterated what I've been thinking. *Can't fly. Can't fly . . .*

44

My head snaps up when Lego and Messy arrive back in the cabin. I don't ask for permission, but set them to work. Their hands are filthy with engine oil, so I have them hold Animal in a position where I can wrap the bandages more tightly around his torso.

"One minute!"

I add layer after layer of dressings until, finally, they remain dry on top. In the background, the loading operations continue. The whole time I've been with Animal, men have walked back and forth carrying boxes and crates, strapping them to the floor.

"Okay, that's it!" Jonas says.

I place my hand over Animal's heart, giving him a small smile before rising.

His tenacious response is communicated with his eyes, which are blazing with determination. If I had to guess, he's saying, *Give 'em hell!*

"Let's move him here," I say to Lego and Messy, motioning farther inside the aircraft.

We turn him so his body is running lengthwise with the cabin, slide his legs under the troop seats, and lay him next to the bulkhead.

"You," Jonas says, pointing at me. "Sit here and don't move."

He directs me to the crew chief's seat next to the main cabin door. The seat itself faces aft, so I have a clear view down the entire cabin.

"You two," he says, motioning to Lego and Messy. "I assume we're operational?"

"Yes," Lego says curtly.

Jonas points to the cargo. "Make sure that gets strapped in."

Lego and Messy grit their teeth and start to work. Collin has resumed guard duty, having followed Lego and Messy inside after their repairs, now standing mid-cabin with a gun trained on both of them.

When Jonas leaves my side, I finally have space to think. Okay, what next? We're going to finish loading, we'll turn up, we'll fly until he's satisfied that the engine is working, and then we're shark food.

I rub my still-gloved hands across the pant legs of my flight suit in an attempt to wipe off the blood, but snag the push-to-talk button against the pocket zipper on my thigh.

The radio. I didn't have time to use it before, but I do now . . . which also means I have time to retrieve the gun from my vest. But then what? Shoot Collin? Bartholomew stands just beyond him, not ten feet further. And the Middle Eastern men—I count eight—who move back and forth through the cabin all carry guns at their sides. The notion of me pulling off some gunslinging miracle surrounded by eleven armed men and who knows how many more onboard the ship is ludicrous.

So I go back to the radio. Best to let Eric know what's happening. I start to press the switch, but realize I can't do this without being overheard. *Okay, okay, okay. Think.*

The idea that pops to mind . . . well, never in a million years did I think I'd actually need this.

When you grow up in a Denning household, you learn certain things— things most kids don't learn. The military alphabet, for one. I didn't learn A, B, C, D. I learned Alpha, Bravo, Charlie, Delta. I also learned the Manual of Arms. I practiced with Ian in our backyard and could complete the entire sequence by the time I was ten. And to covertly communicate with Ian? Morse Code. We played games in our tree house, tapping away and communicating in silence to the befuddlement of the neighbor kids. And, of course, I had to do all these things again once I entered the Naval Academy.

And now, I'm going to use Morse Code officially for the first time ever, and I pray that among the roster of languages Eric keeps tucked in his head, Morse Code is one of them.

I move my hand discreetly behind my back and press the push-to-talk button with my thumb.

"S-O-S," I key using dots and dashes. "S-O-S," I repeat.

"Sara?" Eric's voice runs thick with alarm. "Sara, what is it?"

"S-O-S," I key.

"SOS? What's happened?"

"E-N-G-I-N-E-F-A-I-L-U-R-E."

"Engine failure? Where are you?"

"O-N-D-E-C-K."

"But you reported ops normal."

"F-O-R-C-E-D-T-O-S-A-Y."

"Forced? You were forced? Who forced you?"

"J-O-N-A-S."

My body quakes with adrenaline at the sound of Jonas's voice. "Ah, what's this?" he asks, entering from my left, through the main cabin door.

"Jonas?" Eric's voice is frantic. "Is he there with you now?"

I press and hold the push-to-talk button, hoping Eric can hear whatever happens now.

"Take off your helmet," Jonas orders.

I comply and he pulls my hair aside with an aggravated yank.

"Ahh . . . naughty girl," he says, shaking his head. "Take off your gloves."

When I do, he reaches for the press-to-talk button and presses it himself. Leaning close to my ear, he says, "Hello, Romeo. The little lady is going off line now. And by the way, she's going to pay for this."

The slap across my face that follows is such a shock that the cry escapes before I can stop it.

"Sara!" Eric screams. It's the last thing I hear before Jonas rips the radio from my ear—rips it apart, actually—and throws it across the cabin.

Lego and Messy stand glaring as I put my hand to my stinging cheek.

"Okay, my pretty, you may take your seat and we'll be on our way," he says, pointing to the cockpit.

"Eric will find us," I say. "He'll fly right here."

Jonas starts laughing. "My dear, your Romeo is over one hundred miles away at the moment, searching for a submarine that doesn't exist."

That's why the targets were so far apart. They had to keep Eric and the SEAL team clear.

"He'll radio for help," I say. "He'll send backup. This will never work."

"We'll be long gone before any help arrives, I assure you."

Jonas reaches for my survival vest and removes the radio clipped to my front pocket. He relieves Messy and Lego of their radios in the same manner.

"Can't have you calling for help again. Now, get in."

I breathe a small sigh, knowing I still have Captain Plank's pistol tucked safely inside my vest pocket, out of sight. For what use, I don't know. But at least I have it.

Before I turn to enter the cockpit, I notice something. The radio Jonas pulled from my ear and threw across the cabin is no longer on the floor. I glance up to Lego and Messy and we share a brief look before I take my seat.

"All right, boys," Jonas says. "Time to resume your aircrew duties, if you please."

Jonas climbs into the seat next to me.

"Ah, yes," he says. "I almost forgot." He reaches across the cockpit and unzips my survival vest. I watch, deflated, as he removes Captain Plank's gun.

"I was there when Mr. Plank told Mr. Amicus you were to have this," Jonas says, turning the gun in his hand. "Something about how impressed he was with your ability to perform under pressure. Your *courage* and *bravery*," he says mockingly.

Jonas allows himself a hearty laugh. "What a disappointment! Love, you're supposed to *use* this!" he says, waving the gun in front of my face. "Bloody hell, what the fuck are you carrying it for if you're not going to use it!"

My heart falls . . . I'm about to start up this aircraft and fly him and his team away from here, following his instructions to the letter, enabling this assassination attempt to go forward. I haven't put up the valiant fight, nor have I attempted even one small act to thwart his attempts at hijacking this aircraft.

My god. What would Captain Plank say? Or Lieutenant Colonel Tyson? Or anyone else in the briefing room that day who was sizing up my ability to perform under pressure.

Jonas accurately reads what I'm thinking. "I would pose the same question as Lieutenant Colonel Tyson," he says. "You know, that part about keeping your head together when it mattered. Would you say you're succeeding?"

I stumble, lost for an answer. "I . . . I don't know."

"I think not," he says. "Which is exactly what I was counting on."

He tucks the gun hastily into his waistband even though he wears a vest containing a thousand pockets.

"Knew you wouldn't disappoint," he says with a smile. "Now, start it up."

And here I go again, without hesitation, flicking the switches for the battery and starter units.

But Sara, you do have a plan. It's a long shot, but you have an idea. It's just not time yet.

"Yeah, right," I mutter to myself.

The engines fire up and the rotors begin to spin. Jonas orders Lego and Messy to open the engine cowling to ensure their hose repair is holding. After they report in the affirmative, I scan the gauges, all of which show normal readings. Although I doubt they were able to repair the wiring for the caution panel light and the oil pressure gauge. Wait, check that. Messy is a flat-out genius when it comes to electronics, so there's every chance he did indeed fix them.

"Messy, are the gauges . . . ?"

"Yep, ma'am, those are good readings there."

Incredible.

Before we lift, Jonas reaches to the radio switch and turns it off. He also turns off our transponder. Damn it. The transponder provides automatic radar identification to anyone who's interrogating, like air traffic controllers or other aircraft or ships. He has just shut off the only way we can positively identify ourselves.

"After you lift, stay overhead the ship," Jonas says. "No higher than fifty feet."

As we ascend, I suck in my breath as the tips of the rotor blades pass within a hair's width of the upper decks.

"Let's move it," Jonas commands. "Clear to go."

I exhale once we're clear of the superstructure, and turn the aircraft to arc around the front of the ship. I'm flying with fifteen souls onboard—three SAS members, eight "civilian" men, Lego, Messy, Animal, and me.

"Ma'am, am I clear to get up for the post-takeoff checks?" Messy asks.

"No checks are necessary," Jonas says. "We're only ensuring flyability."

"Uh, sir, I beg to differ," Messy says. "Since you've gone around cuttin' things, I'm a little more concerned than usual."

Jonas pauses here, thinking through the request. "Okay, you may do your checks. One false move, though, and my man Collin pulls the trigger, explosives or no."

"Fuck, you think I'm gonna mess with shit? Take the helicopter down in a blaze of glory just to stop your sorry ass? Fuck no!"

"I'm surprised at your attitude, Mr. Messina. Very un-American."

"Yeah, you've been watchin' too many cowboy movies," Messy says. "So can I get on with this?"

"You may proceed."

"Roger that. My expendable ass is up."

In any other situation, the beauty of the sunrise would have captured my full attention. Pale blues have given way to purples and pinks, the sky now spotted with wisps of cloud that scatter above a flash of orange.

As I fly circles in the light of this new sunrise, the enormity of the yacht comes into clear focus. Three decks rise above the flight deck, including the patio area I noticed earlier, and two decks run underneath. Where the waterline meets the hull at the most aft end of the ship, a flat wooden deck runs across it—a loading platform.

Below the level of the flight deck, but above the waterline, the outlines of several hatches are visible along the hull. The longest must span at least forty feet. I suspect it's the entrance to a cargo bay of some sort. Next to it, a twenty-foot cutout in the hull houses the pontoons of a Zodiac. The opposite side of the ship is structured similarly, but with extra space for a small motorboat stored just adjacent to a second Zodiac.

Judging by the churning roil of white water constituting its wake, the ship is headed somewhere fast. Oddly, it still travels toward Kuwait, even though the ports are closed.

"Drop to ten feet and stay there," Jonas says.

The longer we fly, the more assured he becomes that the engine is indeed working as advertised. He feels comfortable going lower and there's a reason he's doing it. He's hoping our radar signature will get lost in the noise of the waves below us.

I scan the horizon for any hint of land, but see none. Based on the maps we consulted during the brief, we're over twenty miles from shore. And the threat of sharks, sea snakes . . . very real. I've heard many tales from fellow helicopter pilots who have watched hammerheads cruise in schools by the hundreds just under the surface in the Gulf. And the sea snakes? They're regularly spotted feeding on the remains of deceased livestock, tossed overboard from the cargo ships that were transporting them.

Which leads me to thoughts of what's going to happen next. Jonas is going to kick the four of us out of the aircraft. If we're high and fast when he does so, we may not survive the fall. Which, of course, is what he wants. Poor Animal. Even if we're low and slow, he still might not survive the jump. Although, I would have to say that if anyone could survive in the state that he's in now—one, possibly two bullet wounds to the abdomen—it would be him. Tough as nails, Animal.

Other options? Well, the crazy plan I've been thinking about since I bandaged Animal is the only thing I've got. And it's an awful plan because I don't know if I can bring myself to do it.

If I want something else, I only have about five minutes, probably less, to figure it out.

45

"You know, ma'am, we have some un-fucking-believable luck with foreigners, don't we?" Messy says.

I hope he's prolonging his post-takeoff checks. A little stalling now would definitely help.

"I mean, fuck, remember that Italian exchange pilot?" he says. "What was his candy-ass name? Alfredo Francesco Ciarro Signori? Remember that guy? Fuck, I thought he was off. Really *off*. But he doesn't hold a candle to these guys."

"Cut the chatter, Mr. Messina," Jonas warns.

What on earth is Messy talking about? Italian exchange pilot? We've never worked with an Italian exchange pilot. Alfredo Francesco—

And then I feel it. That subtle shift in the aircraft when the automatic flight control system shuts off. I look for the caution light, but it's not on. The AFCS is definitely off, though. Off . . . It's *off*. Alfredo Francesco Ciarro Signori . . . A . . . F . . . C . . . S.

Messy was telling me the AFCS was off. But it wasn't off when he said it. He told me before it happened. Which means he just shut it off. And he must have done it past the junction that sends the signal to the caution panel so it wouldn't light up. He turned it off and nobody knows but the three of us, because Lego would also recognize it instantly.

Why? Why turn it off? I take a chance.

"You know, Messy, I do remember him, and he was *definitely* off. But I don't know why."

"Well, I reckon 'cuz he was an overconfident son of a bitch. Remem-

ber how he thought he could fly anything, anywhere? Even outfly our pilots? What a jackass."

"Enough!" Jonas snaps. "Aren't you finished yet?"

"Almost, sir," Messy says.

Overconfident . . . Thought he could fly anything . . . Jonas. He's talking
about Jonas. Messy's banking on the fact that he won't be able to fly without the AFCS.

Messy was planning on taking them down in a blaze of glory after all,
but only after we'd left the aircraft.

I think I can firmly put Messy in the brilliant category, right alongside Eric and Lego.

And this actually works perfectly with my long-shot plan.

If we're moving fast, at a normal cruising airspeed of eighty or ninety
knots, I'm betting Jonas would still be able to fly the aircraft, even with
the AFCS off. It wouldn't be smooth, the aircraft pitching and bucking a
fit, but it would be controllable.

But if I can bring the aircraft to a hover before transferring the controls, and now especially with the AFCS off, it would seal the deal. I'd
bet my life he wouldn't be able to fly it . . . which is exactly what I'm going to have to do.

"Okay, sir, aft cabin checks complete," Messy says. "Good to go back
here."

"Which means you are also good to go," Jonas says. "My dear, take a
heading of three four five and stay at ten feet."

Ten feet. The low part is there for us. Now for the slow part. Ever since
Jonas ordered the descent, I've been backing off on the airspeed, now down
to seventy knots. It's still too fast.

"Collin, please escort our friends to the aft ramp and be sure to have
them take Mr. Amicus with them," Jonas says.

Thank goodness. He's going to let them jump with Animal. My fear
had been that he would push them out separately. Maybe the guys can
support him somehow during the fall.

"All set aft," Collin says.

"Cheerio, boys," Jonas says in farewell.

Jonas leans over in the passageway and looks into the aft cabin to watch
them jump. This is my chance. I bottom the collective lever and pull back

on the cyclic—a maneuver called a quick stop—that rapidly bleeds air-speed. The airspeed indicator spins down from seventy knots to less than twenty in just a few seconds. I pray that they jump when they realize I'm slowing.

"What the fuck!" Jonas says.

"They're out!" Collin reports.

Oh, no. I can feel the rage from here. Jonas is smokin' mad.

"Okay, tricky girl," he says in a low voice. "Let's speed up then, shall we? You aren't going to have it so easy."

I push the cyclic stick forward, gaining airspeed, thinking five steps ahead to what I need to do next.

"Pity that Marxen won't be here to see this," Jonas muses. "Arrogant prick."

I shake off the thought of Eric, my mind focused on the sea below. Frothy white waves, like milky teeth, accelerate beneath us. . . .

And then it hits me. I can't go through with it.

In another pilot's hands, this plan would work. They would get it done. But this coward is going to hand over the controls without so much as a hiccup, sending an assassination crew on their merry way, all because I don't want to get wet.

We pass one hundred knots. "Okay, your turn," he says.

I continue accelerating.

But you're going in the water anyway. . . . I don't know where this voice comes from, but it's absolutely right. I'm going to be pushed out anyway.

"Now!" he yells, like a bottle that's just popped its cork.

And I react. I drop the collective lever, raise the nose twenty degrees, and roll forty-five. By the time he realizes what's happening, I'm already pulling full aft cyclic and raising the collective to hook around a tiny spot in the sea. Anyone looking from the outside would see a helicopter rapidly decelerating, the nose pitching up and rolling over, turning 180 degrees in a pirouette movement that stops the aircraft on a dime, facing the opposite direction from which it started, tracing the shape of a but-tonhook.

Jonas grabs for the controls now that we're in a hover, but it's too late. I let go of everything and unplug my radio cord. My plan is to exit via the cockpit escape hatch—remove it and step out before he loses control of the aircraft.

The bird pitches down and he overcorrects, pulling the stick back too rapidly. I try to locate my harness release and my hand swipes at nothing as I'm slammed backward in the seat. A quick glance to the left reveals a facial expression from Jonas that is anything but confident. He's frantic and furious.

He tries to nose it over, but the control input is too great. And just like that, I'm hanging in my straps, looking almost straight down into the ocean—a gaping maw, waves churning, lips smacking.

The aircraft pitches up violently when he tries to stop the nose dive, and the sudden movement slams my head into the side bulkhead. My helmet takes the brunt of the collision, but I feel the blood dripping down my face from the gash that cuts across my cheek.

We're sliding backward. Holy god. We're going to hit tail down.

The aircraft lurches, and with a sickening crack, the airframe torques mightily against the sudden stoppage of the rotors. An explosion of sound erupts as the rotors fly apart and the aircraft flips. I'm thrown forward hard against the harness straps, hard enough to expel my breath just before I'm pulled under.

I'm underwater.

I push against the cockpit floor, jerking and twisting, to free myself from the seat. The harness holds fast.

The harness! Release the harness!

I scrabble with the straps, searching for the harness release. *No! No! Wait! Wait . . .*

Wait until all violent motion stops before pulling your harness release.

The instructions come back, just as they did in training three months earlier.

I stop thrashing and clutch the straps as the aircraft rolls over. I wait as long as I dare, probably only a few seconds, but I can't wait any longer. I reach for my harness release, my brain finally recalling its position, and pull, wriggling my way out.

At least I don't have to do the elaborate main cabin door exit. My escape is located less than one foot to my right—the cockpit escape hatch. I push down on the handle. . . .

I push down on the handle again. . . . *Come on! Come on!*

It doesn't budge. I kick it hard. Nothing.

The water smiles as it presses against me. I lash out, slamming my fists against the hatch's window panels, accomplishing nothing. I smash at them again and again. With a crunch, my arm breaks through the glass of the smallest panel, which doesn't do me a lick of good, because it isn't large enough for me to fit through. I tug my hand backward, slicing my left hand in the process. Left hand . . . left hand. *Reach left hand behind you. Grab bulkhead. Right arm across torso to bulkhead on other side. Pull forward.*

The instructions! You know what to do! Go out the back!

I reach in the direction my hands have memorized, still able to make out the walls to the upside-down passageway.

The light dims. The pressure increases in my ears. Oh, no. We're already sinking. The aircraft is pulling us under.

Jonas is struggling to release his harness. As I pull my way through, my eyes unexpectedly meet his . . . Ian's eyes . . . and I'm looking at myself nine years ago. Beyond all reason, I hesitate. Jonas is drowning. The fear, the panic . . . it's all there, reflected in his eyes and in his frantic movements. His harness is snagged on the seat lever.

I shake my head, turning away, and pull myself through the passageway. Halfway, I stop. *Damn it.*

I shove myself back in the cockpit, reach my hand out, and in a what-the-hell-am-I-doing moment, lift Jonas's harness strap over the seat lever.

Without looking back, I thrust through the passageway and into a scene straight out of a horror movie. Bodies are tangled in cargo netting and pinned against the bulkheads by floating crates. The life has left most, while others thrash in the dying throes of a drowning panic.

For the first time in my life, I say a silent thank-you to the navy for the helo dunker. These men don't know what to do. They don't know how to egress, how to escape, while I'm acting and reacting automatically.

Using the bulkhead for leverage, I yank myself forward. My air has long since run out and the pressure descends on my chest, squeezing.

Left hand down to crew chief's seat. Hand-over-hand to main cabin door.

My hands take me to the exit. I pull myself through and turn upward. My arms and legs push and pull, but they're heavy, so very heavy. I'm swimming through syrup.

Come on, Sara! Come on! There's the light! It's right there!

The seawater lightens as I near the surface, but this ascension is endless. The light bends and deflects from its straight path in the air as it travels through the aquatic medium, making it almost impossible to judge depth. The surface that is *right there* is probably still more than twenty feet away. My body wants to turn inside out. All of me is being sucked inward and I'm not going to be able to do this. I'm not going to make it. . . .

Come on! Five more seconds! You can do this!

Ian . . . ? His voice resonates through me, unlocking a final surge of power from I don't know where, until my arms and legs are pulling and stroking as one.

My head breaks through the surface, my mouth opening a second too soon. The act of inhalation almost sends me into shock. The water rushes in. I vomit seawater and enter a fit of coughing spasms. My throat sears with pain as my lungs attempt to do two things at once—expel the water inside and bring the air in.

It's okay. It's okay. It's okay.

As I cough more water out, my inhalations grow deeper. My lungs are working to bring air in now, working harder on this than to cough water out.

Relax. Relax, Sara. Just breathe. Relax.

The heaviness in my muscles begins to dissipate. My arms scull and my legs tread. I breath more deeply.

You can float here. Just float.

I lie back, stretching out my arms and legs, and look to the sky. *You're safe. You're not going to drown. It's okay. Just float here.*

Deep breath in. Deep breath out. Another breath in. Another breath out. Lying on a liquid pillow of salt water, my muscles release, exhausted, unable to carry the tension any longer.

You're safe. You're okay.

My body undulates with the sea. Easy breath in. Easy breath out. The Arabian sky is pink. A beautiful sunrise-pink.

46

The distant purr of an outboard motor brings a smile to my face. As I stare upward into the lightening morning sky, I realize I've actually made it through this nightmare. I picture the small navy rescue craft on its way to pick me up just ten minutes after crashing, wondering which ship it came from and how it could have gotten here so fast. I scull with my arms to bring myself upright, but as I raise my head, the smile is wiped from my face. The behemoth luxury yacht, *Twister,* barrels toward me. I'm so stunned by the sight, I fail to see the Zodiac that approaches from behind.

I turn just as it moves alongside. Rough hands grab my shoulders and drag me aboard. At gunpoint. Two Middle Eastern men stand above me, their semiautomatic weapons pointed directly at my heart. One begins shouting to a third man, the driver, in harsh, abrupt words, giving the order to move, I think.

Lying on my back on the floor of the Zodiac, I spread my arms wide to brace myself as we accelerate. The nose of the raft lifts into the air as it catches a wave, then hurtles down the other side, skipping, bumping, and crashing again.

An eerie snarl alerts me that someone else is aboard the raft. I slowly turn my head.

Jonas, his face bloody, wears a murderous look.

"If I didn't need you, I'd kill you right now, bitch," he growls.

Instinctively, I scooch away, until one of the gunmen steps down on my shoulder with his heavy black boot, pinning it to the deck. I look up, he scowls and presses harder.

We rocket forward, the bounce of the Zodiac slamming my back into the floorboards over and over again. Then, with a rapid whirl and a wide spray of water, we stop abruptly.

Angry voices fill the air and Jonas's is one of them. I'm snatched upward by the men inside the Zodiac and summarily deposited in a heap on the low wooden running board on the aft end of *Twister*.

Two men with semiautomatic machine guns slung over their shoulders "greet" us. An argument ensues and as I listen, the wake behind the ship begins churning in earnest. *Twister* is soon flying. And based on the position of the rising sun, we're headed almost directly west, toward land, toward Kuwait.

My head hurts. I rub my eyes and they start to sting. When I pull my hands away, they're covered in blood. The gash on my face, my hand . . . I'd forgotten.

With a jerk, Jonas grabs my arm and wrenches me upward, shoving me through a hatch and into a passageway that leads to the forward part of the ship. As we move, his grip is tight, and my arm throbs. Another rough push through a final hatch and I stumble into the cavernous cargo bay.

On the far bulkhead, I recognize the cutout shape of the wide cargo bay doors that I had spotted from the outside. Scanning the side bulkheads, I see crates and boxes, similar to those that were loaded in our helicopter, sitting in neatly stacked, ordered rows. Jonas stated we had explosives onboard the aircraft, and there's more of the same here.

A Toyota Land Cruiser, chocked and chained to the deck, occupies the center of the space. Next to it, a workbench scattered with tools and wiring.

Jonas drags me to the car and shoves me into the backseat. The doors click simultaneously as they lock around me.

Jonas disappears out a side hatch and now the cargo area appears to be empty. I slide over to the door to open it. If you're inside, you just open the handle to unlock it, right? Wrong. Maybe that's what the wiring was for that I saw on the workbench outside.

I detect a new car smell, but there's something else . . . like burning rubber. Bits of memory from my time on the USS *Flint* remind me that I'm smelling fumes from a soldering iron. My running mate, Petty Officer Franklin, showed me how to use it when we put together a shortwave radio on that cruise.

I look forward, peeking my head over the front seat, and spy the origin of the strange odors and the more profound reason for the wiring. The dashboard has been removed and rows of shelves behind where the glove box would normally sit are lined with cubed packages. Wires run out of the cubes. . . . Oh my god.

I look up when I hear a familiar whopping sound—muffled, but instantly recognizable. An H-46. The sound grows steadily louder as the rotors beat hard against the air, the pitch change announcing a sudden halt in movement.

Gunfire. Shouts and scuffling. More weapons discharging. And finally, the *whop-whop-whop* of the H-46, growing quieter as it flies away. All sounds indicate a SEAL team has just been fast roped to the deck.

But that can't be. Our team couldn't have gotten here that fast. And the 46? There's only one other in the battle group and she's sitting in a hangar on the *Kansas City* over four hundred miles away.

Rapid footsteps. Scraping and banging. More gunfire. I drop to the floorboards and lay flat. I'm shaking—for a lot of reasons—but mainly because I'm wet and cold. I touch my gloved hand to my cheek and pull it away, bloody, which explains the blood droplets spattered across the leather upholstery. My right hand bumps into my helmet. I still have it on. I remove it and place it on the seat.

Shouts in Arabic. Shouts in English.

This is an awful feeling. Waiting. Hiding. Doing nothing to help myself.

I press up and look about the car, chancing a glance through the tinted windows. The windows . . . I look at my helmet and back to the glass.

Worth a try.

I secure the neck strap to the helmet to make a handle and hurl it across me. I wince and jerk backward as the window shatters—wincing not just to avoid thousands of shards of flying glass, but due to the earsplitting car alarm that now screams through the cargo bay.

I shimmy through the window and begin to run. To where? God, where am I running? Where do I go?

I never have the chance to answer that, as a hand grabs me from behind. I shudder with a surge of adrenaline when I look into Jonas's manic eyes. He wraps his left arm across my chest, twisting me around to face away from him.

We move roughly to a side hatch, Jonas gripping a Heckler and Koch USP 9mm weapon in his right hand. He kicks a door open that takes us into the sunlight, emerging onto a deck that runs along the side of the ship at water level. He turns us to the left, running aft, and then left again into a cutout in the hull that houses the second Zodiac.

The motorboat I saw earlier when we flew circles around the ship is already in the water, five men onboard, all wielding semiautomatic machine guns.

Jonas shoves me in the Zodiac. "Don't move!" he shouts.

He pushes the pontoons from behind and a rough *kerplunk* announces our entry into the water. The motorboat revs its engines and Jonas follows suit, cutting across the stern of the yacht that is now dead in the water. The first Zodiac remains tied to the loading dock, its occupants now speeding away on the motorboat at a much faster speed than the Zodiac could achieve.

Weapons fire originating from the decks of *Twister* is returned from the motorboat that travels in front of us. I take a chance and peek over the pontoon's edge.

"Hold your fire!" Mike yells. "Hold your fire!" He stands with members of his team on *Twister*'s flight deck, weapons aimed.

Jonas gestures to the men in the boat in front of us. We surge forward, lifted and dropped repeatedly by the waves. It's a jarring ride, but even as I'm thrown about, I note Jonas's expression. This is an unbalanced person—an angry, unbalanced person—who is on the run. And his only bargaining chip, the only thing keeping him alive right now, is me.

But I wonder how long he's going to tolerate me. He wants nothing more than to end my life, and I can see and feel the clock of a psychotic time bomb ticking. I know my one chance for escape lies in an option I can't fathom. My gaze moves beyond Jonas to the ever-patient sea.

You've already done it once today, I remind myself.

His head whips around to the distant whopping sound. The sweet, sweet sound of an H-46. And then a second helicopter, the blades beating the air with a deeper, heavier pitch. Scanning the horizon, I enjoy the briefest moment of relief. Rescue is on the way. But that sliver of hope fades with the stark realization that Jonas is getting cornered.

Would he endure a standoff with a hostage? Would he engage in negotiations for his release and mine? I answer no to both. Would he enjoy pointing the gun he holds at my heart? Would he relish pulling the trigger? I answer yes on both counts.

You're going to die in this boat, Sara.

For the second time within the span of an hour, Ian's voice spurs me on. I react before my brain can convince me otherwise. While Jonas's head is turned, I jump over the side.

47

My decision on what to do next is made for me. Gunfire sends me down-ward, clawing my way through the water directly beneath the Zodiac so Jonas doesn't have a line-of-sight target.

This is already a bad idea. No way can I swim fast enough to evade a Zodiac. But worse, every molecule in me wants to swim upward. Up and out of this aquatic hell. Another gunshot. *Shit!* I start a panicked paddle downward through murky water until I can no longer discern the bottom of the boat, hoping this means he can no longer see me, either. Surely I'm out of range if he decides to fire again. I turn parallel to the surface, probably twenty feet below, my arms and legs moving in uncoordinated, erratic strokes.

Slow down! Slow down! Relax!

Despite my protestations, my body bristles with tension, scrabbling and fighting with the water, going nowhere.

Relax. You've got to relax! Breaststroke. You remember the breaststroke? Pull, push, and glide. Pull, push, and glide. Remember?

I extend my arms in front of me, pull them toward my hips, and push back. *That's it! You've got this! Pull, push, and glide. Do it again!* Somehow, muscle movements ingrained from childhood are still there for me.

I'm spurred on by the incessant whirring of the motorboat's outboard engine. I wonder fleetingly why it's sticking around. I can only guess that they feel having a hostage would be a good idea and it would be worth the wait to have me surface.

Pull, push, and glide. Pull, push, and glide.

The sounds from the outboard engines, from both the Zodiac and the motorboat, begin to diminish. Perhaps they don't know in which direction I'm swimming. Maybe they've slowed or changed heading trying to find me. Or, even better, maybe they're running from the approaching helicopters.

Pull, push, and glide. Pull, push, and glide.

I need air. Damn it. And I need it now.

I shift my gaze upward and begin swimming for the surface. My lungs burn. My muscles scream. And I suspect I look like a breaching whale as I explode through the surface.

I whip my head about. Jonas speeds toward me, forty yards away, reaching for his sidearm. I look left. The motorboat converges from the side, twenty yards behind Jonas. Their weapons are up.

An H-60 helicopter races toward us, one hundred yards out. I wonder if they can see me. They must see the boats. At least, I hope they can.

I dive again, but not as deep this time, just trying to move away.

Pull, push, and glide. Pull, push, and glide.

I know I can't do this. He'll catch me soon, but I swim anyway.

Pull, push, and glide. Pull, push, and glide.

I swim and I'm getting heavy.

Pull, push, and glide.

I have to go up. And this is it. He's going to be waiting. Jonas will be waiting this time.

I burst through the whipped-up, whitecapped surface. Rotor blades thwack the air and the outboard motors wail. Jonas raises his pistol. I dive under, but not before a searing, stinging pain rips through my thigh. I grab for my leg, clutching the wound. But I'm floating to the surface.

I can't break the surface. I wind my hands in a reverse propeller-like motion to push me deeper. Wisps of red rise before me.

I try to swim, using arm strokes only, but without my legs to help me kick downward, I start rising again. I scull frantically to stay under, arms swirling through a spiraling column of blood. So much. I look down, afraid to see the wound responsible for this. My survival vest blocks the view of my leg. I tug at it to pull it out of the way.

My hand falls on my left chest pocket. *That's right! I have a gun! I have a—*

I pat at the pocket, squashing it flat. And then I remember. Just prior to jumping out of the Zodiac, I saw Captain Plank's Beretta 9mm still attached to Jonas's waistband.

But my air is out now and I have to swim up.

When I break the surface this time, agitated water stings and whips my face. The rotor wash from an H-60 is stirring the sea into a frenzy. Bright white numbers, 67, reflect in the sun on the tail boom. Jonas balances in the Zodiac ten yards away. His gun is aimed . . . but not at me. I follow his line of sight, watching in horror as he tracks the falling object from Shadow Hunter 67.

Someone has jumped from the left seat of the aircraft. The mission commander's seat. Eric. He doesn't wear a helmet. And he has to be at least fifty feet in the air.

Jonas fires and Eric's body jerks as the bullet hits.

"No!" I scream.

My voice is drowned out by the heavy whopping of an H-46 that passes immediately to my left, ten feet above the water. It's Sabercat 54. Sabercat 54? How—? It splits the distance between the two boats, its .50 caliber machine gun aimed at Jonas. The one doing the firing? I can see him from here. Senior Chief Makovich.

A hailstorm of bullets riddles Jonas's Zodiac, rapidly deflating the pontoons. The weapons fire is returned, but not from Jonas. The men in the motorboat shoot at the helicopter, so Sabercat 54 circles in, pointing its machine gun to its new target.

"Sara!" Eric swims toward me, leaving a wake of blood swirling behind him.

"Eric! You . . . you're . . ."

"I'm fine, but—" He eyes the pool of red that surrounds me. "Oh, Jesus . . ."

"I'm okay—"

"Get down!" he shouts. A protective hand moves in front of my face, while he raises his other arm, Sig Sauer in hand, and fires. Jonas ducks, crouching low in the sinking Zodiac. Taking advantage of the fact that Sabercat 54 has shifted its fire to the fleeing motorboat, Jonas raises his sidearm.

Eric shoots again, hitting Jonas near the shoulder of his firing arm. Jonas folds over briefly, his other hand clutching his shoulder. But Jonas and Eric must have fired almost simultaneously because Eric lets out a grunt of pain and blood sprays from his hand. He can no longer hold his weapon, which dangles precariously on his index finger, snagged in the trigger housing.

The .50 cal from Sabercat 54 pummels the motorboat, only one of the occupants standing now.

Eric looks at his damaged hand. "Fuck!" he shouts angrily.

It affords Jonas the time to pull his torso upright and take aim—not at me, but at Eric.

And the slow-motion sequence happens for the second time today. My eyes are drawn to Captain Plank's Beretta 9mm, the wooden pistol grip visible above Jonas's waist.

"*I was there when Mr. Plank told Mr. Amicus you were to have this,*" Jonas said. "*Something about how impressed he was with your ability to perform under pressure. . . . What a disappointment!*"

I suck in my breath, pull Eric's gun from his hand, and aim it at Jonas. And still, I hesitate, registering that I'm about to shoot another human being.

But the next thing that registers is the smirk on Jonas's face.

An explosion of sound rockets through my ears as I pull the trigger. Jonas's hand recoils from the hit, his pistol jettisoned into the sea. I continue to fire until Jonas drops.

Someone must have called for reinforcements because I see and hear the cavalry approaching. Nighthawks streak toward us, and the destroyer *Leftwich,* along with the frigate *Robert G. Bradley,* speed over the horizon.

The last standing member of the motorboat falls to Sabercat 54's attack. The helicopter circles and dives for us. It moves so fast, surely it's going to fly right by. But the pilot does an amazing 180-degree rotation, a sweet buttonhook, that stops the aircraft dead in front of us. The ramp opens and Lego and Messy are there, soaked, to pull us into the aircraft.

The helicopter accelerates forward and the med bags are out. Lego turns to Eric, a pair of scissors in his hand, while Messy kneels next to me.

"Don't touch me until you've finished with her," Eric orders.

Lego nods, and together, he and Messy start to cut away my flight suit.

I glance behind me. Senior Chief Makovich kneels over Animal, but I'm unable to ascertain more because the effort to hold my head up is too great. I lay back and turn to Eric, who lies by my side, propped on his elbow. His face is blurry. I blink to bring him in focus.

"Sara, you're going to be okay," he says reassuringly. My body starts to shake, freezing. "Guys, let's get her out of these wet clothes."

"Roger that," Lego says.

"I'll get a blanket," Messy says.

My ears . . . the sounds are fading. Black curtains begin to close around my eyes. Eric places his hand on my head and gently strokes my hair.

"You're going to be okay, Sara. You're going to be okay."

I reach for his hand, lace my fingers through his, and the curtains close.

48

It's the familiar drone I recognize first. The whirring, the constant hum, the smells . . . I'm on a Navy ship. My eyes flutter open, focusing on the neatly stenciled ducting running across the overhead. I'm lying in a bed, white curtains hung on either side. Tubing runs from my left arm. I follow it upward to the IV bag that hangs above me.

I feel a squeeze of my hand and roll my head sideways. Glassy green eyes peer into mine.

"Hey," Eric says.

"Hey," I whisper.

He sits in a chair next to me, his head level with mine.

"You're okay," I say.

"Now I am," he says, putting his other hand around mine.

"But you were hit. I remember."

"Yeah." He motions to his leg. Dressed in a T-shirt and shorts, he has a bandage on his right thigh.

I look at the dressings on my right thigh and then back to his.

"We match."

He laughs lightly, his eyes glistening. "That we do."

"And your hand," I say, my eyes drawn to the gauze covering his right palm.

"Looked a lot worse than it was," he says. "And you?" He motions to my left hand, the one that I just now realize is wrapped like his.

"It's fine." I trace my fingers across his bandaging. "Where are we?" I ask.

"In sickbay on *Nimitz*. You have one of the few private rooms here, actually."

I raise my eyebrows.

"You know, special treatment for the female."

My grimace quickly spreads into a grin.

"It's been almost twenty-four hours since your surgery."

"I had surgery?"

He nods. "They removed the bullet."

"And you?"

"Same. I woke up last night, though, so I've been waiting for you for a while now."

He shifts slightly in his seat, adjusting his hands to rest more securely around mine. "How do you feel? Do you need anything?"

I shake my head. "Just you."

He brings one of his hands to my face, running his fingers gently across my skin before combing them lightly through my hair.

"So I guess you were right to be worried," I admit.

He bites his lip.

"Did you know?" I ask. "About Jonas?"

"I had a hunch," he says, bringing his hand back to cover mine. "We had intelligence that something was going down and leads that pointed to Jonas, but not definitively."

"The earpiece? Is that why . . . ?"

"Everyone felt the intel guys were reading it wrong, but I couldn't let it go. I had this gut feeling, so yeah, that's why I gave you the radio."

"But why didn't you tell me your concerns?"

"Because I started wondering if the guys were right. Mike, Animal, they thought I was taking it too personally. That I was too quick to point the finger."

"But why would you do that?"

"Remember when I said Jonas and I had a history? Well, it's a sordid one."

"I remember, but we've never had a chance—"

"I know. The short story is we've conducted joint missions with him and his guys in the past. He didn't care to follow orders. He was reckless . . . dangerous. And the two of us? Butting heads would be an understatement. I had the lead on every mission we did together, and you can imagine how well that went over. And then, the sordid part . . ."

He stops, lifting his shirt, pointing to the bullet wound on his abdomen. Pink and raised and circular, it's just as I remembered. Wait . . .

"Are you saying . . . ? Did he—"

"The bullet that left this scar came from his gun," he says carefully.

My hands fly to my mouth. "No."

"We were trapped in a firefight. One of his men was killed and another severely wounded. But it wouldn't have happened had he stayed in position as I'd ordered. He screwed up, plain and simple. I called him on it right there and I could see it in his eyes. Everything that had built up between us. All those years. Something just snapped. It was about ten minutes later when I went down."

"He aimed at you? He actually fired at you?"

"He claimed it was an errant bullet . . . I don't know. I couldn't prove it. But there was no one near me when it happened, and based on past experience, Jonas only hits what he aims at."

"That's unfathomable."

"Actually, it's even worse than that."

"How could it be worse?"

He runs his hand over the scar and it's some moments before he answers.

"This is an exit wound."

I pause, staring at the scarring. Wait a minute. I look into his eyes and then back to the wound. "An exit . . . ?" And then it registers. "He shot you in the back?"

He nods.

"Eric, I can't even . . ."

"I know it doesn't excuse my actions for trying to keep you off the mission, but I knew he wouldn't hesitate to hurt you. I hope you can understand."

"I do," I say. "Now I do."

He pulls his shirt down again.

"But if you didn't trust Jonas, and if the others didn't either, why were you working on such an important mission together? One that involved a U.S. president?"

"We argued against it, but it was Aussie intelligence that led to the plot discovery, and it got political from there. Our hands were tied."

"I see. But when did you suspect something was up during the mission itself? You got to us so fast."

"After you took off from the *Kansas City*, I called and had five four launch right after you. Something nagged at me. The distance between the targets, I think. And then the whole episode on *Nimitz*. Switching teams around at the last minute. Something wasn't right."

"I know. You didn't look too happy."

"And the sub . . . Well, we realized pretty quickly we weren't prosecuting anything."

"Jonas told me. It was a diversion to keep you away. There's so much I need to tell you, but he was hired, Eric. By someone in U.S. intelligence. Very high in U.S. intelligence. He told me."

"That would make sense. We knew he had to have had high-level help. We had solid intel, normally reliable intel, of exactly when that sub would be there for the rendezvous. But instead, the *Leftwich* boys were left scratching their heads with negative sonar readings and Mike was out there just turning circles. Once we realized we were chasing a ghost, we had ~~five~~ four on scene within thirty minutes. We were already en route when I received your SOS call. That was brilliant, by the way. Agonizing to listen to. But brilliant."

"Did you think we were really ops normal?"

"I did. Even though I suspected something was up with Jonas, I had no inkling whatsoever that his plans would involve you."

"Did you hear what happened?"

"Yeah." He looks down, his thumbs busily rubbing my hand. "God, if I'd seen your bird go down . . ."

It's several long moments before he looks at me again. "You probably don't know this, but Messy radioed me just after you went in."

"Radioed you? But Jonas took their radios."

"He used the radio I'd given you."

"What? But Jonas ripped it apart. He fixed that?"

"Yeah. He gave me all the gory details—well, the quick version anyway. We were only twenty minutes out at the time. It's how we knew you'd been taken aboard *Twister*."

"That means he fixed it while he was floating in the ocean. Unbelievable."

"No kidding."

Floating in the ocean. Floating with Animal . . . I hesitate to ask the question. He was hurt so badly.

"What is it?" he says.

"Animal?" I ask.

A slow smile crosses his face. "He's one tough SOB, I tell you what."

"He's okay?"

"Thanks to you, yes. He told me what you said. What you did. The way he talks, he'll be naming his firstborn after you."

"What about Lego and Messy? Are they okay?"

"Fine. I spoke with them yesterday. They spent most of the day with investigators, giving their statements, and they're doing it again today, but yeah, they're good. They're really worried about you."

"They were both amazing. Lego repaired the engine oil line using who knows what and then Messy with the AFCS. Genius."

"He's really shook up about that, by the way. He's blaming himself for the crash, one that still had you in the aircraft." He stops, his eyes searching mine, his hands squeezing my fingers more tightly now. "Speaking of shook up . . . I've never been so scared in all my life."

I can't imagine Eric being scared of anything. But he looks down at his hands, the ones that cover and surround mine, tightening his lips as he tends to do when sorting out his thoughts. He finally lifts his eyes.

"Remember how we talked about my job as a SEAL? About what I do? Who I am?"

"I remember."

"And the nickname? Lightning? Well, it's energy. This energy that wells up inside and it's all I can do to control it. And then combine that with my feelings for you. . . . Watching you swim away from Jonas . . . you were trying to get away. . . ." He winces, shaking his head at the memory.

"Thank god Brian was at the controls. He saw what was happening to me. We were still a hundred feet above the water when I started unbuckling my harness. I had to do something. Try to draw his fire. Something. And then I'm falling and I'm thinking, did I really just jump? Brian told me yesterday he dropped altitude as fast as he could when he realized what I was doing. He thinks I went out around fifty or sixty feet. I barely remember getting shot. I don't remember hitting the water. And then my arms took me to you."

We share a long look before a grim smile settles across my face. "It probably would have been a lot easier for you to fall in love with someone else, huh?"

He sits back as he regards me, considering the question far longer than I would have liked.

"Maybe," he answers finally.

I flinch at the response.

"But it wouldn't have been real." He leans forward and his eyes are doing the crawl-inside-my-soul thing again. "I'd be lying if I said it wasn't difficult to watch someone shooting at you, but at the same time, when the going gets tough, there's no one I'd rather have at my side. So yeah, it might not be easy. But it'll be real. And I want that. I've wanted that for a long time."

He cups my chin with his bandaged palm, and my vision goes blurry, the moisture spilling over and trickling down my face. He leans forward, touching his lips to mine—a salty kiss, but the sweetest I've ever experienced.

49

The knock on the door startles us both. I reach for his hand.

"Mind if we come in, ma'am?"

It's Lego.

"No, please come in," I say.

Lego and Messy push through the curtain, dressed in their summer white uniforms, clean, crisp, and polished. I don't think I've ever seen them out of their flight suits, so this is a shock.

"What the hell, sir," Lego says. "Are you makin' the lieutenant cry?"

"We can take care of him, you know, ma'am," Messy says.

"Yeah, his sorry SEAL ass ain't a match for us," Lego says.

I look at Eric. "They know?"

"They saw me jump from the helicopter. They said a real pilot would never jump from his aircraft." He laughs. "And with all they've been through, I figured I could let them in on the secret."

"So how are you?" I ask. "I was so worried. Did the jump go okay? Were you hurt?"

"Do you believe this shit?" Lego says, looking at Messy. "She's worried about our candy-ass jump. A jump that wasn't even a jump. More like a step."

"Ma'am, I'm so sorry," Messy says seriously. "I never would have forgiven myself if you hadn't gotten out."

"You were brilliant, Joe," I say. "Just brilliant."

"I almost got you killed, ma'am. That's not so brilliant. I thought we'd all jump out, he'd take the controls, and then botch the landing later. But, my god. A buttonhook?"

"We had no idea you were planning something like that," Lego says. "We were just floating there with our mouths open. That was, bar none, the most unbelievable maneuver we have ever seen."

"Bar none," Messy says. "And even with you ending in a hover and all, I just didn't think our Aussie bad boy would be that . . . well, bad. I thought he'd at least be able to hold it long enough for you to get out, but good god."

"Either that, or she's just that good," Lego says. "I don't know, Mess, I think it's a little of both."

They nod in agreement.

"So look at you two," I say. "You clean up nice."

"Yeah, you won't see this too often," Lego says.

"Fuck, we've been meetin' with the JAGs and the CIA and shit," Messy says.

"Guess our statements don't count if we're in flight suits," Lego says.

"Well, I think it's nice," I say. "You're a handsome lot."

"That's right kind of you, ma'am," Lego says.

"So when are you gettin' outta here?" Messy asks.

I look to Eric.

"That's a good question," Eric says. "I know I'm supposed to be here another three or four days at least, so I'd expect probably the same for Sara."

"Well, just get back as soon as you can, all right?" Messy says.

"Yeah, it's gonna suck not having our favorite pilot on the flight schedule," Lego says. "Although, you have someone else who's gainin' on ya for favorite pilot status."

"I do?"

"Does she know, sir?" Messy asks.

"No, I don't think so."

"Know what?" I say.

"Maybe we should mosey on outta here, Kyle, so she can see her next visitor," Messy says.

"You know, I think I'll mosey with you," Eric says, pushing himself up. For the first time, I notice his crutches leaning on the foot of the bed. Messy grabs them and hands them to Eric.

"Thanks," Eric says. "Come on, guys."

"See ya soon, ma'am," Lego says.

"Yeah, you take care," Messy says.

I look to Eric in question. "I'll be back in just a minute," he says.

I push myself up, not feeling any pain in my leg. I give a glance to the IV bag, wondering what's dripping in there.

"May I come in?" Commander Claggett asks.

"Yes, sir, please."

Like Lego and Messy, he wears his summer whites. He must be giving statements, as well. Wait a minute. Giving statements . . .

"May I?" he asks, pointing to the chair next to me. He continues to look down as he sits, his hands clasped together.

"Sara," he starts, but stumbles over the syllables.

It's the first time I've ever heard him say my name.

"This is going to be harder than I thought," he says, looking up.

"Sir, I'm so sor—"

"No. Please don't. I'm the one who needs to apologize." He leans back heavily in the chair. "I'm sorry. For everything. You've taken so much shit from me . . . all because I couldn't—"

He stops and wipes his face. His light brown hair has been freshly cut, and to anyone else, he would look pressed and clean in his neat, white uniform. But his tortured eyes tell a different story. His razor-sharp outward appearance harbors a wounded soul.

"I never allowed myself—" He looks to the overhead, his quavering lips clamped together. "I . . . I couldn't let her go," he says, his eyes returning to mine. "I don't know how to let her go."

He's blurry in my vision now. I don't even bother wiping my tears, as it would be a fruitless endeavor.

"So I have a lot to work out," he says. "Captain Magruder is allowing me to take some leave so I can get my head together. But I want you to know, it'll be different going forward. You certainly don't deserve to be treated the way I've treated you. Kara would have my ass if she knew." He laughs lightly, but the tears are brimming. He looks away, trying to keep it together.

"I wish there was something I could do, sir."

He returns his glassy eyes to mine. "Well, you can start by calling me Nick . . . if you want."

I nod.

"And you can make the most of the time you have with Lieutenant Marxen."

My breath catches. How did he . . . ?

"I recognized it the first time I saw you together on the *Lake Champlain*. I saw how he looked at you and I remember looking at Kara the same way."

I wipe my eyes, my heart wrenching.

"Anyhow, hang on to that. It's a special feeling that not too many people get to experience."

I'm going to have to ask for a new pillowcase, since mine is now soaked.

"Can I get you . . . ?" He points to the tissue box.

I nod and he crosses the room to the small sink. He grabs the box, places it on the bed, and grabs a tissue for himself.

"I probably need this more than you," he says with a small laugh before blowing his nose.

I smile, realizing that the surreal nature of this moment far surpasses any of my surreal moments with Eric.

"You're in your whites," I say. "Was that you in five four?"

He nods.

"Really? And you were flying?"

He nods again.

"You were amazing! I never knew you could fly like that. And you flew into machine-gun fire—"

"Yeah, the maintenance officer's pissed. Bullet holes all over the airframe."

"I can imagine," I say, looking into his light brown eyes—brave eyes, courageous eyes. "You're the reason we're still alive—Eric and I."

"It was the least I could do. I sort of owed you."

"Well, consider us square."

He looks at me with an expression I've never seen before. Like he's seeing me for the first time. And I have to admit, I probably carry the same expression.

"I need to get going," he says finally. He rises and starts to walk away, but turns. His lips spread into a smile. "I have an award recommendation to write."

I sink into my pillow as I watch him leave. I don't know if I can handle any more emotional upheaval today. I think I'm tapped out.

"What do you mean, I can't see her!" Em's voice grows louder as she nears the room.

"Rest, my ass! That girl is tough as nails! Not like your milk toast–loving jet jocks around here!"

"Lieutenant, please."

"Please, nothing! I need to see her now! I will raise holy fuckin' hell around here if you don't let me in!"

"All right, ma'am," a sailor's voice says. "Five minutes."

"That's more like it!"

She bursts in with enough energy to cure ten of me. And she's in summer whites.

Summer whites? "Were you . . . ?"

"Was I what? You're looking at me like I'm wearing one of your goddamn long-sleeved shirts!"

"Were you in five four?"

"Duh! 'Bout got my ass shot off trying to find you!"

"You were there . . ."

"Hell, yeah, I was there! You think I was gonna let Commander Nick fly off all by his lonesome?"

I shrug.

"You never told me you were being dragged into shit like this," she says accusingly.

"They told me not to tell anyone. I'm sorry, Em."

"See, this is what happens when you saddle up with a badass boyfriend. These things never work out."

"Badass boyfriend? What do you—"

"Hello! He's a SEAL! God almighty, you're with a SEAL!"

I stifle the grin that threatens as Eric silently enters the room behind her.

"He jumped out of his helicopter, Sara, at like a hundred feet! Holy crap! You do *not* need to be with a guy like that. Remember, I *know* these things."

"But he saved my life, Em."

"I know, I know, I know!" she says, grabbing at her hair. "That's the worst part! God, all the romantic shit happens to you! I can't stand it! He jumped out of a helicopter for you! Aghh! I want a guy like that!"

"But you just said that was a bad idea."

"I lied! Every girl wants the badass guy! It rarely works out, but who cares! If they're jumping out of helicopters for you, then what the fuck! We should all be so lucky!"

"Em, you're insane."

"It rarely works out?" Eric says.

"Ah, fuck," Em says, turning to look behind her. "Oh, and look, you have matching bullet wounds. Seriously?"

"So does that go in our favor or work against us?" Eric asks, hopping toward me.

"Well, let's see," she says. "The couple that rides together in the fast lane, danger at every turn. Life-and-death experiences tend to draw those kinds together. But when the adrenaline runs out and you're sitting on your porch in rocking chairs someday . . . I don't see it lasting at that point."

Eric and I share an incredulous look.

"You just heal up fast and get back to the ship so I can have some, you know, details. I need *all* of them," she says, glancing askance at Eric and then back to me.

"It was great to see you, Em," I say. "And, thanks."

She looks at me for a long moment, and then, to my utter surprise, leans over and kisses me on the forehead. "You scared the shit out of me, Sara Denning," she says, with tears in her eyes. "No more of this, okay?"

She turns to Eric and points at him. "Okay?"

She doesn't bother to wait for a response, but rushes out, almost knocking Eric over in the process.

"So how come the sailor outside didn't give *you* any trouble about coming to see me? Em had to resort to threats."

"Probably because I wield a set of crutches and he knew I wasn't afraid to use them," he says, arriving at my side. "Are the pain meds keeping up?"

"Yeah, actually, I'm feeling okay."

"Any chance you'd be up for one more visitor?"

"I have another visitor?"

"Only if you're up for it."

"Well, of course, except I think I've seen everyone."

"Hold on just one second," he says.

He moves agilely across the room, even on crutches, but when he returns, he follows the flight surgeon, who is pushing a wheelchair. My mouth drops open.

"Animal?"

I can't believe he's sitting up. How is this possible?

"Sara, this is Commander Bennett, the flight surgeon who operated on you," Eric says by way of introduction to the man holding the handles of the wheelchair.

"Nice to meet you, sir," I say.

"It's great to meet you, as well," he says. "I'm also the doc who operated on this gentleman," he says, motioning to Animal. "The one who should not be out of his bed now but who threatened to slit my throat in the middle of the night if I didn't let him come see you."

I look at Animal in bewilderment.

"I said he has five minutes," Commander Bennett says. He walks around to the front of the wheelchair, leaning over so Animal can see him directly. "And not one second more."

Animal rolls his eyes.

"I'll be back to get him, Sara, and then I'll come check on you."

Commander Bennett takes his leave and my eyes move back to Animal, who's dressed in a hospital gown, a large blanket covering his torso. Tubes run from under the blanket and connect to an IV bag hanging from a long silver pole attached to the wheelchair above him. His tangled black hair remains in its normal messy state. And everything about him looks tired—his body took a huge beating—but his steel-gray eyes are as sharp as ever.

I look to Eric and back to Animal. "We're quite the sorry lot, aren't we?"

Animal starts to laugh, but grimaces in the process.

"Sir, you should be in bed. I mean—"

"I should be dead."

His penetrating gaze is unwavering.

I look down, nervously spreading the sheets across my lap. The memories, the images—of him in particular—are difficult. It's also hard for me to bear this drawn-out silence.

I take a chance and look up. His eyes haven't moved. This time, I hold his gaze and I realize, finally, this is Animal's way of saying thank you. And he's delivering the sentiment in the most meaningful and heartfelt way I can imagine.

"So how are you feeling?" I ask.

"I'm managing. And you?"

I peer up to my IV bag and back to him. "Whatever they've got going in there is working pretty good."

He stares at me with a heavy dose of contemplation, opening his mouth and then closing it again, as if he has a lot to say and he's trying to pick what comes out first.

"An AFCS-off buttonhook?" His exasperated tone is one of those are-you-kidding-me reprimands.

"Well, you taught me," I say lamely.

"And the attitude? Where did you learn that? 'Just shoot me and get it over with'? Who the hell taught you that?"

"Well, giving in to Australian psychopaths is for pussies, wouldn't you say?"

A satisfied smile spreads across his face. "A chip off the ol' block."

"Uh-oh," Eric says.

"See," Animal says to Eric. "I told you she was perfect for this."

"I already knew she was perfect," Eric says with a sweet glance in my direction.

"So . . . this guy?" Animal asks, motioning to Eric.

"Yeah," I say demurely.

Animal turns his head back and forth, looking between us several times, deliberating the arrangement.

"He isn't good enough for you," he states.

"Uh . . . thanks for the backup," Eric says.

"Anytime."

"All right, time's up!" Commander Bennett says, entering the room. He grabs the handles to the wheelchair and begins to turn Animal around.

"Well, I'll see you around, sir."

"Hell, yeah! We've got more training to do!" He nods in triumph to Eric.

"Max is saying good-bye now," Commander Bennett announces, and without further ado, pushes him through the curtain and out the door.

"You're probably tapped out on visitors," Eric says. "Why don't I give you some space."

"No!" I say emphatically. "Sorry, I didn't mean for that to come out that way."

His eyes light up. "So you don't mind if I hang out a little longer, then?"

I point to the chair. "Sit."

"Yes, ma'am." He leans his crutches against the bed and gingerly lowers himself into the chair. "I was able to corner Commander Bennett earlier, by the way. He said we're looking at another three days here, at least."

"Then what? Back to our ships?"

"I don't know, but I'd guess so. I suspect we'll be flying desks for a while, which is actually good. It'll give me time to arrange the details on a plan I've got brewing for us."

I raise my eyebrows.

"You'll see," he says coyly.

"Lieutenant Marxen . . . what are you up to?"

"Just the usual. Bending people to my will and all that."

"Please tell me that whatever you've got in the works involves just you and me and some alone time."

"You'd like that?"

"I'd love that."

"Perfect. I've got it covered."

EPILOGUE

I stare at my reflection in a Waikiki shop window, not recognizing the person that stares back. This is not the same face I wore three months ago. My hair, worn loose, is flowing over my shoulders—my bare shoulders, that is. Eric just bought me a gift—a halter dress with tiny white hibiscus flowers patterned on the bodice.

I hold his hand as I look up and down at the vision in front of me—a vision, because it certainly doesn't seem real.

"What is it?" he asks.

"I'm just looking . . . at us," I say, motioning to the glass. "I could never have imagined this."

"But what's bothering you?"

I pull my eyes from the window and look up at him. "How do you *do* that?"

His eyes twinkle. "I'm gonna take a wild stab here." He points to the rubber band on my wrist. "May I have that?"

Taking it, he moves behind me and gathers my hair, securing it in a rough version of a ponytail. I smile broadly when he's finished.

"Better?" he asks.

"Yes. Thanks."

"And even though you look freakin' amazing in that dress, remember that wasn't my idea, either," he says. "I just don't want to face Emily's wrath when we get back."

Em made Eric promise that the first thing he would do when we arrived was purchase appropriate beach attire for me. I was good and didn't complain and now Em will be happy. I even had the clerk at the counter take a picture of Eric and me together so I could send it to Em as proof.

"I think I can live with the dress," I say.

He wraps his arm around me and pulls me close, kissing me on the forehead in the process. "Come on."

We turn and stroll with the other tourists along a lengthy promenade of shops, leading past the International Marketplace on Kalakaua Avenue in Honolulu.

That little plan of Eric's? The one he had brewing on *Nimitz*? It was this. A bit of leave in Hawaii. This is one of those things that never should have been approved, and he had to have done a lot of flexing to get this request to fly. But hey, I'll take it.

We boarded a C-9 aircraft in Fujairah, United Arab Emirates, and eighteen long hours later, touched down at Hickam Air Force Base in Pearl Harbor. When the taxi dropped us at our beachfront hotel, the room wasn't ready yet, so we deposited our bags with the concierge and walked directly here.

Before leaving our suitcases, we changed into our swimsuits. Yeah . . . swimsuits. I've decided there's no reason I should feel uncomfortable in a suit, even with scores of military men roaming the beaches of Waikiki. But more importantly, I want to learn to enjoy the water. Eric said he'd help, so that's where we're headed now.

Our wounds have had four weeks to heal, so we're walking more normally now. And even though the hand that holds mine sports a two-inch scar running across the palm, it functions normally, having retained almost all of its strength and dexterity. This hand squeezes mine now as we make our way to the beach. I'm happy for the long walk and the time it affords to mentally prepare for what I'm about to do.

I imagine the feel of wet sand in my toes, small wavelets rushing around my shins. I envision walking farther out, the feel of the water lapping against my thighs. But as I near that point of dropping my head underneath, the scene goes fuzzy, like static on an old TV.

"Here, we can turn down this street to get to the beach," Eric says.

"Hold on a second." I walk closer to the newsstand we just passed, bending to read the headline: US LAUNCHES MISSILES AT IRAQ.

"Do you have fifty cents?" I ask.

Eric hands me the coins, I slot them in the machine, and pull out a copy of the *Honolulu Star-Advertiser*.

My finger moves down the page as I read.

By Emerson Dryer
Special to the *Star-Advertiser*

Yesterday, the U.S. military launched twenty-one Tomahawk missiles at targets in Iraq. White House officials said this was a firm and commensurate response to Iraq's plan to assassinate former president James MacIntyre in mid-March. . . .

I lower the paper, not wanting to read any more. I don't want to remember this. I don't. Especially not now. Not strolling hand in hand with the love of my life in Waikiki Beach.

I find the nearest trashcan and toss it in.

"Hey, I don't blame you," he says. "Besides, our attention needs to be focused on that." He points across the street to the beach and the crystal blue beyond.

Gulp. My hand tightens around his.

"It'll be okay. I'll be with you."

Arriving on the sand, we drop our backpacks. The dress comes off, revealing the suit underneath—one piece, mind you.

Eric takes my hand and we walk to the water's edge. "You lead," he says.

Normally, walking in the water or even wading in a pool isn't a problem for me, as long as there's no danger of submersion. But it's different this time. The memories flood back. Struggling to free myself from the harness . . . the helicopter pulling me under . . . gunfire . . . blood in the water . . .

"Sara?" Eric says.

I look up.

"You're cutting off my circulation."

I look down and his hand is white. *Yikes.* I take a deep breath and slowly release some pressure.

"Honestly, I don't know how you did what you did," he says.

"I don't have the faintest idea."

"You found a way, though, didn't you?"

Normally, I would have chalked it up to that same cosmic deity that comes through for me every two years when I step into the helo dunker. But maybe, just maybe, I've had the power within me all along.

And this is an encouraging thought. The power within . . . I have this.

I have the power to make peace with the water. With what happened nine years ago. With Ian. I even have the power to forgive myself. And with this power, comes freedom. Freedom to live, love, work, and be feminine, be me. I don't have to hide, or shut part of myself off, or become someone else. I have the power within to chart my course, to live my truth, and move forward.

And so, I step forward, gingerly at first, pulling Eric behind me. The warm water rushes around my feet, just as I imagined it would. I scrunch my toes, wet grains filling the gaps. A few more steps and my knees now wiggle in that funny way that objects do when viewed underwater. Eric moves alongside me.

"Not bad," he says. "I can feel my fingers even."

I still have the wherewithal to elbow him in the ribs. A good sign.

"How about a few more steps?" he suggests.

I continue forward, the water rising along my thighs, touching the bottom of my suit, encroaching my waist. My grip tightens and I look up, met with an encouraging smile.

A few more steps and the water covers my chest. I stop, my breathing getting shallow. "I think we're good."

He turns to me, pulling me to him, and wraps me securely in his arms. "I love you," he says, before kissing me so passionately, sparks are surely flying from my head.

I finally break away, coming up for air. "If this is your strategy for helping me deal with where I'm standing right now, it's working."

"Glad to be of service." He says, drawing me to him once more. His lips find mine, and his hands, slippery in the salt water, slide down my back and move around my waist. He pulls our hips together. . . .

Oh, my goodness . . .

I push away, breathing hard. "I think . . . hotel . . ."

"I agree," he says, swallowing.

We share anticipatory smiles before turning to wade to shore. He reaches for my hand and we move slowly against the resistance of the water, attempting to get our breathing under control.

Once ashore, I pull my towel from my backpack and shake it out, but something flips from it, landing lightly in the sand. I start laughing as I pick up a box of condoms.

"What's so funny?" he asks.

I show him what I have in my hand.

"You're prepared!"

I reach into the bottom of the inside flap of my backpack and pull out two more boxes. "I have eighteen."

His eyes grow wide. "I can see that," he says, looking like he's won the lottery.

"Hong Kong. Well, you remember. You couldn't leave the ship without taking them, right? I'd forgotten I had them. But eighteen? Isn't that ridiculous? I mean, seriously."

"Well, let's see, we're going to be here for what, four days? Eighteen . . . yeah, that sounds about right." His grin is a wide one.

"Honestly, you and Emily . . ."

After dressing, we begin the half-mile walk along the beach to our hotel. Hand in hand we stroll, blending into our surroundings perfectly—the couple that ambles along idly on romantic holiday.

I breathe in deeply, relishing the moment.

But the muffled ringing jars me from my reverie.

Eric slides his backpack off his shoulder, unzipping the side compartment. "Just a second."

Phone in hand, he carries on a mostly one-sided conversation. "Okay," Eric says. "Yeah. Yeah. Fuck. Okay, yeah. All right. Okay, got it. Yep, next flight."

He sighs, putting away the phone and taking my hand. We start to walk again.

"What was that?" I ask.

"*That* was our orders to return to the Gulf . . . immediately."

I stop and turn to face him. "What?"

"New intel. New threat. New mission."

"For you?"

"Yes, but for you, too. Apparently we're a package deal now."

"What?"

"They want us both back ASAP. Stupid, too. The mission's not even time critical. They're still in the planning stages."

I look at him, crestfallen.

"I told them we'd be on the next flight out."

"But that's in a couple of hours," I say. "The C-9 that dropped us off was returning late this afternoon."

He takes both my hands in his. "Yeah, too bad we missed that flight."

"But, we still have time—"

"I mean, what could we do?" he says. "I got the call, we were several hours out on a sailboat with no way to return in time for the departure, so we had to take the next flight . . . which is tomorrow evening."

"You . . ." A smile creeps across my face.

"Hey, your badass boyfriend isn't stupid."

But my smile quickly fades, replaced with a sigh. "Is it always going to be like this?" I ask, the resignation in my voice clear.

He moves his hand to my cheek, his thumb brushing softly against my skin. "You mean like this?" He pulls my head closer, his lips forming around mine. His arms encircle me, drawing me to him until my body is molded to his.

The sand is getting hot.

I pull back just slightly, nodding, in answer to his query.

"Then absolutely, yes," he says. "It will always be like this."